BORN TO TROUBLE

Rita Bradshaw

headline

First published in 2009 by
HEADLINE PUBLISHING GROUP

1

Cataloguing in Publication Data is available from the British Library

Hardback ISBN 978 0 7553 4239 6

Typeset in Bembo by Palimpsest Book Production Limited,
Grangemouth, Stirlingshire

Printed and bound in Great Britain by
CPI Mackays, Chatham ME5 8TD

Headline's policy is to use papers that are natural, renewable and recyclable
products and made from wood grown in sustainable forests. The logging
and manufacturing processes are expected to conform to the
environmental regulations of the country of origin.

BORN TO TROUBLE

By Rita Bradshaw and available from Headline

Alone Beneath the Heaven

Reach for Tomorrow

Ragamuffin Angel

The Stony Path

The Urchin's Song

Candles in the Storm

The Most Precious Thing

Always I'll Remember

The Rainbow Years

Skylarks at Sunset

Above the Harvest Moon

Eve and her Sisters

Gilding the Lily

Born to Trouble

This book is for our beautiful Baby Bradshaw, beloved first child for Ben and Lizzi. We never got to hold you, sweet little baby, but one day we will be able to give you all the cuddles and kisses we're saving up. Until then, we know you're safe in the arms of Jesus and take comfort in the knowledge He will work all things together for good. Your photo is my prize possession, precious little one.

Ben and Lizzi, we couldn't be prouder of you if we tried for how you've come through this difficult time. Dad and I love you more than words can say.

Acknowledgements

I was born in 1949, and by then the last true Romany gypsies were being overtaken by the modern world. A proud people with an incredible ancestry which goes back centuries, they had (and have) their own codes and morals, not to mention their own language which still survives today among the small community who haven't been seduced by the twenty-first century. Often discriminated against, most gypsies keep themselves to themselves, which makes research difficult because non-gypsy observers tended to be biased. However, among the many avenues of research to 'flavour' Pearl's time with the Romanies, the following books were particularly helpful: *Incidents in A Gipsy's Life* by George Smith, *The Gypsies* by John Hoyland, and *Travellers Remember Hopping Time*, courtesy of the Romany and Traveller Family History Society.

Man is born to trouble, as the sparks fly upward.
Job v. 7

Contents

PART ONE

The Devil's Playground

June 1898

Chapter 1

Pearl stood backed against the grimy wall of the kitchen, her blue eyes wide with terror. She wanted to call out to her big brother, Seth, to tell him not to make their da any madder, to say that the cuff round her ear hadn't hurt that much – although it had – and that she was all right. However, fear had frozen her voice. All she could do was watch and listen as Seth squared up to the angry, drink-sodden man who was their father.

'I told you.' Seth's voice was shaking, whether with fear or anger, Pearl didn't know. 'I warned you not to hit her again, didn't I?'

Thomas Croft was swearing viciously as he rubbed at his hand where the hot broth had splattered, and for a moment seemed unaware of his son. Then he raised his head.

Pearl's breath caught in her throat. Her father's face always appeared dark and frightening to her; the black stubble around his chin and up the sides of his cheeks, and his great thick eyebrows beneath which the small eyes gleamed, often featured in her nightmares – but when drink had turned the skin a dark red and made the piggy eyes bloodshot, he was terrifying to her eight-year-old gaze.

'Any more of your lip an' you'll get the same.' Thomas reached for a chunk of bread from the plate in the middle of the dirty, food-encrusted table.

'Not any more, Da. I told you the last time you went for Pearl, there's three of us an' only one of you.' Seth indicated his two younger brothers who were standing just behind him, but he didn't look at them; he kept his eyes on his father.

Thomas's hand had stopped just above the plate of bread. He clearly couldn't believe his ears.

'You leave her alone – an' me an' the lads an' all.' Seth was tall for his fourteen years, although Fred at thirteen and Walter at just eleven took after their father, being small and wiry. 'I mean it.'

'You mean it, do you?' Thomas lurched to his feet, kicking back his chair. 'By, I'll skin you alive, lad. You see if I don't.'

It was the flash of silver that stopped him in his tracks. He stood swaying, his befuddled gaze on the evil-looking knife in his son's hand.

Pearl's fascinated eyes went from the knife to her father's face and then back to Seth. She was petrified into dumbness. So, apparently, was Thomas.

'I'll do for you, I swear it.' Seth's voice wasn't shaking any longer, nor did it sound like that of a young lad but someone much older. 'An' I could – you know that, don't you? I might not have had much in the way of book learnin', thanks to you, but I've had a different sort of schoolin', and I've learned well. So I'm tellin' you, Da. You don't touch our Pearl again.'

'Look at my hand.' Thomas's voice held an element of bluster which wasn't lost on Seth. 'That'll be a blister, so it will. Scaldin' hot that mutton broth was, and she sloshed half the bowl over me.'

'It was a drop or two, and she didn't do it on purpose. A bairn shouldn't be doing what Pearl does anyway, cookin' and cleanin' an' the rest.'

'Your mam's up there havin' a babbie, in case you've forgotten.'

Seth kept the knife steady. 'I haven't forgotten, but Pearl's been Mam's lackey from the day she could toddle, an' you know it same as I do. At least we had a bit of schoolin' in the early days, but Pearl's not set foot in school an' it's not right. Even the O'Rileys, bad as they are, send their bairns to school. I tell you, Da, things are goin' to change round here. If you want me an' the lads to carry on workin' for McArthur, then Pearl goes to school an' learns her letters an' numbers. And Mam gets off her backside once the bairn's born and sees to things. It's either that or I'm off makin' me own way, the lads alongside of me.'

Thomas's bullet-hard eyes narrowed. Bart McArthur valued Seth, he'd said so only the other day. Some of the lads were ham fisted with the thieving, but the Croft lads were naturals, that's what he'd said. And it reflected well on him. It didn't do any harm to be on Bart McArthur's good side, not with him controlling most of what went on down at the docks and elsewhere.

Shaking his head to clear the muzziness that umpteen pints of ale in the Boar's Head had induced, Thomas said, 'You wouldn't do that, not you, lad.'

His father's tone had been more conciliatory than aggressive, but Seth's stance didn't soften. His chin thrust upwards, he stood like a fighting cock ready for the ring. 'Aye, I would. Believe me, Da, I would – so think on.'

The two looked at each other for a moment more before Thomas turned, bending and righting the chair he'd sent on its side. Sitting down, he reached out for the bread, only to pause once again as Seth said flatly, 'You tell Mam what I've said, all right? Babbie or no babbie, Pearl's goin' to get some schoolin'.'

'With another mouth to feed it might not be as easy as that.'

'And who brings in the money for rent and food, eh? You answer me that. *Who*, Da?'

'Now look you—'

'If me an' Fred an' Walt walk, you'll be in the mire good an' proper, that's the truth of it.' Bitterly Seth returned his father's glare. 'I'm not stupid.'

Pearl's mouth was agape. She couldn't believe Seth was talking like this to their da. Fearing what her father's reaction would be, and expecting that at any moment he would leap on her brother and hammer him to the floor, she kept as still as a mouse. Her ear was sending shooting pains through her head and she felt sick and dizzy, and she could tell Fred and Walter were scared out of their wits, but Seth – Seth was wonderful, she thought, awestruck by her brother's temerity.

Seth transferred his gaze to her where it softened, like his voice, as he said gently, 'Come an' sit yourself down, Pearl. No one is going to hit you again. Right, Da?'

Thomas didn't raise his eyes from his bowl of broth which he was now guzzling like a pig at a trough, but he nodded. Pearl skirted round him and crept to sit at the far end of the table on one of the two long wooden benches which slid under the table when not in use. There was only one chair in the kitchen, a big, flock-cushioned armchair which her father pulled to the head of the table when they ate and then back to its place in front of the range where he sat toasting himself when in the house.

Seth sat down by her side, Fred and Walter opposite them, but when Pearl stood up to fill her brothers' bowls from the huge pot of broth on the table, Seth said, 'We'll help ourselves, hinny, *all* of us, till Mam's back on her feet.'

Pearl's eyes shot to her father. She knew as well as Seth did that their da expected his food to be placed before him; he'd never so much as poured himself a cup of tea that she could remember, and her mam even stirred in the sugar for him. Thomas Croft was always served first, and with the best bits of meat and such, and not one of them would have dreamed of beginning their meal until he'd taken his first bite. He dallied sometimes, just to keep them all waiting, his hard black eyes darting round each face in turn. The fact that he hadn't done a day's work since Seth and the lads had begun to work for Mr McArthur when each of them had turned nine or ten had nothing to do with it.

Pearl's velvety smooth brow wrinkled. She had once asked Seth what he did for Mr McArthur, but her brother hadn't been forthcoming, merely answering, 'This and that,' before changing the subject. But she knew Seth and the others worked hard because they were never short of food or coal, unlike most of their neighbours.

She ate her food slowly, resisting the desire to put her hand to the side of her head and cup her aching ear in case it started another row. The last time her da had hit her, she hadn't been able to hear properly for days, and every morning there'd been blood and discharge on her pillow.

They had just finished eating when Mrs Hopkins, the midwife, came clattering down the stairs, poking her head round the door to say briefly, 'She's about to have it. I'll need some hot water and towels bringing up,' before disappearing again.

Pearl knew Mrs Hopkins didn't like their da. She had heard her talking quietly to their mam when she was last at the house twelve months ago. That baby hadn't breathed when it was born, and Walter had told her that another one had been the same some years before that. She hoped this one lived. Pearl wiped the last of her bread round her bowl. She'd felt so sorry for the other one when she'd caught sight of it for a moment when she had peeped round the bedroom door. It had been tiny and scrawny and still, lying in the old drawer that should have been its crib on a piece of stained linen. And then the midwife had seen her and quickly shooed her away, shutting the door.

Once the hot water and towels had been taken upstairs, the three brothers filled the big black kettle and two buckets from the tap in the yard they shared with several other families. When the water in the kettle was hot enough, Fred tipped it into the tin bowl which stood on a small table under the window, at the side of which were piled pans and dirty dishes. Pearl began the washing-up without a word. She knew she would be at it for a good little while, but she was used to it; every night was the same. From the moment her mother woke her in the morning and she tumbled out of the desk bed in a corner of the kitchen, her life was one of unending toil. Her parents slept in one bedroom upstairs, her brothers in the other. The front room was kept for lodgers. The family had had a series of these, mostly seamen and often ne'er-do-wells, but the last had been sent packing some months before. Pearl didn't know the reason for this, only that her father had come home unexpectedly and gone into the front room when the lodger and her mother were in there. Since then, the front room had remained unoccupied.

It was another twenty minutes before Pearl heard the sound that made her lift her head and glance at her father, who had moved his chair to its customary place in front of the range. The lads were playing cards at the table and it was Seth who said, 'Aren't you going to go up?' to Thomas as the baby's cry echoed again.

'Aye, I'm goin', I'm goin'.' Thomas lumbered to his feet. 'You got the midwife's money handy?'

'It's in the pot with the rent money.' Seth indicated the little brass pot with bowed legs that stood on the mantelpiece over the range with a flick of his hand.

'I needed that earlier.'

There was what seemed to Pearl an endless silence before Seth spoke, and the expression on his face as he stared at his father again made Pearl wonder what had got into her brother. 'You had your beer and baccy money a couple of days ago.'

'Aye, an' I needed some more.'

Seth stood up slowly. For the first time it struck Pearl that her brother was now taller than their da. 'You're tellin' me it's all gone up against the wall in the Boar's Head yard, is that it?'

Thomas stretched his neck, his eyes narrowing. He was not an intelligent man, but very early on in life he had discovered that fear was a powerful tool and he had used it to great effect, especially with his family. Although small in stature, there was an innate viciousness in his make-up and this, combined with an animal-like cunning, had served to make most people slightly afraid of him. 'Have you forgotten who you're talkin' to, lad, 'cause I'll be about remindin' you if so.'

'You could try.'

Fred and Walter were squirming on their bench and Pearl had her fist to her mouth, biting on her knuckles, but Seth stood as straight as a die. His voice had been quiet and flat, but so cold that Pearl had given an involuntary shiver. Her eyes went back and forth between her brother and father, and to her amazement it was Thomas who dropped his gaze, his voice holding a fawning note when he said, 'What's the matter? What's happened?'

Seth stared at the man he hated, the man who had sold him

8

and Fred and Walter into the brutal care of McArthur with as little feeling as he'd use to swat a fly. He wondered what his father's response would be if he told him what the matter really was. That on the last job, he'd been forced to use the knife McArthur insisted he carry and had left a man lying on the ground with his lifeblood pumping out of the hole in his chest. He'd brought up the contents of his stomach once he and his brothers were clear of the scene, the bag of booty McArthur had sent them in to steal splattered with his vomit.

The house was supposed to have been empty. McArthur had *told* them the owner was abroad. For the hundredth time since the incident the day before, Seth found himself silently crying out in his head. And now he was hooked into McArthur even more surely than ever, all the dreams he'd had of breaking away and getting a respectable job smashed for good. But the terrible thing, the thing that had kept him awake ever since, was that he had ended someone's life. *He, Seth Croft.*

A slight movement from his father brought Seth's mind back to the present and his voice betrayed none of the anguish he was feeling as he said, 'Nowt's the matter. It's just time things changed round here, that's all. We' – the jerk of his head indicated his brothers – 'don't work all hours for you to bolster the Boar's Head coffers.'

He could hear himself saying the words and part of him was as amazed as the rest of them; only two days ago he wouldn't have imagined himself standing up to his da like this. But something had changed in the last twenty-four hours, something deep and fundamental. Perhaps that's what killing a man did to you? Or perhaps it was that when the worst that could happen did happen, it set everything else in perspective. Whatever, the fear that had always paralysed him where his father was concerned was gone. Only hate remained.

It was this same hate leaping out of his son's face that checked Thomas from loosening his belt and whipping the boy into sub-mission. His buckle had marked each one of his offspring for life at some time or other; even little Pearl had a deep scar on the back of one of her legs from her father's belt. But now something told Thomas his control over Seth at least was gone – and with the realisation, bravado born of alarm rose up. 'You'll do as you're told if you know what's good for you, m'lad. You hear me?'

'Oh, I hear you, Da. But let me tell *you* somethin', all right? You don't bring a penny into this house. It's me an' the lads that put food on the table an' boots on our feet, an' you'd be in a muck sweat if we walked. You know it, an' I know it. But we're not going to walk, not with Pearl an' Mam and the new 'un round our necks – not unless you push us too far, that is. You'll get your beer and baccy money, but I'll deal with the rest of it an' there'll be no more of the brass pot. I'll see to the rent man, same as everything else, an' if you don't like the new arrangement, you know what you can do.'

The silence was absolute. But only for a moment. Thomas's face contorted as he came out with a stream of obscenities, flecks of spittle gathering at the corners of his thin mouth as he yelled at his son. It was only the sudden appearance of the midwife at the kitchen door that stopped him, and her shouting, '*Mr* Croft, control yourself. Your wife has just given birth to a bonny baby boy and you're behaving like this! What are you thinking of, man? Do you want her milk to dry up?'

Thomas's next words left the midwife in no doubt as to what his feelings were regarding his wife's milk, and as the woman's outraged, 'How *dare* you swear at me, Mr Croft!' echoed round the kitchen, he stomped out of the back door into the yard.

'Well!' The midwife's glance took in all the children's faces before coming to rest on Seth's. 'What was all that about?'

Knowing that whatever he said would be all round the street in a matter of hours, Seth said shortly, 'He's a bit het up.'

'Aye, I'd worked that out for meself.' The midwife's gaze gentled as it moved to fall on Pearl's little white face. 'Don't cry, hinny,' she said softly. 'It's just a storm in a teacup, that's all. Give me a minute an' then you can come up and see your new baby brother. You'd like that, wouldn't you? Aye, that's right. Now, how about making a nice cup of tea for your mam, eh? There's a good lassie.'

Poor little mite. As Mrs Hopkins bustled out of the room she was mentally shaking her head. The mother was bad enough, if even half the tales concerning the family's procession of male lodgers were true, but the father! Evil, he was. Downright evil. You could see it in his eyes. And the house! It was filthy even for this area. There were plenty of places she visited where the occupants were living hand to mouth but managed to keep up appearances; a bar of soap and a scrubbing brush didn't cost much, now did they? And the bairns, all eyes they were, and each one carrying the stamp of that brute's fists on them, she'd be bound.

For a second Mrs Hopkins pictured her own house in her mind's eye; her husband, back from the pit by now and sitting in his armchair in front of the fire with the cat on his lap, and the aroma of the sheep's-head broth she'd left gently simmering flavouring the air. Counting her blessings, Mrs Hopkins hurried in to see to mother and child, suddenly anxious to be home.

Downstairs, Seth lifted the big black kettle from the hob and filled the teapot before bringing it to the table. He didn't like Pearl doing jobs which involved boiling water; only last month little Beth Ingram a few doors down had been scalded when she'd tipped boiling hot soup on herself, and Beth was a couple of years older than his sister. He glanced at Pearl, who was finishing the last of the washing-up. Her face was still smudged with tears as a result of the recent scene.

His mam worked Pearl to death. He knew it, but until today had felt he was powerless to change the situation. *But his da hadn't gone for him.* The knowledge was warming, like the tots of gin McArthur provided after a job had gone well. And he'd nailed his colours to the mast. Pearl *would* go to school, he'd make sure of it, and provide the necessary funds the penny Methodists asked for. At least she'd be out of the house for most of the day then.

Pearl came to the table, drying her hands on her pinafore. 'Shall I take Mam her tea now, Seth?'

'Aye, you do that, lass.' He glanced at Fred and Walter who were sitting waiting for him to resume their game of cards. It had been as much for them as anything that he'd done for the bloke yesterday; the thought of his brothers being taken away and locked up for stealing hadn't been one he could live with. But could he live with what he'd done?

He straightened, flexing his thin shoulders as though throwing something off. He would have to. There were too many people relying on him to do anything else.

Chapter 2

It was said that Sunderland's East End was the devil's playground, and nowhere was this more true than in the infamous dockside area where Low Street was situated. The parish was immersed in squalor and filth, the overcrowded back-to-back tenements breeding poverty and ill-health, with the consequent foul language, brawling, drunkenness and misery. Every other building was a public house, gambling and prostitution were rife, and the infant mortality rates were the highest in the country. But to Pearl it was home and she had known nothing else. Blessed with a naturally sunny disposition and an innocence which was fiercely protected by her three brothers, her lot was not an altogether unhappy one.

From the first moment she had set eyes on the new baby she had loved him, and James was a placid child, content to lie in the old drawer which was his crib for hours as long as his stomach was full. As soon as she passed through the school gates, she would run all the way home, knowing that James had probably been left in the same nappy all day. Invariably she would have to change him and sort out fresh scraps of linen for his bedding, before getting started on the list of chores her mother had waiting for her, but she didn't mind this. Nor did she object to the fact that she never had time to play like most of the other children. The only thing that saddened her was, however hard she tried, she never seemed to please her mother. And today she was going to be late home. The whole class had been kept in after school until everyone had been able to recite their two times table. She hadn't thought this was fair – everyone knew Eliza Owen didn't know her numbers – and Pearl had suffered agonies of frustration until eventually the other girl had stumbled her way through and the teacher had let them go.

By the time she flew down the back lane and into the yard it was nearly half-past four and she was sticky and hot. The July day had been a scorcher. The foul smell from the privy which was shared by several houses nearly knocked her backwards as she passed it; the scavengers were due the next day with their cart and long shovels.

Gulping and swallowing against the nausea which had risen up, Pearl opened the back door and stepped into the kitchen. The smell in here was nearly as bad as outside, and as she looked down at James in his drawer she saw the baby was covered in his own filth. He was eight weeks old now and immediately he saw her gave a wide toothless smile before stuffing his faeces-smeared fingers in his mouth.

'No, don't.' Pearl's protest was involuntary and brought her mother, who had been sitting slumped in her husband's armchair fast asleep, sitting straighter.

'Where've you bin?' Kitty Croft brushed the hair out of her eyes as she spoke, knocking over the empty gin bottle which had been at the side of her. As it smashed onto the stone flags she cursed, her voice higher as she repeated, 'Where've you bin? It's an hour since you finished school.'

'We were kept in.' Pearl was already kneeling on the floor sorting through the old orange box in which James's bits of rag for his nappies and few baby clothes were kept.

'Don't give me that. You've been off playin' somewhere.'

'No, I haven't. Miss Grant kept us in until we could all say our tables.' Pearl rose quickly and walked across to the kettle placed on the steel shelf next to the range. It was half full of lukewarm water and she tipped some into the tin bowl they used for washing.

'Leave that.' Her mother's voice was strident. 'I'm talking to you, girl.'

Finding the hard brown-veined soap they bought from the slaughterhouse, Pearl set the bowl on the floor after brushing away some mouse droppings with her hand. 'James needs cleaning up, Mam.'

'I said leave it, an' look at me when I'm talkin' to you.'

Itching to get her brother sorted, Pearl straightened and stared at her mother.

Kitty glared at the daughter who'd irritated her from the moment she was born. She had never analysed why this was so, and if anyone had told her that Pearl's cornflower-blue eyes with their long thick lashes and her abundance of wavy dark-brown hair were part of the problem, she would have denied it. In truth, her daughter's prettiness was a constant thorn in Kitty's flesh. Orphaned before she could walk, Kitty had been placed in the workhouse at ten months old and had endured a wretched childhood. At fourteen she had been sent to a big house where she had worked as a kitchenmaid, and two years of mistreatment there by the cook had further embittered her. She had met Thomas on her half-day off a month when she was sixteen, and had seen to it that she was wed within a few months. She didn't love her husband – Kitty Croft was not capable of loving anyone – but she did enjoy the intimate side of their union, and when Thomas's interest in that department had begun to wane, she had made sure that her needs were met elsewhere.

As Pearl fidgeted, Kitty said sharply, 'Take that look off your face and don't come the madam with me, girl, not unless you want to feel the back of my hand.'

Pearl turned her eyes to the floor. She'd learned that silence was the only way to placate her mother when she was like this, and she needed to be able to see to James, who was smelling some-thing awful. 'Sorry, Mam.'

'Aye, I should think so. Now I'll ask again. Where've you been?'

'I told you, we were kept in. We break up for the summer holidays at the end of the week and Miss Grant wants us all to know our two times table afore we go. She's got a bee in her bonnet about it.'

Her mother looked at her a moment longer before relaxing in the chair again. 'Stupid dried-up old crone. What does she know about real life anyway? I could tell her a thing or two. Make her hair curl, I could.' When Pearl continued to stand still, saying nothing, Kitty added, 'Make me a cup of tea. I'm parched.'

'I'll just wash James—'

'Are you deaf as well as stupid? I said make me a cup of tea, didn't I?'

Pearl made the tea. Not to do so would have meant a series of stinging slaps on the backs of her legs but worse, her mother was quite capable of refusing to let her clean up James for hours.

The moment Kitty was drinking the first cup from the pot, Pearl set about washing and changing the baby. Once he was clean and dry she placed him in her desk bed before scrubbing out the drawer and putting it in front of the range to dry off. Next she cleared up the broken glass at her mother's feet and in between all this she poured Kitty two more cups of tea.

The house still reeked of excrement but it was no use opening the door and window, not with the smell in the yard enough to cause you to retch.

When James began to grizzle, she brought him to her mother for his feed and then got on with peeling the potatoes which would be boiled and served up with the leek pudding her mother had prepared earlier and some cold mutton from the day before.

For a little while silence reigned, the only sound an occasional gulp and slurp from the baby at his mother's breast.

She wished her mam liked James. Pearl's bow-shaped mouth compressed at the thought. But she didn't. When she had said the same to Seth a day or so ago, her brother had smiled and ruffled her hair and said their mam didn't like any of them, and she wasn't to worry. But she *was* worried. Pearl's throat swelled and tears pricked at the back of her eyes. It was all right for her and the lads, but James was only a little baby and he was left with their mam all day. But when she had said this to Seth, adding that she didn't want to go to school, he'd got cross with her. She had to go to school, he'd insisted. And then he'd said something which had puzzled her ever since. It was her ticket out of here and she mustn't let it slip out of her fingers. But she didn't have any ticket, so how could she lose it?

She had tried to ask him but he'd gone on, saying she was brighter than the rest of them put together and the teachers would help her if she played her cards right. But she didn't even know how to play cards. The lads did, they played nearly every night, but they'd never shown her how. Seth said ladies didn't play cards, not the sort they did anyway.

She finished the last of the taties and dropped it in the pan with the others. It was too heavy for her to carry, but her mam would put it on the hob in a minute when James had had his fill.

She wished she had a grandma and granda like most of the bairns in her class. A lot of them had two sets and she didn't even have one. Seth had said it was because their mam's mother had died when Kitty was a baby. When she had asked where their mam's da was, he'd said, 'Nowhere,' in the funny tone he used when she wasn't to ask questions. And her da's parents had died of the fever in Scotland when her da was a lad, and he'd been brought to an aunt Sunderland way. She didn't know what had happened to the aunt – she was never spoken of. Perhaps she didn't like their da? No one did.

Pearl contemplated this for a moment or two as she dried her cold red hands on her pinafore. The last time the minister had come to the school and given one of his 'addresses', as Miss Grant referred to the long talks, he'd said God expected you to be kind to people who were nasty. By doing that, you would win them over to a life of good deeds, the minister had explained, and God would change their hard hearts. When she'd put her hand up and said God couldn't know her da if He thought that, she'd got wrong from Miss Grant once the minister had gone, even though he'd just smiled and said there were exceptions to every rule.

'Here, take him.'

James's eyelids were drooping, and as she lifted him from her mother's lap his tiny hands clutched frantically at the air for a moment. Softly, she said, 'It's all right, I won't drop you. Don't worry.'

When the baby was once again lying in the desk bed she stood looking down at him for a moment. His rose-flushed face and downy head reminded her of a dolly she had seen in one of the big shops in High Street West last Christmas when Seth had taken her to see the shop windows decorated with paper chains and bells and baubles. Only the dolly had been dressed in a bonny little dress and coat with bootees on its feet. She frowned to herself. It didn't seem right that a dolly should be dressed better than a real live baby.

'What are you standing there gawpin' at? Take them things an' swill 'em off in the wash-house, they're stinkin' the place out.'

Her mother had stood up and placed the pan of potatoes on the hob, now she pointed to the nappy bucket by the back door into which Pearl had dropped James's dirty clothes and bedlinen. This was another regular job of Pearl's, but it took all the little girl's strength to lug the heavy bucket to the wash-house in the yard which, like the privy, they shared with several other families. If one of their neighbours was possing or mangling or at the big stone sink, they would invariably stop what they were doing and help her, but today the wash-house was empty. Pearl didn't mind this. Most of the other women were kind but she knew they felt sorry for her, and when she heard them muttering under their breath about her mother it made her feel funny.

She stood catching her breath just inside the doorway. The boiler was in one corner and the big poss tub in another, and the table for scrubbing stood in the middle of the room next to the mangle. The deep stone sink was under the window, and it was to this she staggered, wringing the contents of the bucket out and dropping them into the sink before she fetched clean water and the bar of soap to scrub the worst of the stains from the nappies and linen. Some of their neighbours boiled their children's nappies; Pearl often

18

saw the white squares of towelling blowing on the lines across the back lanes. When she had suggested this to her mother shortly after James was born, she'd received a slap round her legs for her trouble.

She had just finished putting the washing through the mangle, the big stiff rollers straining every muscle in her arms and shoulders, when she heard footsteps in the yard and then a man's voice calling her mother's name, accompanied by a hammering on their back door. Startled, she ran to see what was happening and as her mother opened the door she heard the man say, 'Mrs Croft? I think you'd better come quick. There's been a fight outside the Boar's Head.'

'A fight? With Thomas, you mean?'

'Aye, your husband among others. They'd all had one too many but when the dust settled your man didn't get up. I think it's bad.'

Kitty was pulling her shawl over her head and crossing it over her chest as she caught sight of Pearl. 'Stay here an' tell the lads your da's in trouble if they come in afore me,' she called. 'Tell 'em to come to the Boar's Head sharpish.'

Pearl nodded. She watched as her mother left with the man and then went to fetch the washing. For once the length of line in the yard was free – no doubt their neighbours had taken any washing in by now, it being a grand drying day, so she pegged the bits of towelling and linen to the string and hoisted them into the air with the line prop. Once that was done she went back into the house and sorted out James's drawer with fresh bedding and placed the sleeping baby in it. He stirred but didn't wake, and she knelt down by the makeshift crib and stroked his tiny hand with one finger.

It was warm and sticky in the room and she was tired, the ticking of the old wooden clock on the mantelpiece emphasising the unusual quietness. She couldn't remember a time when she had been in the house by herself and it felt strange, but not unpleasant. She watched a couple of mice making darting forays from their hole in the skirting board for crumbs and bits of food. One sat on its hind legs washing its furry face with busy paws and she smiled to herself. Her mam had put down a mousetrap in every room and they'd caught quite a few, which she hated; she felt so sorry for them when they squeaked and squealed, but the ones in the kitchen seemed cleverer than the rest and treated the traps with disdain. She didn't mind the mice, it was the bugs in the wallpaper that came out at night and walked across the ceiling and fell on your face she didn't like. She always pulled her bedcover right over her head, even on the warmest summer night.

She must have fallen asleep for a few minutes because the back door opening brought her jerking up with her heart beating fast. Her mam would give her what for, if she found her slacking.

Scrambling to her feet, she said, 'I – I was just seeing to James's bed . . .' Her voice trailed away. A policeman was standing behind her mother.

Like the rest of the occupants of Low Street and many of the surrounding streets, Pearl knew that the law was something to be feared and hated. Along with her mother's milk she'd imbibed the 'us and them' mentality that pervaded the East End, and believed absolutely that the police existed purely for the upper classes. They were to be avoided at all costs and never, ever spoken to, not unless you wanted to be locked up and never see the light of day again. Her eyes as big as saucers, she stared at the constable, biting on her thumbnail.

'Your mam's not well, lass. She's had a bit of a shock.'

To hear the dreaded figure speak in a broad Northern accent like anyone else made Pearl's eyes open wider. She glanced at her mother who had plumped down in her father's armchair without saying a word, and then her eyes returned to the policeman. He smiled kindly at her but spoke to her mother when he said, 'Is there a neighbour I can fetch? Or family living near?'

Kitty shook her head. The young constable had insisted on seeing her back, but the lads would have a blue fit if they came home to the law in the house. 'Me sons'll be in shortly and I'm all right.'

'I'll wait till they come.'

'No.' It had been too abrupt, and Kitty moderated her tone.

'Thanks very much, but I'd rather break it to 'em meself, calm like, an' it'll be less of a shock if everythin's the same as normal.'

The policeman hesitated. He was well aware that this family, like most of the others in the area, had probably fallen foul of the law at some time or other, and he had it on good authority that the husband had never done a day's honest work in his life, so the wife's reluctance was understandable. Nevertheless, he couldn't just walk out and leave her with that little mite of a lassie. His dilemma was solved in the next moment, however, when the back door opened and Seth walked in, Fred and Walter at his heels.

Kitty spoke quickly, her words running over themselves. 'It's your da, lads. There's been an accident an' the constable here brought me back after I'd gone to see him.'

'An accident?' Seth pulled himself together. For a second he'd almost turned tail and run – and how would that have looked?

'Aye.' Kitty had seen the panic and breathed a sigh of relief that he was acting normally. 'Outside the pub. Your da got in a fight with some others an' he must have cracked his head on the kerb. He – he's gone.'

'Gone?' For a moment Seth didn't understand. Then, as his mother stared at him, he said faintly, 'You mean he's dead?'

'I'm afraid so, lad.' The constable entered the conversation. 'We've a whole bunch of them locked up in the cells, but I doubt we'll get to the bottom of who hit whom, even if they could remember, which I doubt. Once they're sober we'll do our best, of course, but I don't hold out much hope. I don't think any real harm was meant. Your da was just unlucky, that's all.'

Seth stared at the policeman's ruddy face. He knew the man was expecting some show of grief, or at least shock, but the only emotion filling him was one of profound thankfulness. His da had been a vicious, vindictive bully who'd made their lives hell, and been a millstone round all their necks with the amount of money he'd frittered away with his drinking. Lowering his eyes, Seth swallowed hard. 'He was often drunk,' he said shortly.

The policeman's keen gaze rested on him a moment more. Then

he said, 'Well, he won't be drunk any more, lad. That's for sure.' He paused. 'You the oldest?'

Seth nodded.

'Working?'

Seth nodded again, and before the constable could ask any awkward questions, added, 'We'll manage all right, if that's what you're asking. Me an' the lads will take care of things. Isn't that right?' He turned and looked at his brothers, who nodded dumbly, terrified by the policeman's presence.

The constable doubted if these three had seen the inside of a school for umpteen years and the oldest didn't look to be more than fourteen or fifteen, but it was hard to tell; bairns grew up fast round these parts. His gaze moved to Pearl and the sleeping baby. Still, now wasn't the time to go into that, the family had enough on its plate.

Clearing his throat, he said, 'I'll let you know the outcome once we can question the others, but like I said, I don't hold out much hope, Mrs Croft. And you'll need to come to the station to collect your husband's personal effects, of course. Is there anyone who can help with the arrangements for the funeral?'

It was Seth who answered, and succinctly. 'I'll see to everything.'

If this one earned his living by legitimate means, he'd eat his hat. The constable kept his thoughts to himself, merely nodding at Seth, but he made a mental note to keep his eyes open in the future for the Croft lads. 'I'll be going then.' He paused. 'If you need any assistance with the formalities over the next few days, you can ask for me. Constable Johnson. All right?'

Seth made no reply, and it wasn't until the policeman had let himself out that he turned to his mother. 'What the hell were you playing at, bringing *him* back here?'

'I couldn't help it.' Like Seth, Kitty was making no show of false grief about Thomas. Seth and the lads were the breadwinners; Thomas's passing would make little impact except he had kept her warm at night. Mind, for some long time now the drink had affected his performance in that area. 'I could hardly refuse, the way he insisted – it'd have looked funny.'

'Aye, I suppose so.' Seth sat down at the table. Looking at his mother, he said quietly, 'Quick, was it?'

'Your da? Aye, he'd gone before I got there.' Kitty, too, sat down, glancing at Pearl as she said, 'Put the kettle on, I need a cup of tea.' Thomas had looked different, lying there in the street so still and sort of small with the pool of blood about his head. She had known it was him, of course, and yet it wasn't. It could have been a waxwork dummy, like the ones the travelling showmen had. She shivered, a nameless fear making her flesh creep.

It was a full month after Thomas had been buried that Kitty discovered, poor performance or not, his swansong was going to add yet another weight to Seth's shoulders. She was pregnant again.

Chapter 3

It had been nearly eighteen months since Thomas had died. The new baby, another boy his mother had named Patrick, had been born in the spring of 1899. Apart from this event there had been little change in the day-to-day functioning of the Croft family. The role Seth had taken on even before his father's death, that of head of the family, had only been strengthened with the passing of time. When he'd flatly refused to allow more lodgers taking up residence in the front room, Kitty had not argued with him. Instead, on the occasions she knew Seth and the lads were otherwise engaged, she entertained the odd sailor for an hour or two.

Pearl couldn't remember exactly when she'd become aware of her mother's activities and what it meant, but without a word being said between them, she knew she had to keep the knowledge to herself. If Seth had found out what their mother was about, there would have been hell to pay.

He was a strange mixture, was Seth, Pearl mused, one bitterly cold afternoon in January 1900. She now understood the nature of the work her brothers did for Mr McArthur, but Seth was as straightlaced as a clergyman in some things. He wouldn't allow drink in the house, not even a bottle of beer, although Pearl suspected her mother kept a bottle of gin hidden somewhere or other.

It wasn't in their bedroom though. Since her father's death her mother had insisted she sleep upstairs with her and the babies, less for company and more so she could see to James or Patrick if they woke crying in the night. Pearl didn't mind this though, since her mother's bed was a hundred times more comfortable than the desk bed had been.

Her thoughts returning to her brother, Pearl recalled the furore which had occurred after the celebrations to welcome in the new century a few days ago. Fred and Walter had been out on the town with some pals and had come home definitely the worse for wear. Seth had read them the Riot Act good and proper. He wasn't against a drink, he'd insisted, but once you had one too many, it had got you.

Pearl's hands paused in the dough she was kneading. It was their da who'd coloured Seth's thinking, she was sure of it. And Seth was a thinker all right, bright as a button too. If he'd been born with a silver spoon in his mouth he'd have gone far. When he talked about the Boer War and the Troubles in Ireland and things like that, he seemed to come alive. She didn't understand half of what he said but it didn't matter, she could listen to him for hours.

'Pearl? Where are you? Come an' see to the chamberpot.'

Her mother's querulous voice broke into her reverie. Pearl was off school because Kitty was a victim of the influenza epidemic which had hit the country. Hundreds of people a day were dying from it, according to the newspaper reports, but after being ill over Christmas and into the New Year, her mother was now on the mend. Not that you'd know it. All the family had gone down with it in the run-up to Christmas except herself and Seth, but her mother was determined to wring every last ounce out of playing the invalid, even though her two baby sons had been much worse.

She was tempted to pretend she hadn't heard her mother's call – there had already been one for a hot drink and another for her to replenish the stone hot-water bottle at her mother's feet during the last hour – but knowing that she would just keep on and on, Pearl wiped her hands on her pinny and made her way upstairs.

'You've took your time.' Kitty looked up from the penny picture paper she was reading. 'Empty the pot, an' I'll have a sup tea and a piece of that sly cake you made earlier, while you're about it. I need to build me strength up.'

Build her strength up! Her mouth set in a grim line, Pearl reached for the chamberpot under the bed and left the room without commenting. If anyone needed to build their strength up, it certainly wasn't her mother. Lying in bed all day like Lady Muck and reading the *People's Friend* and *The Lady* while stuffing her face with peppermint creams. James and Patrick were still middling but they weren't an ounce of trouble compared to their mother.

After tipping the contents of the chamberpot in the privy, she rinsed the pot out under the tap in the yard before entering the kitchen, where the warmth hit her after the cold outside. James and Patrick were taking their afternoon nap in the desk bed where she could keep an eye on them, snuggled up together under a heap of blankets. She had been so worried about them when they had caught the flu, especially little Patrick. It had been touch and go for a while, but they were both fighters. She stood looking down at the sleeping babies, a faint smile on her lips. That was what Dr Newton had said, and he was right. She and Seth had sat up for several nights when the boys were at their worst, spooning broth into them teaspoonful by teaspoonful when they wouldn't take anything, and pacing round the kitchen, each with a baby in their arms, to try to soothe their crying.

After stroking each velvety forehead Pearl turned away from the desk bed as the kettle began to sing, taking the brown teapot from its place at the side of the hob and spooning in the tea. Once the tea was mashing she fetched the sly cake from the cupboard, putting the plate on the table. The pastry, full of butter and sugar and currants, smelled wonderful and she stared at it regretfully. The sly cake looked so nice and she hadn't wanted to cut it until Seth and the lads were home. It was typical of her mother to have smelled it cooking, she had a nose on her like an elephant.

The dough was ready for the bread tins and so she divided it between them and placed the tins on the hearth to prove. That done, she scraped the last of the elastic dough off her hands and turned to the table to prepare a tray for her mother. As she did so, her mother shouted again. Pearl was about to spring into action when she checked herself. Instead, her movements slow and deliberate, she cut the sly cake and poured the tea at her own pace. By the time she took the tray up to her mother, Kitty had called several times and was red in the face.

'You gone deaf or summat?' Kitty glared at her daughter. 'I've bin callin' me head off.'

'I heard you.'

'Oh, you did, did you?' As Pearl settled the tray on her mother's lap, Kitty's glare deepened. 'Then why didn't you answer me?'

'I was getting the tea as quick as I could.'

'Well, that's not sayin' much. A snail with arthritis moves faster than you.'

'There was the bread to see to and the dinner won't make itself.'

'Don't you give me any of your lip, girl. You might think you can wind the lads round your little finger, but not me. I know what you're like, so think on.'

Pearl stared at the woman in the bed. This was her mother and she couldn't remember ever having one kind word from her. As Kitty began to eat, she turned and left the room.

It was dark and the aroma of fresh bread was filling the house when a knock came at the front door. James and Patrick had been fed and bathed and were now asleep in the bedroom in the wooden cot Seth had bought after Patrick was born. Pearl was in the kitchen, stirring the pan of hodge podge simmering on the hob. It was rich with plenty of neck of mutton, just the way Seth liked it so he could mop up the thick gravy with chunks of warm crusty bread.

Pearl wasn't thinking of anything more important than whether she'd seasoned the hodge podge sufficiently when she opened the door. It was snowing again, the two figures facing her white flecked.

'Hello, lass.' Constable Johnson was bigger, heavier than she remembered and he had another policeman with him who was built like a brick outhouse. 'Your brothers in?'

Pearl found herself stammering when she said, 'My – my younger brothers are in bed,' even though she knew he didn't mean James and Patrick.

'Your older brothers, lass. Seth, isn't it? And Frederick and Walter.'

Somehow the fact that he knew her brothers' Christian names was more terrifying than anything else. Pearl shook her head.

'Your mam then?'

'She's — she's in bed with the flu.'

Constable Johnson looked at his associate. Neither spoke, but then he turned back to Pearl. 'We need to come in and make sure, lass. All right?'

It wasn't all right. If Seth had told her and her mother once he'd told them a hundred times never to let the law into the house. The thought of displeasing her brother overriding her fear of the policemen, Pearl shook her head again. Instinctively knowing she mustn't bring Seth and the lads into it, she said, 'Me mam wouldn't like it.'

What the Constable would have said next, Pearl was never to find out. Kitty, with the uncanny ability any East Ender had for smelling a policeman miles away, had got out of bed and come to the top of the stairs where she peered down at them. 'What's up?' She clutched her shawl against her nightdress, coughing loudly for good measure. 'What do you want?'

'A word with your lads, Mrs Croft.'

'They're not in. Didn't Pearl tell you they're not in?'

'Aye, she did.'

'There you are then.' Kitty's voice had taken on a slightly belligerent tone. 'I'll tell 'em you were askin' for 'em when I see 'em.'

By way of answer to this, Constable Johnson and his colleague pushed Pearl aside and stepped into the hall.

'Here, who said you could come in?' Kitty came down the first few stairs, her voice rising as she said, 'This is a respectable house, this is.'

Ignoring her, the two policemen opened the door to the front room. By the time Kitty had reached them they had moved on to the kitchen, where they turned to face mother and daughter.

'Where are your lads, Mrs Croft?' The other policeman spoke, his voice flatter, harder than Constable Johnson's.

'I told you, they're not in and they don't tell me what time they'll be back. They're not bairns any more.'

'Where do they sleep?'

'What?'

'Which room or rooms do they occupy?'

'Now look, you sling your hook—'

As the policemen brushed past Kitty and made for the stairs, Kitty growled, 'Theirs is the first one at the top of the stairs,' before hissing at Pearl, 'Now look what you've done. You should have slammed the door in their faces an' bolted it.'

Pearl stood in the hall biting at her thumbnail as her mother followed the policemen upstairs. It wouldn't have made any difference if she'd done what her mother said, she told herself sickly as thuds and the sound of drawers being opened came from the lads' room. Look at the Holdens in Fighting Cock Lane. The police had broken the door down when they'd come after Mr Holden, and the neighbours had seen Mrs Holden carried out kicking and screaming because she'd tried to stop them taking her husband.

Her stomach churning, Pearl listened to her mother ranting and raving. Then suddenly, Kitty's voice stopped, and she could hear one of the policemen saying something, his tone grim and sonorous. She was just wondering whether to creep upstairs and listen at the keyhole when the door to the lads' bedroom opened.

Shrinking back against the wall, Pearl watched the two policemen walk downstairs, her mother following. Kitty's voice was plaintive when she said, 'Look, I'm tellin' you, I knew nowt about them things an' nor do my lads. Likely they've bin stuffed up the chimney for donkey's years, long afore we moved in.'

'I doubt that, Mrs Croft.' Constable Johnson was holding a cloth bag. 'Some of this jewellery matches a description of property which was stolen over the Christmas period.'

'Not by my lads.'

'A robbery in which the butler of the residence was threatened with a knife until he showed the three thieves where the safe was hidden.'

'There you are then. My lads wouldn't know one end of a knife from the other. Good as gold they are.'

Constable Johnson stopped and turned in the hall, staring at Kitty who remained on the bottom step of the stairs. She stared back, openly defiant. 'We've had our eye on your lads for some time, so this is no more a surprise to us than it is to you,' he said flatly. 'We just haven't been able to get any proof before.'

'Proof!' Kitty snorted. 'Likely you slipped that up the chimney when I wasn't lookin', to fit 'em up.'

'You know that isn't true, Mrs Croft.'

'The devil I do. You lot are all the same, terrorisin' good, honest, godfearin' souls like my lads while turnin' a blind eye to the goings-on of the nobs. I know, I know.'

'Shut up.' The other policeman was clearly losing patience. He included Pearl in the sweep of his head as he said, 'Go and sit in the kitchen. And quietly.'

'Don't you tell me what to do in me own house.' Kitty's chin was up, her thin lips clamped together, but as the policeman took a step towards her she quickly went through to the kitchen.

Once Pearl and her mother were sitting at the kitchen table Constable Johnson opened the door into the yard and disappeared for a few minutes. Nothing was said until he returned. The other policeman stood in front of the range warming his buttocks as though he had forgotten their presence.

When Constable Johnson walked in, Pearl noticed he wasn't holding the cloth bag any more. Glancing at his colleague, he said, 'No sign as yet, but we're ready.'

'More of you skulkin' about, is there?' Kitty said sharply.

'Worry you, does it?'

Kitty shrugged but she couldn't hide her unease. Pearl's hands were joined on her breast; she was feeling panic-stricken. Wild thoughts darted about her head. Could she jump up and run out before they caught her, and warn Seth and the lads? Or pretend she had to go and see someone? A neighbour maybe?

Or say she had to go to the privy and then creep out and try to get away?

But she didn't know where Seth and the others were or when they were coming back, only that it would be soon and they would enter the house via the back lane. They always did. And the waiting policemen would catch them.

Her mind whirled and spun; although it was hard for her to think clearly, she knew she and her mother were as helpless to change the next hour or two as her three brothers were. They were all caught in a trap.

She could smell that the hodge podge was beginning to catch on the bottom of the pan and so she stood up and walked over to the range to stir it.

'Something smells good.'

Constable Johnson smiled at her but she didn't smile back. She thought she heard him sigh but then from outside came the sounds she had been dreading. Men shouting, a policeman's whistle, Seth's voice and Walter's too.

Constable Johnson's colleague had wrenched open the back door and she and her mother followed them into the yard, Kitty shrieking obscenities. The yard vibrated to screams and yells and to the thud of blows, and in the tangle of fighting bodies Pearl saw her brothers and several policemen. Even as she watched, a policeman caught Fred a vicious blow on the side of his head with his truncheon and her brother went down like a felled tree, another policeman falling on top of him.

The next-door neighbours on either side had come to their back doors and were adding to the din, shouting encouragement to their own and screaming abuse at the policemen. Even the dogs in the immediate area were joining in and barking ferociously.

Pearl's only thought was to get to her beloved Seth. She had flung herself into the fray before Constable Johnson, who was having his work cut out to hold Kitty, could stop her. Seth had undoubtedly been getting the worst of it — there were two big burly policemen to each brother — but he was still on his feet when Pearl reached him. The policeman who had been about to club Seth with his truncheon managed to stop in the nick of time as the small figure came between them, and Seth, his arms opening instinctively to receive her, staggered back a pace or two to land against the yard wall.

It was all over within moments. Fred was yanked to his feet where he stood dazed and bleeding next to Walter, who was being restrained by the simple expedient of having his arm twisted behind his back so far he was doubled up in agony. Kitty had stopped struggling and had collapsed on the icy ground, wailing like a banshee and slapping at Constable Johnson's hands when he tried to pick her up.

Pearl was now wrapped around Seth's chest like a small monkey, her body heaving with silent sobs as the blood from a cut above his eyebrow dripped on to her hair. When one of the policemen tried to take her from Seth she clung all the tighter, nearly strangling her brother in the process. It was a signal from Constable Johnson that made the other policeman step back.

'It's all right, lass, it's all right.' Seth's head was swimming and he felt nauseous from the blows he'd received. 'This'll get sorted, don't you worry.'

She didn't believe him. She had seen the cloth bag and the expression on the face of Constable Johnson when he had looked at her mother. They were going to take Seth away and she couldn't bear it.

'I need you to look after James and Pat for me.' The fight had gone out of Seth as he stood swaying with Pearl in his arms, and he knew he was in a bad way. He had never passed out in his life but he was a breath away from it. 'Will you do that, eh, lass? Till I'm home?'

She didn't answer for a moment and then a trembling, whispered, 'Yes,' reached him.

'There's a good girl.' He didn't want to give way and let himself slide to the ground, the coppers would love that, but he felt as weak as a kitten. He managed to unwind her from him and set her on her feet a moment before the ground rushed up to meet him, the last sound he heard before losing consciousness her frantic cries.

Chapter 4

Seth came to in the police wagon. He was propped between two big policemen, and Fred and Walter were sitting opposite him. As he raised his head and tried to focus, he remembered what had happened and in answer to Fred's, 'You all right, man?' he nodded before shutting his eyes again, as much to think as anything.

'They've found the stash up the chimney.'

Walter's voice brought his eyes opening again. He felt muzzy and sick, but his mind was clearing. 'Shut up, Walt.'

'It's no good, Seth.'

'I said shut up.' As his brother did as he was told, Seth looked at them both, his voice softer as he said, 'You know nowt, all right? Nowt. Anything I did, I did on my own. Got it?'

'You don't seriously think the judge'll buy that, do you?' the policeman on Seth's left said scornfully. 'The three of you are going down the line, make up your minds about that.' He jerked his head towards his companion. 'Interesting what we found on him when he was out cold, eh?'

'Very interesting.'

As Seth's hand went instinctively to his trouser leg and the hidden compartment where he kept his knife, the first policeman laughed. 'Too late, son. Much too late.'

Seth's lower jaw moved from one side to the other but he said nothing. They had him, sure enough, but if his brothers played their cards right they might still walk away. Someone needed to take care of things at home.

He was still thinking this way right up to the moment the next morning when he was taken out of his cold miserable cell in the bowels of the police station. He was flanked by two policemen and led up a flight of stone steps into a narrow corridor which had several doors opening on to it. One of the policemen opened the first one and pushed him into a small, windowless room which had a bench attached to one wall. The only other furniture consisted of a square wooden table behind which two policemen were sitting on large padded chairs. He knew immediately that these were not ordinary flatfoots but men of authority, even before one of them said, 'Seth Croft, isn't it? I'm Inspector Taylor and this is Sergeant Atkinson. I hope you don't intend to waste our time.'

The two policemen who had escorted him from the cells had gone to stand by the door, leaving him in the middle of the room facing his inquisitors. He turned and glanced at their impassive faces before staring at the two sitting men. The Inspector had spoken in what Seth would have described as a la-di-dah voice, but when the Sergeant said, 'Well, lad? Going to make a clean breast of it, I hope?' the Northern burr was strong.

Seth's head was still pounding and he felt sick to the depths of his stomach, but his voice was steady. 'Clean breast of what?'

'The little matter of certain valuables taken from Highgrave House being found stuffed up the chimney in your bedroom, along with other objects we know to be stolen. That's what.' The Sergeant paused. 'It's no use denying it, lad. The knife even matches the description of the one used by the three assailants to threaten the butler.'

Seth returned the man's stare but said nothing.

'If you're canny you'll plead guilty and save us all a lot of time. Always goes down well with the judge, a guilty plea. He don't like folk trying to mess him about, any more than we do.'

All through the long night hours when he'd been chilled to the marrow and feeling like death, Seth had thought about what he was going to say. Now it came easily. 'Aye, well, it looks like you know it all, but you've got it wrong about me brothers. I *was* with two other blokes, but Fred and Walt aren't involved in this.'

'Oh, come, Mr Croft.' The Inspector's smooth voice suggested amusement. 'Do we look as though we were born yesterday?'

'It's the truth.'

'Your brothers accompanied you on that spree and others.'

'No.'

'They are your partners in crime in every way.'

'No, they aren't.' He appealed to the Sergeant. 'They aren't, I swear it. He's got it wrong.'

'Tell him.' The Inspector looked briefly at his colleague. 'I haven't got all day.'

Tell him? Tell him what? As Seth stared at the Sergeant, fear gripped his vitals.

'We had a tip-off, lad. About you and your brothers. They put you down for the Highgrave job and two others. I'd say you've upset someone, someone who knew a mite too much for your good.'

McArthur. Seth's stomach turned over. Somehow McArthur had found out about the couple of recent jobs they'd done on their own. But how could he? They'd been careful, dead careful. They hadn't even tried to get rid of the stuff through the normal channels, knowing McArthur had long fingers, but had hidden it for the time when they left Sunderland for good. That's what he'd been working towards. Getting the family away down South where they could make a new start.

'Well?' The Inspector leaned slightly forward over the table and Seth noticed how cold his eyes were. Glassy almost. Like a fish. 'What do you say now?'

His mouth was dry. He had to swallow before he could say, 'My brothers weren't with me. They've never been with me.'

'Get him out of here.'

The Sergeant nodded at the policemen behind him and the next moment Seth felt himself hauled backwards out of the room.

Despite his protests that he could walk by himself they didn't relinquish their grip on his arms until they thrust him back into his cell. When the door banged closed behind them Seth stood for a moment with his eyes tightly shut. Then he opened them and walked across to sit on the wooden pallet bed which was devoid of even a straw mattress. Besides this there was just a bucket in one corner and it stank to high heaven.

Would Fred and Walter do what he'd told them and keep to the story that they were innocent of all charges? He sat gripping his knees, his mind racing. They *had* to – it was the only hope for Pearl and his mam and the babbies.

Perhaps he'd been crazy to think he could do anything without McArthur finding out, but he'd never imagined in his wildest dreams it would result in this. A beating from one of McArthur's thugs perhaps, even a kneecap job, but not this. And of course McArthur would have known he wouldn't have dared to try to get rid of the stuff through the network of fences in the town, so he'd probably assumed it would be in the house somewhere. *Damn it.*

Seth dropped his head in his hands. How could he have been so stupid? Better to work for McArthur for ever and a day than this. The three of them banged up together. *What was he going to do?*

In the event he could do nothing. Three weeks later, on a bitterly cold February day, Seth, Frederick and Walter Croft were sent to prison for eight years apiece.

Kitty had left Pearl minding the children and gone to the courthouse to hear the verdict, at which time she caused such a commotion she had to be forcibly removed from the building. It was Constable Johnson who told her on the steps of the courthouse that she could count herself lucky; but for the fact that the judge's wife had presented him with a bonny baby boy the night before, her lads might well have received fifteen years or longer. And now her best bet was to go home and look after her family, he added grimly. If the judge hadn't been in such a good mood, she would have found herself in contempt of court and in the cells with her lads.

Kitty watched the constable as he made his way back inside the building, rubbing her arm where his fingers had gripped her as he'd manhandled her out of the court. Stinking copper. She spat on the ground. All alike, they were.

Pulling her shawl over her head, she began walking home, the grey afternoon made more miserable by the freezing fog which had enveloped everything in a shroud. She wasn't far from Low Street when, on passing one of the rough, spit-and-sawdust pubs in the area, the door opened and a burly sailor half fell into the street, righting himself by holding onto her shoulder.

'Hey, get off, you,' she began, only to stop and peer at him. 'Seamus?' she said. 'Is that you?'

'Kitty?' Seamus had had more than a few. 'The fair Kitty? Well, you're a sight for sore eyes.' He belched a gust of beer fumes into her face. 'Your lads around, are they?'

She knew what he was asking. And the idea that had begun to take shape from the day Seth and the others were arrested, crystallised. 'No, they're not around. They'll not be around for many a long day.' Swiftly she explained what had happened, adding, 'So things'll be a bit different from now on, lad. I've bairns to feed, so I can't give it away for fun no more, if you get my drift.'

Seamus got her drift and it didn't bother him an iota. He had paid for his pleasure since taking to the sea as a youth, leaving his seed in accommodating bellies in every port he'd docked at. Smiling, he said, 'Suits me, lass. An' I take it I can stay the night for the right price, being as we're old friends, as it were?'

Kitty smiled back. Seamus was a good sort, he'd always brought a couple of bottles of gin with him in the past, and she had other 'friends' she knew would be as reasonable. 'Don't see why not. It's up to me now, isn't it?'

He put his arm round her waist, drawing her against him. 'How about we get some gin on the way back, eh? An' how are you off for grub? I could eat a horse.'

Kitty hesitated. The bit of money Seth had put by for what he'd called a rainy day was fast disappearing, and if Seamus was prepared to fork out . . .

Seamus took the hint. 'Come on, lass, we'll call and get a few victuals, how about that? I sail the morrer but I'll see you all right afore I go. Can't say fairer than that.'

The fog had drawn in an early twilight and Pearl had already lit the oil lamp in the kitchen when Kitty walked in. The relief at seeing her mother swamped everything for a moment and she didn't realise Kitty wasn't alone.

'Oh, Mam, what happened?' She had been like a cat on a hot tin roof all day, but since her mother had left earlier, her anxiety had known no bounds. After shouting at James for no other reason than that the toddler wanted some attention, she'd tried to pull herself together. Settling James on the clippy mat in front of the fire with a saucepan lid and a wooden spoon, she'd let him bang away to his heart's content while she'd seen to Patrick, propping the baby up in the desk bed with a crust to chew on. He was teething hard and miserable with it. Once her baby brothers were occupied she had made the pastry for the cow-heel pie they were having for dinner, using the leftover pieces for a few jam tarts, but when it had begun to get dark and her mother still hadn't returned, each minute had seemed like an hour.

As Seamus followed Kitty into the kitchen, Kitty said, 'This is a friend of mine an' he's stayin' the night,' without answering Pearl's question.

As Seamus plonked a sack holding items of food on the table, Pearl's eyes went to it and then the bottles of gin in her mother's hands. She had seen this man before. He was one of her mother's visitors. When he smiled at her, saying, 'Hello there,' in a friendly voice, she stared at him for a moment before again saying to her mother, 'What happened?'

'What do you think happened?' Kitty began to unpack the groceries as Seamus sat down in the armchair that had been Seth's since Thomas's demise, ruffling James's curls as the child looked up at him. 'They've bin sent down.'

'How — how long for?'

'Eight years.' Kitty reached for one of the bottles of gin and after pouring a good measure into a cup, she passed it to Seamus before doing the same for herself. Without looking at her daughter, she said, 'Now go an' light a fire in the front room. It'll be as cold as the grave in there.'

'The *front* room?'

Pearl's voice had been high, and now in one swift movement Kitty took hold of her arm and pulled her out into the hall, shutting the kitchen door behind her. 'Take that look off your face an' do as you're told,' she hissed. 'Seamus is a good pal of mine an' he's already set us up with enough grub for the week, so you mind your manners.'

Pearl jerked herself free. 'How can you have him here and let him sit in Seth's chair when the lads—'

A ringing slap across the side of her face cut off her words and then she felt her head bouncing on her shoulders as her mother shook her. 'Don't you come the madam with me. Who do you think is going to pay the rent an' put food on the table now? Not your precious Seth, m'girl. We're on our own now, an' things are going to change. When I say do somethin' you'll do it, no questions asked. Now get in there an' light the fire, an' then see to putting a hot-water bottle in the bed. An' you be polite to Seamus unless you want more of the same.'

Pearl could hear Patrick beginning to grizzle; the baby would be wanting his tea. That, more than her mother's threats, made her do as she was told. Once the fire was blazing in the front room and the hot-water bottle was in the bed, Kitty picked up the half-full gin bottle and inclined her head at Seamus before glancing at Pearl who was feeding Patrick a bowl of thick rabbit broth. 'You can dish up our dinner an' put it to warm – we'll have it later,' she said, and left the room without waiting for a reply.

Pearl continued feeding Patrick whilst keeping an eye on James who was sitting in his highchair eating small chunks of bread soaked in the broth. Since he had begun to feed himself after recovering from the flu it had been a great help, although occasionally he stuffed too much in his mouth and ended up choking.

What would Seth and Fred and Walter be eating tonight in that terrible place? And Pearl knew it was a terrible place — she'd heard stories about what went on in gaols from Humphrey Fraser at school. Half of Humphrey's family were in some gaol or other, and he was inordinately proud of it. And her mam, letting that man sit in Seth's chair and then taking him into the front room! She wasn't too clear about what went on in the front room, but she knew it was all to do with the big bed the lodgers had slept in, and her mother allowing liberties. That's what she had heard Seth say to Kitty just after their father had died: 'There'll be no more liberties taken by the scum of the earth with you, in this house, not while I've breath in my body.'

But whatever it was that went on, her mother didn't intend to do it secretly any more, not now Seth had gone.

To stop her tears falling, she applied herself to washing Patrick's face — a procedure to which he heartily objected — and then got both of her brothers ready for bed.

She could hear her mother laughing in the front room and the deep sound of Seamus's voice, along with the bedsprings twanging. It made her stomach twist and tighten. How could her mam laugh like that on the day Seth and Fred and Walter were locked away? Eight years. *Eight years.* She would be eighteen years old by the time they were free, and that was old.

Carrying Patrick in her arms, she stood behind James each step as the toddler clambered up the stairs on his hands and knees. Once in the bedroom she lifted both little boys into the cot and then sat on her mother's bed as they snuggled deeper under their blankets. There was ice on the inside of the window and her breath was a white cloud in front of her when she breathed out, but although James and Patrick were already half asleep she continued to sit and watch the mound of their bodies by the light of the streetlamp directly outside their window.

Her mam was doing bad things in the front room with the sailorman. She had been doing the same for years, but this was different somehow. Pearl didn't put the word 'brazen' to it, just 'different'.

She rocked herself back and forth with her arms crossed over her stomach, making no sound so as not to disturb her brothers, in spite of the tears coursing down her face. *And she didn't know what to do. She was frightened, so frightened, and she didn't know what to do.* And then Seth's words came back to her. 'I need you to look after James and Pat for me. Till I'm home.'

Slowly she took control of herself. She had promised Seth, and a promise was a promise. Drying her eyes on her pinny, she brushed a few damp tendrils of hair from her cheeks. James and Patrick were now her responsibility, and she would do all she could to keep them safe and warm and fed. School didn't matter. Nothing mattered, except her promise to Seth.

She slid off the bed, a thin little figure in the shadowed room, and made her way downstairs to get the dinner ready for her mother and the sailorman.

PART TWO

The Romanies

July 1901

Chapter 5

The pavements and buildings were radiating heat, and the evening sun was still hot as Pearl pushed the creaking perambulator through the dusty streets in the direction of home. The country was in the grip of a heatwave, and when Pearl had risen very early that morning, it had promised to be another baking July day. Her mother and a woman named Cissy Hartley, a new and seemingly bosom pal of Kitty's, had been 'entertaining' in the front room for most of the night, and when the men and Cissy had left just before dawn, her mother had come upstairs to tell her she expected the boys to be kept quiet all day so she could sleep. James and Patrick had been irritable and tetchy with the heat for the last week, and so Pearl had determined to take them out for the day, Tunstall Hills way.

After packing a basket with some food and a bottle of water, she'd lifted three-year-old James and two-year-old Patrick into the rusty old perambulator they'd bought from a neighbour for a shilling or two the year before, and off they had set.

They'd had a wonderful day. Pearl smiled to herself as she looked at the two little boys, rosy cheeked and fast asleep in the depths of the pram. The long walk to the outskirts of Bishopwearmouth had been worth it. Once they had left the noise and dirt of the town behind, the essence of summer had been everywhere. The still air had been heavy on the hills with the perfume of eglantine, the wild briar; the bright sunshine warming the foxgloves and brightening the dog roses and daisies, clover and forget-me-nots which had painted the banks and meadows. The boys had rolled and tumbled and frolicked like two excited puppies when she had found a spot to settle at, loving the freedom and softness of their surroundings after the grim streets and stinking back lanes.

When they had worn themselves out she had let them sleep before lunch under the shade of an oak tree in the scented grass; sitting with her arms wrapped round her knees, she'd gazed into a shimmering heat-haze before falling asleep herself.

They had picked armfuls of wild flowers in the afternoon to take home, sweetly scented in both leaf and bloom and glowing with colour. These were now lying at one end of the perambulator by the boys' heads, and although they were beginning to wilt, they were still lovely.

She would do this again. Pearl mentally nodded to the thought as the smells and squalor of the East End began to make themselves felt. She rarely went to school now. Most days she took care of the boys and saw to the house and meals, sometimes while her mother slept and sometimes because Kitty hadn't come home the night before. On those occasions her mother would return at some time during the morning smelling of drink and smoke and demanding a hot meal before falling into bed after drinking more gin. Pearl had learned to take the money for rent and food out of her mother's purse while she slept, because once she was awake there were always arguments. Funnily enough though, her mother never challenged her on this practice.

The nearer they got to Low Street, the more the stink of festering privies and brooding decay impinged on the lingering beauty the day had produced in her mind. The smell of the docks hung in the air, a composite of stale fish, filth and polluted water, and for a moment Pearl was seized with the wild notion of turning the perambulator round and wheeling it as fast as she could away from the East End, away from her mother, for ever. But there was nowhere she could go. And so she walked on.

Kitty was slumped at the kitchen table when Pearl entered the house with the boys after leaving the perambulator by the back door. She looked dirty and unkempt, and her features had coarsened over the last couple of years. She was fanning herself with one of the penny magazines she loved to read, her blouse half undone and her breasts hanging slack.

'Where the hell've you bin?' She reached for the glass of gin at the side of her, knocking it back in one gulp. 'There's the dinner to see to.'

'You said you wanted the bairns out of the way so I took them out.' Both boys were holding a bunch of flowers, and as they offered them to their mother, Pearl said, 'Look – they picked them for you.'

'What do I want with flowers?' Kitty flapped her hand at the children. 'Put 'em on the table.'

'I'm taking them straight up, they're tired out. I'll see to the dinner when I come down. It's cold meat and potatoes. I didn't think you'd want anything warm with the weather being like this.'

When her mother made no reply to this but poured herself another tot of gin, Pearl took her brothers upstairs. She and the boys shared their older brothers' room now, all sleeping together in the double bed the room held. James and Patrick were barely awake when she undressed them, and fell asleep as soon as their heads touched the pillow. She stood looking down at them for a moment before kissing each small brow. They were growing so fast, they wouldn't be babies much longer, she thought with a pang. She wished they could remain babies for ever, ignorant of anything outside their small world of eating, sleeping and playing.

Turning abruptly, she made her way downstairs and brought out the smoked bacon and potatoes which had been left over in the pantry on the cold slab from the previous day's dinner, adding a loaf of bread and pat of butter to the table.

It was as they were finishing their meal that Kitty said nonchalantly, 'Mr F is comin' by shortly, so make sure the front room's clean an' tidy. He likes things proper, Mr F.'

Pearl put down her knife and fork; she suddenly had no appetite for the remainder of the food on her plate. Her mother always referred to her regulars by the first letter of their surnames – Mr T, Mr W, Mr A – but of the several or so men who called at the house on certain nights, it was only this one individual, Mr F, she was frightened of. If any of the others caught sight of her, they would often smile and say hello, and even toss her a coin or two and tell her to buy some sweets, but Mr F wasn't like that. She shivered deep inside. He just stared at her with that funny look on his face, his eyes going all over her and making her feel she had to wash wherever they'd touched, as though they'd left a trail of slime like the slugs did.

'I don't like him,' she said flatly.

'Don't start that again. You don't know when you're well off, that's your trouble, madam.' Kitty glared at her daughter, taking in the sunflushed cheeks and luminous eyes with their thick lashes. It seemed as though with every month that passed, Pearl got lovelier, and the dislike she had always felt for this flesh of her flesh verged on something stronger these days. 'Get your backside off that chair,' she went on, 'an' earn your keep – an' you can change the sheets on the bed while you're about it. Mr F likes clean sheets.'

As Pearl looked at Kitty, there came to her a strange thought. Her mother would have done what she did in the front room sooner but for marrying at sixteen, and she would have been happier. It was only her father, and then Seth, who had prevented her from going down this road years ago. There had been talk in the wash-house among their neighbours for months now – she'd heard them whispering when they thought she wasn't listening or didn't understand. But her understanding had been broadened considerably since Seth had gone. The neighbours thought her mother was a trollop, and Mrs Cook next door had said she'd got more time for the dockside dollies because at least they had the decency to keep their bairns out of it.

Slowly Pearl turned and went into the front room. The old three-quartersize iron bed the lodgers had used stood against one wall, the covers in a heap, and the horsehair sofa took up most of the remaining space. The floor was littered with empty gin and beer bottles and cigarette stubs, and it was stifling, the stale smell which was a composite of many things making her swallow hard. She hated this room.

She stripped the worn sheets from the bed, wrinkling her nose in distaste as her hand brushed against one of the patches of dried matter staining the bottom sheet in several places, and then gathered up the bottles and other large items of debris. That done, and the soiled sheets in soak, she began to clear the cigarette stubs and other bits and pieces with a dustpan and brush.

Quite when she became aware that she wasn't alone she didn't know, but a sixth sense had her flesh creeping even before she turned and saw the fat, greasy-looking figure of Mr F standing in the doorway. Quickly she straightened, her voice a stammer as she said, 'I – I'm clear – clearing up.'

He nodded, his small dark eyes never leaving her face, and then for the first time in the twelve months or so since he had been visiting the house, Pearl heard him speak. 'There's a good little lassie,' he said softly.

Pearl glanced at the unmade bed. The clean sheets she had fetched from the cupboard in her mother's room were neatly folded on top of the mattress. Her mother would expect her to see to it before she left, but the thought of making the bed while this man watched her was mortifying. 'I – I'll see to the rest of it in – in a minute.'

He nodded again but continued to stand in the doorway. Pearl wondered where her mother was and why she hadn't come to join him. Every sense in her body heightened and her face scarlet, she put the dustpan and brush to one side and approached the bed. This man was Kitty's best payer, her mother had told her so before when she'd voiced her unease about him, clipping her across the ear for good measure. She had to be polite to him. Clearing her throat, she said, 'My mother's in the kitchen.'

'I'm aware of that.'

Not knowing what to do, Pearl unfolded the bottom sheet. It had been dried outdoors and for a moment the elusive scent of fresh air reached her nostrils.

'Let me help you with that.' He shut the door as he spoke.

'No, no – it's all right.' Panic uppermost, Pearl wondered if her mother knew he was here. Should she call her, or would she get into trouble? He was so near now she could smell the acrid odour of his sweat, but she didn't dare look at him. Her hands trembling, she shook the sheet over the bed.

'You're a bonny little lassie but then you know that, don't you?' His voice had changed. It had become thick, excited. 'Oh aye, you know it all right.'

Her terror increasing, Pearl mumbled, 'My mam – she – she wants me to get the room sorted.'

'Your mam wants you to please me. That's what your mam wants.'

She opened her mouth to scream but his hand came hard over her lips. He was a big man, in stature as well as girth, and Pearl was slender for her years, her child's body as yet showing no signs of puberty. When his free hand came out and grabbed her dress, heaving her onto the bed, she fell into the middle of it like a rag doll, her limbs sprawling. She tried to roll away but he slapped her so hard across the side of her head she saw stars, and then he was on top of her, tearing at her clothes as he stripped her, one hand again over her mouth.

She fought him but her wild flailing had no effect as he crouched on top of her, muttering obscenities. When he released the hand over her mouth in order to unbutton his trousers she wriggled backwards, falling off the bed and hitting the floor. The pain that shot from her coccyx was so acute she passed out for a few moments, regaining consciousness to find she was again on the bed and his full weight was on top of her. Then her body was rent in two, pain that was all-consuming causing her to scream and choke as she struggled to escape the thing ripping her apart. His hand came across her nose as well as her mouth, cutting off her air supply, and as she tried to bite at it he slapped her again.

She knew she was dying. The pain was so terrible she couldn't bear it. And then he began groaning and shuddering, and the mad pounding lessened as he became still before rolling off her. She lay limp and helpless, the agony between her legs and in her belly causing her to shake uncontrollably.

'You shouldn't have fought me.' The soft thick voice came to her but she didn't open her eyes or speak, wanting only for him to be gone. 'You made me hurt you by fighting me.'

When she felt the touch of his fingers on her inner thigh she jerked, her eyes opening involuntarily. He raised his hand to his mouth, sucking his fingers which were covered in red.

'We'll have some good times, you and me, and I can be generous, you'll see.' He stood up, buttoning his trousers before extracting some notes from his pocket which he threw on the bed beside her. 'You wouldn't get many who'd pay as much as that for a breaking-in – you ask your mam.'

Curling herself into a little ball and with the tears raining down her face, Pearl didn't answer, terrified he would come at her again. It was only when he had left the room that she found the strength to pull the sheet round her, cocoon-fashion, the red stain between her legs vivid on the bleached linen.

Kitty raised her head as the kitchen door opened. She had been dozing in the armchair, the gin bottle at her elbow. 'Well?'

Leonard Fallow looked at the woman he had forced himself to service for the last year, ever since he had caught sight of the daughter on his first visit to the house. He had been drunk that night or he would never have come back with Kitty in the first place. He liked them young, very young and fresh. All the things Kitty wasn't. But his body had needed release and when he was in his cups, anything would do. And there had been the child. Like a rose on a dung heap. And he had known he had to have her.

But this old biddy had made him pay, and not just in the amount she had demanded for the breaking-in. She was wily enough to know that once he'd had the daughter, her own usefulness was over, and so she had made the most of delaying that time, using one excuse after another.

Straightening his jacket, he said, 'It's done.'

'Put up much resistance, did she?'

'A little.' He didn't intend to discuss the details and his tone reflected this.

'Where's me money?'

His voice cool, he said, 'I left it with her.'

'With *her*? You give it to me, all right? I take it you do want to come again?'

He let a small silence grow before he said, 'Possibly,' whilst knowing as well as she did that he'd be back within days.

'Then in the future you give it to me.'

He nodded. He didn't want to get on the wrong side of the mother, not now. He had one or two friends who would be very grateful for an introduction to the child, but he had intended to have his way with her first. It was better than any drug or drink, being the first.

'You want to stay for a while?' Kitty stood up, swaying slightly, as she gave him what she thought was a beguiling smile. 'You can have it for free after what you've stumped up the night for the lass.'

Leonard looked at her lank hair, the creases in her neck lined with dirt and her pendulous breasts. Only the thought of having the child had enabled him to achieve the act in the past, and once or twice it had been beyond him. Using this, he said, 'You know me, Kitty. Once is all I can manage, and sometimes not that.'

She stared at him. He didn't fool her. She'd seen the way he looked at Pearl – fair licked his lips, he did. For a moment resentment burned, deep and bitter, and then she told herself it didn't matter. Mr F had paid a small fortune for the lass tonight, and although she might not get that much again, her being broken in now, there would still be men who liked them young who would pay plenty.

'I'll be off then.' Leonard picked up his hat and gloves from where he had left them on a kitchen chair on entering the house earlier. Even on the hottest day he wore gloves as his position in life demanded.

Kitty had sat down again, reaching for the gin bottle. 'Aye, so long.'

★   ★   ★

52

Leonard had been gone some time before Kitty rose, draining the glass and smacking her lips. She hadn't known how long Leonard would expect to stay and so she hadn't arranged to meet Cissy or see another customer. Her thoughts on the money Leonard had left with Pearl, she opened the door to the front room. Her daughter was curled in the middle of the bed with the sheet round her, and in spite of the humid night Pearl was shivering convulsively.

Kitty looked at her with dispassionate eyes. 'Get off there, you'll stain the mattress,' was all she said.

Pearl opened her eyes. 'I hurt.'

'Aye, we all hurt the first time, but you'll live.' She came closer to the bed and it was then she registered the amount of blood Pearl had lost. Damn that Leonard, she thought irritably. He'd clearly been brutal. She'd been hoping Pearl would be able to accommodate another punter she'd got in mind for her tomorrow, but if she was too badly torn he'd have to wait for a few more days. 'Where's my money?' she said testily, before catching sight of a number of notes scattered on the floor where they had fluttered when Pearl had pulled the sheet round her.

She went down on her hands and knees and retrieved the notes, stuffing them in the pocket of her serge skirt as she stood up. 'Did you hear me?' she said to the small mound on the bed. 'I said get up.'

Pearl sat up, blinking through swollen eyelids. 'Did you know?'

'Know?'

'What he was going to do to me?'

Kitty put her hands on her hips. 'Course I knew. It had to happen some time or other, didn't it? And far better we got a good price for it than you giving it away to some lad or other who took your eye in a few years. There's some men who like bairns, that's just the way of it, and once you've turned fifteen or sixteen they'll lose interest.' She turned away. 'There's some warm water in the kettle. Clean yourself up and get to bed, and we'll see if you're fit to look after another gentleman I know tomorrow.'

Pearl was all eyes as she stared at her mother, her hair a cloud about her white face. The shock and anguish Kitty's words had

caused overrode everything, even the pain between her legs. 'I –
I can't, Mam. I can't. Please . . .'

Kitty turned at the door. 'You can and you will, girl. Make no
mistake about that.'

'Please, Mam—'

Kitty inclined her head impatiently. 'And none of your dramatics,
they won't wash with me.' So saying, she opened the door and
Pearl heard her footsteps going upstairs, and then the sound of the
bedroom door opening and closing.

How long she sat there before she could find the strength to
move Pearl didn't know, but when she hitched herself off the bed
still wrapped in the sheet and saw the red stain on the flock mattress,
she gave a little whimper of distress. Her mam would go mad if
she came down and saw that.

Stumbling about the room, she picked up her scattered clothes.
She had to sit down for a while before she could dress herself;
when the faintness receded she pulled her cotton dress over her
head only to find every button had been ripped off the bodice.
Her shift was torn beyond repair, as were her drawers.

Once in the kitchen, she filled a bowl with water and found
the soap, returning to the front room and scrubbing at the mattress
until the blood had dulled to a faint pink colour. The smell was
in her nostrils but the odour of Mr F was worse, clinging to her
so that every movement she made brought him wafting closer.

By the time she had emptied the bowl and filled it afresh with
water to wash in, twilight had fallen. Taking off her dress, she stood
in the shadowed kitchen and washed herself all over, scrubbing at
her skin until it was red and sore. She could hardly bear to touch
between her legs; when she dabbed at the area, her flesh stung so
badly it brought tears streaming from her eyes and made her shake
again. Tipping away the soapy water, she filled the bowl again and
then sat down in it, hoping to ease the soreness.

Eventually she felt a little relief and after a while she steeled
herself to stand up and get dry, pulling on her dress again and then
going to the back door and opening it. It was quiet outside, since
most children had been called in and put to bed, but high in the

mauve- and charcoal-streaked sky, the swallows were calling to each other as they skimmed and dived in the thermals, skilfully swooping on airborne insects the hot weather had brought out and gorging themselves in a feeding frenzy.

She stood listening to their cries and watching their graceful dipping and rising until it was dark and they were gone, and slowly the numbness born of shock and trauma which had paralysed her mind began to dissolve. And she knew she had to get away.

Her mother had been paid for letting Mr F do what he'd done to her. Not only that, but her mother was going to let it happen again and again. She shut her eyes for a moment. She'd rather throw herself in the river than suffer that.

She felt sticky between her legs and knew she was still bleeding, but now panic at the thought that her mother might somehow constrain her was high. She couldn't wait until morning – she had to go now, tonight. It didn't matter where, she told herself frantically. But she had to change this dress for her other one, and put on her spare shift and drawers – and that meant going upstairs.

Once she was standing on the landing she could hear her mother snoring. The sound was reassuring inasmuch as it meant she could leave the house undetected, but now, as she put it to herself, she was feeling bad right through. Just climbing the stairs had made her sick and giddy, and as she entered the room she shared with James and Patrick, she had to hold onto the door handle when the floor shifted and everything spun. Sitting down on the edge of the bed, she looked at the sleeping faces of her brothers in the dim light. They were lying facing each other, James's arms about Patrick. They often slept like this.

She had promised Seth she would take care of them both, so she couldn't leave them. But she couldn't take them with her either. How was she going to feed them and look after them? Where would they sleep? No, she couldn't take them. Silent tears ran down her face. Her mother would *have* to look after them when she had gone, and it wasn't as if they were any trouble, they were good little boys. And at least here they would be clothed and fed and have somewhere to sleep. The neighbours would keep an eye on them once they knew she'd gone; they were all aware what her mother was like.

She sat with her hands clenched in her lap in an agony of indecision, but really she knew she had no choice. She had to go, and she had to go alone. She didn't care what happened to her – in fact, right at this moment she wanted nothing more than to hide somewhere and go to sleep and never to wake up again – but the boys needed a roof over their heads.

She was hurting so much she wanted to creep under the covers and lie down, but she mustn't. Taking her spare set of clothes from the orange box under the bed, she slowly got dressed, pulling on her boots and replaiting her hair which had come loose in the struggle with Mr F. Then she bent over the sleeping children, laying her face against one little tousled head and then the other before straightening, the ache in her heart a physical pain.

Silently she left the room and once downstairs took her hat and coat from their peg in the hall. It was summer and she didn't need them, but she took them anyway.

In the kitchen she paused. The bunches of flowers were where James and Patrick had left them on the kitchen table. They belonged to another lifetime, another world. She stood, a small figure in the dark room, whispering, 'Seth, Seth, I want you, Seth. Please help me,' but the only sound was the uncaring tick of the mantelpiece clock and a rustling in the corner which meant the mice were hunting for crumbs of food. Her mother had never told her which prison Seth and the others were in, and her requests to visit them had been met with cuffs round the ear until she had learned to stop asking, but never had she longed for her brothers so desperately.

She had to leave the house. She couldn't stay and let *that* happen again. She would walk into the country and hide somewhere and go to sleep. That was as far as her bruised mind could plan and it was enough.

The night was dark but not as black as she had expected; when she looked up into the sky she saw the moon was high and the stars were bright. She had always been frightened of the dark – Seth had used to tease her about it – but she knew she would never be frightened of the dark again. There were much worse things than ghosts and ghouls.

When she started to walk she didn't know how she was going to get to the end of the back lane, let alone to the country. Any movement was excruciatingly painful, and the feeling of nausea had her swallowing hard.

There were still a few people about once she came into High Street East, but no one paid her any attention and she kept to the shadows, using the alleys and back ways as she forced herself to walk on. After a while the pain seemed dulled, the fear of what was behind her if she didn't escape the town driving her limbs. When she came to Ashburne House and then Hendon Burn she was surprised she had got this far; it was as though she had been in a dream, unthinking. She was on the outskirts of the town now, not far from where she had brought the boys earlier. The odd farm and big house were interspersed with old quarries and disused clay pits, the country-side stretching before her. She breathed in the warm night air, her senses heightened even as her mind remained in the vacuum where it had taken refuge.

She walked until she couldn't walk any more. If she had but known it, the birds were a few breaths away from beginning the dawn chorus when she crawled into the shelter of an ancient tree, the bottom of its trunk almost hollowed away and providing a small cave-like structure. Spreading out her coat, she fell asleep the moment she lay down.

When Pearl awoke, late-afternoon sunlight was slanting through a tiny crack in her hidey-hole. The day was very warm, but lying as she was inside the tree, the sun had not burned her. She lay looking out of the hole she'd crawled through. Tall grasses were swaying gently in the mild breeze and she could hear birdsong. On raising her head she felt so sick and dizzy that she was glad to shut her eyes again. This time though, her sleep was punctu-ated by strange dreams and disturbing images, and although she was uncomfortable and in pain she didn't have the will or strength to do more than toss and turn. She knew she was unwell, but it didn't matter. She didn't want to wake up properly and leave her sanctuary, she just wanted to sleep.

Night fell. A vixen with her cubs passed the tree and paused, sniffing the air before hurrying her offspring away. An owl hooted, the creatures of the night went about their business as they always did, and eventually the pale pink light of dawn began another day. And in the hollow of the tree Pearl got sicker and sicker, the fever that was ravaging her body sending her temperature soaring.

Chapter 6

The sun was at its height. It shone on the raven-black hair of several brightly dressed young girls with Gitano complexions and big gold hoops in their ears, sitting in a giggling circle plaiting rush baskets with deft brown fingers. In the field behind them were horse-drawn caravans and tents of all shapes and sizes, the smoke from numerous woodfires and the shouts of squabbling children and barking dogs filling the air.

The gypsy encampment had arrived early that morning, but to an onlooker it would have appeared they'd been settled in place for some time, such was the order prevailing. Horses had been put to grass, washing hung on lines constructed between trees, fowls were pecking about for scraps, and children were being bathed in the big wooden tubs the clothes had been washed in. Clothed all in black, gnarled old women with saffron skin and forbidding eyes sat on the steps of gaily painted, round-roofed caravans with babies on their knees, while younger women with harassed faces were bent over great black pots suspended above woodfires, stirring something or other in the cavernous depths. A group of men were sorting through a number of salvaged pans, metal buckets and kettles for those worth mending and selling; others were preparing rabbits and hedgehogs for cooking, still others chopping wood for the fires or inspecting the horses they intended to trade later. All was bustle and life, noise and chatter.

Some fifty yards or so from the encampment, three young boys were returning home with two pheasants caught by their lurcher dog. They were brothers, the eldest sixteen years old, and all had the swarthy fresh complexions, sturdy limbs and bright eyes which came from living and working in nature's own atmosphere. The two younger boys having gone slightly ahead, the eldest's attention was caught by the dog which was behaving strangely, whining and pawing at the foot of an old tree higher on the bank.

'We've got all the food we want for today, Rex. Leave it.' Byron Lock whistled to the dog and then frowned when he continued to scratch at the tree roots, grumbling deep in his throat. This wasn't like Rex. Byron had trained the dog himself from a puppy, and he responded immediately to his every command. Calling to his brothers to take the birds they'd poached back to the camp where his mother would soon have them plucked and in the pot, the youth climbed up the bank and made his way to the dog. At his approach, the animal became still and sat down, but did not budge from the spot.

Byron crouched down and looked into the base of the tree, which he saw was one big cavity. A good storm and it would be down, he thought, in the moment before he saw the small figure of a child curled up inside. He started, making the dog jump and bark, but the child – a girl – didn't move.

His heart thumping hard, he put out his hand and felt the little body. It was warm, and when he slid his fingers under the chin, he could feel a rapid pulse. She was alive then. Breathing out his relief, he sat back on his heels. As he did so, the child stirred, muttering something unintelligible. 'Wake up, little 'un.' Byron reached into the hole again and shook her gently. 'Come on, wake up. Time to go home, wherever home is.'

She stirred again, giving a low moan, and as his hand moved to her forehead he felt it was burning hot. Again he sat back sharply. They'd moved camp from their usual summer place near Newcastle because the hot weather had caused the fever to become rampant in the town.

Byron stood to his feet, glancing at the dog who stared back at his master trustingly. 'Guard.' Turning, he slid down the grassy bank and began to walk towards the camp. He didn't need to check if the dog had obeyed him.

The laughing circle of girls called to him in the gypsy tongue as Byron passed by, but although he raised his hand in acknow-ledgement, he didn't pause. He made his way to the far corner of the field where his mother and one of his sisters were already busy plucking the pheasants. Theirs was not a large family compared to some within the tribe. It consisted of his parents, two older sisters – Leandra and Ellen, who were both married with children of their own – Madora, his twin, who at sixteen was due to be married within the year, and his two younger brothers, Algar and Silvester, who were fourteen and thirteen respectively. Freda was the baby of the family, and she was eleven years old. Many of their relations had families of double numbers, and his mother had been one of twenty-two children, twenty of whom had survived to adulthood.

His mother stopped what she was doing at his approach, seeing from his expression that all was not well. Corinda Lock was a fine-looking woman, her thick shiny hair still as black as the day she had married twenty-three years ago, and her figure as firm and lithe as a woman half her age. Born a Buckley, and the eldest daughter of the Buckley clan, Corinda could trace her ancestry for many generations, and her heritage showed in her noble bearing.

'What's the matter?' Corinda asked as Byron reached her. 'Algar and Silvester said the dog was after something.'

'Not exactly.' Corinda was tall for a woman at five foot seven, but even at sixteen Byron was several inches taller than his mother. Swiftly he explained what he had found, adding, 'She's in a bad way by the look of her, Dai.'

Corinda stared at her son. Wiping her hands on a piece of sacking she gestured to Madora to continue with what she was doing. 'I'll get your dad – and keep this to yourself for the moment.' Her husband had been tending a foal since they had camped; it had been born a few days before and was on the small side.

Mackensie Lock listened intently to what his son had to tell him. He didn't hesitate. 'Fever or not, we can't leave a child out there in that condition.'

Byron made no answer but looked towards his mother. Quietly and in level tones, Corinda said, 'Until we know what's what, she had better be isolated in the caravan with just myself seeing to her. She can have Madora and Freda's bed, and I'll sleep in your grandmother's. The three of them can have our bed and you' – she looked at her husband – 'can sleep with the lads.'

Corinda and Mackensie slept at one end of their long tent, a strong waterproof construction made with wooden hoops fastened into the ground and covered with canvas. At the opposite end, Byron and his brothers occupied a curtained-off area, and the two girls and Halimena, Mackensie's old mother, slept in the caravan. Although the boys would strip to the waist in the open for a wash and think nothing of swimming naked in a river or lake, Byron had never so much as seen his sisters in their undergarments, and the most perfunctory toilet was done with the carvan door closed.

By the time Byron carried the small figure into the camp, Rex bounding and jumping beside him, Corinda had been joined by the wizened figure of Halimena. At seventy-six, Mackensie's mother was still as nimble as a young girl. As her son had often remarked wryly to his wife, Halimena was quite capable of seeing them all out. Not that Mackensie didn't love his mother, he did. They all did, and Halimena was greatly respected within the community owing to the fact it was generally acknowledged she had the Second Sight. However, she could be difficult to live with. As the eldest son, it had been Mackensie's responsibility to take his mother under his protection when his father had died, but it had been a while before Corinda and his mother had co-existed comfortably.

Flatly refusing to stay outside, Halimena followed her long-suffering daughter-in-law into the caravan once her grandson had laid the child on his sisters' bed and left. Looking down at the little girl, she stated, 'She's in a bad way.'

Corinda nodded. She hadn't needed her mother-in-law to point that out. The child was burning up and clearly unaware of her surroundings.

'If they come looking for her and find her here, it'll mean trouble, you know that.' Halimena sniffed. 'She's got the smell of death on her.'

Ignoring Halimena, Corinda began to examine the child for injuries. When she lifted the cotton dress and saw the bloodstained underwear sticking to the little body, her head shot up to meet her mother-in-law's eyes, and for once Halimena was silent. Carefully now, the two women stripped the little girl, but they had to soak and bathe the drawers from her. Once they had done so, they were silent for a moment. Then Halimena said, 'This is bad, Corinda. Byron should never have brought her here.'

'What was he to do then? Pretend he hadn't seen her?' Corinda had spoken too sharply and she knew it, but she was feeling sick to her stomach. For someone to do this to a small child! She had been violated – and savagely, too. Goodness knew what damage had been done. She now drew in a great long breath, her voice quieter when she said, 'Would you get your box?'

Halimena nodded. 'She'll need careful tending.'

'I'll stay with her. Madora is quite capable of seeing to the meals and so on, with your help.'

When Halimena said no more but left to fetch her chest of herbs and potions which she used to treat every malady under the sun, Corinda knew the little girl's condition had affected her mother-in-law too.

Once a soothing and healing ointment consisting of elder-flower, green willow bark, foxglove and other ingredients in home-cured lard had been applied, and Corinda had spooned a few drops of Halimena's nettle and barley tea into the child to bring her temperature down, she covered the little figure with a loose sheet and stepped outside, where Byron was waiting. Halimena had told only Mackensie and Byron what they'd found. Although Mackensie was shocked and upset, it had been Byron who'd been most deeply affected. Probably because he had found her, Corinda thought now, saying, 'She's lying quiet but I'll sit with her for the time being.'

Byron rubbed his hand across his mouth. 'Will she be all right? She will get better, won't she?'

Corinda stared into her son's kindly face – for he was kind, was her Byron – and she couldn't answer him.

His voice harsh, Byron said, 'And there's some out there who call *us* savages. How old do you think she is?'

'Hard to tell, she's a thin little thing. Nine, ten, mebbe a bit older. We'll know more if –' Corinda paused and then went on '– when she's able to speak.'

Over the last hour, thunder had begun to rattle the distant hills, gathering stormclouds showing deep grey against an increasingly sullen sky. Corinda looked up as the first fat raindrops began to fall. 'It's as well you found her when you did, love.' She guessed – rightly – that his grandmother had made her feelings known to him. 'Whatever happens, you did the right thing.'

His shoulders lifted in a shrug but she saw something relax in his face. 'Do you think the law'll come sniffing about?'

So that's what Halimena had berated him with. Concealing her anger, his mother reached out and placed her hand against the side of his face for a moment. Such gestures were rare; they were not a demonstrative family. 'Whether they do or whether they don't, we've done nothing wrong. Remember that.' The heavens had opened, the rain a deluge now. Turning from him, she went back inside the caravan.

Byron continued to stand for a few moments more before making his way – not to the tent, where Madora had the meal waiting – but across the campsite to the wood beyond, Rex at his heels.

By the time he reached the other side of the wooded area, the cloudburst was past. It had left pockmarked patterns on the dry soil, the much-needed drops of water yielding the gratifying smell only fresh rain on parched ground can give. He sat down over-looking a pale shimmering field of freshly mown hay, others behind it making a mosaic against grainfields which had mellowed to the bronze of harvest. Rex dropped down beside him without a sound. He always knew when his master was troubled.

Dog roses rambled abundantly in the hedgerow, but Byron was oblivious to their sweet perfume. At sixteen he was well versed in the ways of the world, since gypsy children were born wary and shrewd, and trusted no one but their own kind – but this act of brutality to a child had turned his stomach. That being said, he knew he had brought danger into their community. He would have known this even if his grandmother had not laboured the point.

His mother had said he'd done the right thing. He sat quite still, thinking about this, long hours of poaching having taught him how to become as still as stone. Only the next days and weeks would tell if that was true.

A small shrew emerged along the hedgebank, rearing up on its hind legs to sniff the summer air with its long, twitching snout. His grandmother believed that a painful disease of the limbs resulting in lameness would occur if a shrew ran over a person's leg. To remedy this she had told them the creature must be buried alive in a hole bored into ash bark, and she was adamant that the tree had the power to cure the ailment if its leaves or twigs were rubbed against the affected area. Byron had had many shrews run over him in his time when they'd been intent on pursuing their insect prey, but he had never followed his grandmother's advice and he was as healthy as the next man.

His eyes narrowed as he watched the little creature clutching a grass stem, its attention focused on a big fat grasshopper. He had proved that his grandmother was not always right. Besides which, and this was the crux of the matter, he couldn't have lived with himself if he had done anything else.

The girl would have died if she had been left.

He breathed out slowly, the barely perceptible sound enough to send the shrew scurrying for cover and for Rex's eyes to focus on his master's troubled face. The child was safe now. If nothing else, he had enabled her to be cared for by his mother, and if the law came in their great hobnailed boots shouting the odds, he would tell them how she had been when he'd found her, and ask them if they could guarantee her safety if she was returned whence she'd come. They wouldn't pin this on him; he wouldn't let them. Nor would he let that little child be given back without setting a cat amongst the pigeons. Someone should pay for what they'd done.

His hand reaching into his trouser pocket, he brought out his whittling knife and a small wooden owl he had been working on. From a young boy he had cut and hand-polished pieces of oak and beech, making rough platters and ornaments which he'd sold at fairs and markets. As he'd grown older he had fashioned cradles on rockers, and stools, as well as the smaller items, and they always sold well and for a good price. He loved the look and the smell and the feel of wood; in fact, sometimes he thought he was only truly happy when he was working at his sideline — as his father disparagingly called it. For generations the Locks had been horse dealers, travelling all over the country and as far as Ireland as they plied their trade. As the firstborn male he was expected to follow in his father's footsteps. So were Algar and Silvester, to be fair, but if one of his brothers had expressed an interest in something else, it might have been considered. Not so with the eldest son.

Shaking his head as though to clear his mind, Byron began whittling, and after a while the wood worked its magic, soothing and calming his spirit.

The child might not have been reported missing if she had been hurt by those she lived with, and even if that was not the case, there was nothing to say the police would look for her here. If they did come, there wasn't a man, woman or child within their community who would breathe a word if he spirited her away until the coast was clear. She was in his safekeeping now.

His shoulders came back and his head lifted, and buoyed up by this train of thought, he stuffed the knife and the little wooden owl back into his pocket. It would take more than a few coppers with their truncheons and whistles to prise her away if he didn't see fit.

Feeling something of the conquering hero, and with his grumbling stomach reminding him about the meal waiting for him, he returned to the camp, only to find that Madora — with the prickliness of all sisters when their efforts are unappreciated — had given his dinner to one of their neighbours' dogs.

★　★　★

It was a full week before Pearl really became aware of her surroundings. For four days after Byron had carried her into the gypsy camp she was delirious most of the time, then came a period where she slept deeply and was too exhausted to open her eyes. But on the eighth day when she awoke and stared into the strong, compassionate face of the woman who had been attending her, her mind was her own again.

'Don't be frightened.' Corinda smiled at her, gently stroking a tendril of hair from Pearl's forehead. 'You're with friends, you're safe.'

She remembered this voice, it had featured in her dreams. It had been cool, soothing; when it had spoken, she had felt comforted. She tried to speak but her mouth was too dry. The woman held a cup of water to her lips, and when she had swallowed, Pearl whispered, 'Where am I?'

'I told you, with friends. My son found you in the woods. You were –' there was a brief hesitation '– you were hurt. Do you remember?'

So it hadn't all been part of the nightmares. Her mother *had* sold her to that man. Pearl shut her eyes but not before a tear had slipped down her face.

'Don't worry.' Corinda sat down on the bed, her hands gripping those of Pearl. 'You're all right now. Do you understand? No one will hurt you here.'

She was tired. She was so, so tired. She tried to force her eyelids open but it was beyond her.

'That's right, sleep a bit. Sleep's the best medicine, and soon you'll be feeling like yourself again.'

The voice continued to speak as she let herself slip into the place where she didn't have to think, but just before she allowed oblivion to take her, Pearl was conscious of thinking the lady was wrong. She would never feel like herself again.

It was another two days before Pearl ventured outside the caravan. The damage to her coccyx was the main problem. It had set up an inflammation in her back and pelvis which made every movement extremely painful and kept her temperature volatile. But in those two days she learned a lot about where she was and the people she was with. The caravan was so spotless you could have eaten off the floor, and from the tiny window next to her bed she could see the Romanies going about their business.

Besides the caravans, all with little ladders going from the ground to the small doors, she could see a number of round tents in various sizes. An indefinite number of dark-eyed, olive-skinned children tumbled about, sometimes playing games or often sitting together making wooden clothes pegs or small baskets which she watched them fill with wild flowers early in the morning, presumably to sell that day.

On the whole the children were poorly dressed but clean. None wore shoes but then it was the height of summer. From what she could see of the women, it appeared the younger ones were like a host of brightly coloured butterflies, their blouses of pink or mauve or bright blue over a full-pleated skirt of indeterminate hue, and their strings of beads and long earrings catching the sunlight as they moved about the camp. The older women were invariably clothed in black or dark colours, but some of them had a brightly coloured scarf knotted about their neck or waist, and wore black hats with long feathers coming from the brim. In comparison the men's garments were decidedly unimposing, their trousers, shirts and waistcoats occasionally enlivened by a scarlet or gaily spotted necktie. On their heads sat workingmen's caps, full-brimmed hats, even a top hat on one old gentleman. But what struck Pearl most about the gypsies as she peered out of her window was their smiling faces and laughter, the noise and general coming and going seemingly good natured and with purpose.

The day before she got up out of bed, Corinda sat with her while she ate her evening meal of stew and a kind of flatbread flavoured with herbs. When she had finished and Corinda had removed the bowl, the older woman took Pearl's hands in hers. They had spoken the day before about how Pearl had been found by Corinda's son and that only he, Corinda and her husband and an old grandmother knew of the nature of her injuries. As far as everyone else was concerned, Corinda had quietly said, she had been beaten badly. Pearl had nodded, knowing it was meant kindly, but once the camp had settled down for sleep she had lain awake with tears running down her face, feeling dirty and ashamed.

That feeling intensified now when Corinda said, 'Pearl, I think you understand I need to ask you about what happened. Who attacked you and where have you come from? Where is your family?'

She had known this moment was coming. Twice before, Corinda had broached the subject, but she had been feeling poorly then and when she had started to cry, Corinda had said it didn't matter. But of course it mattered. Before she had woken up in the gypsy camp she had never met any real live Romanies, but she had heard talk about them. It was well known that they had their own language and their life was a mystery to non-gypsies; some of the folk in the East End had spoken of them disparagingly as nothing less than itinerant thieves and natural vagabonds, loose in their morals and without cleanliness or decent habits. From what she had observed, once she was able to look out of the window, Pearl knew this was not the case. Certainly her daughters' virtue was dear to Corinda. She had not said this directly, but the normal sleeping arrangements for the girls and the fact that the old grandmother acted as both chaperone and guard once the sun went down spoke volumes. When she compared the gypsies' life to the higgledy-piggledy herding together of men, women and children in the East End, along with the squalor and filth and brutality such conditions evoked, she knew who were the civilised beings. And what must this woman be thinking about her?

Her head bowed, Pearl mumbled, 'I – I don't want to go back.'

'No one is saying you have to go back.'

'I didn't want him to do that. He – it wasn't my fault. I'm not – not bad.'

Corinda squeezed the small cold hands. 'Of course you're not bad. Now stop crying.' She waited until Pearl raised her eyes before she said, 'But I need to know what happened if you're to stay with us. Your being here could bring trouble down on our heads if folk come looking for you.'

'It's not like that.'

'Then tell me what it *is* like.'

Pearl's voice was a whisper when she said, 'Well, it started when my brothers were put away . . .' The telling didn't take long. When Pearl finished with: 'People will think I'm bad if they know,' Corinda let go of the thin hands and drew the child against her breast.

'You've got nothing to be ashamed of,' she said quietly. 'Do you understand? Nothing in the wide world to be ashamed of. Remember that.' Silently she was reflecting that it was worse than she had expected. For a mother to be party to such a thing was unbelievable. But she did believe Pearl. Every word. 'And I see no reason why you can't come along with us, if that's what you want.'

Pearl's arms around her waist was her answer. Softly, Corinda said, 'I'll need to tell Mackensie and his mother what you've told me, but if you don't want Byron to know, that's all right.'

Pearl thought for a moment. 'Byron found me. It's – it's right he knows.'

'Then it will be the four of us and you who are aware of the full facts, that's all.' Corinda stood up. 'I think you're well enough to get up tomorrow, and in the evening Madora and Freda can move back in and we'll get back to normal. There'll be three of you to the bed, but in the past it was four before Leandra and Ellen wed, so you'll manage.'

This meant the old grandmother would resume sleeping on the bed that became a long seat in the daytime. As yet she hadn't seen the grandmother, although Madora and Freda had come to say hello, and Byron and his brothers had stood waving outside the window the day before. Mackensie had popped his head round the caravan door several times in order to talk to his wife, but he hadn't ventured inside and for this Pearl was grateful. She knew he was a nice man – he must be, if he was Corinda's husband – but everything inside her had shrunk at the proximity of a man. This was the main reason she was terrified at the prospect of leaving the womblike confines of the caravan, even though logic told her she couldn't hide away for ever.

Perhaps Corinda had sensed how she was feeling because now

she said briskly, 'Madora or Freda will keep you company and show you how things are for the next little while. You won't be left alone. You understand you will be expected to work to earn your keep? All the children do once they've reached five summers. Are you good with your fingers?'

Pearl stared at her. 'I don't know.'

Corinda smiled. 'There's a skill to making the things we sell but it's not difficult, and then there's always the cooking and washing and suchlike.'

Pearl nodded but said nothing. Although she had done the cooking at home she had seen enough from the window to know things were different in the gypsy camp. Probably because it was summer, all the meals were cooked outside the caravans and tents. Iron pots suspended over open fires was the order of the day here. The pots hung from a rod which was shaped like a shepherd's crook and placed at an angle over the heat of the fire, and she had seen potatoes pushed into the ashes as well as skinned hedgehogs, and fish roasted over the flames on split hazel sticks. Rabbits and pheasants and other meat the gypsies poached always disappeared into the pots shortly after arriving in camp, presumably, Pearl supposed, so that if any gamekeepers came asking awkward questions, the evidence was gone.

Corinda had turned and was making up the narrow seat bed. She brought Pearl's attention to her again by saying, 'Go to sleep now, child. Tomorrow will be a new beginning. That's how you must look at this. The past is gone and nothing can change it, but the future will be what you make of it.' She straightened, smiling at Pearl who smiled back before obediently sliding under the covers and shutting her eyes.

She knew when Corinda was asleep – Byron's mother snored, for one thing – and with the camp settled for the night and the moon high in the sky, thoughts crowded into Pearl's mind. She was feeling much better physically. The dreadful soreness inside had gone, and the pain she'd had when she emptied her bladder had been cured by one of Halimena's potions. The bottom of her spine still hurt, but it was a dull throb now, like toothache. But as she had got better, the gnawing guilt about leaving James and Patrick had got worse. Today she hadn't been able to think about anything else. And yet she couldn't have stayed and done what her mother would have insisted she do. Curling into a little ball, she stifled the sob in her throat by sticking her fist into her mouth and biting hard.

But she would go back one day, she thought as scalding tears flooded down her face. When she was old enough to be able to stand against her mother and her plans, she would go back and take care of her brothers. Maybe she could find work and earn enough to rent a room so they could live with her? They could manage on very little.

Pipe dreams. The words her mother used to fling at her when she was being scathing about something or other were loud in her head. And anyway, it was now that the little boys needed her. Who would play with them and tell them stories, and wipe their tears when they hurt themselves if she didn't? Oh, James, Patrick. James, Patrick. How could she have left them? She was wicked, that's what she was.

It was nearly dawn before she went to sleep, an unquiet sleep filled with hopelessness, heartache and remorse.

Chapter 7

The next morning, Pearl was visibly trembling as she followed Corinda down the caravan steps. It was one thing to view the gypsy camp through the small window in the caravan, quite another to be thrust into it. It was early, the dawn chorus hadn't been long finished, but already it promised to be another scorching hot day. All round the camp, fires were lit and the women were preparing breakfast. Mackensie, Halimena and the rest of the Lock family were sitting in the opening to the tent, and as Corinda and Pearl joined them everyone smiled and nodded at her – everyone but Halimena. Byron's grandmother merely stared long and hard at her before taking the bowl of porridge, stiff with salt, which Madora handed her.

'Feeling better?' Eleven-year-old Freda hitched herself closer. 'I got kicked by a dray horse once and had to stay in bed. I was black and blue all over, wasn't I, Dai?'

Pearl had gathered by now that 'Dai' was the gypsy word for Mother, and as Corinda said shortly, 'And whose fault was that?' Pearl smiled at Freda, aware that the other girl was trying to make her feel comfortable.

'Freda got too close to the milkman's horse when we were in a town. It had its feeding bag on and she'd been told to stay away from it.'

This snippet was provided by Byron. When Freda turned on her brother, saying indignantly, 'It wasn't *my* fault, it was a mardy old nag,' he shook his head at Pearl.

She wanted to smile at him but her face felt stiff with nerves. She longed to jump up and run away, go up the caravan steps and shut the door.

Halimena rattled something off in the gypsy tongue, and when Corinda said, 'All in good time,' Pearl felt that Byron's grandmother had been talking about her and that it hadn't been complimentary. Telling herself she couldn't cry – not here, not now – she forced herself to eat the porridge, hoping no one would notice how her hands were shaking.

The porridge being washed down by a mug of hot tea which had neither milk nor sugar in it, the family scattered about their business. Mackensie and his sons were going into the next village to do some horse trading outside the public house, Corinda and Madora were tackling the weekly wash, Halimena was sitting in the tent entrance weaving a cabbage net, and Freda had told Pearl to accompany her to where a group of girls about their age were busy weaving rush mats. Later in the week, Freda told her, the camp would be on the move. There was a big fair on the outskirts of Durham where they would be able to sell their wares, trade horses and tell fortunes to the townfolk and ladies of social standing.

The other girls fell silent as Freda and Pearl approached, eyeing Pearl curiously. All of them had brown skin, dark hair and gold hoops in their ears, and were dressed in blouses and skirts, but some were more raggedy than others. The soles of their bare feet had the appearance of being as tough as leather, and they glanced at Pearl's boots and faded summer dress which she realised made her stick out like a sore thumb from the gypsy children.

'This is Pearl. She's living with us now.' Freda plonked herself down and waved her hand for Pearl to do the same. Starting with the girl nearest to her, she introduced each one. 'Betsy, Naomi, Sarah, Etty, Jemima and Repronia.'

The names whirled in her mind; she knew she wouldn't

remember who was who. As the other girls began to chatter in their own language, Freda showed her how to begin working the prepared rushes together on a mat which was already half finished. It looked easy, but it wasn't. The rushes seemed to have a mind of their own and they were sharp and unforgiving on her soft flesh. Furthermore, she couldn't seem to get them tight enough so they didn't promptly spring loose and go out of shape. And she knew the other girls were looking at her and laughing at her efforts. She couldn't understand what they were saying, but she didn't have to, to know they didn't like her, that they considered her an outsider. Which she was. She bit down on her bottom lip so the pain would prevent the tears that threatened.

At midday everyone returned to their own caravans and tents for a quick meal. Mackensie and the boys weren't back and Madora had a pan of potatoes and meat ready which was heavily augmented by mushrooms she'd picked earlier from the fields beyond the camp. In spite of her morning in the fresh air Pearl wasn't hungry, since misery was weighing her down, but she ate the bowl of food she was given before returning to her task with Freda.

She fared no better with the rushes in the afternoon, and although Freda talked to her now and again, the other girls barely glanced at her. Her fingers were sore, and by evening she had three large blisters. Her back was aching too; the hours of sitting on the ground in one position had set off the nagging pain at the bottom of her spine again. The only thing which gave her a faint trace of comfort was the way Freda had slipped her arm through hers as they walked back to the tent.

A summer twilight richly flavoured by the smell of the camp-fires had fallen by the time the whole family settled down to eat their evening meal. Mackensie and his sons were in fine fettle; the trading had gone well and one of the landed gentry had bought all four animals for a handsome price and expressed an interest in doing further business the next time the Romanies were in the district.

While they had been waiting for the menfolk to return, Freda had taken Pearl inside the tent. It hadn't been at all as she had imagined. In fact, the interior had presented an air of luxury. Woven matting covered the whole of the floor, and on top of this reposed a large square of carpet in bright, rich colours. In the middle of the tent a row of cushioned seats sat either side of the carpet with a low table between them, the bedroom areas being curtained off. Several large wicker baskets, presumably holding clothes and bedding, stood behind the seats. Besides the horsedrawn caravan, the family owned an enormous farm cart, pulled by another horse, and it was this which transported the tent and most of their belongings from place to place.

Pearl had stared at the interior of the tent, awed by the comfort and cleanliness, and was overwhelmingly thankful that Freda and the others hadn't seen Low Street and her beginnings.

''Course, not everyone's as particular as us,' Freda said with some pride. 'And some don't have a caravan *and* a tent, just one or the other, but Dai was a Buckley and she brought a fine dowry with her. Lots of men wanted her, but she set eyes on Dad when the Buckleys were visiting a horse fair in Ireland at the same time as the Locks – and that was that.' This was said in a manner which told Pearl it was a favourite story. 'If Dad had been just a tinker or pedlar like some, likely there'd have been trouble, but the Locks were already the head of ten gypsy families, so that was all right.'

Pearl nodded without really understanding anything other than Freda's satisfaction in her family's position within the gypsy community; it was obviously very important to her.

Halimena had been sitting in her chair at the entrance to the tent still weaving cabbage nets to sell as she listened to the two girls' conversation. Raising her head, she glanced across at her granddaughter. 'The Locks are as old a tribe as the Buckleys and others. Don't forget that.'

'I know.'

Freda's voice carried a note of indignation but Pearl felt the words had not really been intended for Freda but meant as a message to her. She caught Halimena's eye; the old woman might be shrunken and wrinkled, but there was something in the round hard eyes that was strong and vital, something she couldn't put a name to but which filled her with trepidation.

As the sun went down, with blue smoke from the fires curling into the darkening sky, the noise within the camp began to decrease. Younger children were put to bed and the dogs, well fed with scraps from the evening meal, settled down with bones to gnaw under the caravans. Horses which had been having kicking matches or baring their teeth at each other now stood docilely munching at the thick sweet grass at the edge of the camp, and the men sitting by the campfires had something stronger than tea in their mugs. It was the time for pleasure.

Hitherto, confined to the caravan, Pearl had only heard the sound of music and laughter and seen the figures whirling and dancing in the shadows as the twilight had thickened. Now she was part of it. Songs were sung in a soft chant, with violins and mouth organs and the spoons accompanying the dancers, as well as one or two piano accordions. She couldn't understand what was being sung, it was all in the gypsies' own language, but it was beautiful. Beautiful and so haunting, at times it caused a physical ache in her chest. She sat quietly beside Corinda and Mackensie as Madora and Freda and the three boys joined in the dancing, even though Freda kept calling to her until spoken to sharply by her grandmother, still sitting at the mouth to the tent behind them.

It was just after this that Corinda said softly, 'It is our way to have a time together after the work of the day, Pearl. Stories are told and songs are sung and passed on from generation to generation. It's important our history is kept alive for our children and our children's children. We have been part of the countryside and lived in harmony with the land for hundreds of years, but the new towns are taking what was once ours. It makes some of our old folk angry and bitter.'

There was a snort behind them but Corinda ignored her mother-in-law and went on, 'Some of our community are suspicious and wary of non-gypsies because of this. They don't accept that the only thing we can do to protect our way of life is to adapt to what is happening.'

There was a rustle as Halimena stood up and said something in her sharp voice, to which Mackensie replied, just as sharply. At this Halimena disappeared into the caravan, banging the door behind her. Pearl looked at Corinda but Freda's mother continued to stare into the flames, her work-roughened hands clasped round her knees and her stance pensive.

Nothing more was said, but shortly after this Corinda called the children and they all went their separate ways, Mackensie and Corinda and the boys into the tent, and Madora and Freda and Pearl into the caravan where Halimena was already stretched out on her narrow bed, apparently asleep.

But Halimena was not asleep. She lay completely still and silent until she was sure the three girls were no longer awake, and then rose, pushing her feet into her boots and pulling her shawl around her shoulders.

It was only Rex, lying outside the entrance to the tent wherein slept his master, who raised his head as Halimena closed the caravan door. When the old woman sat down on the last wooden step he closed his eyes again.

The night was soft and warm, the glow from the dying camp-fires and the sweet fragrance of woodsmoke drifting on the air as the small, black-clothed figure stared out over the sea of tents and caravans.

It was a bad day when Byron brought that girl into the camp, she thought, her mouth tightening over her full set of teeth, most of which were still strong and whole. She patted her knuckles against her closed lips and looked up into the night sky. And Corinda, allowing a gorgie to sleep and eat and live with them! How could any good come out of that? That child, with her blue eyes and fair skin, would bring down a curse upon them.

Halimena muttered an incantation to ward off the evil spirits that constantly observed human beings in their foolishness, her gnarled fingers making the signs that had been passed down from her mother and her mother before her to those possessed with the Sight. It was a great disappointment to her that none of her children had inherited the gift, but she lived in hope that one of her grandchildren would show signs of it in the years to come. Of course, most of the women in the camp practised fortune-telling at the fairs and country markets at some time or other, but that wasn't the true Sight. She sniffed her scorn.

Her thoughts returning to the object of her agitation, she turned her head as though she could see through the caravan door to where Pearl slept between her granddaughters. In her grandmother's day, even in her mother's day, this would never have happened. They would have given succour to the child, maybe even taken her to the gates of the nearest church or habitation, but to allow her to remain with them and learn their ways? Never. *Never.* There were one or two gypsy families she knew who had allowed their sons or daughters to marry gorgies and dilute the blood, but she would rather die than see such a thing within her own. Not that they were talking about that here, not yet, but the girl was too pretty for her own good even now, her skin as smooth as satin and the colour of fresh cream touched with rose.

Halimena ground her teeth irritably. Corinda was a fool and Mackensie more so for being led by her. No good came from the woman wearing the trousers and the man the petticoat.

She continued to sit brooding for another full hour, thinking up ways and means of forcing Pearl to leave the camp. The blood of two newts, mixed with early-morning dew and a fresh spiderweb, enclosed in an acorn cup and placed under her pillow, would do it, but sleeping with Madora and Freda as she did, that was out of the question. The magic wasn't discriminating – and what if her granddaughters up and left too? A longer-term remedy would have to do. The wings and antennae of an Emperor Moth crushed to dust and placed in a person's boots was known to give them the wanderlust, the same as the seeds of rose-bay willowherb spread over the tailfeather of a swallow and hidden in a person's belongings ensured that they'd be on the move before the month was out. Mind, the chit had no belongings to speak of, so perhaps the

Emperor Moth solution was the one? She could easily sprinkle the powder into Pearl's boots once she was asleep. And if that didn't work there were other – stronger – methods she could employ.

There was a potion she could slip in the child's food to make her restless and agitated, another to induce sleeplessness and irritation of the skin, or maybe even one that would cause a severe loss of appetite and bring about a steady decline . . . Yes, there was plenty she could do.

Heartened at having come to a decision on the matter which had been troubling her since she'd first seen Pearl, Halimena stretched her legs and stood up. As she did so, the ghostly white flash of a barn owl flew across the clearing, its great wings lit by the moonlight before it disappeared into the trees. Clutching her scrawny throat, Halimena stared after it.

The guardian. She sat down again, her legs suddenly weak and her heart racing. Why had it come at this moment, if not to tell her it was aware of her intentions?

She fumbled inside the bodice of her blouse, her trembling fingers finding the amulet she wore at all times and which had been passed down the female line of the family for generations to those who had the Second Sight. She was mortally afraid.

The silence of the barn owl's long, rapid wingbeats had earned the predator its association with supernatural powers, and its eerie reputation had been enhanced through the ages by the bird's traditional choice of nesting places – church towers. As guardians of the church, the owls were known to have their favourites among the sons and daughters of mankind, and to cross such a one would bring down the wrath of the bird's protector – the God of Ages – upon that unfortunate soul. Halimena believed this folklore to the core of her being, and she had no doubt that the bird was warning her to hold her hand with the child who had come among them.

Muttering another invocation, she stared into the night, her fingers working on the amulet's hard stone surface as she sought comfort. What she saw as the bird's patronage of the stranger in their midst did not cheer her or ease her mind; rather it endowed

Pearl with powers equal to her own. The bird was respected and feared for its mysterious ability to catch its quarry without any warning of its presence, its silent flight and loud shrill shriek terrifying to its prey and those who observed it. It bequeathed favour on those it protected and it could curse any who came against them, with devastating results. Her hands were tied.

Chapter 8

Over the next few days Pearl did her best to adapt to the new and strange life into which she'd been thrust. Her natural affinity and love of babies and very young children soon saw a little clutch of devotees gathering around her in the rare moments she wasn't working. Everyone above the age of five or six worked from dawn to dusk, stopping only for meals, but once dinner was over in the evenings the gypsies relaxed around the campfires. It was then the younger children would make for Pearl, sitting on her lap or playing with her hair as she told them stories, their initial shyness gone. It was in this way she got to know some of the other families; mothers and older children stopping to talk to her for a moment or two when they fetched their little ones for bed.

She no longer felt awkward with Corinda and her daughters; Halimena and the menfolk were a different kettle of fish though. She was well aware that Halimena didn't like her and wished her gone, a blind man could have seen it. Freda had explained her grandmother's coldness and refusal to talk to her by saying Halimena didn't like anyone who wasn't a Romany. Pearl accepted this excuse – there was nothing else she could do – but the old woman's gimlet stare made her feel uncomfortable and nervous. Mackensie and his sons she was fearful of, but in a different kind of way. Every time she shut her eyes at night she had to fight against reliving the violation she'd suffered at the hands of her mother's 'friend', but her dreams she couldn't control. She often woke up shaking and terrified beyond speech, only to realise she was with Madora and Freda; she was safe.

And on top of all this she longed, she *ached* for James and Patrick, her thoughts a constant torment of regret and guilt. She had told Corinda she wasn't bad, but what was it if not bad, to leave her little brothers the way she had? And that man, Mr F. Had he sensed something in her, something that had made him think he could do what he'd done? Had she made him imagine she would allow it? Perhaps if she had fought harder, he would have stopped? And so her thoughts went round and round until she felt her head would burst.

When Byron and his brothers laughed and joked with her, the same as they did with their sisters, she knew they must think her a halfwit, the way she put her head down and became tongue-tied. But she couldn't help it. Even the slightest touch from one of them panicked her beyond coherent thought. She was spoiling any chance of fitting into the family, that was what logic told her. But it didn't seem to make any difference to how she *felt*.

Things came to a head the day before the camp took to the road again. One of the older boys about Byron's age had a pet jackdaw he'd taught to speak. It sat on his shoulder and was rarely parted from him, hopping up and down and cackling as it entertained everyone. Pearl couldn't understand half it said, as it lapsed into the Romany language most of the time, but just watching it perform was enough to make her smile, even if its sharp beak was slightly intimidating.

Logan, the owner of the bird, and several of his friends had come to sit with Byron and his brothers once the singing and dancing began in the evening. They were playing a game Pearl had noticed before. She supposed it was a form of gambling because coins changed hands for the winners and losers. She didn't quite follow what went on but it involved the throwing of small smooth pebbles with signs and numbers painted on them which the player aimed through small hoops made of woven reeds and wood.

Madora and Freda had edged closer to the group of lads to watch the game and Pearl had followed them, smiling when the jackdaw became as animated as his master when Logan won three times running. At those times the bird did a little dance and almost seemed to pirouette in its excitement, gabbling away and whistling as it twirled round. And then suddenly, with no warning whatsoever, it flew at Pearl and landed on her shoulder, taking a beakful of her hair in its mouth and pulling.

It didn't exactly hurt, but the surprise made her scream, and as Logan jumped up and came over, admonishing the bird which immediately flew back to him, she recoiled violently as he went to pat her arm. No one could have mistaken the fear in her face, and for a moment an embarrassed silence reigned, then Byron stood up and came to her side. 'It was your hair reflecting the glow from the flames of the fire,' he said very gently. 'It would have attracted the bird, as they like shiny things.'

Her cheeks flaming, Pearl nodded, first at Byron and then at Logan, who was standing awkwardly by. 'It's all right,' she said weakly. 'It made me jump, that's all.' Forcing a smile, she sat down again but a little further away from the others. She stiffened when Byron chose to sit down beside her, Logan returning to the game, and she didn't look at him.

'You know you are safe here? No one will hurt you, you have my word on that.'

His voice was very low but nonetheless she glanced about her before she whispered, 'I know.'

'We respect our womenfolk.'

Again she murmured, 'I know.' And then, almost in spite of herself, she added, 'But I'm not – not one of you.'

Byron frowned. 'My father and I and my brothers would protect you the same as we would my mother and sisters.'

84

'I didn't mean . . .' She paused, wishing the ground would open and swallow her. He knew what had happened to her and in this moment she was bitterly ashamed.

Byron found himself at something of a loss. This was rare and he didn't like the feeling, but over the last days since Pearl had been on her feet and among them, he had found his thoughts returning to her constantly no matter what he was doing or who he was with. Initially he had been full of anger and outrage when his mother had told him and his father what had happened to the girl. For a man to do that to a tiny little thing like her was unimaginable. He had been full of pity at first – he still did pity her, but as the feeling of wanting to protect and look after her had grown, so had the desire to be her friend and confidant. Her refusal to have anything to do with him most of the time had caused deep frustration. He wanted to tell her he wouldn't let anyone so much as lay a finger on her again, but how could he when just catching her eye made her tremble?

Clearing his throat, he said gruffly, 'You know it was me who found you in the hollow of the tree? Well, it was Rex to be fair, but what I mean is, I feel responsible for you.' Aiming to lighten the moment, he added, 'Rex does too. He's always close to you these days. Have you noticed?'

The big dog had crept from under the caravan in the last minutes and was lying by her side; her fingers were idly tangling and untangling in his grey fur. Byron saw the glimmer of a smile touch her mouth and, encouraged, he went on: 'What happened wasn't your fault and I can understand it's made you afraid, but—' Now it was he who paused before adding even more gruffly, 'Don't be afraid of me. Dai said you've got older brothers –' he didn't mention that he knew they were in prison '– and until you see them again, I'd like to take their place, me and Algar and Silvester.'

She moved her head once, then said, 'I – I feel frightened.'

Realising the admission was some kind of a breakthrough, he warned himself to go careful. 'Of course you do. Anyone would. I got caught by a couple of gamekeepers once some years ago when I was in the fields. They said I'd been poaching –' they had been right too '– and they beat me to within an inch of my life and left me in a ditch. The first time I went into the fields again after that, I was running scared, but it got better as time went by.'

She continued ruffling the dog's fur, her head drooping and her eyes on the ground. 'That's different.'

'You're right, it is.' He rubbed his mouth, his pity for the child swamping him. 'But what I mean is, you can't let this spoil everything. You have to fight back. You got away, didn't you? That was the first step. Lots of people wouldn't have had the guts to do that.'

Slowly now, she turned towards him. 'But I left my little brothers.'

'Because you had to. We all have to do things we'd rather not do because we've got no choice.'

He watched her consider this, before she said haltingly, 'They – they won't understand that.'

'They will one day when you tell them. And you *will* tell them when you're older.' He didn't know why he said that, but it seemed right. 'And they'll be older too, capable of understanding why you couldn't stay.'

'You really think so?'

'I know so.'

His reward for the lie was the way she smiled at him as she touched him, naturally and of her own volition. 'Thank you.'

He looked down at her small fingers gripping his arm and smiled back. And that was the beginning of their friendship.

The next morning all was bustle and unbelievable noise as the travellers departed. The poultry was gathered into large wooden crates which were slung between the back wheels of caravans or wedged on the rear of a cart, the sound of the birds' squawks and indignant cries adding to the mêlée. It was a morning of men shouting at horses, dogs barking incessantly, women yelling at enraged and screaming children, and an incessant rumbling as one after another the caravans and carts

86

began to roll on their way. Large and small, like ships at sea, the exodus continued.

Most of the carts were heavily laden, the most trusted, stoical horses straining as they pulled their load over the uneven ground, and in the caravans the wives and mothers leaned out of the half-doors, holding the reins, as their menfolk led the horse on its way. Children were everywhere, some peering out at the scene beside their mothers or balanced precariously on top of a cart laden with furniture, others sitting on the shafts of the vehicles or running behind. Youths led ponies and horses which the families hoped to trade at the next town or village, and dogs ran back and forth between the horses' legs, miraculously escaping the lethal hoofs.

Pearl was amazed at how swiftly the camp had got underway, but she supposed it was part and parcel of the gypsies' lives. Perched beside Freda in the back of the cart which Byron was driving, the sun hot on her face and the air full of shouts and cries and men whistling to their dogs, she felt a moment's panic at the thought of moving further away from James and Patrick. But slowly a sense of, if not exactly peace, then inevitability stole over her.

She was sitting on a sack of oatmeal with a stack of pots and pans at her feet, and as one of the wheels of the cart bumped down into a pothole, jerking her so she rose up in the air and landed back on the sack with a little gasp, Byron turned his head, his deep brown eyes meeting hers. 'All right?' He grinned at her and she smiled back as she nodded. 'It'll be easier when we get nearer Chester-le-Street and the Great North Road. The roads are always better nearer the big towns.'

'Is that where we're stopping again? Chester-le-Street?' She had heard of this place. Mr McArthur had sent Seth and Fred and Walter there one time on some business, and Seth had been full of the way the railway line crossed the deep valley of the Chester Burn, on an impressive eleven-arch brick and stone viaduct, nearly a hundred feet high and hundreds of yards long. She had wondered what business Mr McArthur had, so far away, but when she enquired,

Seth had changed the subject. He had talked about the viaduct for days though.

'We're only stopping there overnight. It's Consett we're making for,' Byron said over his shoulder. 'The red town.'

'Red town?'

'That's what it's known as. The dust from the ironworks is red and it covers everything.'

'It's horrible.' Freda wrinkled her nose. 'I hate the towns, they're so dirty and they smell.'

Byron laughed. 'The townfolk think we're the dirty ones. Anyway, there's a summer fair held on the outskirts of Consett at the end of the month, and there's always plenty of buyers for the horses. We'll get some good trading done there, dirt or no dirt. You'll be able to sell your baskets and mats, and I dare say there'll be some fine ladies who will be after having their fortunes told.'

'They have hurdy-gurdies and swingboats and coconut shies and all sorts.' Freda beamed at Pearl, her disgust with the towns forgotten. 'It's a branch of Dai's family who run the fair. They travel all round the country, so we get to see our cousins and aunts and uncles. Last year, Byron got drunk and had a fight with Aunt Lily's eldest.'

Byron's head shot round. 'That wasn't my fault! Erin started it – you know he did.'

Freda ignored her brother's glare. 'Dai and Dad were furious with him 'cos once they started, all the other lads joined in and we ended up leaving before the end of the fair.'

'I told you, it wasn't my fault.'

'Whoever's fault it was, you shouldn't have drunk so much of Uncle Noah's brew. Dad said it has the kick of a mule.'

'Shut up, Freda, or I'll make you walk.'

Byron didn't turn round but his voice was a growl and his shoulders were hunched. Freda grinned at Pearl, completely unabashed at her brother's fury. Pertly, she said, 'Dai said you'd got to have us with you.'

Aiming to pour oil on troubled waters, Pearl pointed to a sunny woodland slope beyond the track they were following, where hundreds of foxgloves, tall and magnificent, waved their dappled bells in the breeze. 'Aren't they lovely? I've never seen so many.' Apart from the odd walk Tunstall way, she had never seen anything of the countryside and certainly not what she termed real countryside, like this. The scent of wild flowers and trees was sweet on the lazy air, and just a mile or so before, they'd passed fields of ripening corn rippling in the warm breeze. 'I can understand why you prefer to travel around rather than live in houses.'

'No true Romany could live in one place for long.' Byron seemed glad of the change of subject. 'Neither would they be idle or expect anything they haven't worked for. Those who give us a bad name are not of the blood: we're not thieves or vagabonds.'

Pearl thought about the poaching she had seen but already she had lived with the gypsies long enough to understand that they considered it their right to hunt for food as their ancestors had done for hundreds of years. The land belonged to every man and woman, that was the way they looked at it, and be it a farmer's fields, an estate owned by the gentry or wild land, it was the same to them. It was a convenient way of thinking, she admitted, and when last night there'd been a communal feast and venison had been on the menu, she had felt on edge until it was all gone and no trace of the young deer remained, but that was the Romanies' way and that was that. Certainly it didn't seem wrong in the same way as her brothers' thieving had, but she didn't doubt there was a gamekeeper or two who would disagree with her.

'It can be hard in the winter.' Freda entered the conversation again. 'We stay inland then, Penrith way. We were snowed in for weeks last year.'

Pearl wanted to ask a thousand questions. How did the camp manage with food? And what about fuel, if all the woodland was knee-deep in snow? How did they provide hay for the horses and shelter for the animals in the worst of the winter? Were there any friendly farmers in the district, and did they winter in the same location each year? Questions buzzed in her head but she didn't voice any of them.

She would find out soon enough. Mentally nodding to the thought, she shut her eyes and let the glare of the sun play over her face for a minute or two before reaching for the wide-rimmed black hat Corinda had lent her until she could get a straw bonnet to protect her fair skin. None of the gypsy girls seemed to have need of protection from the sun, their complexions ranging from a light tawny shade to a deep, dark brown.

Everything about her proclaimed she was different, that she would never be able to fit in. The thought had been in the back of her mind for days, but now it was jabbing away like a needle into soft flesh. *And she had to fit in.* This tribe of people who had taken her in, this strange clan who looked so fierce and yet could be so gentle, they were the only folk in all the world she could trust. If Byron hadn't found her, she would have surely died, curled up in that tree – and that would have been the end of all her problems.

'Look, over there.' Freda caught her arm, pointing to a field of scarlet poppies blazing their glory with every twist and turn of their silky heads amid the corn. 'I love to see the poppies, don't you?'

Pearl nodded. She didn't tell the gypsy girl she had never seen a full field of the crimson flowers before, only the odd one or two blooming alongside bindweed and purple spear thistle when she had taken her baby brothers for a walk Tunstall way. Distant elms shimmered beyond the golden corn, and above, the deep blue sky provided a breathtaking contrast of colour.

Pearl felt something swell in her breast and travel to her throat. Whatever happened in the future, she was glad Byron had found her. *She wanted to live.* It was as though she was answering a question within herself which had been there since she had first woken up in the Romany caravan. There would be more days like this, when the sky was so high that even the larks seemed unable to reach it, and the light was so bright it wiped everything dark clean away.

Byron turned round again, his eyes tight on her as he said, 'You've gone very quiet.'

She smiled at him, the ache in her heart easing still more at his obvious concern. 'It's all so beautiful,' she said softly. 'I never knew it was so beautiful.'

PART THREE

The Blossoming

May 1908

Chapter 9

The first eight years of the new century had seen changes within the world in general and England in particular. There were many men of influence who believed that with a new King on the throne and a victorious conclusion to the Boer War, Britain was set to grow more powerful than she'd ever been.

These same stalwarts of the Establishment were not so happy about the changes in other areas. The disgraceful affair of Mrs Emmeline Pankhurst forming a new militant movement called the Women's Social and Political Union stuck in many a man's craw. Everyone knew giving the vote to women would not be safe. Men and women differed in mental equipment, with women having little sense of proportion, as one MP put it.

Equally dangerous was the notion to put more of these machines called motor cars on the road. The agreement between the Hon. Charles Rolls and Mr Henry Royce to sell motor cars under the name Rolls-Royce was nothing to get excited about. Rattling about the countryside and frightening the horses, whatever next? So said the members of the old guard as they sat in their gentlemen's clubs, smoking their cigars and drinking fine brandy, their coach and horses waiting outside.

There were many too within the Romany community who

sensed the winds of change beginning to blow. The towns of the Industrial Revolution were growing, swallowing large parts of the surrounding countryside. Hamlets were turning into large villages and large villages into small towns. Some of the old Romany routes and byways were being lost, and the old folk in particular felt it keenly, becoming fierce in their desire to protect their heritage and discourage anything they saw as a watering-down of their way of life.

None were so passionate in this regard as Halimena. Always a woman of indefatigable opinions, she had become more dogmatic and bigoted with each passing year, and Pearl's presence within the camp and especially her own family was a constant thorn in her flesh. A gorgie living with them, learning their ways and secrets, summed up everything that was bad about their changing world, and the old woman never missed an opportunity to make her feelings known. It was due to her relentless opposition that Pearl had not been taught the Romany language, something which did not trouble Pearl particularly but which did serve as a constant reminder to both her and the others that she was not one of them. Not that a reminder was needed. One only had to look at Pearl to see she was different.

Now eighteen years old, the beauty which had been apparent in the child was fully developed in the woman. Although only five foot four inches tall, Pearl carried herself very straight and with a natural grace that was not lost on an observer. Her thick, dark-brown hair fell to her shoulders in glossy waves and the colour touched on a deep chestnut in places. The smooth natural cream and pink of her skin had changed to pale honey from a life in the fresh air, but this only served to accentuate the cornflower-blue vividness of her heavily lashed eyes and the redness of her full lips. Even the palest of the gypsy girls looked dark next to Pearl, their jet-black hair and deep brown eyes adding to the contrast. This was not without its problems in that it brought Pearl to the attention of outsiders when they stayed in any one place for more than a few weeks, the local male population in particular. At those times Byron was never far from her side.

It was Byron Pearl was thinking of as she deftly skinned and prepared several rabbits for the pot late one cool May afternoon. She had taken over the cooking, cleaning and washing for the family a couple of years ago, leaving Corinda free to weave the mats and baskets they sold. Try as she might, Pearl had never become as adept as the gypsies at these tasks, but had discovered she had a natural gift where cooking was concerned. Even Halimena had been heard to give grudging praise on one or two occasions, ostensibly when Pearl was not within earshot. Corinda had been generous in sharing the Romany knowledge of natural herbs and plants and cooking methods which could enhance a dish, but she was the first to say Pearl could make the most ordinary dish extraordinary.

The stew underway, Pearl stood up and stretched, glancing across the campsite in the direction Byron had taken that morning. He and his father and brothers had left at first light. The gypsies had arrived at the site on the outskirts of Newcastle the day before. It was a spot the community had been coming to for decades, and Mackensie and his sons were sure they'd have no trouble trading the horses they'd brought over from Ireland a few weeks ago. Byron had told her there was one wealthy landowner in particular who didn't quibble at the price for the right horse.

Byron . . . Pearl bit down hard on her bottom lip as she was apt to do when troubled. She wished there was someone she could talk to about this matter which had been slowly coming to the surface over the last three years – ever since Freda had got married, in fact. Now both Algar and Silvester were betrothed, and she knew Byron would speak soon.

He liked her. She shut her eyes and then opened them to stare up into the cloudy slate-blue sky. It had been a bitterly cold March, and April hadn't been much better; now it was nearly the end of May and she was still going to bed with several layers on. That was another way in which she was different, since the gypsies prided themselves on not feeling the cold. It had been the week before, when a few rare hours of sunshine had lit up the wood close to where they had been staying, that Byron had persuaded her to go for a walk with him. The countless drifts of bluebells reflecting the deep blue of the sky that day had been a sight to see in the clearing they'd come to, the pyramid blossoms on the horse-chestnut trees and the dazzling green and gold of oak trees making the woodland magical.

She had been laughing at Rex cavorting amongst the bluebells when she'd become aware that Byron had fallen silent. She had glanced at him and the look in his eyes had made her immediately turn her head and call to the dog, acting as though she hadn't heard Byron when he spoke her name in a deep thick voice. But then he had taken her hand and she had been forced to look at him. Before he could speak, she'd said, 'I want to go back. Please, Byron. The evening meal won't cook itself.'

He had stared at her, his dark attractive face the same as usual, the fierce, hungry look gone from his eyes. Quietly, he had murmured, 'There are things I need to say, Pearl.'

'Not now.' She had smiled at him, pretending not to understand. 'I need to get the dinner on or your grandmother will be on her high horse.'

He'd sworn softly – in his own language, but she knew a profanity when she heard one. 'Then soon, all right? I want us to talk, really talk.'

She had nodded rather than prolong the conversation, but since that day had been very careful not to be alone with him. But that couldn't go on for ever. Again she shut her eyes for a moment. It wasn't that she didn't like Byron, she did. Loved him, even. But not – not in *that* way. She heaved an unsteady breath. The feeling she had for Byron was similar to that she'd felt for Seth, that was the only way she could describe it to herself. And although she might not know much, she knew the love between a man and a woman was made up of more than that.

Not that she ever wanted to be married. She gave a little shudder. She couldn't imagine letting anyone lay their hands on her and do what Mr F had done, let alone *want* them to. But the gypsy women were happy with their menfolk; she had lived among them long enough to know that Freda and Madora and the other girls she'd grown into womanhood with both loved and desired their husbands. Madora already had three bairns and Freda was expecting her second come September.

Holding her hands against her chest, she pressed them as if to assist her breathing while she asked herself whether, loving babies and little ones as she did, she could be content with life as a single woman.

The answer came strong and harsh in her mind. *More content than if I was being pawed and slobbered over by a man.* She didn't name Byron in her head at this point. It was merely a man. Any man.

Turning sharply, she went to the pile of wood behind the caravan for more fuel for the fire. It was as she returned with her arms full of twigs and small logs that she saw Byron and his father and brothers, and she gauged immediately from their jaunty manner that the day had been a good one. Byron's gaze met hers and she knew he had been looking for her. He always searched her out with his eyes the moment he was back. When she was younger, this had been reassuring; it was as though Seth was still around. Lately, it had become unsettling.

She busied herself with seeing to the fire and only looked up at Byron when he reached her side. She answered his smile with one of her own. 'I gather the trading went well?'

He nodded. 'Tollett knows a thoroughbred when he sees one.' The Romanies had been dealing with the manager of the Armstrong estate, Wilbert Tollett, for years and always for a tidy profit.

Pearl stirred the stew. 'Dinner won't be ready for a while yet but there's some suet pudding and cold meat if you're hungry,' she offered, adding some field mushrooms to the pot.

Byron looked down at the slender wisp of a girl he had loved for years. More times than he would care to remember, he'd lain awake all night planning the words he'd use when he asked Pearl to marry him, but then in the cold light of day he'd cautioned himself not to rush her and spoil their friendship. She needed more time, he could see that. He had told himself this when she had reached fifteen and he had danced with her at Freda's wedding. Then when she was sixteen, then seventeen. Most of the gypsy girls were wed and bedded by the age of fifteen or sixteen, but Pearl wasn't a gypsy girl. And the ill-treatment she'd suffered which had been the means of bringing her into his life was also the means of keeping him from speaking.

When he had recognised his feelings for what they were some years ago, it had taken him a while to get past the fact that he wouldn't be the first – but that didn't matter now. None of it was her fault – she'd been a child still, and in one way what had happened then had no bearing on the woman he wanted as his wife. In another way it had huge relevance because it had scarred her, if not physically then emotionally. But he could break through her fear and reserve, he knew he could. And now she was eighteen and he couldn't wait any longer. Here he was, twenty-five years old, and never yet had he taken a woman, because from the age of sixteen he had been waiting for Pearl. If he wasn't careful, one of his brothers would marry before him – and that would reflect badly on him, as the eldest son. Suddenly he knew he couldn't wait another day, another minute. His voice determined, he said, 'Leave that,' as he turned her away from the fire and the big iron pot. 'You're coming for a walk with me.'

Her eyes wide, Pearl stared up into his face. For a moment a protest hovered on her lips but something in his manner told her he wouldn't take any excuse. The day she had dreaded had come. Silently she passed him and fetched her thick shawl from the caravan, wrapping it around her shoulders as she joined him again.

They didn't speak as they left the field where the campsite was, walking side by side but without touching. Pearl was conscious of a whirl of thoughts milling about her head but they all boiled down to one thing. Could she bear what she would have to bear if she said yes to Byron? And if she said no, what would happen to her? She wouldn't be able to go on living with these people she had come to think of as her family and friends. It wouldn't be right or fair on Byron.

She glanced down at Rex who was following at Byron's heels. The big dog was showing signs of age, with white appearing round his muzzle and a rheumy quality to his eyes, although he was still

100

as lean and fit as ever. She owed her life to Rex and Byron. The knowledge had been hammering away at her for months, years – ever since the night she had danced with him at Freda's wedding. That had been the first time she had seen what was in his eyes. *How could she refuse him anything?*

Byron opened the wooden gate which led into another field full of cows, and just before she passed through it she glanced back once at the caravans and tents. The blue smoke from the campfires rising into the sky and the noise of children fighting, dogs barking, men shouting and horses neighing was all suddenly infinitely precious and familiar.

Swallowing hard she stepped through the gate to where Byron was waiting and they walked on.

Halimena had been sitting in the entrance to the tent apparently dozing, her hands resting on the cabbage net she was making. The nets were her forte and she was very skilful at them; they were always in great demand with the villagers to protect their garden crops from rabbits and birds and other pests. But she hadn't been asleep; she rarely slept in the day and she almost always never missed anything that went on around her. She had watched Byron and Pearl leave together and she thought she knew what her grandson was about. That girl had played him like a violin for years, fluttering her eyelashes but keeping her distance until he was fair foaming at the mouth. But he'd been restless of late, she'd seen it, and likely the girl had decided he was ripe for pulling in.

Halimena's teeth ground together in anger.

Well, she had taken no direct action, she had merely prayed to the spirits of the wind and sun and stars to come against the forces that protected the girl, but now it looked as though she would have to take matters into her own hands.

Her thin lips moved one over the other, since the thought was frightening. No mortal interfered with the destiny of one of the guardian's chosen ones: retribution could be swift. But she couldn't let Byron, the eldest son and the keeper of his father's name, marry the gorgie. Not while she had breath in her body. The old ways were being cast aside – even Mackensie had fallen whim to looking on the girl as one of his own – but the blood couldn't be diluted.

Sitting quietly, looking over the busy scene in front of her, she hatched her plans. It would have to appear as an illness. Her mind jumped from one potion to another. Something undetectable. Something which would not affect the rest of the family. It had to be so innocuous that no trace would remain. But how would she be able to introduce it into the girl's food or drink?

The celebrations on Midsummer's Day. Halimena's black eyes narrowed. Admittedly it was a month away, but that would be all right. It wouldn't be seemly for the couple to marry before gathering the Buckleys and the Locks together – and that would take some time. Months, in fact. No, nothing would be done before Midsummer's Day. And it was the custom for the oldest member of the family within the Lock tribe to cook the sun bread in the bonfire that was lit to honour the Sun God, then at his highest ascent. Everyone ate the unleavened bread she would serve to them, and who was to know if Pearl's plait was made with corn mixed with darnel grass containing ergot? She had noticed the black fungus on the darnel's seedheads in a field near Gateshead last summer and, knowing it to be a powerful poison when digested, had carefully preserved a bundle of darnel grass on which the parasitic growth was prevalent.

Her hands beginning to automatically work at the cabbage net, she considered the idea. She had never seen it herself, but it was said that victims of the fungus became insane and subject to all manner of strange delusions. Severe spasms affecting the working of limbs resulted in gangrene and the loss of fingers and toes, and some folk screamed like wild animals. Even Byron, besotted as he was, would shy away from marrying a woman who had suffered a bout of madness.

Of course, she would have to be extremely prudent. It wouldn't do for the girl's portion of bread to fall into the wrong hands. But once eaten, all evidence would vanish, and with no subsequent nausea or stomach upset to suggest that anything untoward had been digested.

Her eyes gleaming, Halimena's fingers sped on as nimbly as a young woman's. Her own grandmother had told her that once on their travels, when she was a small child, they had come across a whole village affected by eating bread made with polluted corn. People had been deluded into the belief that they could fly, throwing themselves out of upstairs windows and smashing to the ground, only to try to get up to dance and run on broken limbs. It would be interesting, she thought, to see for herself the result of consuming the fungus.

Standing up, she walked to the pot of stew which was simmering over the open fire, stirring it vigorously before throwing a few sticks on the flames. The girl might be able to cook but she would never make a good wife for any man, let alone Byron. Pearl was bad at bottom — she felt it in her water. If Byron did but know it, she was saving him from a life of misery. There were plenty of good gypsy girls who were ready and willing to comfort him — he could take his pick — and if he married one of them, the pure line would continue. Which was all that mattered.

Less than a mile away, Pearl was saying much the same thing. 'I can't marry you, Byron. You know I can't. Your family have been kind to me and I'm grateful, but I'll always be an outsider. They're expecting you to marry well, one of the daughters of a respected Romany family, you know that.'

'As my wife you *will* be respected.' His voice was soft. He had expected opposition but he wasn't about to give up.

'It wouldn't be enough.'

Ignoring this, he said even more softly, 'I love you, Pearl. I have for a long time. Do — do you love me?'

Her long lashes swept down over her eyes. 'As . . . a brother.'

'You have the same feeling for me as you do for Algar and Silvester?'

'No. Yes. Not exactly.' He was confusing her. 'What I mean is, you're special.'

'Special is a good start.'

'But I don't think of you in *that* way.' She raised her eyes and he saw they were swimming with tears. 'I don't think I'll ever want to marry anyone.'

He knew what she was trying to say, and now his voice came low and gentle as he took her hands. She had long since stopped trembling when he touched her, and he had always rewarded her faith and trust in him by restraining himself. He did so now, merely keeping her fingers in his, but without pulling her into him as his whole being wanted to do, when he said, 'If you give us a chance I can make you want to marry me. I promise. I won't hurt you, Pearl.'

She shook her head. 'Your family—'

'I'll take care of my family.'

'But you can't, don't you see? Even if the others accepted me as your wife, your grandmother never would. She – she hates me.'

He didn't deny this, he couldn't. It was the truth. Instead, he said, 'My grandmother will die sooner or later – she's an old woman.'

Again, Pearl shook her head. 'I want us to be friends like we were. I – I like you better than anyone else in the world, but I can't be what you want me to be.'

'I want you to be yourself and I can be patient. Now don't cry. Please don't cry, Pearl.' Tentatively he drew her into his arms, wiping her tears with his handkerchief before moving her to rest against him, his chin nuzzling the top of her head. It took all his willpower not to crush her against him and kiss her. After a little while, he said, 'This isn't so bad, is it?' although he was aware that she was holding herself stiffly.

Her voice was small when she said, 'No.'

He held her for a few moments longer before stepping back to look into her face, still with his arms loosely about her. 'I love you and I can wait, but I want you to start thinking of me differently. I'm not your brother, Pearl. I don't want to be your brother. Do you understand? This can be just between us for now. Nobody else needs to know, but I want you to try.'

'But—'

'What?'

'If – if I can't think of you in that way, what then?'

'You will.' He sounded very confident. 'Now you go back and I'll see you later.'

They were standing apart now and she stared at him uncertainly. She had expected . . . She didn't know what she had expected, but not this quiet reasonableness. 'You're not angry?'

He moved his head slightly. 'No, Pearl. I'm not angry.'

'I – I do care about you, but – but not . . .'

There was a long pause before he finished, 'Not in that way. You've said.'

Pearl hesitated for a moment more and then turned, walking swiftly away.

Once he was alone, Byron held his brow in his hand and, closing his eyes, remained still for some minutes. It was Rex pawing at his boot that made him take his hand from his head and bend down to pat the dog. 'It's all right, boy. It's all right.'

But it wasn't all right. He clicked his fingers at the animal and began walking in the opposite direction to the campsite. It was far from all right. He hadn't expected her to fall on his neck with delight at his offer of marriage. He'd known he'd have to tread carefully, woo her, reassure her, but he'd thought . . . What had he thought?

He came to the grass-covered bank of a weedy stream and flung himself down, Rex flopping down beside him.

He had thought that when he declared himself, there would be some answering spark in her eyes, something to tell him that at the bottom of her she felt the same. That under the layers of fear and shyness and timidity, she wanted him.

His fingers reaching for his whittling knife, he brought it out of his pocket along with the small figure of a child at prayer that he was working on. He always found this went down very well with the fine ladies, a child at prayer. His dark eyes concentrated on the wood in his hand, he allowed the peace and quiet of his surroundings to steal over him.

She had asked him what he would do if she couldn't see her way clear to accepting him. The truthful answer would have been he didn't know. All his thoughts and dreams of the future had been wrapped up in her for so long he hadn't contemplated anything else. *He wouldn't contemplate it.*

His face hardened, his full, sensual lips thinning. She *would* become his wife, nothing else would do. He had waited for her longer than any man would have done; she was his by rights.

And what if Pearl didn't see it that way? What if another man came sniffing about? She was so beautiful, she grew more beautiful each day. What if she looked at another man and liked what she saw?

He answered the devilish little voice in his head by standing up so abruptly that Rex growled and barked. No one else would have her. She was his.

His knife had slipped on the figure as he had jumped to his feet. He looked down at it in his hand, one finger stroking the surface of the child's face which now had a deep groove in the wood. His mouth set in a grim line, he drew back his arm and flung the wooden figure into the stream, the weeds and lilies closing over it and hiding it from view beneath the dank green water.

Halimena was surprised to see Pearl return alone. Her gimlet eyes took in the girl's posture, the droop of her shoulders and the downward curve to her mouth. Well, well, well. Her aged gums ruminating like a cow chewing the cud, she watched Pearl attend to the stew. Perhaps Byron wasn't so foolish as she'd thought. It would appear that whatever had gone on wasn't to m'lady's liking – and that could only mean one thing. He hadn't been prepared to give her his name.

She smiled to herself, her eyes gleaming under the wrinkled lids. Her grandson was a strange mixture, and she had long since come to understand there was a streak of independence in him that could threaten the following of the old ways if they didn't coincide with what he wanted; however, in the case of the girl it would seem she had misjudged him. And that was good. She had no wish to go against the forces of the guardians if she didn't have to.

She sat mulling the matter over in her mind for some time, her fingers busy. She knew the moment Byron walked back into the camp, and one look at her grandson's face confirmed there would be no announcement made of a betrothal.

But she would watch and listen as to how things progressed. Mackensie and his wife were worse than useless; there were none so blind as those who did not want to see. And in the meantime she would summon up all the charms and incantations she knew to cause her grandson's desire for the gorgie to wane and die, and for him to become bewitched by another pretty face. There was Margaritt, Wallace's daughter, or Scicily Young – she was a fine Romany girl with wide hips for childbearing.

At twilight when the evening meal was ready, Halimena did not wait for her portion to be brought to her at the entrance to the tent as was her custom. Instead she rose and went to sit beside Byron, slipping the contents of the small vial she'd concealed in her pocket into his stew when he wasn't looking. The love potion was powerful, and she would make sure she had something from both the girls of her choice to slip under his pillow come bedtime. A strand of hair perhaps, a thread or two from an item of clothing or a handkerchief. Something for the potion to focus on while he slept.

Relief that the worst had not happened made her mellow, her cackling laugh sounding now and again once the meal was over and the music began. Pearl's sombre face was food for her soul, further confirmation that the girl's nose had been put out of joint and that her grandson had seen through the chit's wiles.

She shouldn't have doubted him, she decided, after several glasses of Mackensie's strong, woody-tasting ale. He clearly wasn't so daft as he looked. But just in case, she would keep the darnel grass safe in her chest along with all her herbs and elixirs and charms. Just in case . . .

Chapter 10

Christopher Montgomery William Armstrong watched his father shovelling food into his mouth like a pig at a trough and wondered for the umpteenth time how his mother – his elegant, genteel mother – endured living with such a man.

But he already knew the answer, he told himself in the next moment, and it certainly wasn't love – unless you counted the love of money. When his father's father – a moderately rich man with a burning desire to become much more than moderately rich – won this estate with its house, farm, labourers' cottages and 100 acres of grounds on the turn of a card, he had promptly brought his wife and only son here, determining that it would be the beginning of a new life.

He'd bought himself a leatherworks and flour mill on the banks of the River Tyne in Newcastle, and later a string of warehouses on the waterfront. He'd seen his power and influence grow yearly, becoming respected and not a little feared, but the one thing he hadn't been able to boast was a wife from the aristocracy. And so he had made sure he bought one for his only son from a noble family who were on the verge of becoming insolvent, and then promptly got himself and his wife killed in a boating accident when they were doing the Grand Tour, leaving his son the master of everything he surveyed at the age of twenty-five.

'Christopher, dear.'

His mother's calm voice brought the young man's eyes to her face. 'Yes, Mother?'

'You aren't eating. Are you unwell?'

'I'm quite well, just not particularly hungry.'

'Huh!' Oswald Armstrong raised his eyes from his breakfast to glare at his son. 'Not hungry! You'd be hungry if you did a decent day's work, m'boy. You can be sure of that. Can't work up an appetite burying yourself in books with your grand friends.'

'No, I suppose not.' Christopher didn't take offence at this. He, along with his mother, could hear the pride his father was aiming to conceal by belittling the very thing he was immensely proud about. A son at Oxford might not be much benefit in his father's many businesses, but it was something to boast about over dinner parties and at his club. His father, like his father before him, was a social climber who was very aware that his beginnings had not been in the top drawer. Added to that, Oswald Armstrong had another son, Nathaniel, to take over his little empire when the time was right.

As though his thoughts had conjured up his older brother, Nathaniel strolled into the breakfast room a moment later.

'I was just saying, if Christopher wants an appetite he'd better work alongside us every day.' Oswald spoke with his mouth full, and Nathaniel glanced over at his brother with raised eyebrows.

When Christopher merely smiled, Nathaniel said lazily, 'He'd only get in the way, wouldn't you, Chris?' This was said with affection. At twenty-five years of age Nathaniel was four years older than his brother but the gap had always appeared wider. Nathaniel was like his father in nature – strong willed, determined and selfish – but from the moment Christopher had been born, his brother had taken on the role of protector and friend. When Christopher had proved to be a gentle dreamer of a boy with a passion for books and poetry, it had been Nathaniel who had stood between his brother and father when Oswald got irritated with the son he didn't understand and had little time for. Indeed, if there was one person in the whole world whom Nathaniel truly loved, it was his brother, and the feeling was reciprocated. Their father was a hot-tempered bully and their mother merely a vague presence in their lives, content to leave her sons to the care of the servants when they were younger, and each other and their friends as they reached manhood.

Once Nathaniel was seated, one of the maids brought his coffee and the soft white rolls he favoured, made with honey that morning by the cook. He always ate these before he helped himself from the covered dishes at one side of the room. In all, there were fifteen indoor servants to see to the family's needs, and seven outdoor men from the coachman down to the stable boy. The farm was a separate entity, under the control of their manager, Wilbert Tollett. He was responsible for the buying and selling of stock and also the fine hunters which were Oswald Armstrong's one weakness. They had a stable full of superb horses but Oswald could never resist another one. The farm hands numbered a dozen, and several of their wives were employed in the dairy.

'So, all set to enjoy your vacation, little brother?' Nathaniel spread one of the split rolls liberally with crab apple jelly, made from their trees in the orchard. 'I'm sure Adelaide will be pleased to see you safe and well and in the bosom of your family.'

Christopher grimaced. Adelaide Stefford was the daughter of his parents' oldest friends, and with only a year's difference in their ages the two had been pushed together since they could toddle. Both sets of parents were shameless in their desire to see a union between the two, but although Adelaide was willing – more than willing – Christopher's tastes didn't run to big, voluptuous women who liked nothing more than a day's hunting in the fresh air followed by a hearty meal most men couldn't finish. Adelaide was voracious in more ways than one, and he'd had enough sexual experience – courtesy of Nathaniel's introduction to a couple of his ex-mistresses and one or two ladies of the night – to know he preferred women who were happy to be led rather than those who insisted on taking the dominant role.

'I haven't made any plans to call on the Steffords,' he said, only to regret his ill-chosen words at once as his mother said reproachfully, 'I really think you should, Christopher. Adelaide was here only the other day, enquiring as to when you were home. She is so looking forward to seeing you again.'

Ignoring the wicked sparkle in his brother's eyes, Christopher smiled at his mother. 'Perhaps when I've had time to settle in?'

'Well, don't leave it too long. The Steffords are such dear friends.'

If he had voiced what he was thinking, Christopher would have said, 'The Steffords are typical of the incestuous breeding which produces dull minds and animal appetites, and I would rather walk through Oxford naked than call on Adelaide.' Instead, he nodded. 'Perhaps in a few days.' Looking at his brother, he asked pleasantly, 'And how's Rowena?'

Nathaniel's laughing blue eyes said, *'Touché.'* His voice was circumspect, even prim, however, when he said aloud, 'Very well.'

'That's good.' Rowena Baxter's family had connections with royalty, and their parents had made it very plain that that was where Nathaniel's duty lay. The fact that Rowena was as thin as a pikestaff and twice as plain, and twittered like an empty-headed bird given half a chance had nothing to do with it.

Oswald Armstrong could hardly be called the most intuitive of men, but he had always been aware of the strong bond between his two sons and it grated on him. Now his small round eyes, which were as hard as black granite, moved between them. 'If you've nothing better to do then I suggest you accompany Tollett on his rounds today and see how the farm is faring,' he said to Christopher, his tone making it clear that this was an order. 'It won't do you any harm to put yourself out for once.'

Christopher's quiet, faintly benign stance did not waver. He knew his father intended the exercise as a punishment. Oswald's interests were totally centred on his business assets in Newcastle, the Stock Market, and his horses – and not necessarily in that order. The farm, in spite of being a successful and rewarding venture in its own right, interested his father not an iota, and because of that he couldn't imagine either of his sons displaying a fondness for it. Which happened to be right, in Nathaniel's case. Christopher himself had always enjoyed walking round the fields full of livestock and seeing the new additions in the spring, or strolling on the edge of the wheatfields when the warm summer sun wafted air rich with the smell of warm grass and golden crops. He knew most of the men by name, and Wilbert Tollett he liked and respected. He considered him a good, honest man and thought his father was fortunate to have secured his services umpteen years ago. Expressionlessly, he said, 'I'll do that, Father.'

His father inclined his head sharply at him and then continued to guzzle his meal, pieces of food falling from his mouth to his plate. Christopher didn't look at his mother but he knew her face would be remote and her gaze concentrated anywhere but on her husband. She never looked at him unless she had to.

He left the house immediately after breakfast, walking swiftly through to the stableyard where the groom quickly ordered the stable boy to saddle his horse. He'd had Jet for years, resisting his father's attempts to buy him a better and grander stallion. He and Jet were fond of each other, that's how he felt, and he didn't share his father and brother's desire to outdo their neighbours by owning the best hunter in their circle.

The August sun was already hot as he rode out of the yard, directing the horse through an ivy-covered arch and along by a tall wall covered with roses in full bloom. The scent of the flowers was heavy in the still air; on the other side of the wall his mother's pleasure gardens would be a picture. By the time he left the grounds of the house and turned into the cobbled lane leading to the farm, the claustrophobia his parents' home always induced was falling from him.

The sky was a deep blue, but billowing white clouds drifted aimlessly across the fields, a gentle reminder of the weather's capacity to flatten the crops. Years ago, Tollett had told him England had one of the best climates for growing crops but one of the worst for harvesting them, and he had never forgotten those words of wisdom. The cornfields stretching in front of him made him stop for a moment, his gaze relishing the vivid golden sea of grain. A kestrel, rigidly suspended in the still air and motionless save for its quivering wingtips, was scanning the ground in search of prey.

As he watched, it swooped into the corn, only to emerge again grasping something in its talons as it returned to the sky. Tollett had taught him that these birds were useful allies of the farmer, catching many rodents and insects, but he preferred the songbirds to the russet-flecked predator, magnificent though the birds of prey were.

The lane ended where a copse began and he continued through the small wood and into a meadow which had been left to the riot of wild flowers that starred the thick grass for as long as he could remember. Beyond this he joined a dirt road. At one end of this the farm could be seen in the distance, a big old sprawling farmhouse where Tollett and his wife and family lived. At the back of the farmyard stretched the labourers' terraced cottages, and behind them lay the fields containing the livestock. The other end of the road veered sharply away from the grounds of his parents' house, eventually leading to a road that went to Newcastle. This meant that no trace of the farm, or its noises and smells, intruded on his parents' house and immaculate grounds.

Tollett was in his study working on the farm accounts when Christopher arrived at the farmhouse, flustering Mrs Tollett and exciting her little brood of children who were off school for the summer. As she bade him sit in the pleasant, oak-beamed sitting room, the children peeped round the door at him, giggling and whispering until their mother shooed them away. 'We don't get many visitors to the house,' she apologised in her warm Northern drawl, immediately adding, 'ee, Mr Christopher, I didn't mean you're a visitor, not as such – not being the master's son.'

'It's all right, Mrs Tollett. I knew what you meant.' He smiled to put her at her ease but the woman was all a-flutter, and they were both glad when Wilbert appeared in the next moment, hastily doing up the buttons of his cloth jacket.

'I'm sorry, sir, I didn't know you were coming this morning.' He held out his hand and Christopher shook it. 'Nowt wrong, is there?'

'Not that I know of, Mr Tollett.' He always gave the man the courtesy of the 'Mr' as befitted his responsible position, although his father and brother never did. 'My father suggested I might come and see how things are, but to tell you the truth I was planning to come anyway, just to get away from the house.' He smiled. He'd known Tollett all his life and the man had spent many days allowing him to tag behind him about the farm when he'd been a child. As he had grown, he had felt the two of them had become friends. He hoped Tollett thought so too, although he knew Wilbert would never presume to claim this out loud.

The manager's face relaxed and he smiled back. 'Walls pressing in on you already, sir?'

'Something like that.'

'Then a ride in the fresh air'll be just what the doctor ordered.' Wilbert paused. 'The wife was just about to make some coffee when you came. Can I tempt you to a cup and a slice of her fruit-cake?' This was said with an element of pride. The drinking of coffee denoted the manager's station in life, and elevated him above the men working under him.

'Sounds good to me.' Suddenly Christopher felt hungry.

They chatted about his life at Oxford and how the farm was doing while they ate, and then the two of them left the farmhouse, Christopher sending Mrs Tollett into a further tizzy when he complimented her on the fruitcake and declared it was the best he'd tasted since he'd been here the last time. 'I'd like to take a couple back with me when I leave, if that's all right?' he said to the pink-faced little woman. 'There's nothing like your baking, Mrs Tollett.'

It was as they mounted their horses that Wilbert said, and warmly, 'It's good to have you back, Mr Christopher, and you haven't changed a bit in spite of being down at that grand university and all.'

Christopher raised a quizzical eyebrow. 'Did you expect me to?'

'I don't rightly know, sir, but there's many who might have. Hobnobbing with lords and ladies and the cream of the crop.'

'If you looked into the ancestors of the "cream of the crop", as you put it, there's more villains and rogues than they'd like to admit to,' Christopher said drily. 'Not to mention a few murderers and torturers for good measure.'

'Oh aye, you're right there, sir. And not too far back in history neither.'

Their talk was easy as befitted old friends as they began a leisurely tour of the farm. The pigsties were full of little piglets squealing and clambering over each other, and big fat contented sows lying on their side as their offspring fought each other for the exposed teats. The hen coops were producing more and more eggs each year; the vast open area the wooden coops led on to was full of happy hens busily scratching about in the dirt and clumps of grass.

The two men sat chatting for some time as they watched the cattle lazily ambling about in the livestock fields beyond the buildings close to the farmhouse. It was a hot, sultry day, and as Christopher listened to the manager detailing the facts and figures and the profit the farm had made in the first half-year, he knew he wouldn't remember anything Wilbert had said later. He was at peace, a rare occurrence when at home and one almost always confined to moments such as these when he was with Wilbert or riding Jet in the surrounding countryside.

Where was he going to fit into the overall scheme of things, once his time at Oxford was done?

The thought was an unwelcome intrusion, spoiling the moment and bringing his parents' world into the tranquil scene in front of him. Was he destined to marry Adelaide and become one of the privileged country set? All hail fellow and well met? And Nathaniel. The only way his brother could stomach being wed to Rowena would be if he had a mistress or two in the wings, supplying his carnal needs. Was this it? Was this the sum total of the future?

'. . . tidy, respectable folk, none of your riff-raff. They might snare a few rabbits and take the odd pheasant or two, but they're an honest lot.'

'I'm sorry, Mr Tollett.' Too late, Christopher realised he'd been miles away. 'What were you saying?'

'I was explaining about the gypsies I've hired to help out with the haymaking, sir. They're the same ones who sell the horses to us each year, and I can vouch for 'em else I'd never have took them on.'

'I'm sure you wouldn't.'

'The thing is, sir, this good weather is going to break soon, I feel it in me bones, and them gypsies work like the devil. They show our lads up, I can tell you. They're camping where they usually do, up by Lot's Burn, and seeing as they were around I thought I might as well use 'em, but . . .' Wilbert hesitated. 'I haven't mentioned it to your father, Mr Christopher.'

Christopher nodded. Wilbert didn't need to explain further. His grandfather Armstrong had been nothing more than a shopkeeper who had been successful enough to buy a string of shops before he struck lucky with his gambling and won the estate, but this was never mentioned at home. To hear his parents talk you'd think the Armstrongs had always had blue blood, and his father was worse than his mother in this regard. Oswald seemed to think it necessary to show he had a contempt for the working class as though this somehow reinforced his superior position, and on the subjects of minorities like the gypsies or the Irish or indeed any person who wasn't English upper-class, he was scathing.

'There was no need to mention it, Mr Tollett.' They both knew his father and Nathaniel only visited the farm once in a blue moon. 'My father leaves the employment of seasonal labour in your hands and is only interested in a job well done.'

'Oh, it'll be that, sir. Like I said, them gypsies work like the dickens, their womenfolk too. Very comely some of 'em are an' all, very comely, but there's never no trouble with our lads, their menfolk see to that. They're not ones for mixing, the Romanies. Sell you their horses, oh yes, and the womenfolk their posies and baskets and such, but by and large they keep themselves to themselves and their noses clean.'

'You sound as though you approve of them.'

'Aye, well I do, sir, to be truthful. There's some tinkers and pedlars who give the whole lot of 'em a bad name, but this particular group are a pleasure to deal with, compared to some of the scum in the town. I'm not a one for towns, never have been.'

They had left the livestock fields and followed the winding path in the direction of the acres of ripe golden wheat as they had been talking, and now, as the horses took them closer, they could hear in the distance a song being chanted in the motionless corn. Christopher brought Jet to a halt, straining his ears. 'That's not English, is it?'

'No, sir. That's the gypsies singing; they sing all day and in their own language most of the time. I like it meself, but some of our lads say it gives 'em the willies. Mind, they don't like the gypsies showing 'em up workwise.'

They passed several fields where the sheaves were already stacked and ripening in the blazing sun before coming to the area where the reapers were at work. The farm hands were working in one field, the gypsies and their womenfolk in another.

Christopher did not comment on this. What he did say was, 'I remember a day when you let me help out with the harvesting, Mr Tollett. Do you? I was ten years old at the time.'

Wilbert nodded. 'I do, sir. The sun turned you as red as a beet-root but you wouldn't stop work till the men did.'

'I told my mother I'd been reading by the lake all day and I still got into trouble for that. What she would have said if she knew I'd been haymaking, I don't know.'

'If your parents had known half of what you got up to we'd both have been in trouble, sir.'

The two smiled at each other before sitting back on their mounts and letting their gaze wander across the working men and women. A golden haze hung in the air, the sickles of the reapers moving rhythmically and the Romany chant rising and falling in the still air. Christopher breathed in the evocative scent of cut corn. It was better than any manufactured perfume.

He watched a group of gypsy women gathering the corn and deftly binding it into sheaves, their faces and arms nut brown and their bright blouses splashes of colour against the acres of gold. Most of them were bare headed, their blue-black hair shining in the sun. One of the women, a young girl, was wearing a large floppy straw hat that hid her face, and for no other reason than that the hat made her different, his gaze focused on her. As it did so she straightened, flexing her slender shoulders. Her back towards him, she took off her hat and held her face up to the sun for a moment, a mass of thick, luxuriant dark-brown hair with glossy chestnut highlights falling about her shoulders.

Christopher's breath caught in his throat. His eyes glued to the figure, which seemed almost ethereal compared to the other gypsy girls, he watched her run her fingers through her hair several times. Then she wound it up and piled it on her head again, before stuffing her hat on and continuing with her work.

Letting out his breath in a silent sigh, he said, 'That girl, the one with the hat on. She's one of the gypsies?'

'As far as I know, sir.' Wilbert's gaze had moved behind Christopher to the farm buildings in the distance. 'It's the men's lunchtime – here comes the wife with their victuals.'

Christopher turned in the saddle to look to where Mrs Tollett and some of the other women and children were coming laden with baskets. He recalled the year he'd helped with the harvest: the bottles of cold tea and huge slabs of sticky fruitcake and ham and egg pie had seemed like the best feast he'd ever had. They still did, come to it.

'I want a word with the men, sir. Will you wait here, and then you're welcome to come back to the house and share our meal?'

Christopher nodded. 'Go ahead and thanks, I'd like that if it's no trouble for Mrs Tollett.'

'Oh, she'll be tickled pink and so will the bairns.'

Christopher watched Mrs Tollett approach and as he did so he reflected that Wilbert was a lucky man. As a young boy he had enjoyed the times he had sneaked away to visit the manager's home. There had always been plenty of children to play with; Wilbert's oldest son was twenty-nine now and the Tolletts had fifteen children in all, the youngest having been born six years ago. But it wasn't this which had drawn him but the tangible atmosphere of warmth and laughter prevalent in the home.

From the beginning he'd sensed something between husband and wife he hadn't been able to define as a child, never having witnessed love and friendship between a married couple before. He'd always left the farmhouse on leaden feet, wishing with all his heart he'd been born a Tollett as he'd walked back to his own home. He'd made the mistake of saying this to Nathaniel once. His brother had laughed at him, teasing him about it for weeks. He hadn't mentioned the subject of the Tolletts to Nathaniel again, but the incident had brought home the fact that, much as he loved Nathaniel and his brother loved him, they were fundamentally different. It had made him feel even more of an outsider within his home.

His gaze returning to the gypsies, he saw they'd followed the farm hands' lead and were now sitting down in small groups eating their lunch. One or two of the girls had poppies threaded in their dark hair. He'd picked a bunch of poppies on his way to the Tolletts' once as a child, and although Mrs Tollett had taken them with a word of thanks, one of her children, a pert young miss called Gladys who'd been a year younger than him, had told him he shouldn't have done it.

'The poppy's the protector of the crop, isn't it, Mam?' she'd said to her mother. 'Da says the poppies grow to make the Corn Goddess sleep so she doesn't wander and forget to grow the wheat. If you pick them before harvest you'll bring down thunder and rain and flatten the crop. That's what Da told us.'

Mrs Tollett had shushed her precocious daughter and told him it didn't matter, but he'd later discovered that all the country folk thought the same. The following week had seen several violent thunderstorms and he had never picked the poppies again. Gladys had married the son of a local farmer at sixteen and was happily bossing him about and having a child every twelve months, according to her father.

A slight smile on his lips, Christopher came out of his reverie to find he was staring at the girl in the straw hat and she was staring back at him. He blinked, and the brim of the hat swiftly lowered, hiding her gaze, but not before he'd seen two great azure eyes set in a heart-shaped face, the beauty of which took his breath away for the second time that day.

Who was he? Pearl was glad of the hat to hide her burning cheeks. A gentleman, obviously, from his clothes and manner. And she had been staring at him. She bit into a piece of flatbread, mortified at her forwardness. It had been obvious he'd been miles away, lost in thought, and there she'd been gawping at him like a hussy.

It was another few minutes before she dared to raise her head and then it was to see Mr Tollett, the manager, and the young gentleman riding away. Her eyes followed them until they disappeared from view. The gentleman hadn't been wearing a hat. That alone denoted his class. His hair had been beautiful, golden, like ripe wheat or perhaps just a shade or two darker. Beautiful, anyway. *He* had been beautiful.

Her thoughts again made her lower her head in embarrassment and she was thankful none of the girls around her could read her mind. Who was he? she asked herself again. Someone important from the way Mr Tollett had acted. Anyway, it was none of her business.

She continued to tell herself this throughout the rest of the day as she worked in the fields, but still her mind kept returning to the handsome stranger. Every little while she found her eyes scanning the distance to catch a sight of him, but although Mr Tollett returned late afternoon, he was alone.

The twilight was deepening rapidly when she arrived back at the campsite with the others. Most of the able-bodied among them had gone to help with the harvest, but Byron and his father and a couple of the other men had ridden up the coast after hearing about a horse fair further north. They were expecting to be away for a few days.

Corinda had taken on the task of cooking the evening meal for as long as the harvesting continued, but Pearl found she wasn't hungry. She felt odd, restless – and when Halimena made a show of complimenting her daughter-in-law on the dinner, adding that it was the best food she had tasted in a long time, Pearl found she couldn't ignore the old woman's scarcely veiled hostility as she usually did. After saying she was going to bed and leaving the others, she suddenly balked at the thought of the hot stuffy caravan and decided to go for a walk instead, slipping silently away. This in itself was a rare treat, and something she wouldn't have been able to do if Byron had been around. To be fair, she qualified in her mind, none of the gypsy girls were allowed to wander far without a male escort from their family accompanying them.

The daylight had all but gone as she strode along the lane leading away from Lot's Burn. She had thought she was tired on the walk back to the campsite, in fact she had wanted nothing more than something to drink and her bed, but now she felt invigorated, even exhilarated at walking alone in the cool of the late evening. A missel thrush, its beak holding the last meal of the day for its fledglings, flew past her – and in the distance she could hear cows mooing as they settled for the night. Somewhere in the near hills a fox barked. She breathed in the air, warm and holding a hundred summer scents, and suddenly took off at a run, leaping over a low stone wall as she laughed out loud and crossing a meadow of thick grass on feet that seemed to have wings.

She reached a hill but didn't stop, scrambling up the steep path and keeping going until she reached the top, whereupon she gave in to the stitch in her side. Throwing herself down on grass still warm from the heat of the day, she looked up into the sky where the first star was twinkling beside a crescent moon.

She hadn't run like that in years, not since the time she had left the East End. When she had taken James and Patrick out Tunstall way she had made her brothers laugh sometimes by running up and down hills and around them while they'd clapped their hands and shrieked, infected by her joy of the moment. James and Patrick . . . She sat up, clasping her knees, the joy she'd felt draining away and the old familiar sadness taking its place. She had long since given up any thought of going back to Low Street. Her place was with the Romanies now, with Byron. She owed him her life.

She swallowed hard against the knot of fear that accompanied such thoughts. When she looked into the future she became panicky at what lay before her, but since Byron had spoken she knew deep within there would come a day when she'd have to say yes to him. She didn't doubt that he loved her and he was kind, handsome too, in his dark swarthy way. As the eldest son of the most powerful family in the community, she was well aware it would be considered a great honour to become his wife.

She plucked a blade of grass, idly chewing at its sweetness and enjoying the warm breeze after the fierce heat of the day.

She had always known deep down that Byron was in love with her, but she had been able to pretend he merely thought of her as a sister before he'd declared himself. Now that comfortable deception was gone, and with its passing she'd had to face up to the fact that she was afraid of him, afraid of his body and what it would do to her when she became his wife. The last few weeks she had been trying to make herself love him as a woman should love a man, but instead even the warm affection and trust she'd always felt for him was dying. Which made her feel doubly wretched. But for him, she would have died curled up in that old tree like a hurt animal; he deserved her undying gratitude. And love. But how could you make yourself want someone in *that* way? The feeling was either there or it wasn't, surely?

Sighing, she rose to her feet. She'd have to get back. If Halimena went to bed and found the caravan empty, she'd take great pleasure in raising the camp and causing a fuss, just to put her in a bad light. Oh, she knew Halimena's little ways sure enough, and it would serve the old woman right if she married her precious grandson and spoiled the purity of the blood. In fact, the thought of Halimena's outrage and fury at hearing that Byron wanted to marry her was the only bright spot on the horizon.

Telling herself she'd end up as bitter and twisted as Halimena if she wasn't careful, Pearl began to retrace her footsteps, but slowly. At the bottom of the hill she stood for a minute or two, drinking in the solitude. For some time now she'd felt as restricted as a dog on a short leash, but the other unmarried gypsy girls didn't seem to mind the limitations their society put on their movements. But that was it in a nutshell, she supposed. She wasn't a gypsy, not by blood – as Halimena took great pleasure in reminding her at every opportunity.

By the time she reached the lane that led to the campsite at Lot's Burn, she was walking more swiftly, suddenly anxious to get back before her disappearance was discovered. The fox was barking again, nearer now, the harsh sound jarring on the whispering stillness of the night. Whether it was because she was listening to the fox or thinking about how she would creep into the caravan undetected, Pearl wasn't sure, but she didn't hear or see the horse until she jumped over the low stone wall into the lane and landed almost under its hoofs. It reared up on its hind legs, neighing loudly and almost unseating its rider, and Pearl fell backwards in her fright, landing with a jolt on the grass verge.

'Are you all right?'

The breath had left her body in a whoosh and she couldn't answer for a moment. The rider had dismounted and coming to where she was, said, 'Are you hurt?' as he crouched down in front of her.

Blue eyes met grey. 'You?' The voice was deep and without any discernible accent. 'The girl in the straw bonnet.'

She stared at the man who had featured in her thoughts all afternoon and evening and who was the reason for her earlier restlessness. Pulling herself together, she managed to say, 'I – I'm sorry. I didn't see you.'

'Nor me you. In fact, you seemed to materialise straight from Jet's hoofs.'

The voice had a touch of laughter in it and it provided the adrenaline needed for Pearl to ignore the hand he held out and scramble to her feet unassisted. The moonlight was very bright, and standing as close to him as she was, she was aware of several things all at once. He was tall and his shoulders were broad under his fine coat; there was a faint smell emanating from him – not exactly perfume but something very pleasant; he was even more handsome than she'd imagined, and there was something else she couldn't put a name to. It wasn't frightening and yet it was sending tremors down her spine and reminding her that she was out here alone. Again, she said, 'I'm sorry.'

'Don't be sorry, I'm just relieved you've come to no harm.' He looked in the direction she had come from. 'Is there no one with you?'

She shook her head. 'I was just taking a walk.'

After working in the fields all day? Had she been meeting a secret suitor she didn't want her family to know about? A local? Ridiculously, Christopher found the idea rankled. His suspicions made his voice stiff when he said, 'I was led to understand such freedom would be frowned upon in your community. For an unmarried girl, that is,' he added, as the even more unwelcome thought hit him that she might be married.

'It is.' Pearl shrugged her slim shoulders. 'But I needed some time by myself and it's such a bonny night.'

'So there is no lovelorn farm boy waiting in the shadows?'

She looked at him, a straight look, and her voice was as stiff as his had been when she said, 'I told you, I wanted some time by myself.'

Oh dear, he had offended her. 'I apologise,' he said at once. 'That was presumptuous of me. Will you forgive my impertinence?'

Pearl didn't answer for a moment, as she wasn't sure if he was making fun of her. Then she saw he was deadly serious. It flustered her and to her chagrin she knew she was blushing. 'I must be getting back before I'm missed,' she said weakly.

'May I escort you home?'

'*Oh no!*' The words had left her lips before she had time to consider how such a vehement reply sounded. He had been half smiling but now his face was sombre. 'No one knows I'm out, you see,' she explained hastily, 'and if they saw me with you they'd think . . .' Her voice trailed away. It wasn't seemly to say what they'd think.

He nodded, and to her relief the smile was back when he said, 'Then may I suggest I walk you to the bend in the lane before the campsite? None of your family could possibly see us if I leave you there.'

Pearl hesitated. The risk was still there. What if one of the men or some of the lads were out poaching and spotted them?

'I saw you earlier and I would have liked to speak to you then, but it wasn't possible,' he said softly. 'This opportunity seems heavensent.'

It was a reflection of her own thoughts and the inflection in his voice made her shiver inside. She wasn't doing anything wrong, she told herself silently. Just by allowing him to walk with her a little way, she wasn't doing anything wrong.

Again he spoke quietly. 'I don't even know your name.'

'Pearl. Pearl Croft.'

'And I'm Christopher Armstrong, at your service.'

'Armstrong? That's funny, the owner of the country estate where we're harvesting is . . .' The penny dropped. This must be a member of the family.

Ignoring this, Christopher said swiftly, 'Well, now we've been formally introduced, so I think it's quite proper for me to escort you part of the way home. I'll tell the horse to tiptoe, how about that?'

His eyes were twinkling and Pearl couldn't help but smile. 'He must be very well trained to tiptoe to order.'

'Absolutely, but then you have no idea how often he and I come across a damsel taking the air late at night.'

Pearl's smile widened. She was feeling strange – happy, excited, apprehensive. She didn't really know how to explain it. But from the first moment she had caught sight of him, she had known that this was what she had been hoping for when she'd left the others tonight. And it had happened. She had met him, she was talking to him, and he was walking her down the lane . . .

Chapter 11

Pearl and Christopher didn't arrange to meet the next night, but when she slipped out of the camp again she knew he would be waiting at the bend in the lane. When she turned the corner he was standing stroking his horse's muzzle, talking to the beast in a low voice, and for a moment her heart stopped. Then it raced madly as he raised his head and saw her.

She had brushed her hair until it resembled raw silk and changed into a clean blouse, but her old skirt and ugly stout boots she could do nothing about. She had noticed the previous evening how his clothes were of the finest quality and cut, his knee-high leather boots shining and without a mark to blemish the smooth surface. Everything about him was wholesome and fresh. When he'd led the horse the night before, she'd looked at his hand on the reins and his fingernails had been short and spotlessly clean. A gentleman's hand, one that had probably never done a day's hard labour in its life. But he couldn't help what he was born to, she'd chided herself, as though the thought had been a criticism. Which it had, in a way.

'Hello, Pearl.'

Again the sound of his voice made her shiver inside. She looked into his face. It was slightly flushed and his eyes were bright. 'Hello,' she murmured shyly.

'I was hoping you might decide to take the air again.'

He spoke as though she was a highborn lady strolling around her manicured gardens. A silence ensued between them for a moment, then Christopher unfastened the horse's reins from a branch of a tree, saying, 'Shall we walk a little?'

He had thought of nothing but this moment all day. And what course of action he would take if she didn't come. But she *had* come. Struggling to keep the elation from sounding in his voice, he said, 'You were able to escape your fetters once more then?'

He'd spoken lightly but he knew immediately he'd said the wrong thing, even before Pearl replied hotly, 'If you're implying I'm a captive then you're wrong, Mr Armstrong. The gypsies respect their womenfolk, that's all, and they have good reason for making sure they're protected when close to the towns. Some folk seem to think gypsies have loose morals and they tar them all with the same brush.'

Her phraseology was interesting. This time Christopher considered his words. 'Forgive me, but you speak as though you are more of an observer than one of them.'

'I – I wasn't born a gypsy, if that's what you mean.'

So he'd been right. All day he'd been trying to reconcile how she fitted into the Romany community. Her fair skin and blue eyes and slender build was at variance with the sturdy, black-haired individuals he'd seen working in the fields. Carefully, he said, 'May I ask how you came to join them?'

There was a long pause, the silence broken only by a pair of male blackbirds fighting noisily in the hedgerow, one of which flew away as they approached, with the other hot on its tail.

'They found me when I was ill and alone and took me in,' Pearl said quietly.

'How long ago was that?'

'I was eleven years old.' The tone of her voice warned him not to pursue this line of conversation. Restraining his burning curiosity with some difficulty, Christopher acknowledged that he would have to tread carefully if he didn't want to spoil things. He didn't qualify in his mind what he meant by 'things', he only knew if he frightened her off now he would regret it for the rest of his life.

Casually, he said, 'They've obviously been good to you.'

'Aye, they have, very good. And kind.'

'I should imagine you're someone it would be easy to be kind to.'

'I don't know about that.' She gave him a small smile.

They walked on in the deep twilight until they came to the place where they'd met the night before. Motioning towards the wall with his hand, Christopher said, 'Shall we sit a while?' As she nodded, he quickly took off his coat and laid it on top of the dusty stone, saying, 'There, that should be comfortable enough.'

The simple action brought home to Pearl that he was from a different world, not that she really needed to be reminded of it. She'd been saying the same thing to herself all day long. It had been folly to come tonight; a man of his class would want one thing and one thing only from a gypsy girl. And yet . . . he didn't seem like that.

Christopher now looked at her and saw she was perturbed in some way. Her earlier comments about how people viewed the gypsies in mind, he said gently, 'I'm glad you decided to take a walk again tonight. I was hoping we might talk a while.'

'You – you're the son of the Mr Armstrong who owns the estate, aren't you?' Discreet enquiries under cover of casual conversation out in the fields that day had elicited this information. There were two sons of the present landowner and his lady wife, she'd been told, although one, the younger lad, was away at university down South for a large part of the year.

'Yes, I am. One of them anyway. I have an older brother, Nathaniel.'

Having tied up his horse, Christopher came and sat down beside her. The faint scent of woodsmoke hung in the still air. The woodman had been felling the straight, eight-year-old chestnut underwood growing at the back of the estate earlier in the day, the grey smoke from his woodfire billowing out into the blue sky. If Byron had been here, Pearl knew he would have skulked around once it was dark to see what he could salvage. Walking sticks cut from chestnut always sold well and took no time to fashion, unlike his carvings. But she didn't want to think of Byron, not now.

'I've been longing to see you all day.'

Christopher's quiet confession brought Pearl's eyes to his. Then she turned her gaze away, looking towards the hedgerow on the other side of the lane, her cheeks pink.

'Do you mind me talking like this?' he asked after a moment or two.

'I – I don't know. I don't want you to think—' She stopped abruptly, not knowing how to continue.

'I don't.' He replied to what she'd been unable to voice. 'Please believe me when I say this, I only wish for us to be able to get to know each other a little. I wouldn't harm a hair of your head. You have my word on that.'

His coat was thick and soft, she could feel the beautiful material beneath her hands where they rested either side of her on the wall. She had never felt cloth like this; she had never met anyone like him before. She was trembling inside but not with fear; she somehow knew he was speaking the truth when he said he wouldn't hurt her. 'What is your university like?' she asked.

'My . . . ?' He stared at her. 'Do you really want to know?'

She did. She wanted to know everything about him, starting from when he'd been a little boy and right up to the present day. She didn't say this though, merely nodding her head.

'Well, the university is full of men like me whose family don't really know what else to do with them.' Then he shook his head. 'No, that's not fair. There are plenty of good, intelligent men who are following a worthwhile goal and who will emerge at the end of their education equipped to follow the career of their choice. I envy them, I suppose.'

'Because you don't feel like that?'

He shrugged his shoulders, privately amazed he'd told her so much. 'I'm the younger son. This means my brother inherits and takes over the estate and my father's business enterprises in due course. Which is all to the good, I might add. Nathaniel is as ideally suited to this role as I am not.'

Pearl's brow wrinkled. 'What will you do then? When you leave the university?'

'The truthful answer to that is I don't know.'

Pearl stared at him. It seemed amazing that a young man of his wealth and power had no clear idea about his future. He could do anything, couldn't he? 'What would you like to do?' she asked. 'If you could choose anything, regardless of your position?'

He smiled. 'Regardless of my position? I would like to have a bookshop, a dusty little bookshop where people could browse all day long without having to buy anything if they didn't want to. It would house the works of writers which span centuries, from Anglo-Saxon laments to Tudor husbandry, and from Regency *fêtes-champêtres* to the modern day. Dickens, Addison, William Blake, Wordsworth . . . Beautiful literature, particularly that which has a powerful feeling for the countryside, as I do. Words paint pictures, you know. Like yesterday. When I saw you in the cornfields I was reminded of a poem which finishes,

"Speak but one word to me over the corn,

Over the tender, bowed locks of the corn." That's how I felt.'

Pearl was entranced. 'Who wrote the poem?' she asked a little breathlessly. 'What was it called?'

'Summer Dawn by William Morris. He was a poet and novelist and painter.'

'And you learned about him, about poetry and books at university?'

Christopher nodded. 'I'm studying for a degree in English Literature.' He didn't mention the magnificent library at home, a room which – to his knowledge, at least – his father had never entered and Nathaniel only once or twice.

English Literature, thought Pearl. Even the sound of the words was daunting. He was as far removed from her as the Man in the Moon.

But of course he was, a part of her mind answered harshly. What had she expected? He was a fine gentleman, used to servants and beautiful clothes and sitting on a horse watching others work.

'What's the matter?'

His grey eyes were tight on her face when she looked up. 'I – you shouldn't be here. Your family wouldn't like you talking to me.'

He didn't deny this. What he did say was, 'My grandfather was a shopkeeper, as was his father before him. They both had a penchant for gambling though, and my grandfather was particularly good at it. Some said he cheated – but it could never be proven. One night he staked everything he had in a game of poker. He won. It would seem he always won when he needed to. Overnight he rose to the dizzy heights of a rich country gentleman and within a few short years he had convinced himself that others saw him as he wished to see himself. He made sure his only son – my father – married into an old aristocratic family who needed his money to keep the wolf from the door and were prepared to sacrifice their daughter for the right sum. Distasteful, isn't it?'

She did not reply, and he went on, 'Shortly after the marriage, my grandparents were killed and my father inherited. My mother dutifully bore him two sons and then retired to the west wing of the house, leaving my father to his quarters in the east wing. At a social function they are cordial to each other, the rest of the time they rarely speak or acknowledge each other's presence. My mother has her circle of friends and enjoys her dinner parties, bridge clubs, balls and other gatherings; my father has his little empire, his club and an elegant hostess who knows all the right people and says all the right things at the right time. That, Pearl, is my family.'

'And your brother?' she asked softly.

He hesitated. 'Nat is Nat. We've always rubbed along well

together, although we're quite different.' He turned to her, his hand close to her fingers on the wall but without touching. 'What I'm trying to say is, the Armstrongs are not what they seem. If that game of cards had turned out differently, my grandfather would have been forced to work down the mines or in the steel yards – anything to earn a crust like thousands of other working-class men.'

'But it didn't turn out differently.'

'No, it didn't.'

It was dark now, but the moonlight was as bright as the night before. It painted moving pictures where the faint evening breeze rustled the leaves on the trees and the shadows danced. The fragrance in the air and the warm balmy night were soothing, but the silence which had fallen between them stretched and quivered until Pearl found herself saying, 'I was born in Sunderland and Seth, my eldest brother, looked after the family when my da died.'

'Is he living with the gypsies too?'

'No, no. Seth and Fred and Walter were sent to prison. For thieving. But they did it for us, for my mother and baby brothers. They weren't bad, not really.' She made a wide sweeping movement. 'That's what people always say, isn't it, when one of their own gets into trouble? But in this case it's true. My da set them on with McArthur when they were just bairns . . .'

As her voice faltered and died, Christopher stared at her. He'd known from the moment he set eyes on this girl that she would make an impact on his life, even if it was only that he'd forever carry the memory of her standing in the golden corn under a brilliant sun with her hair cascading down her back. But now he'd spoken to her, he knew that wouldn't be enough. His voice little more than a whisper, he said, 'Tell me. Tell me everything, from the beginning.'

Pearl brought her hands into her lap and looked down at them as she began speaking. She told him everything. Afterwards, she was amazed at herself but there, in their quiet shadowed little world, the words came easily because it didn't seem real. It was as though they had stepped out of time.

At some point Christopher's hand took one of hers but he didn't interrupt her. It was only when she finished speaking that he said softly, 'I'm glad the gypsies found you, Pearl. They have my undying gratitude.'

Slowly now she looked at him. Two days ago she hadn't known he was alive, but now she had the strangest feeling that she knew him better than anyone in her life. She didn't smile when she said, 'I'm glad too, but I must go back now.'

'Will you come again tomorrow?'

'If − if I can.'

'You must.' As they stood up, he said again, 'You must. Promise me you will.'

'I promise.'

She watched him untie his horse and when they began to walk and he took her hand again, she didn't demur. Nor did his touch raise any fear in her, nothing but a warm, pleasant sensation. They stopped at the bend in the lane. 'Till tomorrow then.' His voice was soft and deep. 'I'll be waiting for you.'

Pearl nodded. Shyness was overwhelming her and she almost snatched her hand away now in her haste to be gone. Suddenly, the enormity of what she'd confided, of what he must be thinking was making her hot. He had been born to comfort and ease, used to servants attending to his every need from when he could toddle. How could he envisage what it was like to live in Sunderland's East End? Whatever he said to the contrary, privately he must be thinking she came from a bad lot.

She turned, running along the lane without looking back, and she didn't stop until she was sure he wouldn't be able to see her any more. Then she leaned against the trunk of an old oak tree, her chest heaving. She was stupid, so stupid. She shouldn't have told him anything, there'd been no reason to, not really. Now she had spoiled everything. Even if he came again tomorrow, he would look at her differently. He had seen her as a girl, a pure young gypsy girl, and in the space of an hour she'd confided that she came from the slums, that her father had been an evil bully who had sold his sons into a life of crime which had resulted in their imprisonment, that her mother was . . . she closed her eyes and then made herself say the word – *a prostitute* – and that she, herself, was not the innocent maiden he had supposed.

She slid to the ground, her hands over her eyes, and as the sobs came they were silent but nonetheless bitter because of it.

When Pearl nerved herself to approach their trysting place the next evening, she felt sick with fear. Fear that Christopher wouldn't be there, that if he *was* there he'd be different. All day as she had worked in the fields under a blazing sun she'd told herself it would be for the best if he didn't come. Then this thing between them, this thing she didn't dare put a name to, would have to die.

And really, she'd asked herself, what had he said to make her feel he thought of her in a special way? A few kind words, words he'd probably said to other girls, girls of his class who were free to meet him on an equal footing. He was a kind man, she didn't doubt that, and likely when she'd confided her past to him he'd felt sorry for her. Sorry and embarrassed. The thought made her squirm but it kept hammering at her mind, along with the little voice of conscience, which stated that she shouldn't meet him. That way, he wouldn't be put in a difficult position if he was regretting their assignations and she could walk away knowing she had done the right thing – for Christopher, for herself, and for Byron.

She made up her mind during the course of the long day that she wouldn't go for a walk that evening, but as the twilight deepened and the songbirds sang their accolade to their Maker, she slipped out of the campsite once more.

He was waiting for her. But then he would be, she reasoned as her heart thudded so hard it threatened to jump out of her chest. He was that sort of man. It didn't mean he was glad she'd come. Merely that he'd felt obliged.

As Christopher saw her come towards him he read the doubt and uncertainty in her bowed head and measured walk. It made him throw away all caution and decorum. As she reached him he took her hands in his, his voice husky when he murmured, 'I was terrified you might change your mind. Oh Pearl, Pearl. Can you believe what's happened to us?'

She raised her head, her eyes seeking his. What she saw there took her breath away. And then she was in his arms, his lips smothering her face with his kisses as he whispered her name.

Part of her was standing back and exclaiming that she was in a man's arms, that he was kissing her, holding her, and all she felt was an overwhelming urge for it never to finish. It was only then that she realised how frightened she'd been that she would never feel this way about anyone, that the attack which had taken her innocence had in some way crippled her, stolen from her the pleasures of love between a man and a woman.

'I love you.' His voice was broken. 'Please believe me when I say I love you. I know it's madness, that we've only known each other for three days, but I've never felt this way before about anyone.'

'I love you too.' She didn't care that this was folly. This was Christopher, and she felt she'd known him for ever, that in some shining place beyond the confines of class and wealth and time, they'd been waiting for this moment.

'I was here two hours ago. I'd almost given up hope you'd come and I was thinking up a hundred excuses to go and find you.'

'You mustn't, you mustn't.'

'I know' – he shook his head – 'but I was desperate.'

'Promise me you'd never come to the camp.'

'I can't do that.' He took her face gently between his big hands and as gently kissed her. 'But I can promise you I wouldn't do it lightly.'

'They wouldn't understand, none of them.'

'I know,' he said again.

Of course he knew; his own family and friends would feel the same about her. Pearl stared at him. This couldn't work. He knew it and she knew it, so what were they doing?

'Come and sit down a while.' He drew her towards the grassy bank, spreading out his coat like the evening before. The moonlight lay in patches about them and Jet was munching contentedly on the thick sweet grass at the edge of the lane. When they were seated, he took her hands in his. 'In a perfect world we'd have all the time we need to get to know each other, but this isn't a perfect world, is it?'

'No,' she whispered.

'And soon the harvesting will be over and you'll move on. I – I don't want that to happen, Pearl.'

'Don't talk about that now.'

'I have to, I've thought of nothing else all day.'

'Mr Tollett's arranged for us to help with the harvesting at the farm whose fields are next to yours, so we'll be here for another few days at least.'

'A few days.' He brought her hands to his breast now, pressing them tightly there. 'I can't let you go, Pearl.'

She stared at him for a moment and then bit on her lip. His hair was shining almost white in the moonlight, his even, classical features in shadow. He kissed her again, and following this they were silent for some little time, their fingers interlocked. She looked down at her hands. She had scrubbed them and scraped her finger-nails clean before she'd left, but her flesh was rough and reddened by her work in the fields. Christopher's hands were tanned and smooth. Quietly, she said, 'Tell me the whole of that poem you spoke about yesterday, "Summer Dawn".'

He smiled. 'It begins, "Pray but one prayer for me 'twixt thy closed lips; think but one thought of me up in the stars" . . .'

She barely breathed until he'd said it all. Then she murmured softly, 'It's sad. I didn't expect it to be sad.'

'I find most poetry on the sombre side. There's one that's apt for tonight though.'

Warned by the quirk to his mouth, Pearl said warily, 'Oh yes?'

'"Come live with me and be my love, and we will all the pleasures prove that hills and valleys, dales and fields, or woods or steepy mountain yields" . . .'

There were seven verses in all and Pearl was smiling when he came to a halt, although her cheeks were pink. *Come live with me and be my love.* If only that were possible, she thought behind the smile. But in spite of what he'd said about not letting her go, Christopher knew as well as she did that all they could hope for was a few stolen hours together. But she wouldn't think of that now – she couldn't bear to think of it now. Not when he was with her and they had the promise of another few nights like this.

As though he had read her thoughts, he now said, 'I meant what I said, Pearl. I can't let you vanish out of my life.'

She stared at him. 'You said yourself we've only known each other three days.'

'And once upon a time, if anyone had told me they felt like this about a girl after so short a time, I'd have advised them to have their heads examined, but not now. Not since I've met you. I've been attracted to women before and I have to confess I've known several intimately – I was even infatuated once or twice – but what I feel for you is as different to that as chalk to cheese. Pearl,' he took her in his arms, his face close to hers, 'this is no passing fancy.'

She did not answer but leaned upon him, her face uplifted for his kiss.

When their lips parted, he said huskily, 'We'll face them together, your people and mine.'

'No!' It was involuntary, and in that moment she was thinking of Byron and what this would do to him rather than herself.

'*Yes.* Look, I've got it all worked out. I have an allowance – it's not much, just a few hundred a year that a Great-Aunt left in trust for me – but now I'm twenty-one my parents couldn't stop that. We can live on it until I decide what I can work at.'

A few hundred a year? That was a small fortune. Pearl's heart began to race. She hadn't expected this, not in her wildest dreams. Never for one moment had she allowed herself to imagine he saw a future for them.

'We could be married within the month, Pearl. Would you? Would you marry me?'

The proposal was so unexpected that for a second she remained silent, although her face had lit up. 'But – but your family would never allow it.'

Christopher made no attempt to gloss over his parents' reaction. 'They couldn't stop us and that's what counts.'

'But what about Oxford and your studies?'

Again he didn't try to pretend his father would continue to pay for his education. 'That doesn't matter. It's only you and I that's important here. If you leave in a few days I might never see you again, and I couldn't bear that. Could you? Could you bear to say goodbye?'

She shook her head, but still she had to say, 'Your family and friends, everyone – they wouldn't understand you wanting to marry someone like me, and we don't know each other. Not really. You might regret –' she couldn't bring herself to say 'marrying me' but changed it to – 'meeting me in time.'

'Never.' He pulled her fiercely into him. 'Never even think that, Pearl. I love you, I adore you.' He kissed her again. 'It might be madness, but I feel I've known you since the beginning of time, that you're the other part of me.'

His words melted the barriers of class and wealth, and now Pearl kissed him with a touchingly inexpert hunger. They clung to each other, swaying a little, lost in a world of touch and sensation. It was several minutes before she found the strength to pull away. Part of her wanted to agree to what he was saying without any more protest, but another part – a part born of her beginnings and her experience of life thus far – couldn't let him take such a step blindly. In a strange way she felt years, decades older than him.

'Your circle would never accept me as your wife,' she said gently. 'You would find yourself stuck between two worlds without belonging to either. Mine would label me an upstart and you a fool, and yours . . .' She shrugged. 'I can't even talk properly, Christopher. I know nothing about society or how to behave.'

He caught her hands. 'That's the first time you've said my name,' he murmured softly. 'And I don't care about my world, or yours either. We'll make our own world.'

'I'd never be able to live up to what would be expected. You – you'd be ashamed of me one day.' Why was she saying this? she asked herself wretchedly. She loved him, and in a way she knew she couldn't love any other man. Far from being frightened of his touch, his lips, she wanted more. So why was she pointing out the pitfalls? 'You've always been used to fine houses and refined company, going to dinner parties and balls, and what about your place at Oxford? You wouldn't be able to give all that up, and if you did you would long for it one day.'

Christopher didn't speak immediately. A full ten seconds crawled by before he said, 'Tell me you don't really think so little of me as to believe that.'

When he saw the tears in her eyes, he softly cupped one side of her face as his other hand took hers. 'Listen to me, Pearl. This wonderful world that you seem to think I inhabit is like a flower that's been dried and preserved – beautiful on the outside, but when you touch it, it crumbles away. I don't want a marriage like my parents have, I don't want a wife like my father has or others in his circle have. Women who give their children to nursemaids and nannies and see them for an hour in the drawing room before they're taken away to the nursery suite. And these dinner parties and balls you speak of. I listen to the conversation at such events and it sickens me, the bigotry, the shallowness. I've never fitted into my world.' He smiled. 'Nathaniel has always said I'm a changeling and perhaps he's right, I don't know. What I do know is that the only time I was happy when I was growing up is when I was with the Tolletts on the farm or escaping into a storybook. But I don't want to live the rest of my life trying to escape. Can you under-stand that?'

The urgency in his voice had stilled her and as she looked into the grey eyes she saw the aloneness behind the facade he presented to the world. It swept away any further opposition. Her answer to him was the covering of his mouth by hers . . .

★   ★   ★

139

Well, well, well. Halimena was part of the dark hedgerow, invisible in the blackness of the night. So still and silent was she that a harvest mouse which had poked its head out of its neat spherical nest of woven grass and wheatblades, slung between thick grass stalks and positioned a few inches above the ground, brought its babies out of the nest for their first excursion into the big wide world, passing within a foot from where she crouched.

Hadn't she known something was afoot behind that one's big blue eyes when she'd seen the girl slip into the caravan last night when she'd purportedly been abed an hour before? But this was better than she could ever have hoped for, Halimena told herself gleefully. Wait till Byron heard that the girl had got herself a fancy man – and what a fancy man! Gentry for sure. But then she'd get a good price for her favours from such as him.

The hard black eyes narrowed. That butter-wouldn't-melt-in-her-mouth guise had never fooled her, unlike some. In spite of what Corinda had said about the girl's virtues, she'd always known it was a case of like mother, like daughter. There were some who were forced into it and some who were born to it, and she knew which fitted that little chit. *And to think Byron would have stooped to mix his blood with hers.*

Her indignation had no visible form, but such was the power of her malevolence that the last of the baby mice sensed danger and skittered off after the others as fast as its tiny feet would carry it.

But not now. She knew her grandson well enough to be sure what his reaction would be when he found out Pearl had been making merry with another man. Besotted he might be, but no Lock would take being made a fool of. And that's what the chit had done: she'd made a fool of them all. All her love potions had been like water where Byron was concerned, the gorgie's hold over him was undiminished.

Halimena brought her eyes from the young couple and as silently as she'd followed Pearl, began her retreat. It wouldn't do for the girl to know she'd been rumbled, not yet. It might give her time to think up some story that Byron would find half-plausible. And it would take only the weakest tale for Byron to clutch at straws. That was men for you. They always let what was between their legs rule their head. No, he had to catch the girl in the act.

Like the dark mist that rises from wet, treacherous ground, Halimena melted into the shadows.

Chapter 12

For the first time in his life Byron had found the haggling and negotiations that went on at a horse fair irritating. He had watched his father and Horace and Edgar Lee driving a hard bargain, and his only emotion had been one of frustration. He wanted to get home. Home to Pearl. Nothing else mattered.

Since he'd declared himself and brought this thing that was between them out into the open, he couldn't bear to be separated from her for any length of time. He knew that if he could just persuade her to forget her fears and inhibitions, she would admit she loved him like he loved her. She'd told him he was special, hadn't she?

They were nearing the campsite now and behind his impassive face his emotions were at fever pitch. They'd been travelling all day, stopping only for a quick lunch of bread and cheese washed down with ale, but the sun was already set. In the days they'd been gone she'd been at the forefront of his mind constantly, and he knew his father had been annoyed at his lack of fervour regarding their business. Edgar, Horace's son, had been on top form, but the normal spirit of competition which existed between Edgar and himself had been absent, at least on his part.

The curling blue smoke of the gypsy campfires was apparent

some distance away, but now the twilight was closing in swiftly, and as they rode into the camp, mothers were already marshalling little ones to bed after the evening meal. After securing the horses at a grassy patch on the perimeter of the caravans and tents, Byron and his father made their way to where the family were sitting round the fire. Algar and Silvester jumped up at their approach and for a few minutes all was bustle and talk. It was only when Byron and his father were seated with a bowl of thick rabbit stew each that Byron felt able to say casually, 'Where's Pearl?'

'Oh, she's taken to going to bed early since the harvesting began.' Corinda's voice was indulgent. She neither liked nor agreed with her mother-in-law's opinion that Pearl was lacking the stamina and strength of a gypsy girl, but she had to admit the work in the fields seemed to have taken it out of the girl the last little while. According to those women who worked with her she more than held her own, but come evening time she was very quiet and subdued.

'She's not ill?'

'No, she's not *ill*.' It was Halimena who replied, and something in the tone of her voice caused Corinda to look sharply at her mother-in-law, the expression on her face saying, 'Don't start.'

Halimena tossed her head. She had watched Pearl slip away into the field behind their caravan a short time ago, but she didn't want to say anything in front of them all. What she had to reveal was just for Byron's ears and it had to be at the right time. The trouble was, she wasn't sure how long this fancy gentleman would put himself out to come this way. She hadn't dared get close enough to hear what the pair were saying the night before, but from the way the chit had been clinging hold of him, he might have been cooling off a bit. To a man like that, girls like Pearl were ten a penny, after all.

Controlling her impatience with some effort, Halimena waited until Byron had finished his meal and was gazing pensively across to where several of the lads were playing their fiddles while couples danced and laughed in the firelight. Algar and Silvester had joined the circle and were standing talking with their arms round their girls' waists, and Mackensie and Corinda had moved to the entrance to the tent where they sat close together, Corinda's head on Mackensie's shoulder. Rex, tired out by the last few days and the journey home, was deeply asleep, snoring and twitching under the family caravan.

Seizing the opportunity, Halimena touched her grandson's arm, bringing Byron's gaze to her. 'There's something I think you should see,' she murmured under her breath.

'What?'

'It's to do with Pearl and I'm not sure how to handle it, that's the thing. I know I've made no secret of the fact I think it's unwise to have a gorgie among us, but your mother's fond of the girl.' She had decided to pretend she was unaware of Byron's feelings and used her daughter-in-law as a smokescreen. 'I don't want to upset her.'

'What are you talking about?'

'Ssh, keep your voice down.' Halimena glanced round at her son but Mackensie and Corinda had disappeared into the tent. 'Pearl's not abed, she hasn't been abed these last few nights either − not since you went, in fact. I didn't know at first, but then last night . . .'

Byron stared at the woman he respected and loved but whom he'd come to find intensely aggravating since Pearl had come into his life. He had been careful to keep his feelings for Pearl hidden from his grandmother because he knew the fury she'd pour over his head if she guessed he loved the 'gorgie'. He just didn't under-stand the desire − which bordered on obsession, especially in Halimena's case − most of the older folk had to keep their blood-line pure Romany. There had been all manner of shenanigans a few years back when one of the girls from another tribe had run off with a clockmaker from Gateshead, even though the man was well respected and had immediately made her his wife. His grand-mother had been a prophet of doom then, predicting the marriage would be an unhappy one and any children born of the union would be shunned by both sets of families.

Reminding himself she was set in her ways, he said dutifully, 'What's the matter?' thinking he didn't blame Pearl for wanting some time to herself. Maybe she'd been missing him? His heart beat a little faster. Perhaps she'd wanted to sit quietly in the cool of the evenings after a hard day's work and think about him? He knew she found his grandmother's constant criticism wearing. In Pearl's eyes Halimena was the main obstacle to them getting together, he was sure of it, and as things were the poor girl even had to sleep in close proximity to his grandmother. But everything would change once they were married. He would make sure everyone, especially Halimena and the older generation, gave Pearl the respect due to her as his wife.

Halimena read her grandson like a book. What she saw as Byron's obstinate determination to see only the best in the gorgie brought a touch of asperity to her voice when she said, 'Come and see for yourself.'

Somewhat wearily, Byron said, 'Don't be silly, just tell me.' If Pearl wanted a few minutes in peace he'd wait till she returned and seize the opportunity to spend a little time with her without the rest of the family around. Suddenly the night was beautiful.

'I said, come and see for yourself.' Halimena's eyes bored into his, and as he stared at his grandmother the expression on her wrinkled face brought a strange numbness into his being. Without further protest he stood up. Once they left the campsite, the two of them moved through the shadows without a sound. It came naturally to move thus; even the very youngest Romany children were capable of roving through the countryside they inhabited undetected, their progress as silent and stealthy as the wild animals they hunted and poached.

Afterwards Byron was often to ask himself if he had expected what he found. On reflection he thought not, and yet when he saw the outline of a man and a woman against the charcoal-streaked sky embracing by the low stone wall bordering the lane, he felt no surprise. He stared at them, his eyes wide as he took in the handsome horse tethered some yards away. By the look of the animal, its rider was no common labourer or farm hand.

At this realisation there swept over him a feeling of such rage he must have made a sound in his throat because the horse stopped its munching of the thick sweet grass at its feet and raised its head.

Halimena placed a restraining hand on his arm, warning him to be quiet, but Byron shook her off. He was damned if he was going to skulk in the shadows. Stepping forward, he'd walked a few steps before the couple noticed him, and then it was only the horse whinnying and pawing the ground which alerted them.

He heard Pearl's exclamation of dismay but his eyes were focused on the man who still held her in his arms. Now he was closer, Byron recognised him as one of the sons of the big house. He'd seen him a couple of years back when he and his father had been delivering a horse to the estate. The man had been sitting on his horse talking to Tollett but had ridden off at their approach. When he'd asked Tollett about him, Tollett had described him as a grand young man, adding that this son was the only member of the big house he had any real time for. Now the recollection of the manager's approval made him even angrier.

'Take your filthy hands off her.' His facial muscles working, he was now so close he could see the amazement in the man's face. A handsome face, aristocratic.

'Byron, no. Let me explain.' Pearl had wrenched herself out of the fellow's arms and twisted herself in front of the man in an attitude of protection.

It added fuel to the fire, the more so when the fellow gently but firmly moved her to one side, saying, 'I don't know who you are but this isn't what you think. It's no idle flirtation. We are going to be married.'

With a deep oath, Byron was on him. It was an uneven fight from the start. Byron was a gypsy, used to hard work and hard living. From a boy when he'd fought he'd used both fists and feet and given no quarter. Furthermore, Christopher was not a violent man and had been taken by surprise; he had expected to reason with his adversary.

When Christopher fell to the ground and Byron continued to hammer him with his big hobnailed boots, Pearl's screaming rent the air. Rex had appeared from nowhere, barking madly, and added to the mayhem were the horse's panic-filled cries as it pranced and stamped, attempting to free itself from the constraint of the reins Christopher had tied to the branch of a tree.

Dimly Christopher realised the gypsy had murder in mind, and as his groping hand found a thick piece of wood, he grabbed it and brought it swinging against Byron's legs. It wasn't a hard blow, since from his position on the ground Christopher had little impetus, but it was enough to make Byron lose his balance. As he fell, Christopher rolled and staggered to his feet, dazed and shocked by the ferociousness of the onslaught. As Pearl flung herself at him, one arm went automatically round her waist, and by the time Byron sprung up it was to see the two of them facing him.

Halimena was screeching profanities at Pearl, and in the distance was the sound of cries and shouts; the furore had obviously raised the camp. All the dogs were barking in answer to Rex's din, and that alone was deafening in the sleeping countryside. Byron was aware of none of this. A red mist had come before his eyes at the sight of the gentleman with his arm once more about Pearl.

He didn't remember reaching for his whittling knife, but suddenly there it was in his hand. With a sound that could have come from an animal he sprang forward, lunging wildly. He felt it pierce the body in front of him, and as the man flung Pearl to one side he lunged again. This time the knife went in to the hilt.

Christopher once more hit the ground, but now he was groaning horribly, one hand clutching the top of his chest and bright red blood pumping through his fingers. Pearl crawled to him from where she'd fallen, sobbing as she cradled his head in her lap, and Halimena hung on to Byron's arm to prevent him striking again. Not that he would have. Even as they were joined by some of the others the knife fell from his limp fingers.

'Get help. You must get help, he's bleeding.' Pearl was trying to staunch the blood with her petticoat now, looking up at the circle of faces above her. Mackensie arrived at that moment, and taking in the situation at a glance, his face as white as Byron's, he took control.

'Ride the horse and get Tollett.' He pushed one of the men towards Jet who was calmer now the barking and screaming had stopped. 'And you two, get Byron back,' he added grimly, nodding at Algar and Silvester who were now standing either side of their brother. 'Tell your mother what's happened – he'll need to be got away fast before the law comes. She'll know what to do.' Glancing at Halimena, he bit out, 'Do what you can for his wound. If he dies it could be a hanging job if they get hold of Byron.'

A hanging job. And Christopher, her Christopher dead. As Halimena roughly pushed Pearl out of the way, she stood, her face ashen as she glanced about the men and boys in front of her. No one spoke a word. They didn't have to. The condemnation was so thick she could taste it.

Chapter 13

The next morning Pearl was summoned to the big house. The police had arrived at the camp before first light, but Byron had long since been spirited away. Edgar and Horace Lee had volunteered for the job of making sure he got safely to a distant branch of his mother's tribe way up in Scotland. He hadn't said more than a word or two since the fight; he'd appeared as one stunned, except when he had cried on his mother's breast like a baby.

The police had spent some time questioning the gypsy community. Young Mr Armstrong was hanging on to life by a thread, and had been unable to say much, merely that he had been attacked by persons unknown and left for dead before the gypsies had found him. The police did not believe this. It was as plain as the nose on your face that he'd been the victim of a vicious assault by one of the Romanies, but why? That's what they didn't understand. The gypsies had been working for the estate and according to the manager they'd done a good job and had been paid well, both parties being satisfied. And this particular Romany tribe dealt mainly in the buying and selling of horses and had been in the habit of doing business with the Armstrongs for years. One thing the gypsies didn't do was to cut off their nose to spite their face, so the whole thing was a mystery. Of course one of the tribe might have had a

149

grudge against the young man, but according to his parents he was away at university most of the year and out of it.

The demand for Pearl to go to the house was brought by one of the male servants – the butler, no less. He had been more autocratic than his master when he'd arrived at the camp in a horse and trap. Looking down his nose disdainfully, he'd ordered that a female by the name of Pearl Croft was to accompany him forthwith. When Pearl climbed into the seat beside him, her eyes swollen and puffy and her hair tangled from the times she'd run her hands through it in her distress, he made a point of shifting so that no part of her came into contact with him.

The butler said not a word on the way to the house. Pearl, sunk in misery and remorse, did not notice his frostiness or even raise her head. The lodgekeeper opened the massive iron gates which led onto the long winding drive and stood looking after them once the trap had passed through. Another two hundred yards and the Armstrong residence stretched before them – a huge, stone-built house with four imposing wings and turrets.

The butler drove the trap round the side of the house, passing through the stableyard which housed numerous horse boxes, most of them occupied by noble beasts who watched them over the half-doors. They passed through an arch into a wide, stone-flagged courtyard, and here another servant hurried to take charge of the horse when they came to a halt. The butler made no effort to help Pearl dismount, his voice cold as he said, 'Follow me.'

Walking across the yard he opened a door and Pearl followed him into a vast kitchen, the like of which she'd never seen before. In spite of her anxiety about Christopher and fear for Byron, she couldn't help being awestruck by her surroundings. A long white table ran down the centre of the enormous room with a continuous bench beneath it on either side, but it was the profusion of shining pans, the massive range, the huge dresser crammed with gaily coloured china and dishes, the side tables and overall sparkling cleanliness that rendered her dumbstruck. She had no time to stop and stare, however. The butler nodded to a personage Pearl assumed was the cook before continuing straight through the kitchen and opening a door into a narrow corridor. At the end of this was a green-baize door. This led into a wide hall which seemed to be all colour and light, the deep red carpet, enormous paintings on the walls and brightly upholstered chairs next to tables holding fresh flower displays overwhelming to her stunned senses.

The butler continued without a pause to a door at the far end of the hall. There he stopped, knocking twice, before opening it and motioning her through. He followed her into the room and shut the door behind him.

The room outdid anything she'd seen thus far in splendour, but Pearl was taken up with the three people staring at her. One she knew to be Christopher's brother, since the physical similarity was so strong, and the woman seated on the sofa next to which the two men were standing must be his mother, because again the resemblance to the brothers was marked. But it was the older man who held her attention. He was small and dark, and his presence seemed to fill the space between them with seething fury. He looked behind her to the butler. 'You fetched her yourself and kept your mouth shut?'

'Yes, sir.'

'The rest of 'em out there can think what they like, but if a word's said you get rid of them immediately. Got that?'

'Yes, sir, but none of them would be so foolish.'

'They'd better not be.' The hard little eyes switched to Pearl. 'What is the name of the man who tried to kill my son?'

Pearl blinked. 'I – the police said—'

'I know what the police said. They were told what was appropriate. Now I ask you again, what's his name?'

'I – I don't know.'

'This man is . . . what? Your lover? Your betrothed? And you don't know his name? I warn you, girl. Don't play games with me. My son confided in his brother that the two of you were together when this gypsy attacked him, so I'll ask you one more time. His name?'

Pearl gave no answer but her chin rose a fraction.

'Do you realise I could have the lot of you arrested? Do you?'

Then why hadn't he? As Pearl stared into the glowering face she warned herself to keep quiet although her legs were trembling so much she was frightened she'd sink down onto the carpet.

'So, there's honour among thieves, is there?' It was not laudatory. 'Well, let me tell you, you dirty little slut, if my son dies you'll swing along with the man who killed him, because I'll make sure of it. I know your type. Thought you were on to a good thing, didn't you? Leading him on until he didn't know which end was up. But I'm not like that, girl. Believe me. In my father's day you'd have been horsewhipped until you begged for mercy or were put six foot under or both.'

Clarissa Armstrong hadn't taken her eyes off the gypsy girl who had ensnared her son. It had been she who had decided that not a word of this dreadful affair must become public when her husband had wanted to tell the police what Nathaniel had told them. It would be the end of an alliance with the Steffords, and there was talk of Algernon getting a knighthood before too long. Furthermore, they'd become a laughing stock; their social standing would never recover. It was one thing for the sons of gentlemen to make merry with servant girls and the like, quite another to be involved in this sort of scandal. And according to Nathaniel, Christopher had said he loved the wench, even that he wanted to marry her. She still felt faint at the thought of it.

Her voice thin and cold, she said, 'My son is engaged to a gentlewoman, a lady of the utmost good taste. I trust you are aware of this?' Without waiting for a reply, she went on, 'Even now she is at his bedside, willing him through these dark hours. For her sake we have held our tongue about the true facts of this matter, not wishing to add to her grief. You can count yourself fortunate in this instance, but should you make any attempt to see him again then both you and the man you are attempting to shield will be brought to justice. Have I made myself plain?'

'He − he's not engaged. He would have told me.'

'How *dare* you,' Clarissa hissed. 'Your effrontery is shameless.'

Nathaniel stared at the girl who was the cause of his brother even now fighting for his life. He wanted to leap across the room, put his hands round her neck and squeeze the life out of her. Christopher was a gullible fool and he blamed himself for not sensing what was going on. But his mother was handling it the right way. A sly little baggage like this one wouldn't be intimidated by his father's blusterings, but he could tell she'd been shaken when his mother had spoken. Yes, the girl had thought she was on to a good thing, that much was obvious, and by disabusing her of the notion, there would be no reason for her to stay.

He watched his mother rise to her feet. He had to hand it to her, he thought with admiration, she looked every inch the ice queen.

'You will return to your dwelling with Parker,' Clarissa said in a clear, ringing tone, 'and we shall expect to see and hear no more of you and your kind. Is that clear?'

'I — I can't go. Not till I know Christopher's going to be all right.'

'You most certainly will.' Clarissa nodded her head to the butler who took Pearl's arm.

Shaking his hand off her, Pearl stepped forward a pace. Everything Christopher had told her about his parents was true. They were cold, unfeeling, and she didn't believe a word his mother had said. Looking straight at Nathaniel, she said, 'If Christopher told you what happened, he must have said we love each other and want to be together.'

Nathaniel studied her for a moment. 'He was anxious that no whisper of your liaison reached his fianceé, that's all.'

'That's not true. You know it's not true.'

Oswald, his patience gone, growled an order to the butler, who now took both her arms and with a strength that belied his thin frame, whirled her round and out of the door he had opened. He didn't let go of her until they were outside standing by the trap and even then, after he had pushed her unceremoniously onto the seat, he drove with one hand, the other gripping one of her wrists. He only let go when they were well clear of the house.

Pearl said nothing until they were approaching the campsite. She had sat stiff and still beside the butler, but this time her head had been up and her shoulders straight. They were on the coach road, and before the man turned the horse and trap on to the dirt track leading to Lot's Burn, she said steadily, 'You can stop here. I will walk the rest of the way.'

'I'm to see you back.'

'I said, you can stop here.' Her tone had been authoritative, her voice crisp. 'Please do as you're told.'

The butler's face flushed with colour. 'Don't you talk to me like that, you little hussy. I know all about your kind – vagabonds and thieves the lot of you.'

He had nevertheless stopped the horse, and as Pearl jumped down from the trap, she stood facing him. 'And you're so much better, are you?' she said bitterly. 'Toadying to them up there. They're liars, every one of them.'

The butler looked as though he was going to burst. His voice losing its polished edge and dropping into a brogue which proclaimed his working-class roots, he shouted, 'Get out of here afore I put this whip across your shoulders.'

'Just you try.' Pearl didn't know what had got into her, but whatever it was, she welcomed it. 'And you can tell your master and the rest of them that I'm not going anywhere. I don't believe a word about Christopher having a fiancée. I'd have to hear it from his own lips first. They're all snakes in the grass up there. My brother used to say you can't make a silk purse out of a sow's ear, and they're sows' ears if ever I saw any.'

The man was now apoplectic. Such was the fury in his face Pearl prepared herself for the whip being used, but instead he jerked on the reins so hard the horse reared up, narrowly missing her with its lethal hoofs, before cantering off in a whirl of dust and grit. She stood staring after the trap, her lips trembling as she fought back the tears. She felt desolate. It had been a long time since she'd felt as desolate as she did right now, and then Byron had found her and saved her. Byron, oh, Byron. And Christopher. If he died, she'd want to die too. She had ruined all their lives . . .

The gypsy camp was unusually quiet when she made her way to the tent where Corinda and the others were waiting. A number of men and women were standing about and Pearl knew she was being stared at, and in a manner which would have made her afraid if she hadn't been so bereft.

Corinda's eyes betrayed her fear, but her voice was low and normal-sounding when she said, 'Well? Do they know it was Byron who stabbed him?'

Pearl shook her head. 'Chris – Christopher said it wasn't one of us to the police but he told his family what happened.'

'One of us!' Halimena spat the words. 'Don't you claim to be one of us, girl.'

Corinda raised her hand and the old woman fell silent. 'What are the family going to do?'

'Nothing.'

'Nothing?' Mackensie looked at his wife. 'I don't believe it, that's not natural. They'll want their pound of flesh all right, especially if he snuffs it.'

'They're saying . . .' Pearl took a deep breath. 'They told me Christopher is engaged to – to a lady and she doesn't know the truth of what's happened. They want to keep it that way.'

'So it all depends on the lad pulling through.' Again Mackensie was speaking to his wife. 'And from the look of him last night, that's questionable.' Turning to Algar and Silvester who were standing to one side, he said, 'Spread the word we're leaving tomorrow at first light but quietly, all right? If the law come sniffing around again today I don't want it to be obvious.'

Both young men nodded, looking at Pearl as if she was the devil or something before turning away.

'I'm sorry.' Pearl reached out to touch Corinda, but as the woman shrank from her touch she let her hand fall to her side. 'I never wanted this to happen.'

'You're bad, girl. Right through.' Halimena's eyes were pinpoints of black as she narrowed them at Pearl. 'I knew it from the first.

Born to trouble, you were, and you'll take trouble wherever you lay your head. It's a curse that's on you and woe betide any man who's drawn to you.'

Pearl stared aghast at the old woman. 'No.' She wrenched her gaze from Byron's grandmother, her eyes imploring as they met Corinda's. 'No, I couldn't help what happened. Please, you have to believe me.'

'All I know is that because of you, my son is exiled from us.' Corinda's voice was still low but it trembled when she said, 'I wish we had never set eyes on you.'

The gypsies were gone by noon the following day and Pearl did not go with them. With her few belongings tied up in her shawl she made herself a bed of moss and grass under a hedgerow and spent the night under the stars.

The next few days were hot and sunny, and with the knowledge she had gained in her years with the tribe and the fact that it was the height of summer, she had no trouble feeding herself from the land. She did not venture far.

On the fifth day she washed all over in the burn before washing her hair too. Once it was dry she wound it into one thick, long plait and tidied herself as best she could, brushing the dust and grass from her clothes and cleaning her boots. When she was as respectable as she could make herself, she set off for the big house. She had to know what had happened to Christopher. She held out no hope now that they could be together, but she had to find out whether he had pulled through. If he hadn't . . . She didn't dare let herself imagine he hadn't.

She didn't try to enter the grounds by way of the lodgekeeper, knowing instinctively that she would be turned away. Instead she climbed over the high stone wall which surrounded the house and grounds and skirted through the gardens, making sure no one saw her. Once the house was in sight she stood looking at it for some time.

She *had* to know and she would do whatever it took to find out. She would shout and scream and fight them all if necessary.

Her heart beating fit to burst, she left the shelter of the bushes and trees and set off across a smooth green lawn which led on to the drive that curved round the side of the house. She was on familiar territory here. Moving swiftly but not running, she came to the stableyard where two men and a boy were working. Her chin up and her walk purposeful, she nodded briskly at them as she passed, and such was her stance they didn't think of challenging her. Once she was in the courtyard beyond, she went straight to the kitchen door. Here she hesitated. If she knocked and waited she might not be admitted into the house but she could hardly just walk in.

Her dilemma was solved in the next moment when the door was pulled open and a young kitchenmaid carrying a bucket of kitchen slops emerged. When the girl's look of surprise changed to one of recognition, Pearl knew it was no use pretending.

'You're the one Mr Parker brought here a few days ago, the one all the fuss is about. What are you doing here?' The girl was young, fourteen or fifteen by the look of her, and as she spoke she took a step backwards as though she was frightened Pearl was going to leap on her and rend her limb from limb.

Struggling to remain calm, Pearl appealed to the girl's mercy. 'I'm not supposed to be here but I have to know how −' she stopped herself saying Christopher, changing it to − 'the young Mr Armstrong is, whether he's better.'

'We were told if we saw you we had to tell Mr Parker at once.' The girl was still wary but something in the bright eyes told Pearl she was a perky piece. This was confirmed when she added, 'Mr Parker told the housekeeper who told the cook that you cheeked him. Did you?'

Pearl nodded.

'By, you're a one.' This was said with a touch of admiration and something approaching friendliness. 'He's a real tartar, is Mr Parker.'

'Do you know how Mr Armstrong is?' Pearl asked again.

The girl leaned forward, her voice a whisper. 'We're not supposed to know owt, but is it true you an' him were . . . well, you know?'

Again Pearl nodded. She wasn't quite sure exactly what she was admitting to, but it didn't matter in the circumstances.

'And he caught his toe when one of your lot found out.' The girl didn't wait for an answer, a note of bitterness coming into her voice when she said, 'Makes a change for the gentry to come a cropper – it's normally the other way round. My sister was in service at a big house Sunderland way, and when she came home with her belly full by the master, an' him old enough to be her granda, it was the workhouse for her. Me mam says I've got to scream an' keep screaming if anyone tries it on with me.'

For the third time, Pearl said, 'Mr Armstrong, how is he?'

'Poorly.'

'He's alive then?' She felt the world turn upside down for a moment and reached out a hand to steady herself on the wall of the house.

'Oh aye, he's alive, or he was when he left this mornin'.'

'Left?'

'The mistress went with him. He's supposed to be con – convales – getting better abroad. Cook says it was foolhardy to move such an ill man. She says the upstairs maid told her Mr Christopher didn't know what day it was – rambling all the time, she said. She can't understand what possessed the mistress to insist they leave.'

Pearl stared at the girl. She knew what it was. Christopher's family were determined to get him as far away from her as possible. No matter if the journey might kill him.

'And we've bin told to say he fell off his horse while out riding and did himself an injury, if anyone asks.' The girl made a 'Huh!' sound in her throat. 'Think we're half sharp, the gentry do.'

No, they didn't think their servants were half sharp, merely bought and paid for, body and soul. As Christopher's father had said to the butler that day, the servants could think what they liked as long as they didn't voice it. Their servants' opinion of them mattered so little it wasn't worth considering.

'Do you know when they're expected back?'

The girl shrugged. 'Not for months, Cook said. The housekeeper told her she wouldn't be surprised if Mr Christopher decides to live in Italy or somewhere foreign where there's plenty of art an' books an' such. A great one for poetry and art, Mr Christopher is. But then I suppose you'd know all about what he likes,' she added slyly. 'He hasn't left you with a belly full, like my sister, has he?'

Pearl straightened. 'No.' And then she softened the brusqueness of her tone when she said, 'And thanks – thanks for talking to me.'

'That's all right. It fair broke me mam's heart when our Betsy was taken down,' the maid said by way of explanation.

Pearl walked away from the house in the same way she had approached it, with her head held high, and this time she continued down the drive. When she reached the iron gates, the lodgekeeper came running out, his eyes wide as he spluttered, 'When did you come in, lass?'

Pearl walked to the narrow side gate and waited until he had unlocked it. 'Earlier,' she said briefly.

She left him scratching his head and muttering to himself, but he didn't try to detain her. Once she was clear of the lodge she veered off the road and into the fields, and it was then she felt free to sink onto the ground and give way to a paroxysm of weeping. She had ruined Byron's life and lost Corinda and the family in the process, and now she would never marry Christopher, never marry anyone. If she couldn't have him, she didn't want anyone else.

She cried until there were no more tears left and she was limp and spent. The grass was warm and sweet-smelling under her face, and the air carried the fragrance of ripe blackberries from the hedgerows. She sat up eventually, her eyes tired and heavy as she gazed into the distance. Along the wayside, elms and sycamores were faintly touched with yellow, and the landscape in front of her was chequered in a patchwork of subtle tint and mellow hue which indicated autumn was round the corner. The summer was all but gone.

There was nothing left to live for. The thought came in with the swiftness of an arrow and just as swiftly she thrust it aside. A few weeks ago, days even, she wouldn't have thought herself capable of surviving without her adopted family, but she had and she would. Halimena had said she had a curse on her. Holding her hands tightly against her chest, she swayed back and forth several times. She didn't know about that. What she did know was that life was a battle and you couldn't stop fighting until it was over. And her life wasn't over. She was still breathing and feeling, wasn't she? She had her eyes and her ears and her limbs, which was more than some poor souls had.

Looking up into the blue, blue sky, she longed for Seth like she hadn't done for years. And with the thought of one brother, memories of James and Patrick crowded in. They had been little more than babies when she had been forced to flee the East End, now they'd be lads of nine and ten. She was old enough to stand up to her mother this time round, so why shouldn't she seek her brothers out? She was free now, free to do what her heart told her. Once she was reunited with James and Patrick, she could make enquiries and see if she could find out which prison Seth and the others were held in. Or maybe they were back in the community? Whatever, she'd try to trace them.

The melancholy calls of lapwings in the stubblefields picking off the plentiful supply of grubs and beetles drifted on the air. Halimena had taught her that those birds were the host of departed human spirits who could find no rest and were doomed to wander the earth; their cries, which sounded like, 'Bewitched, bewitched!' were proof of this and were thought to bring evil down upon all who heard them. Halimena had plenty of stories like this and all contained gloom and destruction.

Pearl closed her eyes for a moment. She had always thought the birds beautiful with their distinctive raised crest and prominent black and white markings shot with iridescent specks of metallic turquoise. Halimena had seen death and darkness, while she had seen beauty and grace. The lapwings were birds, that was all. Halimena was wrong.

She opened her eyes. And if she could be wrong about the

lapwings, she could be wrong about the curse. Christopher would live, Byron would be reunited with his family in time, and she? She would find James and Patrick and the others.

Rising to her feet, Pearl picked up her small bundle of belongings and set her face for the town she had left behind eight years before.

PART FOUR

Atonement

October 1908

Chapter 14

It was the first week of October – a cold, bleak October with icy rain and bitter winds. Pearl was standing outside the forbidding building of the Union Workhouse and she was trembling, not so much because of the weather, although her thin coat and felt hat offered little protection, but because she had every reason to believe James and Patrick were incarcerated behind its walls. She had knocked on the workhouse doors earlier in the week but had been told to come back on Visiting Day by the porter who had barred her way.

Like all working-class folk, Pearl had a fear of the workhouse which bordered on horror. Everyone knew that to enter its walls was to give up hope. Men were separated from women, thus breaking up families, and both groups were divided into the able-bodied, the aged and children. The sick and mentally ill had their own quarters, and this ward could be smelled as soon as you stepped through the workhouse doors. She knew this, along with the fact that all inmates wore hideous uniforms, and the hair of both boys and girls was cropped, subjecting them to ridicule if they were taken out of the workhouse confines, because her mother had told her so. Many a time Kitty had threatened to leave her children at the workhouse doors where they'd be taken in and made to eat food infested with cockroach droppings.

Pulling her hat more firmly on her head, Pearl nerved herself to go inside. It was the only way she could check if her brothers were really inmates, and although she didn't want them to be there, if they weren't she didn't know where else to look for them.

She hadn't arrived back in the town until the middle of September due to the fact that on her journey she had found a few weeks' work picking fruit at a big farm. The farmer's wife had been a kind, genial soul, allowing Pearl to sleep in one of the hay barns at night and providing her with the leftovers from their evening meal. With the fruit she'd eaten whilst working this had meant Pearl had been able to save every precious penny of the wages she'd earned, rather than spend anything on food and lodging. The work had been exhausting but welcome; she'd fallen into the hay each night too tired to think.

When she had left the farm and reached the town, she'd had enough money to rent a room in a lodging house in the East End. She had visited the Old Market and bought herself some cheap second-hand clothes and once she was tidy immediately looked for work, procuring a job at the pickling factory two streets away the next day. She hated the work; the brine was so strongly impregnated with salt that it made her hands raw, and the overpowering smell of fish worked its way into her hair, skin and clothes, but the worst thing was the fact that the four walls of the stinking factory seemed to press in on her after years of living in the fresh outdoors.

That very first weekend, she'd made her way to Low Street only to find strangers living in the house in which she'd been born. They hadn't any knowledge of what had become of her mother and brothers. She had knocked on neighbours' doors but got no joy that first visit, but when she'd returned later in the week she had recognised a face from the past, a Mrs Weatherburn who lived at the end of the street. Mrs Weatherburn had invited her in and made her a cup of strong black tea, after which she'd informed Pearl that her mother had died years ago after falling into the fire whilst drunk and badly burning herself.

'Dreadful business it was,' Mrs Weatherburn told her. 'Lingered for days, she did. Everyone said it was a merciful release when she went.'

And her brothers? Pearl had asked. What had happened to James and Patrick?

Mrs Weatherburn had looked at her compassionately. 'Why, the workhouse of course, lass. They were put in the workhouse as I recollect, there being no family to take 'em.'

No family. Pearl swallowed hard and then stepped up to the front door. Well, James and Patrick *did* have family – and if they were in this terrible place, she intended to get them out.

The officer on duty in the vestibule was sitting at a long wooden desk with several big heavy ledgers in front of her. Two more female officers were standing by a pair of wooden doors which led into the hall of the building. There was a middle-aged couple in front of Pearl and a short stout man in front of them. Pearl watched as the man gave his name, then the name of the person he'd come to visit followed by a number. A ledger was opened, pages turned and then the sitting officer called a name and ward number to one of the officers by the door as the stout man walked across to them and disappeared into the hall. Pearl had never been to a prison but she couldn't imagine the procedure was much different.

The couple in front of her repeated the process and then it was her turn. Nervously she looked at the thin-faced officer. 'My name is Pearl Croft and I've come to see my brothers, James and Patrick Croft.'

'Ward?'

'I'm sorry?'

'The ward number.'

'I – I don't know the ward number.'

'They've been recently admitted?'

'No.' Pearl was conscious of other folk behind her. 'It was years ago.'

'Which year?' the officer asked woodenly, seemingly uninterested.

'I think it was 1903 or maybe the beginning of 1904.'

'Ages on admittance?'

Pearl gulped. 'James would have been five or thereabouts. Patrick's a year younger.'

A ledger was opened and pages flicked. 'Croft, James and Patrick, West Five,' the officer called without looking up.

Pearl walked over to the wooden doors, her heart pounding.

The smell which had been faint in the vestibule was stronger in the hall. A composite of urine and cabbage was the only way Pearl could describe it to herself. She was directed to a small wooden table which had two pairs of stools either side of it. There were many of these dotted about the hall. The stout man was sitting with a very old couple, probably his parents, Pearl thought. The old folk looked to be holding hands and they were sitting in silent misery, staring at the man who was talking jovially. The old man must have come from the men's quarters and the woman from hers. This visiting time, once a week, would be the only time they would see each other.

Tearing her eyes away from the pain in the old people's faces, Pearl stared down at her hands clasped in her lap. She felt sick with horror and guilt that her baby brothers had ended up in such a place, terrified they would hate her, confused as to how she'd go about getting them out, and wildly elated that she was going to see them again.

The couple who had been in front of her had just had a young girl brought to them by an officer. She was an odd-looking girl and appeared to be simple minded, but she was dressed in the distinctive yellow uniform which stated she was an unmarried mother. Pearl could hear her begging her parents to take her home. Her mother was crying but her father's face was stony and the next moment he had seized his wife's arm and pulled her up from her seat, literally dragging her out of the hall as their daughter's wailing increased. The girl was ushered away by one of the officers present but no sooner had the door at the far end of the room closed than it opened again to reveal an officer with two children.

Pearl's heart lurched and jumped up into her throat. She had been frightened she wouldn't recognise her brothers but they both bore a strong resemblance to Seth. She hadn't expected that, and it tore afresh at her heart. They walked silently towards her, and although she was smiling through her tears there were no answering smiles on their pale thin faces. The calico shirts and trousers they were wearing looked clean enough, but James's shirt was too small, his arms extending in an ungainly fashion from the sleeves like two sticks on which his red, chapped hands appeared too large.

'Sit down.' The officer's voice was not unkind and she glanced at Pearl as she added, 'They haven't had a visitor before so the procedure's unfamiliar.'

Pearl kept her eyes on the small pinched faces in front of her as she said, 'I'm their sister but I've – I've been away for a long time.'

'Is that so? Well, you have an hour.' With that the woman turned away and walked off.

'Hello,' Pearl said softly as she wiped her eyes on her handkerchief. 'Do you remember me?'

For a moment she didn't think they were going to respond as they stared at her. Then as Patrick slowly shook his head, his eyes never leaving her face, James whispered, 'There was a pram an' you used to push us.'

'That's right.' She wanted to gather them up in her arms and hug and kiss them. 'We used to go for walks and play games and sing songs. Can you remember any of the songs we knew?'

James did not reply to this. What he did say was, even more quietly, 'Mam said you left because we were naughty and you didn't like us no more.'

Pearl jerked as though she had been slapped across the face. Her mother had been a wicked soul. She had, she had. And she was glad she was dead. 'That's not true and Mam was very bad to lie to you like that. I was ill, I had to go far away to get better. I hated leaving you both. I cried every night for a long, long time. I – I missed you very much.'

Patrick shot a quick glance at his brother but James kept his eyes on Pearl. 'You didn't say goodbye.'

'I couldn't.' How could she explain what had happened to two small boys? But then as she looked into James's tense face, the eyes that stared back at her willed her to try. Bending forward, she swallowed to dislodge the lump that was choking her. 'I was ill when I left because I'd been hurt. I – I'd been attacked, by one of the men who used to come and see Mam. Do you remember them?'

Both boys nodded at this and Pearl told herself that of course they'd remember; their mother had been on the game right until she had died and the boys had been big enough at that point to recall how things had been.

'Well, this man hurt me so badly I nearly died. For a whole week I was unconscious. Do you know what that means? It's . . . it's like when you sleep and don't know anything that's happening around you, only with unconsciousness you can't wake up until you're made better. The people who looked after me did make me better but they took me far away. I was only a little girl, James. Two years older than you are now. I wanted to come back to you and Patrick but I couldn't.'

'They wouldn't let you?'

It was simpler to nod and agree. 'No, they wouldn't let me. But they were kind and looked after me so I grew strong again.'

James's strained stance didn't relax. He was mechanically rolling and unrolling the corner of his shirt. 'Are you going away again?'

'No, hinny. I'm never going to go away again, I promise.'

The child tried to speak, but couldn't. Such was the look on his face that Pearl forgot about everything and everyone else. Rising, she moved to their side of the table and knelt down, putting her arms round their thin bodies and squeezing them close. For a moment both boys were as stiff as boards and then as one they relaxed. Pearl sent up a swift prayer of thanks as their arms went round her and they buried their faces in her breast.

'I'm going to get you out of here as soon as I can.' After they'd stopped crying and she had wiped their faces, she continued kneeling between them. 'You'll come and live with me. It'll be a squeeze, as I've only got one room, and we'll have to manage carefully if we're going to have enough for food and rent, but we'll get by somehow, won't we?'

Both boys nodded vigorously, Patrick a few seconds after James.

Pearl had the feeling he took the cue from his big brother in everything.

'I don't know how soon it can be arranged, so you'll have to be patient for a bit, but you can do that, can't you?'

This time James was slower to nod. 'But you will let us come and live with you?'

'I promise.' How they would manage she didn't know. Her room was only large enough to take a single bed, one rickety chest of drawers and one small armchair which was so moth-eaten she was constantly picking up the straw filling and stuffing it back inside the holes in the arms and seat. But it was because of this it was so cheap to rent – that and the poor district. 'But you'll have to be good boys until it can be sorted out.'

The hour passed quickly and when a bell clanged signifying the end of visiting time, both boys clung to her again. The officer who had brought them to her reappeared, and at a word from her James and Patrick immediately let go and stood with their heads down like small whipped dogs.

No amount of blinking could keep the scalding tears from falling as Pearl watched the boys being led away, and once they had disappeared through the far doors she took a moment or two to compose herself and dry her eyes. Then she left the hall which was full of people saying goodbye and went to the desk in the vestibule. A different officer was sitting there but like the first one, her face looked as though it would crack if she smiled.

'Yes?' She looked up as Pearl stopped in front of her.

'I wonder if you can help me?' Pearl began politely. 'I need to know the procedure for taking my brothers out of here.'

The woman looked her up and down. 'Taking them where?'

'Home. Home with me.'

'You say you are their sister. You have proof of this?'

'Proof?' Pearl repeated, slightly nonplussed.

'A birth certificate?' the officer said, speaking in such a way that suggested she suspected she was talking to a simpleton. 'And we would need to know your address and the name of your husband's employer. I take it you are married?'

Pearl shook her head. 'No, I'm not married.'

'But you are living with family?'

Again Pearl shook her head. 'I have a job,' she said desperately. 'I can keep the three of us.'

The woman sat back in her chair. 'How old are you?' she asked baldly.

As Pearl didn't have a birth certificate she thought she'd lose nothing by adding three years to her age. 'Twenty-one,' she lied, without blinking.

A small smile touched the stern mouth. 'You're game, lass, I'll say that for you,' she said, quite kindly now. 'But you haven't a snowball's chance in hell of getting your brothers released into your custody. There's rules and regulations, see? And we have to be seen to abide by them. What if you took these lads and put them to work on the streets or something like that? Oh, I'm not saying you would, not for a minute, but you'd be surprised how many try and pull the wool over our eyes.'

'But I have to get them out – I've promised them.'

'What's this job you've got?'

'It's in the pickling factory in the East End.'

'And you earn what? A few bob a week?'

Pearl nodded. Four shillings to be exact, and one shilling and thruppence went immediately on rent.

'Lass, forget all about this notion. It'll be kinder to you and them in the long run. In here they're clothed and fed. They have a roof over their heads and schooling. Come and visit them when you've a mind, but leave it at that. Without a man behind you a young lass like you wouldn't be considered a suitable person by the guardians, not in a month of Sundays.'

Pearl was wringing her hands in her despair. 'But I promised them.'

The officer straightened, her eyes dropping to the papers on her desk. Her voice brisk, she said, 'Well, you shouldn't have.' It was clearly the end of the conversation.

As Pearl stood undecided, the outer doors opened and a man and woman strode through. The officer she'd been speaking to sprang immediately to her feet and the ones by the wooden inner doors opened them, nodding deferentially as the two sailed past.

The couple hadn't noticed her or glanced her way, but Pearl felt the blood draining from her body. She would know Mr F anywhere, and such was the shock she felt sick and faint.

As the officer sat down again she glanced at Pearl. 'You all right, lass?' she asked, her voice kind again. 'Look, don't take on so. Your brothers are all right.'

'That . . .' She had to swallow and hold on to the edge of the table. 'That couple, the man and woman. Who – who are they?'

The officer, after casting a glance at her colleagues, a glance which said all too clearly, 'We've got a right odd one here,' said soothingly, 'That was the workhouse master, Mr Fallow, and his wife, the Matron, but it's no good thinking they'll say any different to me 'cos they won't. Rules are rules and Mr Fallow is a stickler for doing things to the letter.'

'And how.'

This mutter came from one of the women by the door. Pearl looked over to them and both were staring at her sympathetically. Pulling herself together, she nodded to them and the officer she'd been speaking to and then quickly left the building. Outside, the bitingly cold air smelled clean and fresh. She breathed it in in great gulps, aware she was trembling and that her legs felt weak. It wasn't until she had passed through the main gates of the workhouse that she came to a halt. She stood for some minutes fighting the waves of nausea.

She wasn't going to be sick, she wouldn't let herself be. Once she was walking she continued to tell herself this all the way home, but then she had to hurry to the brick-built privy at the bottom of the small yard.

By the time she emerged white faced and shaking, her stomach was empty and she was chilled to the bone. The rain had turned to sleet and as she looked up into the sky it was dull and heavy, like her heart.

Wearily she entered the house and climbed the stairs to her room. It felt as cold inside as out, but once she had put a match to the fire in the small grate which she'd laid before she'd left for the workhouse, it began to warm up. She placed her kettle over the steel shelf fixed above the grate which was her only means of heating the water she had to bring from the tap in the yard, and when it was boiled made herself a pot of tea. She drank two cups scalding hot without milk and sugar, standing with her back to the fire as she soaked up the warmth.

Once the fire was glowing red she put a piece of bread on her toasting fork and held it out to the hot coals. She ate this and two more slices spread with beef dripping.

The hot tea and food revived her, and slowly the numbness receded which had gripped her since seeing the face of the man who still haunted her dreams. Pulling the battered armchair close to the fire, she sat down. She had to *think*, she told herself. Mr F – Mr *Fallow* – wasn't as important as getting James and Patrick out of the workhouse. This room wasn't much – she glanced round the cramped confines made worse by the dingy wallpaper under which hundreds of bugs lived – but anything was better than that place. The lads could sleep in her bed at night, she'd be comfortable enough in this chair, and she'd just have to make a penny stretch to two or three.

She ignored the voice in her mind which pointed out that she could barely manage now. It wasn't an option to leave them where they were, and that was that. The stigma of the workhouse had sat upon them like a mantle and they'd already had years of it. She didn't question whether it was right or wrong to remove them from the institution. She didn't have to. It was only the means of *how* this could be accomplished that was troubling her.

A grey twilight came early but Pearl didn't light a candle; she rarely did unless she absolutely had to. Normally she was so tired in the evenings she went straight to bed after she'd had something to eat, the glow from the fire she always lit on walking in sufficient to enable her to see what she was doing. Candles were a luxury, and if it was a choice of them or coal for the fire, warmth always won.

She had bought a thick eiderdown for the bed from the Old

Market, delving into the small hoard of money she had left from the farmwork. Now she undressed down to her shift, keeping her woollen stockings on, and slid under the covers, hugging her knees as she curled into a little ball to keep warm.

Since arriving in the town her thoughts had centred on Christopher and her brothers, and Byron to some extent, but tonight it was the fat, greasy figure of Mr Fallow who filled her mind. He was even more repulsive than she remembered. She shivered, but not with cold. And the way he had marched into the building as though he owned it . . . which he did in a way, she supposed. Certainly the workhouse master was someone who was greatly respected and feared, a man with untold power. And to think Mr F had a wife! Not only that, but she was the Matron of the workhouse, the second-in-command so to speak. Pearl had only glanced at her briefly because she'd been focusing on Mr F, but she had taken in that the woman was enormously fat.

The old fear of the man who had abused her so savagely was making her insides writhe, along with worry about James and Patrick, and she had never felt so alone. Alone and helpless. She was beyond tears.

She must have fallen asleep because when she next opened her eyes, the fire had gone out and the room was as black as pitch. She could hear shouting and cursing from one of the rooms below where a family of six were packed in like sardines, but it wasn't that which made her sit up in bed, her eyes wide.

She knew what she was going to do now.

Chapter 15

The next day was a Sunday. At eight o'clock in the morning Pearl was standing outside the locked workhouse gates insisting to the porter that she be allowed admittance. When he tried and failed to persuade the 'stiff-necked little madam' – as he later described Pearl to his wife – to see reason, he gave up and fetched the admittance officer on duty. The officer took Pearl to the Assistant Matron. When Pearl still continued to maintain that what she had to say was for the ears of Mr Fallow only, adding she was sure he would see her when he was told she had information regarding a Mrs Kitty Croft of Low Street, she was shown to a small brown-painted room which had a backless form running round three walls.

Half an hour later, a half an hour in which Pearl oscillated between blind terror and controlled panic, the door to the room opened and Leonard Fallow walked in. He was alone.

Staring at the young slim girl standing so straight and still in front of him, he bit out one word. *'You!'*

She had wondered if he would recognise her. Eight years was a long time and she had been a child. Strangely, because she was trembling inside, her voice held no tremor when she said, 'Yes, Mr Fallow. Me.'

He had shut the door behind him but now he turned and

opened it again, poking his head out into the empty corridor beyond before he closed it again. Without any preamble, he said, 'What do you want?'

Pearl's face was deathly white but her manner was composed, even calm. 'I want my brothers released into my care.'

'What?' The shiny brow wrinkled, his black eyes disappearing into the fat of his face. Whatever he had expected it clearly wasn't this. 'What the hell are you on about, girl?'

'My brothers, James and Patrick, are in here and I've been told I can't get them out. You're the workhouse master, you can release them to me.'

Leonard Fallow found he couldn't take his eyes off the girl in front of him. He didn't desire her any more – once they reached a certain age that predilection was gone – but this girl had been an ache in his loins for years. She'd made him a laughing-stock with the group of men who shared his weakness; he'd told them about her and offered to share her with them, and then the mother had told him she'd vanished into thin air. He hadn't visited the house again, but that hadn't stopped him thinking about her, morning, noon and night. She'd been like a curse on his life.

His eyes as hard as bullets, he drawled, 'And why would I do that, pray?'

Pearl's anger was overcoming her fear. The Mr F of her imagination had assumed the power and ability of an omnipotent monster over the years. Mr Fallow, workhouse master, was just a man. A repugnant, oily, dirty-minded man who had ruined her life and been the means of her having to leave her brothers and ultimately them ending up in this hell-hole.

Without faltering, she said, 'Because if you don't, I will make it my business to see that your wife and everyone else knows about your secret life, a life which involves visiting whores and violating little girls. I don't think the guardians would be pleased to know what their workhouse master is really like.'

'You're threatening me?'

'Yes, that's exactly what I'm doing.'

He took a step towards her and in spite of herself she shrank back; the thought of any part of him coming into contact with her was insupportable.

Leonard smiled. 'You and your mother are the scum of the earth, m'dear,' he said softly. 'Who do you think would listen to you? And if your brothers are in here as you claim, I'll make sure they don't get out a day before they are able, and then I'll send them to a master who'll make their days in here seem like a holiday in comparison to what he'll put them through. Now I suggest you get back to whatever hole you've crawled out of and continue obliging those men who pay for your services – unless you want me to call the law and tell them you are mentally unfit and ready for the asylum.'

'I am not like my mother, Mr Fallow.' Pearl didn't know where the words were coming from, she only knew this man was her last chance of getting her brothers released. 'She *was* a whore as we both know, and weak and cowardly too – unless she was bullying her children. I have a respectable job and my own home –' she didn't see why he should know it was only a rented room – 'and I would be only too pleased for you to call a constable. I'm sure he would listen to what I have to say, as would your wife. She'll believe me, I'll make sure of it.'

He swore, a foul profanity, lifting his arm with his fist clenched, but this time Pearl held her ground. After a moment his arm dropped to his side. 'You leave my wife out of this.'

'That's not my decision, it's yours.'

'Who do you think you are, to talk to me like this? Whether you have a job or no, you're a trollop born of a trollop and blood outs. I'm a respected member of the community, people look up to me.'

'They look up to the person you profess to be, but no one would look up to a pervert who rapes bairns.'

'Shut up! *Shut up!*' Leonard Fallow was practically foaming at the mouth but Pearl glared back at him, her eyes blazing. It was even more important now that she got James and Patrick out of this place; by his own admission Fallow would make their lives even more miserable than they were already. After a few moments during which he ground his teeth, he said, 'How do I know you won't be back next week asking for something more if I let your brothers go?'

Wild elation surged through her but she was careful to let no trace of it show in her face or voice. 'I want nothing to do with you, Mr Fallow. Nothing. You disgust me, and if I never have to set eyes on you again I'll be content.'

He stared at her, tugging down his waistcoat over his balloon-like stomach and straightening his morning coat. He always dressed thus and his clothes were of the best quality and cut; after all, a man was judged on his appearance. His lower jaw moved from side to side a few times. 'How do I know I can trust you?'

'You don't.' Still unflinching, she looked back into his perspiring face. She felt sick to her stomach that this gross man had had her and used her; she wanted to shout and scream and cry and scratch his eyes out, but that wouldn't get her James and Patrick. 'You'll just have to take my word for it.'

'The word of a whore? That's a joke.'

Hating him, she didn't answer, merely swallowing hard as the stench of his sweat came to her nostrils. He was frightened of calling her bluff, she could see it in his face.

Nevertheless she had her work cut out to hide her surprise when he suddenly said, 'All right, you can take the boys and be damned, I don't care – but if you repeat a word of this, it won't be only you who suffers. Do you understand me?'

Hardly daring to believe he meant what he said, she nodded. 'I understand perfectly.'

'You'd better. A loose mouth can be shut permanently.'

'I told you, all I want is my brothers.'

He stared at her a moment more before turning and opening the door. 'Wait here.'

Once she was alone again Pearl sank down on the bench. The trembling she'd hidden from him now wouldn't be denied, and her hands were shaking as if with the ague. Telling herself she couldn't afford to give way until she was sure he wasn't playing a trick on her, she forced herself to stand up and begin pacing, taking great gulps of air as she did so. Eventually all outward agitation was gone, even though her head was whirling as she went over what had been said.

When the door opened, she prepared herself to face him again, but it was the Assistant Matron who entered, carrying a bundle of clothes. 'Mr Fallow says it's imperative you take your brothers home today, Miss Croft. As you have given him the necessary documentation I don't see that as a problem, although it is highly irregular.'

Pearl did not reply. She couldn't. She was feeling faint.

'Your brothers will be brought here shortly, where they will change into these clothes. Please concentrate while I lay them out for you.' So saying, she began to make separate piles on the form. 'One pair of drawers each, one vest each, one pair of woollen socks each, one linen shirt each, one pair of short trousers each, one knitted pullover each, one jacket each, one cap each. They will retain the boots they are wearing at present.' She straightened after adding a small Bible to each pile. 'Please sign this form to say you've received this and add your current address. You can write, I take it? Good. Now, any questions, Miss Croft?'

Numbly, Pearl said, 'I don't think so.'

'You understand that the contents of the abode your brothers were taken from were sold and the money given to the guardians as a small – and in the case of the Croft brothers I understand it was very small – donation towards their keep?'

Pearl hadn't given the matter a thought but she nodded.

'Mr Fallow has expressed his satisfaction that the boys' welfare will be adequately taken care of.' The Assistant Matron's tone suggested she suspected otherwise. However, she had no chance to say anything further because after a knock on the door it opened and one of the officers led James and Patrick into the room.

Pearl wanted to reach out and take them into her arms, but conscious of the two women's eagle eyes, she contented herself with saying, 'You're coming home with me today,' as she tried to smile naturally.

They nodded but appeared too overwhelmed to speak.

The Assistant Matron instructed the officer: 'You will see Miss

Croft and her brothers to the gates, Miss Ferry.' Turning her gaze on James and Patrick, she said, 'I shall expect you to conduct yourselves with propriety at all times. You were most fortunate to come under the care of this establishment, so please see you reflect the values which have been taught to you.'

Again they did not reply, which caused the woman to frown. Quickly, Pearl said, 'Thank you. I'm sure they will.'

After exchanging a glance with the officer, the Assistant Matron nodded sharply and left the room.

'Take off your uniforms and fold them neatly and leave them on the bench.' The officer pushed James and Patrick towards the two piles of clothes. 'Here are your new clothes. Make sure you look after them.'

The boys did as they were told. Once they were fully dressed, Pearl held out her hands to them and they came and stood with her. The clothes they had been given would have been taken from lads their age who had come into the workhouse, and were far from new. Patrick's jacket was verging on threadbare. But she still had a little money left from her farmwork, Pearl thought. She could buy them each a warm coat from the Old Market if nothing else.

'Follow me, please.' The officer opened the door and led them along a corridor which opened into a wider passage. The smell Pearl had noticed in the hall the day before was stronger here, verging on a stench. She glanced at the double door as they passed and the officer said, 'Infirm ward for the chronic patients,' as though that explained everything. Which it did, she supposed.

Pearl didn't speak to James and Patrick as they walked along clutching her hands so tightly it hurt, and they still hadn't said a word. Two more corridors later and they reached doors which opened up into the hall. Once they reached the vestibule, which had no officer sitting at the table which had been pushed against the wall, unlike on visiting day, the grip on her fingers became even more intense. And then they were outside in the fresh air and walking towards the main gates.

The porter came out as they approached, nodding at the officer and then speaking directly to Pearl. 'Got what you came for then?' he said, glancing at James and Patrick.

She nodded. 'Aye, I got what I came for.'

He grinned, opening the gates. 'Good on you, lass.'

Pearl had only been in the place just over a couple of hours but even so she felt she had been let out of prison. Goodness knew how James and Patrick were feeling.

As the gates clanged behind them she looked down at her brothers. Patrick was crying but James looked like a sleepwalker, his little face holding an expression that made her stop and gather them both against her chest. As James's body began to shake and tears erupted from his eyes and nose and mouth, his arms went round her neck in a stranglehold, and the three of them nearly ended up sprawled on the pavement.

It was another five minutes, a time of whispered comfort and hugs and kisses before the boys calmed down, and by then all three faces were wet. 'Come on, we're going home.' Pearl straightened their jackets and caps, smiling tremulously into their upturned faces. 'It's not much, like I told you, just one tiny little room and you'll have to share a bed and bring water up from the yard for washing and drinking, but it'll be ours. Yours and mine.'

'And we won't ever go back?'

Her face solemn now, she crouched down in front of James again, taking his cold little hands in hers. 'I promise you – both of you – you won't ever go back to that terrible place. Whatever happens. All right?'

They nodded and as James hugged her again she put out a hand and drew Patrick to them. She would work till she dropped, beg the foreman at the pickling factory for a double shift when any were in the offing, anything, but no one would take her brothers from her. She had let them down once, she would never do so again. They were her life now.

For a moment the mental image of a handsome male face topped by a shock of corn-coloured hair was strong, but as she stood up she told herself that that dream was in the past and gone for ever.

She had to concentrate on the present, and that meant James and Patrick.

Blinking away the tears, she took the boys' hands in hers. 'How about if we get a bag of chitterlings and a hot meat pie apiece on the way home, to celebrate?' she said brightly. 'And maybe a crusty loaf and a pat of butter to go with it?'

The boys' faces lit up.

'Mind, I've only got one knife and fork and spoon at present. We'll have to buy another two sets next week.'

'We like eating with our fingers,' said Patrick chirpily, 'although the kitchen officer, Miss Ratlidge, used to rap our knuckles with the cane if she caught us. Rappy Ratarse, we used to call her.' He stopped abruptly, obviously wondering if he had said too much.

Pearl stared at him and then burst out laughing. 'Well, I won't rap your knuckles,' she promised, 'but I shall expect you to use your knife and fork when the King comes to tea.'

All three were laughing now and it was like that, with the boys' hands held in hers and smiles on their faces, that they walked home.

Chapter 16

On Monday evening Leonard Fallow left his very comfortable quarters and roaring coal fire after telling his wife he was going to his Monday-night card-game. The card-game was a front; he and his friends used their Monday nights for quite a different purpose.

He walked briskly along Chester Road away from the workhouse and towards the east of the town, making for the Station Hotel in Prospect Row. The railway line from Durham built in the 1830s terminated at the staiths in Low Quay, and the railway station stood near the town moor; it was after this wooden structure the public house was named. The Station Hotel was in the heart of the warren of streets close to the docks, transit sheds and warehouses in the East End, and after dark the dock dollies plied their trade in dark corners and alleyways or on the strip of town moor which remained behind the almshouses and orphan asylum. On arriving in Sunderland as a young man, Leonard had very quickly nosed out the less salubrious part of the town and carefully, over a period of years, made the acquaintance of men of like mind. Due to the nature of the area, he'd also rubbed shoulders with villains and ne'er-do-wells, contacts which had proved useful on occasion.

When he entered the public house the others were already gathered in one corner drinking. This was part of the ritual. It was important to establish exactly who was present before they went their separate ways, in case an alibi was needed. Occasionally, as had happened the week before, one of them had heard of a new young girl being offered in one of the whorehouses, and they had all visited it together. And she *had* been young, as young as Pearl had been. He licked his lips, his body hardening. But tonight he had a different agenda in mind and one that wouldn't wait.

The group of men spent an hour in the Station Hotel and then left together, as though intending to go on to a different pub. Once the others had dispersed, Leonard cut through Silver Street into Low Street. The street's location along the riverside meant its pubs were especially popular with sailors and shipyard workers, although there were only a handful of those pubs left these days, compared to forty or more at the begining of the previous century. The houses that were occupied by families often had rooms to let for seamen, as Pearl's had once done, but as he walked by the Crofts' old house Leonard didn't spare it a glance.

The bar he entered was small and smoke filled, the sawdust on the floor and pockmarked face of the bruiser of a barman suggesting it was not an establishment for the faint-hearted. Glancing round, Leonard spotted the person he had been hoping to see. He made his way over to a corner of the room near the grimy window where an old man with an unkempt beard and rheumy eyes was sitting nursing a pint of ale, an equally ancient bull terrier fast asleep under the table.

'Hello, Arthur.' Leonard smiled. 'What can I get you?'

Faded blue eyes surveyed him for a moment. 'That's very nice of you, Mr Fallow. A tot of the hard stuff wouldn't go amiss.'

Once Leonard returned with a double whisky for Arthur and one for himself, he sat down beside the old man. No one glancing at Arthur Bell would imagine that the benign-looking, somewhat down-at-heel elderly gentleman knew every crook and felon – not to mention what they were up to – in the East End of Sunderland. On taking over as workhouse master, Leonard had first heard Arthur's name mentioned when he had been offered a supply of meat by a contact at the slaughterhouse, no questions asked. As it was a third of the price the then present supplier, a reputable butcher, was asking, Leonard had jumped at the chance to buy inferior meat and pocket the difference in money. No matter that the slaughter-house meat was ofttimes diseased or of equestrian origin; he made sure the meat for his own household and that of the officers' mess was obtained from the original source and then doctored the butcher's bill once he had paid the man, in case the Guardians checked the accounts. The contact at the slaughterhouse had put him in touch with Arthur for other supplies from questionable avenues; flour sacks which regularly fell off the back of lorries, vegetables which were so spotted they looked to have the pox, and so on. And Arthur had been very helpful. As he always was for the right price.

Leonard leaned forward, his voice low when he said, 'Arthur, I've a problem and you're the only one who can help me.'

'Is that so, Mr Fallow? Well, you know me. If I can oblige, I will.'

'I need someone to do a job for me. A very private job.'

'Oh aye?'

'There's someone who's out to cause trouble for me.' Leonard knocked back his whisky and set the glass on the table. 'I need them to disappear.'

Arthur didn't bat an eyelid when he said, 'Permanently?'

Leonard nodded. 'And there might be more than one. This woman could well have her brothers in tow.'

'A woman, is it?' Arthur had finished his whisky and now looked pointedly at his empty glass.

'Same again?' Leonard was already standing and reaching for the old man's glass. Once they had two more whiskies in front of them, he continued, 'This woman, Pearl Croft, has already blackmailed me once, Arthur, and likely she's told her two brothers what she's got on me. They're young lads, ten or thereabouts, but if they open their mouths once she's disposed of . . .'

'Three's as easy as one, Mr Fallow, if you know the right people to do the job.' Arthur didn't ask what it was this woman had on his client, it wasn't his business. 'But it'll cost you, you know that? This isn't like a spot of moonlightin' or creamin' off the odd sack or two of flour, and it'll take more than one to pull off a job like this with no disturbance or repercussions. Know what I mean? You pay for silence in this game.'

'I know that, Arthur, and I've a bit salted away.'

'Aye, well, you'll need it an' all. Like I said, these blokes don't come cheap. Look, I'll see what I can do. Meet me here tomorrow about the same time and I'll have an answer for you. They'll want payment before the job's done, but you say that's no problem?'

'No problem at all, Arthur.' Leonard's words tumbled over themselves in his eagerness.

'Where does she live, this Pearl Croft? Local, is she?'

Leonard pulled a piece of paper out of his pocket. 'That's her address and I've written her name and her brothers' too.'

'Aye, well, leave it with me till the morrer. 'Tis likely I know the very lads for this job but I'm thinkin' they'll want twenty pounds a head or more. You up for that?'

Leonard swallowed hard. He had more than that under his mattress but it was galling to think he was having to fork out to get rid of that little baggage. Still, needs must. 'Aye, I'm up for that.'

By the end of the week it was signed and sealed. Leonard had paid over seventy pounds – the wily Arthur had demanded a nice bonus in view of the nature of the business and Leonard hadn't thought it wise to quibble – and in return received an assurance that he'd be notified when the job was done.

'Efficient, are they, these blokes you know?' Leonard asked as he watched the wad of notes disappear into Arthur's trouser pocket.

'Oh aye, sir, don't you worry about that.' Arthur reached down and patted his dog as the animal expelled wind loud and long. As the tail end was by Leonard's feet he received the blast full in the face. 'Aye,' Arthur went on, 'when these lads take a job they look on it as honour bound. Know what I mean?' He smiled, the blue eyes complaisant.

'Honour among thieves?' There was an edge to Leonard's voice. 'Exactly.'

'And you impressed on them it's urgent?'

'I did that, Mr Fallow. They'll see to things this weekend. By Monday morning, all your troubles will be over.'

'I hope so, I'm paying enough,' Leonard said irritably. Handing over the money had been painful. 'There's plenty on the march for jobs – likely a couple of them would have done it for less.'

'You don't want amateurs for something like this, take it from me. And you're paying for discretion, don't forget. There'll be no comeback with these lads.'

'Aye, you're right, Arthur. Of course you're right.' Leonard stood up, anxious to be gone. This was the third time this week he'd left his fireside. Delia was beginning to smell a rat. Only this evening she'd proved a little difficult when he'd said he was popping out again. 'And I will know when the job's done?'

The gentle blue eyes surveyed him over the rim of a whisky glass. 'You'll know, Mr Fallow. Rest assured, you'll know.'

Leonard nodded at the old man and turned for the door. This place and the people who inhabited it disgusted him. He glanced down at the sawdust at his feet, splattered with phlegm and dog's pee. He was better than this. And that girl, daring to threaten him and put him in this position! It was all down to her, Pearl Croft. She was the root of all his troubles. Once he knew she had been taken care of, the thorn in his side which had been troubling him for years would be gone.

He paused at the door, turning and raising his hand to Arthur, who nodded an acknowledgement. Then he pushed open the door and stepped out into the black night.

Chapter 17

Pearl finished work at the pickling factory at midday on a Saturday, and James and Patrick were waiting for her when she emerged into the grey October afternoon. The last days had been something of a worry, but she had kept any trace of concern from her brothers. She was finding herself hard pressed already to make ends meet, and the lads had only been with her five days. They ate so much, that was one thing. It was as though now the meagre and unappetising food of the workhouse was no more, they were making up for lost time. They seemed to be forever hungry. And although she had seen to it that they were enrolled in the Methodist church school, they were home long before her in the evening, which meant the fire was lit earlier and more coal burned. Already she could see that her present wage wouldn't be enough to keep the three of them in food and fuel, and that was without things like clothes and boots for the boys taken into consideration. She had asked the foreman at the factory to keep her in mind for extra shifts, but these didn't crop up too often. With so many folk out of work perhaps that wasn't surprising.

She had left the boys curled up snug and warm in bed that morning, only their noses visible as they'd said a sleepy goodbye. When she had stepped out into the dull light of early morning her normal optimism had been flagging and the work at the pickling factory had seemed twice as arduous as normal.

Sleeping in the chair at night was taking its toll too. She tended to catnap for part of the time in spite of being exhausted, and invariably woke up with a crick in her neck.

Now, as she looked at her brothers' bright faces, her worry and fear for the future lifted temporarily. Somehow they would manage. Against all the odds they were together again and she wouldn't let anything part them, not while she had breath in her body.

'Look what the lady in the cake shop gave us.' Patrick was hopping from one foot to the other in his excitement as he thrust a bag full of cakes and rolls under her nose.

In answer to the expression which had come over Pearl's face, James said quickly, 'It's all right, honest, Pearl. We were looking in the window and she came to the door an' asked us if we wanted anything and we said no 'cos we hadn't any money. Then she come back with these. She said they were old and stale, and the manageress had told her to put them in the farthing bin but there were lots more and the manageress wouldn't miss these.'

When Pearl looked at her brothers, she could see what had melted the cake lady's heart. Their pudding-basin haircuts under their caps spoke only too plainly of a brush with the workhouse, and their thin faces made them look all eyes. No doubt they'd had their noses pressed against the windowpane. She glanced again into the bag and then smiled widely. Lunch was taken care of at any rate, and she wasn't too proud to look a gift horse in the mouth, especially if it was bringing food.

'How about if we go to Mowbray Park and have a picnic?' she said gaily. 'And after we could visit the museum and the Winter Garden.' Admission was free, and they could spend the afternoon in the warm looking at everything in the museum and the antiquities and art galleries, and in the large conservatory adjoining the rear of the building called the Winter Garden there were tropical plants and cages of foreign birds, and a pond well stocked with goldfish.

It began to drizzle as they sat on a bench in the park munching their way through the stale cakes, tarts and rolls, but they didn't mind. The boys were still heady with the excitement of being free of the workhouse, and everything was an adventure. Pearl, looking at the world through their eyes for a while, felt her spirits lift.

Once inside the museum the boys wandered around fascinated, and she was content to follow them, their happiness like balm on her sore heart. She held out no hope that she would ever see Christopher again – maybe his parents would make sure he didn't return to England for many a long year – but that didn't stop her looking for him wherever she went. She knew it was madness but she didn't seem able to help it.

Patrick was entranced with the goldfish pond in the Winter Garden, especially when one of the attendants let him sprinkle some special powdery food on it and the fish almost jumped out of the water in their eagerness to eat. Pearl found a bench where she could sit down when the boys showed no signs of wanting to leave and she must have dozed a little; suddenly the museum was about to close and it was dark outside.

On their return journey, the earlier misty drizzle settled into persistent rain, and by the time they approached the Old Market in the East End it wasn't so busy as usual in spite of the fact it was all under cover. The market didn't close until midnight, but one or two of the traders were already beginning to pack up. Pearl and the boys hung around a while. There were bargains to be had at such times.

By the time they left they had a big bag of scrag ends and yellowing vegetables which would see them over two or three days when cooked slowly in the black pot Pearl had bought and which sat neatly on the steel shelf over the fire. The stallholder who had sold them the ageing vegetables had thrown in some pieces of spotted fruit too, and all her purchases hadn't cost Pearl more than four pence.

She was thinking of their dinner that night as they trudged home towards the house in Long Bank through the back ways and alleys. She had some stale bread left from yesterday, and once she'd lit the fire and it was glowing nicely, they could have toast and dripping – that was filling. And the boys could have the fruit for afterwards. She still had a few spoonfuls left of the quarter pound of tea she'd bought before the boys came, but at two shillings a pound they'd have to eke that out until she got paid again next week. And they were getting low on coal. She squinted through the rain, her mind grappling with the problem of filling the boys' bellies and keeping them warm.

They'd almost reached Long Bank and the smell from the kipper-curing house on the corner was strong as she became aware of the men behind her. Before she could react or even open her mouth, she was manhandled against the wall of the alley they were in, James and Patrick being grabbed from behind by two of the men, who had their hands over the boys' mouths.

'Don't scream.' The man who had pushed her against the wall wedged her there with his hand over her mouth, her bags having fallen to the ground. 'It's Seth, Pearl. All right? It's me – Seth. I'm not going to hurt you.'

Half fainting with terror, she remained rigid against the slimy bricks. It was dark in the alley but she could see the man's outline. He was tall with broad shoulders.

'Listen to me – it's your brother, Seth. Do you understand? And Fred and Walter. We're not going to hurt you, but I have to talk to you and you mustn't scream.'

Dimly she made out familiar features, features which she'd last seen a long time ago and which had changed, coarsened. But it *was* Seth. As the terror drained away she went limp against him, and he removed his hand from her mouth as he gathered her into his arms. 'Come on, you're all right,' he muttered thickly. 'Breathe deeply, that's a good lass.'

James and Patrick were still wriggling and twisting like eels in their brothers' arms but they were no match for the muscled men Fred and Walter had become. Nevertheless, as a kick from James's hobnailed boots made his captor swear, Pearl revived enough to straighten and say, 'Don't be frightened, lads, they're not going to hurt us. It's your big brothers.'

Seth had let go of her and now, as Fred and Walter released

James and Patrick, the boys flew to Pearl as she put out her arms to them. For a moment she stared at her three brothers over the heads of James and Patrick. She could hardly take in the fact that they were here, in front of her. After rescuing her younger brothers, finding Seth and the others had been next on her agenda. But they'd found *her*.

As Fred and Walter came either side of Seth, she said faintly, 'I don't understand. What are you doing here, and why frighten us like this?'

Seth didn't answer this directly. His voice gruff with emotion, he said, 'It's better you and the lads aren't seen with the likes of us, lass, and if anyone asks – which they won't, so don't worry – you haven't seen us.'

'You – you haven't escaped from prison?'

She saw the flash of white teeth in Seth's face and his voice held amusement when he said, 'No, lass. We did our time and were released nice and proper so don't fret on that score.'

Pearl nodded. 'Then why . . .'

'The secrecy?' Seth's voice took on a rougher tone. 'Pearl, when you've been inside for any length of time there's not too many folk over-anxious to give you a job, not one that's above board leastways. It's dog eat dog and you either sink or swim. Me an' the lads didn't intend to sink.'

Now her eyes were becoming accustomed to the shadows she could see more clearly the faces of the men who were her brothers – and yet not her brothers. They looked – she couldn't bring herself to say frightening – they looked hardbitten, but then of course they would be, with all they'd gone through. Now Fred and Walter smiled at her, their voices low when they said, 'Hello, lass.'

She wasn't aware that she was crying until Seth got a handkerchief out of his pocket, his voice gruff again as he said, 'Here, wipe your eyes, lass, an' don't take on. There's nowt to cry about. Against all the odds the six of us have survived an' that's something to be marvelled at, considering where we come from.'

'You know Mam's been dead these past five years or so?'

'Oh aye, we know all about Mam,' said Seth grimly.

Pearl peered at him in the darkness. The look on his face told her the three of them were under no illusion about Kitty's activities after they had been sent to prison. Then he caused her to gasp and put her hand to her throat when he said softly, 'We know about Fallow an' all, lass.'

'It's all right, Pearl.' One of the others, she wasn't sure which was Walter and which was Fred, spoke now. 'He's been dealt with.'

'Dealt with?' she asked in bewilderment.

'Aye.' Seth made a sharp movement with his hand and his brother fell silent. 'Look, we need to tell you what's what, but it don't make pretty hearing. Fred —' he gestured to his brother — 'take the bairns up the alley a bit.'

'We're not bairns.' James's voice was indignant and both he and Patrick had tightened their hold on Pearl.

Seth surveyed the two brothers who had been babies the last time he'd seen them. 'No, mebbe you're not at that, but can you keep your mouths shut?' he said quietly. 'Young 'uns have a habit of speaking out of turn.'

'Not us.'

'Aye, well, likely it's as well you know, all things being equal. It'll save any questions about this.' He handed Pearl a brown paper packet which she accepted gingerly. 'Look on that as a form of atonement, even if it is years too late.'

Her confusion and fear must have spoken aloud from her face, for Seth saw it. Moving closer but without touching her, he said urgently, 'You got the bairns out of the workhouse by threatening Fallow, didn't you, with what he'd done to you all those years ago? He told us.'

'He *told* you?'

'With some . . . persuasion.'

'Seth—'

'Just listen, will you? He went to someone, someone who arranges for things to happen. For a price. Only this man recognised the surname of the woman and bairns Fallow wanted out of the way, so he came to us first. Honour among thieves,' he added with grim self-derision.

'He – Fallow – paid for someone to *kill* us?' She felt faint with horror.

'It happens, lass, believe me. Only he caught his toe, see? He didn't expect us to turn up and thank him personally for his blood money.'

'Sang like a canary, he did,' Fred said with chilling satisfaction. 'Once we'd convinced him confession is good for the soul.'

Pearl stared at them aghast. She felt as though she was in the middle of a nightmare she couldn't wake up from. 'You – you didn't . . .'

'He was rotten through and through,' Seth said dispassionately. 'He won't be missed.'

'You topped him?' James and Patrick had been listening with avid interest and Patrick couldn't keep quiet any longer. 'How? Was there blood everywhere?'

'Ssh.' Pearl pulled Patrick round, bending down close to him. 'This isn't a game, Pat, this is serious.'

'I know.' The boy stared at her earnestly. 'But that man wanted to hurt us, didn't he? They just got him first. I think that's fair. We didn't start it.'

This was all beyond her. Helplessly Pearl straightened.

'My sentiments exactly.' Seth wasn't smiling. 'While Fallow lived, you'd never have been safe – take it from me. But for Arthur putting two and two together, the three of you could simply have disappeared. Would you have preferred that?'

'Of course not, but . . .' She waved her hand weakly. 'This is all . . .'

'Forgotten. As of now. Right?'

Forgotten? How could she forget that a man had been murdered, by her own brothers and for her? And then she was thrown into further turmoil when Seth reached out and touched her face gently. 'I'd have done the same thing ten times over if I could, once I found out what the dirty so-an'-so had done, lass. Me and the lads are not ones for preachin', we know what we are only too well, but scum like Fallow . . .' He paused. 'I couldn't have done anything else. Me guts used to turn inside out them first few months in gaol, thinking about how you and Mam and the bairns were getting by, but never in a month of Sundays did I think she'd sell her own daughter to a devil like him.'

'Oh, Seth.' What could she say? What should she do? He was her big brother and she loved him; at times there had been an ache in her to see him again because even as a bairn she had recognised the honesty of the feeling he had for her and the rest of his siblings. He was a good man. And then she caught at the thought in despair. How could she think he was a good man when he had just told her he was part of the criminal community and hadn't thought twice about killing a man?

'We're going to disappear and you won't see us again.'

'No, please.' She caught at his sleeve. 'No, Seth. Please don't leave us.'

'It's for the best, lass. There's enough there for you to be set up till these two are out earning, and then some. And you're canny, you were always canny. You'll make sure these two don't end up like their big brothers.'

'Seth, no. Don't go.' She didn't care about Fallow or what Seth had done, she only knew she couldn't bear him to leave her again. Clinging hold of him she buried her face in his neck, shaking them both with her sobs.

He stood, stroking her hair and comforting her, much as he'd done when she'd been a child and he had been her only defence against a violent world. When he pressed her from him it was to hold her at arm's length while he stared long and hard at her. 'Lass, it's a mucky road me and the lads are on, and the way I see it we're set for life,' he murmured thickly after some moments. 'There's no way back for us but you, you an' them, you're different. Forget – forget you ever had three older brothers.'

'Never.' She stared back through swimming eyes. 'I love you – and you two,' she added to Fred and Walter, who were standing silently by. 'I don't care what you've done in the past, the future's different. We can all be together, we *can*.'

Seth's face was working and for a moment the tough mask lifted and she caught a glimpse of the boy he'd once been. His lower lip trembling, he said, 'Let me do one thing in my life that's decent, Pearl. One thing that helps me rest easy at night.'

'Seth—'

'*No.*' The mask was back in place and as she tried to fling herself on his chest he shoved her roughly aside. 'You don't know what we've done, what we still do and it's better you don't. An' I'm not bellyachin', it's how things are. You two —' he turned to James and Patrick — 'you keep your noses clean and look after her, you hear me?'

Pearl wanted to hold on to him but now Fred and Walter were awkwardly embracing her and the moment was lost. As the three melted into the darkness she called out, 'Seth!' but he didn't answer. Short of running after him there was nothing she could do, and instinctively she knew the end result would be the same. He wasn't going to stay. She was losing him and Fred and Walter once again, but this time because Seth had determined it that way. How could he be so blind, so stupid? He was cruel. No, no, he wasn't. He was doing this for her, for the three of them. But she didn't want to be alone again. That was how she felt. She had James and Patrick, but in this moment she felt numbingly alone. She wanted Seth. She wanted to be cared for and protected. She was tired and frightened and cold.

'Pearl?' James and Patrick were standing in front of her and she forced herself to respond as Patrick tugged at her wet coat-sleeve. 'Are they really not coming back?'

'No.'

'They're our brothers, aren't they? Why can't they stay?'

Wearily, Pearl picked up the bags she'd dropped when Seth had appeared. 'They just can't, that's all.'

'That — that's not fair.'

Patrick's voice broke and it was the spur which enabled her to pull herself together. Taking a deep breath, she squared her shoulders. 'Come on, we're going home. You two are wet through and you'll catch your death if we don't get you out of these clothes. You'll have to strip off and get into bed while I light the fire and the room warms up, and then once the fire's going we'll have toast and dripping. How about that?'

In the bustle of sorting her brothers out and lighting the fire and getting some hot tea down them once the kettle had boiled, Pearl didn't open the brown package immediately. They only had one candle left, and although she lit it initially because the room was as black as pitch, as soon as the fire gave sufficient light she snuffed it out.

While they waited for the fire to die down to a red glow so they could toast the bread, Pearl let the boys eat the fruit they'd bought that day. It was then, sitting in the armchair, that she reached for the brown package, holding it against her chest for a second because it was a link with Seth.

She still couldn't seem to take in that Mr Fallow was dead. That Seth and the others had murdered him. Murder . . . She shivered. But Mr Fallow had wanted her dead, and the lads. It was only because of that he had come to Seth's attention in the first place. And this was the money Mr Fallow had paid out for her demise. He had thought he'd been buying men to kill her.

The slim package was tied with string and Pearl fumbled with the knot for a moment. Then the string was loose and she folded back the brown paper. The sound she made as she saw the wad of notes brought James and Patrick scrambling out of bed to her side as naked as the day they were born.

'Holy Joe . . .' Patrick reached out a hand and touched the money reverently.

Pearl was too taken aback to admonish him about his language. She stared at the notes and then raised her gaze to Patrick and James. Their faces reflected her amazement and disbelief.

'How much is there?' James, the ever practical one, asked.

'Light the candle.' If ever an occasion demanded sufficient illumination, this one did. Once the candle was lit and at her elbow, she counted the notes slowly. Sixty pounds. She was holding in her hand *sixty pounds*. It was a fortune. She could get the boys' boots mended tomorrow, perhaps even buy them new boots, and some warm clothes, too – they needed another set. These thoughts raced through her mind even as she said flatly, 'We can't take it.'

'What? Why? It's ours, Seth gave it to us an' it was his to give.'

'James, you heard what he said and how he got it. It – it's not right.'

'Seth said it was at- atone-'

'Atonement.'

'Aye, that's it. That means makin' up for something, don't it? An' that's why he gave you it. And whatever you say, our Pearl, it *was* his to give. Mr Fallow had paid him with it, him and Walter and Fred, so it was theirs. It's not like they robbed someone.'

She stared at her brother in the flickering light from the candle, her head whirling. She didn't know what to do. *Oh, Seth, Seth, I don't know what to do.*

Patrick settled the matter. 'Anyway, you can't give it back,' he said with immense satisfaction. 'There's no one to give it to. Mr Fallow is dead and Seth has gone, and Seth wouldn't take it back even if you knew where he was. He said he wanted you to have it till we could work and look after you, so that's that.'

Pearl became aware that the boys were shivering, and as she shooed them back into bed James paused to hug her. 'Did Mr Fallow hurt you very much?' he asked hesitantly.

Ushering him into bed where he snuggled down beside Patrick, Pearl nodded. She didn't want to elaborate on what she had already told them. Maybe if they asked when they were older, she might feel differently.

'Then this is all his fault, isn't it? The workhouse schoolmaster used to say that everything we did had consequences . . .'

'Normally before he caned us,' Patrick put in.

'. . . And that if we didn't want bad things to happen, we had to be good.'

Pearl smiled at the two little faces looking at her so earnestly. Out of the mouth of babes.

Pearl didn't sleep much that night. Long after the candle had burned away and the fire was reduced to glowing embers, she sat in the darkness listening to the boys' heavy breathing, her mind racing. The precious brown package was tied up and hidden under her shawl in the chest of drawers, but although she couldn't see it, it filled her vision.

Slowly the enormity of what her brothers had done for her dawned. Not only had Seth and the others saved her and the lads from something terrible, but they'd given her the means of taking James and Patrick out of this tiny cramped room and hand-to-mouth existence. Sixty pounds would enable her to rent two good-size rooms in a respectable house. The boys would be old enough for Saturday jobs soon, and with what she earned and their extra bit they'd manage fine until the lads left school and started earning properly. They could furnish the rooms with bits and pieces bought cheap from the Old Market or secondhand shops, and they'd be set up. The worry of the immediate future had been taken away in one fell swoop.

Or – her heart began to thump – she could go with this idea that had been gathering strength all night, the idea that carried a certain amount of risk with it.

All through Sunday she pondered what she was going to do, changing her mind umpteen times before once more sleeping badly, in spite of the fact that she and the boys had gone for a long walk in the afternoon. Then she woke up early on Monday morning, her mind made up. At six o'clock she lit the fire and a little while later woke her brothers with two steaming cups of tea.

'I'm not going into work today,' she told them. If her idea worked out, her days in the pickling factory were over. 'Once you're dressed and ready for school, we're going to buy our breakfast from that little café in High Street East before you go to school, and I'm going into town. I'm going to get you both a thick winter coat and new boots, as your old ones are like colanders. But first –' she paused, looking at them as they stared at her over the tops of their cups – 'first I'm going to look into renting a shop.'

She really had their attention now. 'A shop?' Patrick's hair had been cut so short in the workhouse that it shouldn't stick up, but somehow it always managed to. 'What sort of shop?'

'I'm going to sell pies and puddings and soup, and brawn, definitely brawn, and meat rolls.' She stood up and began to pace back and forth. 'Corinda, the Romany lady I told you about, she taught me all about herbs and things, and I was better than her in the end. She said I had a flair for cooking that was born in someone rather than learned. I could do wonders with the toughest meat, and some of the stews and soups the Romanies cooked were better than anything you'll ever taste, I promise you. And I know how to do it. I *can* do it. It'll be hard work at first, of course, and I'll have to buy all the stuff I need and pots and pans.' She paused for breath. 'What do you think?'

Before they could reply, she went on, 'We'll rent somewhere with living space above if we can, as it'll be better to live in, especially at the beginning. Once you get home from school you can help me and at weekends. And I can show you what I do. For the future, you know? When you leave school you can work with me.' Again she paused, and this time when she said, 'What do you think?' she waited for them to speak.

Their faces were wreathed in smiles. Neither boy could think of anything better than living above a shop that sold food. James answered for the pair of them when he said, 'How soon can we go?'

'Soon.' There was a well of excitement bubbling up inside her and it went some way to quelling the words which had come to haunt her through the dark night hours. '"Born to trouble, you'll take trouble wherever you lay your head. It's a curse, and woe betide any man who's drawn to you."' She knew Halimena had always hated her, but in the middle of the night when the human spirit was low she'd had to fight against the old woman's denunciation.

She wouldn't believe there was a curse on her. She looked at James and Patrick's bright faces. But even if there was, she could break it and make a good life for these two. She could say with hand on heart that she wouldn't have wished Mr Fallow to die at the hands of her brothers, but in all honesty she wasn't sorry he was dead. That might be wicked, but that's how she felt. If just one little bairn was saved from what she'd suffered because he was no more, it was worth it.

As for Christopher and Byron . . . She turned away from the boys, saying, 'Come on then, out of bed and get dressed and we'll see about that breakfast.' Christopher and Byron were lost to her, each in their own way. She knew now things would have come to a head with Byron sooner or later. She couldn't have wed him – meeting Christopher had shown her that would have been a terrible mistake for them both. And in refusing him, she would have been forced to leave the gypsies. But Christopher. Oh, Christopher . . .

None of that. The little voice that had talked sense during the night switched on in her mind. *What is done is done. To dwell on it weakens you, and you can't afford to be weak, not with the boys looking to you. You go on from here, and who would have thought even a couple of days ago that such power would be placed in your hands.*

And money was power. She had always known it – bairns in the East End were born with the knowledge – but the confrontation with Christopher's family had cemented the fact. James and Patrick weren't going to go the way of their big brothers, nor were they going to spend their days down a mine or in the steelworks where fatalities were commonplace. She couldn't protect them from everything in life, she knew that, but she could equip them with the sort of power Seth had given her last night. That was why she had to make this money work for them. A fortune it might be, but even fortunes could be lost. She wouldn't let that happen.

Breakfast was a merry affair, although Pearl was a little worried Patrick might be sick with the number of sausages he'd consumed as she waved them off in the direction of school.

When they were lost to view she crossed High Street East and turned into the tightly packed terraced streets south of the river. She knew where she was making for. It would have been nice to look for somewhere in the main part of town and escape the East End, but commonsense told her she couldn't compete with the grand shops and eating houses already there. In the East End she would still have competition with the pie shops and places like the Old Market which had stalls selling hot food along with everything else, but she hoped that with the skills she'd learned from the Romanies and her own natural ability she could produce superior food at low prices.

She had recently noticed that a little shop not far from the pickling factory had become vacant – she'd passed it on her way to work in the mornings. It was situated on the corner of Zion Street and had been a 'pot' shop, selling anything from pots and pans to paraffin oil and sweets, although the window had been so thick with grime you could barely see inside.

She had brought the brown-paper package with her, tucked down the front of her bodice inside her petticoat next to her skin. She didn't dare leave it in the chest of drawers. Not that she really thought anyone would go poking and prying in their room, since those who lived in the area would know that no one had anything to steal, but still . . .

There were the normal snotty-nosed bairns playing their games when she reached Zion Street. In spite of the freezing weather and dull sky several of them had no coats or hats, and a couple of little boys were barefoot. She glanced at these two, their straggly hair white with nits. This could have been James and Patrick five years ago, because she had no doubt that her mother would not have lifted a finger to keep them clean.

The shop was different from the terraced houses stretching down the street inasmuch as it had a large bay window made up of little panes of glass. The bottom left-hand pane had been cleaned and a notice stuck to it which read, *Premises to let or buy. For further information kindly contact Charlton & Son, estate agents, no. 42 Fawcett Street.*

'Ain't no use you lookin' in there. Old Ma Potts is six foot under an' the shop's shut up.'

One of the two lads she'd noticed had left the others and was standing looking at her. 'Is that so?' She smiled at the dirty face but a pair of dark brown eyes surveyed her solemnly.

'Aye. Dropped down dead over there by that lamp-post, she did.'

'Oh dear, I'm sorry to hear that.'

'Had to fetch the Constable to her.' A lingering amazement was evident in the boy's tone. Pearl could understand this. It wasn't often any of the East End residents voluntarily called a policeman. 'And then she was took away.'

'I see. Well, thank you.'

The lad nodded at her, evidently pleased to have been able to help. He couldn't have been more than seven or eight. On impulse, Pearl fetched out her purse and gave him a thrupenny bit. It fitted the occasion somehow. The beginning of a new order.

'What's that for?' The dirty little paw had closed over the coin immediately and he clearly couldn't believe his luck. It was probably the first time in his life he'd been the recipient of such wealth.

'For taking the time to come and tell me what had happened to – to Ma Potts.'

He stared at her a moment longer before grinning and darting off to his pals who were standing in a group waiting for him, the old pig's bladder they'd been using as a football in the middle of them. Pearl didn't hang about. As a native of the East End she was fully aware that all the children would be badgering her for pennies, given half a chance.

When she reached Fawcett Street she found she had to summon up all her courage to enter the impressive facade of number 42. Once inside the foyer, however, she discovered that the building housed various businesses. There were plaques on the wall for a writing academy, an architect, a shipowner and an iron merchant besides Charlton & Son, who were situated on the first floor.

She climbed the stairs slowly, her heart thudding. Suddenly it seemed horribly presumptuous to imagine she could make a success of forming her own business. She was just a ragamuffin from the East End, the lowest of the low in polite society. What had she been thinking of? Nevertheless, on reaching the first floor she found the door inscribed *Charlton & Son* and after gathering her courage, knocked twice.

It was opened by a portly barrel of a man with rosy red cheeks and a bald head. Pearl took one look at his immaculate clothes and gold pocket-watch and almost turned tail and ran. Instead she managed to stutter, 'Mr – Mr Charlton?'

'I'm afraid not, ma'am. Mr Mortimer Mallard, assistant to Mr Charlton – the young Mr Charlton – at your disposal.'

'Oh.' She nodded. 'I'm – I'm here to enquire about a property, a shop in Zion Street.'

'I know the very one. Come in, come in.' If she had been royalty he couldn't have treated her with more respect. Ushering her into a somewhat cluttered room which had two desks either end of a number of filing cabinets and bookcases crammed with papers and cardboard boxes, he led her to a well-padded leather chair in front of one of the desks. Once she was seated he walked across to a filing cabinet and extracted a folder which he then placed on the desk in front of him before sitting down. 'Zion Street, you say? Desirable property. Very desirable.' He opened the folder, studying the papers within before he raised his head, surveying her with bright blue eyes. 'And you're interested in it, you say?'

'Aye, yes. I'm – I'm thinking of opening a shop.'

'Admirable, admirable.' There was a pause, a distinct pause. 'You and . . . ?'

'I'm sorry?'

'Who would be joining you in this venture?'

'No one. At least, there are my brothers but they're still at school. They'd help in the evenings and weekends though.'

'Good, good.' The pause was longer this time. Pearl was conscious that although Mr Mallard was examining the papers in front of him he had taken in every inch of her appearance. Suddenly she was very aware that her clothes had been bought secondhand at the Old Market and her boots needed mending. She could feel herself shrinking into the leather chair, and even the feel of the package rough and scratchy against her skin didn't help. She had a strong desire to make some excuse and leave, but the memory of Seth's face when he'd asked her to accept the money was uppermost. She'd be letting him down if she left now.

Mr Mallard cleared his throat and looked at her again. 'Would you be looking to rent or buy the property?'

'How much is it?'

'The rent would be eight shillings a week. To buy we'd be looking at a hundred pounds or more. The property has six rooms.'

Pearl swallowed. 'I see. I'd definitely be renting for the time being, in that case.'

The blue eyes moved over her hot face. Suddenly Mr Mallard's professional manner softened. 'Lass, I have to ask. Can you afford to look at such a property? You need some capital behind you if you're thinking of running a shop.'

'I know.' She had thought about what she was going to say to explain her wealth. 'And I do have some capital. I've been left a sum of money. More money than I ever thought I'd have in the whole of my life,' she added candidly, glad that in this she could speak the truth. 'I want to open a pie and soup shop. I'm very good at cooking.'

Mortimer Mallard smiled kindly. 'There's a lot more to running a business, and that's what we're talking about here, than being good at cooking. What if – and I'm not saying it will, of course, no, heaven forbid – but what if you can't make a go of it and you lose all your money?' His gaze took in the beautiful young face and unworldliness of the girl in front of him. 'What would you think then?'

'That I had tried.'

He blinked. 'But, m'dear—'

'My parents are dead, Mr Mallard, and my two brothers only have me.' She made a mental apology to Seth and Walter and Fred. 'We – we come from the East End and I feel this is our one chance to make something of ourselves. I won't let it fail.'

He sat back in his chair. 'How much have you got?' he asked baldly.

Pearl thought swiftly. It wouldn't be wise to state the full amount. No one from her background would come into such a sum. 'Twenty-five pounds.'

He nodded slowly. 'And you think that would be enough to set yourself up? You will need to buy equipment, don't forget, and raw materials.'

'I shan't buy new equipment if I can get secondhand. And I know how to make a penny stretch to two.'

Their conversation was interrupted by the door opening. A younger, sharp-faced man came into the room, his gaze going from Pearl to Mr Mallard. It was the latter who said, 'This is a new client, Mr Charlton. She has her eye on Zion Street.'

'Excellent.' Mr Charlton gave a smile which didn't touch his eyes. 'I trust you are taking the young lady to view?'

Half an hour later Mr Mallard opened the front door of the property and stood aside for Pearl to precede him. She stepped directly into a large room that had obviously been the main shop premises from the bits and pieces still scattered about. The stone floor was filthy and there was a smell of damp, but it was when Mr Mallard led the way into the back of the shop that Pearl realised old Ma Potts had clearly been struggling for a long time. She was standing in what once might have been a nice kitchen, but now was coated with the grime and dirt of years. Even as she glanced around, a couple of cockroaches scuttled out of sight. The range was encrusted with a decade of food and hadn't been black-leaded for at least that long, the curtains at the window were ragged strips of wasted cloth, and as she stepped down into what was a storage room or scullery she had to swallow hard against the smell. Worse was to come. When they walked out into the small backyard, the stink from the privy was such that Pearl asked Mr Mallard not to open the door.

Stairs from the kitchen led on to a landing, and the first door Mr Mallard opened revealed a sitting room. Besides this there were two bedrooms. The rooms were every bit as bad as the ones below.

Mr Mallard hadn't said a word as he had showed her round. Once they were standing in the main room of the shop again, he cleared his throat. 'You didn't hear this from me, lass, but in properties like this one it isn't unusual for a lower offer to be made to the owner, who in this case is a cousin down South. For someone who wants to take it on I'd say a rent of six shillings a week would be reasonable. And if you were buying, maybe, eighty pounds. The owner might say no, of course, but a client doesn't lose anything by asking.'

Pearl stared at him.

'It looks bad now, but the building is sound enough,' he went on. 'Plenty of elbow grease and a whitewash brush'd work wonders – that and some fumigation pellets from Skelton's store. The privy . . .' He shook his head. 'That'll need a strong stomach for sure.'

'I've got a strong stomach, Mr Mallard.'

He smiled at her. 'Aye, I don't doubt it. But it'll be a job and a half to start with, lass.'

'My brothers will help.' Six shillings a week. And six rooms. 'It's a large property, isn't it, Mr Mallard?'

'Two houses knocked into one, apparently. Miss Potts was worth a bit once – her father was a wealthy man, I understand – but she had a love affair that ended badly and she went a bit . . . doolally for a while. Her father died and she inherited and came here to live, and it was then she bought both houses and made one property out of them. But she was never quite right, by all accounts. Sad business. Anyway, she left everything to this cousin who she hadn't seen in fifty years and who has no intention of visiting the North. Very well off herself, I understand. But like I said, you didn't hear any of this from me.'

'Of course not.'

He was nice. He was really nice. 'So if I ask you to put in an offer of six shillings . . .'

'I'll do that.' He grinned at her. 'Mr Charlton prices the properties. He's a little . . . ambitious on occasion.'

At the end of the week Pearl was notified by Mr Mallard that the cousin would accept a rent of six shillings and sixpence a week, take it or leave it. She took it.

Chapter 18

Christopher sat quietly beside his mother as the coach bowled between the iron gates the lodgekeeper had opened at their approach. The journey home from Italy had been a frosty one, mainly due to what his mother called his 'ingratitude' in insisting they return to England rather than see the winter out in Europe. When he had pointed out that he'd had no wish to leave England in the first place, and it had only been the fact that he had been as helpless as a kitten that had enabled her to whisk him away, she hadn't spoken to him for a full twenty-four hours.

When the carriage stopped, a footman was there to help his mother descend, but Christopher waved the man's hand away when he tried to assist him in turn. He was feeling tired, deathly tired and ill, but he held himself straight as he followed his mother into the house. He wasn't about to give her more ammunition to fire at him. Not that she ever shouted or even raised her voice, she didn't have to. The icy silences and reproachful looks were more than enough to contend with. Until the last few weeks when he had been in her presence all his waking hours, he hadn't realised he actually disliked the woman who had borne him. He wasn't proud of himself for feeling that way, but he could do nothing about it.

The housekeeper and Parker the butler were waiting for them in the hall, along with a little maid who took their coats and hats. His mother merely inclined her head as the butler expressed his hope that the journey had been a tolerable one before she walked regally into the drawing room. Christopher hesitated for a moment and then followed her. He was very aware that he was going to have a battle on his hands over the next weeks, but if it could be deferred until he was feeling stronger, so much the better.

The doctor who had attended him in Italy had been first class but blunt. He was lucky, very lucky to be alive, Signor Rotondo had said gravely. One knife wound had damaged the muscles and ligaments in his left shoulder, which might cause problems with his power to grip in that hand, but it was the wound which had missed his heart by a millimetre which would take some recovering from. And you couldn't rush such things. But then, why would he want to? The Italian doctor had smiled at Clarissa, who had inclined her head graciously. He was in Florence, was he not? With its wonderful churches and architecture. If they were still here at Easter they mustn't miss the celebrations in the Cathedral square when a great cart, bearing a large wooden edifice encircled with fireworks, was drawn by four huge white oxen before coming to rest between the main portal of the Cathedral and the Porta del Paradiso of the Baptistery. On the stroke of midday, the doctor told them, a mechanical dove began a journey down a wire from the high altar to the edifice, and as it reached the first firework, it set off a display that was truly *magnifico*.

Christopher had made some polite comment to the worthy doctor, but the thought of remaining in Florence to the end of the month, let alone until the following Easter, had been completely insupportable. He had to see Pearl. He *must* see her. Thoughts of her and what she might be going through at the hands of the madman who had attacked him tormented him day and night. He had written to Nathaniel, expressing his fears, and his brother had written back to say he mustn't worry. He had it on good authority that the gypsy had fled to distant climes on the night of the attack. Christopher had felt a little better after that, but he knew he wouldn't be at peace until he held Pearl in his arms again. He intended to make her his wife at the earliest opportunity. Nothing else would do.

Twice he had compromised his recovery by attempting to show his mother he was well enough to make the journey to England. The second time, when he was confined to bed for a week, convinced him that Signor Rotondo had a point. Nature wouldn't be rushed, and the healing process would dictate the time he could leave. When that time came, he would be ready.

It was now early November. Turning his head, he looked out of the drawing-room windows. There had been sleet in the rain which had accompanied them ever since they had set foot on English soil. But he was home. He had done it. Now he could track down the gypsy camp, which Nathaniel had written had moved on. And when he found Pearl, they would never be separated again. His thoughts continued in this vein until exhaustion caused him to lean his head against the winged back of the chair and shut his eyes.

Clarissa sipped the tea the maid had brought her and watched her son as he slept. Wind and rain buffeted the windows and the late-afternoon sky was black with thunderclouds. By contrast, the roaring fire in the great hearth and the mellow light from the lamp behind her made the vast room almost cosy. None of this impinged on Clarissa's thoughts, however. She was angry. So angry she found herself wishing Christopher had died from his wounds in Italy, where some excuse could be made for his demise once she'd returned home. As it was, the problem of her son consorting with that creature still existed, because she knew Christopher well enough to gauge that he didn't intend to give the girl up. And it wasn't as though he was prepared to be discreet about the matter. If he had set the girl up in a house somewhere quiet and visited her on occasion, that would have been one thing. But to talk of marriage – that was indefensible.

The sleet had turned to snow when Oswald and Nathaniel walked in an hour later. Christopher awoke with a start to see his mother offering her cheek to his brother, who then strode over and clasped him warmly as he stood up. 'Chris, Chris, how are you?' Nathanial asked, clapping him gently on the back.

'Much better.'

'He is not.' Clarissa's voice cut like a knife. 'Signor Rotondo was most unhappy about our undertaking such a long journey, but your brother would not listen to reason.'

It was on the tip of Christopher's tongue to say that if he could survive the journey out – of which he had no recollection save moments of excruciating pain – the return one was a piece of cake, but he did not. Looking across to his father who had just given Clarissa a perfunctory kiss on the cheek before plonking himself down in the chair nearest the fire, he said quietly, 'Hello, Father.'

If Oswald had but known it, his feelings regarding his younger son resembled those of his wife at this moment. Nathaniel had shown him the letters Christopher had written, and it was clear the gypsy trollop was still in his blood. Oswald's countenance was dark, his lips drawn in tight against his teeth and his bullet-hard eyes unblinking. 'Is that all you have to say for yourself? You drag your poor mother back from a much-needed sojourn in the sun and half kill yourself in the process, and all you can say is "hello, Father"? Hell, man, take a look at yourself. You're a walking skeleton and as grey as clay. You're determined to break your mother's heart by going to an early grave, is that it?'

His father's words didn't fool Christopher. He'd had his twenty-second birthday while in Italy, but as he stood silently surveying his father he appeared much older to the three people watching him. It was as though the incident which had nearly taken his life had aged him a decade.

'I have no intention of going to an early grave, Father,' he said, after some moments had ticked by. 'None at all. And Mother was bored stiff in Florence – too much culture and not enough bridge parties.'

'And why do you think she went there in the first place, you ungrateful young cur, you? It wasn't for *her* health.'

'Nor mine,' Christopher shot back. 'Signor Rotondo himself said it was amazing I'd survived the journey. We all know why I was taken abroad, so don't let's play games.'

His father glared at him, then muttered thickly, 'Games, is it? You, to talk of playing games when your tussles with a gypsy wench could have ruined our good name.'

'Good name?' Christopher's upper lip curled, but before he could say anything more, Nathaniel took his arm.

'Don't say anything you'll regret, Chris,' he said, his voice low and urgent. 'You're ill, and no wonder. That journey would have taken it out of someone in rude health, let alone you. Come and have a rest before dinner.'

'I don't want to rest. I've done nothing else but rest.'

'Then come and tell me about Florence and I'll tell you what's been happening here.' Nathaniel was urging his brother across the room as he spoke. 'Oxford have written to say they've given you a year's leave in view of the accident – did Mother tell you? They've been very decent about it, so all's not lost there. And Rowena's mother is expecting a baby. Can you imagine, at her age? The scandal's rocked the county.'

He was still talking as he ushered Christopher out of the room, turning in the doorway to give his father a swift warning glance before he shut the door, leaving Oswald and Clarissa alone.

Oswald sprang to his feet, assuming his favourite stance with his back to the fire and his coat-tails held up as he roasted his buttocks. His voice a growl, he said, 'I'm not going to be able to stand this kid-glove treatment. Just setting eyes on the young fool makes my blood boil.'

'I thought we all agreed to tread carefully? I told you in my letters how he's reacted to me, Oswald. Nothing will be gained by behaving as you've just done.'

'This is my house and I'll behave as I want, woman.'

'Ignore him if you can't be civil. At least that way you're not inflaming him.'

'Inflaming him? By, I'd like to inflame him all right! The Catholics' idea of souls in purgatory being forced to sit on burning-hot gridirons would do a certain part of his anatomy the world of good.'

'Oswald, please.'

'A trollop like that pert little piece . . . after all we've done for him! It'll make Rowena's mother's lapse seem like nothing at all if it gets out.'

'Well, it won't get out, will it. You said the gypsies are gone. And it's been months, Oswald. Girls of that kind aren't without a man for long.' Clarissa didn't believe what she was saying, but for the moment she felt nothing would be gained by Oswald losing his temper. Besides, she hadn't heard the news about Henrietta Baxter. She couldn't believe Oswald hadn't mentioned it when he'd written to her, but that was men for you. Rowena's mother must be over forty – and to find herself in a delicate condition at that age! It was dreadful, quite dreadful. Poor woman.

Her voice holding a throb of delight she couldn't quite hide, Clarissa said, 'Anyway, enough about Christopher for now. We'll discuss it tomorrow when you're feeling calmer. Tell me about Henrietta. Who knows – everyone? What did the Steffords say?'

'Tollett doesn't know where they've gone, Chris. I had a word with him like you asked me to, but he couldn't help.'

Christopher sighed heavily. They were standing in the sitting room in Nathaniel's bedroom suite and his brother was busy pouring two glasses of brandy. 'I thought he might have some idea.'

'Well, he hasn't.' Nathaniel handed him a glass, saying, 'Sit down. You look ready to drop.'

'I have to find her.'

The hell you do. If Tollett had known where the Romanies had gone, Nathaniel had been prepared to buy his silence. As it was, he'd saved himself a few pounds. Now he shook his head. 'Chris, you know I'm for you. Always have been, always will be, but—'

'What?'

'She's a gypsy, man. All right, she might not have been born one if you believe what she said, but she's one of them now and they don't let their own marry outside their tribe. Tollett told me that himself. Tight knit, they are. Tighter than nobility. If you found her, they might turn nasty and do her harm. Have you thought of that? Look at what happened to you. You could put her in harm's way and you don't want that, do you?'

Christopher downed his brandy in one. 'I have to find her,' he repeated obstinately.

'What if she doesn't want to be found?'

'What does that mean?'

'Look, I don't want to upset you, but have you wondered why, if she thought as much of you as she said she did, she didn't come to the house to see if you were alive or dead after that maniac had attacked you?'

'They wouldn't let her.'

'But she managed to slip out and meet you each night, didn't she?'

'That was different. They didn't know about us then.'

Nathaniel poured them both another drink. 'If you persist in looking for her I'll come with you. There's no way you're going near those devils alone, all right? Promise me.'

'I promise, but I'm going to find her, Nat.'

'All right, all right, you're going to find her.' Nathaniel had seen how the muscles of his brother's face had tightened. Their father was right, Chris was nothing but skin and bone and all because of that little madam who'd had her eye on the main chance. She'd nearly had him killed, playing fast and loose with this gypsy lover of hers, but Chris just couldn't see it. *Wouldn't* see it. He hoped to blazes the gypsies had covered their tracks so they wouldn't be found, but if he and Chris did find them, and if she still fluttered her eyelashes at him, he'd be at his brother's side this time. And no matter what it took, no matter who he had to buy, that little whore wasn't having him.

It was another week before Christopher was sufficiently strong enough to begin the search, a week of snowstorms and thaws and more snowstorms. But then the weather turned bright and dry, although bitterly cold, and with Nathaniel at his side Christopher rode out of the claustrophobic confines of the estate.

Nathaniel had primed his parents to make no objection and let matters take their course, assuring them he'd see to it events played out as they would wish. Clarissa had suggested they take the carriage, but when Christopher had said he preferred to travel on horseback she hadn't argued. The less the servants knew of this latest venture the better, and the use of the carriage would have necessitated the services of Briggs, the coachman.

As it happened, it wasn't difficult to track down the gypsy encampment for the simple reason the gypsies had made no effort to conceal their whereabouts. Within two days and an overnight stay in an inn, the brothers saw the thin blue smoke of the camp-fires late one afternoon on the outskirts of Carlisle. They had travelled slowly, since Christopher had needed to rest often, but he hadn't once considered turning back.

'It must be them. That farmer in Talkin was right.'

Nathaniel nodded but said nothing. He was worried about his brother. This had been too much for him. If he saw the girl, he'd have a job to keep from wringing her neck.

The camp was situated at the end of a narrow lane and the horses stepped carefully on the big ridges of frozen mud. Long before the camp itself came into view the brothers could hear it – shouts and calls and laughter, children crying and dogs barking. Nathaniel was feeling distinctly uneasy now the moment had come, not so much about the danger they were in – although bearing in mind the events of the last two or three months, that could be considerable – but how he could persuade the girl to leave his brother alone. He was carrying a large sum of money sewn into the lining of his coat, but she might think she could obtain more by hanging on to Chris. If so, he would have to convince her otherwise. He had already determined to tell her that an associa-tion with her would mean his brother being cut off without a penny, and this was not altogether fiction. His parents were angry enough to do just that. But it would be getting the girl alone which would be the problem. He'd just have to play it by ear.

His heart thumping, he let Christopher lead the way, and as they came to the end of the lane and the campsite stretched out in front of them, he could see tents and caravans and horses and amid it all men, women and children. He bent down and undid the saddlebag as the horse clip-clopped on and a hush fell over the site. Unbeknownst to Christopher, Nathaniel was carrying a loaded gun in the bag and he wouldn't hesitate to use it, should it become necessary.

Halimena was sitting at the entrance to the tent as usual, and she recognised Christopher immediately, her keen eyesight which was as good now as it was eighty years ago picking him out across the field. *Him.* Her eyes narrowed as she watched the figure on horseback stop to speak to a group of children who pointed her way. She was aware of Corinda leaving a group of women she had been talking to and hurrying towards her, clearly agitated. As her daughter-in-law reached her, she said softly, 'Calm, child. Calm.'

'What do you think he wants?' Corinda's voice was shaking. 'For this to happen when our menfolk are in town.'

'Mebbe it's just as well,' Halimena said quietly. Mackensie was missing his eldest son more each day, so who knew what he might do if confronted with the reason Byron had had to leave them. 'You leave the talking to me, you hear? Whatever they want, I'll deal with it.'

A few months ago Corinda would have argued with this, but now the stuffing had been knocked out of her. She had a constant fear on her that Byron would be sought by the police and locked up, and that would kill him. To be unable to go where he wanted, live under the stars with nature about him, he'd die. She knew it.

Halimena stood up as the riders approached and she saw a flash of recognition in Christopher's eyes as he saw her. So, he remembered her, did he? As well he might.

She watched both men dismount but she didn't speak, her lined, tawny face inscrutable. The last time she had seen the gorgie's lover he had been lying on the ground with his clothes covered in blood, looking as though he would breathe his last. But he hadn't died. He was obviously tougher than he looked.

'I'm sure you remember me?'

She still didn't speak, merely inclining her head as she kept her eyes fixed on him. He had glanced at Corinda too but her daughter-in-law had her head down, looking at the ground. The old woman could smell the fear coming off her.

'I'm not here to cause trouble, believe me on that. What is done is done, and I bear no one ill-will. I – I'm looking for Pearl. I have to see her.'

So that was it. She'd got under his skin, had she, the gorgie? But then, those whom the guardians protect had powers to equal her own, she knew that. She'd heard it said they could tell the guardians to send a man mad, and this one looked well on the way. Aye, the girl had put her poison in this one, sure enough. He'd never be rid of the need of her till the day he died; it'd shrivel him up inside.

'Can I speak to her?'

Halimena looked at the ill young face. He was sick, grieving in his soul, and without the girl, he'd remain that way. He might take up the threads of life again, but nothing would be the same. Her thin lips moved in a terrible smile. 'Not you nor no one else,' she said softly. 'She's dead, drowned many a long day. Went wandering off by herself once too often and fell in the river when it was in flood.'

She watched as his brother – it had to be his brother, they were so alike – reached out and took the sick man's arm as he swayed. Huskily, Christopher said, 'I don't believe you.'

But he did believe her. It was his worst nightmare come true.

'Search every inch if you like.' She waved her hand to encompass the campsite. 'But you won't find hide nor hair of her. Found her body with her hair all spread out about her head like a veil, we did. Cold and lifeless. There's nothing for you here.'

Christopher's eyes went from her to Corinda, but the younger woman didn't raise her head or make any movement.

'Where is she buried?' he asked, his voice breaking.

It was the final victory. 'We don't bury, we burn, otherwise the spirit returns and haunts us. We make a funeral pyre and—'

'Enough.' The brother stepped forward. 'Keep your ghoulish details to yourself, you gruesome old crone.'

'He wanted to know.'

'And now he does. Come on, Chris.'

For a moment she thought he wasn't going to leave and then he turned blindly, his brother leading him to the horses where he helped him mount.

Halimena turned to Corinda as the two men rode out of the field and into the lane beyond, the first shadows of a cold winter twilight touching her face as she said, 'Now – *now* he'll suffer.'

Chapter 19

For four weeks after she had taken on the shop premises, Pearl and her brothers continued to sleep in the rented room while they got to grips with the mess Miss Potts had left. Every morning Pearl went straight to Zion Street and the boys joined her there once they had finished school. The three of them worked by the light of candles when it got dark and never returned home before ten o'clock. At weekends they arrived at the shop at first light.

Pearl tackled the downstairs of the property first. Once each room had been emptied and swept of debris, they scrubbed the floor, walls and ceiling of layers of dirt. They purchased practically the whole stock of Skelton's fumigation pellets, dissolving the eyewatering toxic yellow tablets in hot water before brushing the liquid on every inch of the surfaces they'd prepared. Once the downstairs was clear of bugs and mice they moved upstairs and repeated the process. The smell worked its way into their skin and hair and clothes; they tasted it when they ate and smelled it in their dreams, but eventually the whole place was as clean as a new pin.

Pearl had to spend the whole of one day on the range, but by the time she'd finished she was thrilled with it. James and Patrick bravely declared war on the privy and worked with handkerchiefs tied across their noses. They declined supper that night.

The floor of the shop and kitchen was stone flagged and scrubbed up beautifully; once the walls and ceilings had been white-washed and the massive white sink scoured, Pearl felt they were getting somewhere. There was a further sink in the scullery, along with a large walk-in cold pantry and rows of shelves on one wall. These were white-washed along with the walls and ceilings upstairs. At one time there had been wallpaper in the two bedrooms, but when they'd stripped it off, the number of bugs which had been hiding behind it had turned Pearl's stomach. Now everything was sparkling clean and white and fresh, and she wanted it to remain that way.

The fourth week was the most enjoyable. Apart from the long built-in counter which ran down a third of the main room, they'd been able to salvage nothing in the shop space. A couple of rickety tables had had to be cut up for firewood and stacked in the cleaned backyard under an old lean-to, but the ancient paraffin heater had been falling apart and even the shelves on the walls had been crumbling. The kitchen was the same. The table had fallen to pieces when they'd attempted to move it, and when Patrick had sat on the bench the legs had disintegrated under his weight, much to James's amusement. The kitchen cupboards either side of the range had been cleaned and lined with scalloped-edged newspaper, providing some storage, but Pearl knew she would need much more.

After making a list of everything she would need right down to the last teaspoon, she marched off to Casey's Emporium on the fourth Monday morning. This store had a reputation of being the best second-hand shop in the district. It was slightly more expensive than some of the other second-hand shops and pawnshops, but Mr Casey guaranteed that none of the furniture he sold had woodworm, and all upholstery and cushions were devoid of bugs. Pearl had had enough of bugs to last her a lifetime.

When she showed Mr Casey the list he nearly fell over himself with delight. Escorting her to a chair as carefully as though she was made of Dresden china, he had his assistant fetch a cup of tea. 'If I buy most of what I need here, I trust I'll receive a good discount?' Pearl enquired sweetly once she was sipping her tea.

Mr Casey shook his head sorrowfully. 'Well, lass, I keep my prices at rock bottom as it is so I don't think—'

'Mr Casey, I was born in the East End,' Pearl interrupted. 'I know full well I can go to several other shops and get what I need, but I like your reputation. However, I have to say I don't like it enough to pay through the nose, and I'm putting a considerable amount of business your way today.'

Mr Casey smiled. He knew when he'd met his match, besides which this young lass with the sad eyes interested him. He'd always been a man who admired folk with a bit of get up and go. 'I tell you what, let's see what's what and then we'll talk about coming to some arrangement. How about that?'

By the time she left the Emporium later that day, Pearl had bought everything she needed. Some of the items had not been on display in the shop, but Mr Casey had escorted her to a row of premises by the docks where he rented a small warehouse. They'd agreed a 15 per cent discount and he had thrown in a stack of good quality bedding for the three single beds Pearl had purchased. The whole endeavour had taken half of her precious sixty pounds, but Pearl knew she had got a good deal. She had been determined to give the boys a bright, comfortable home after what they'd been through, and she didn't regret one penny.

Mr Casey had agreed to deliver the furniture for their living quarters the next day, and the shop and kitchen furniture and pots and pans and crockery and so on, the following day. This meant they could get straight upstairs before organising the shop premises and the kitchen, which would be an enormous task.

The following morning the boys were delighted when Pearl told them they could have two days off school. Mr Casey was true to his word, and his horse and massive covered cart trundled to a stop outside the shop at eight o'clock. There followed a wonderful time.

By the end of the day the sitting room boasted a large gold square of carpet which exactly fitted the floor space. Upon this, a pair of mahogany-framed armchairs upholstered in gold and a matching sofa sat, along with a mahogany secretaire bookcase complete with books. A small occasional table with a large aspidistra on it stood between the full, green velvet curtains which framed the window, and on the wall above the fireplace a carved and gilded mirror with a pattern of leaves and berries hung in splendid isolation. Patrick was drawn to the mirror again and again, fascinated by his reflection as he practised pulling faces.

Besides the beds, the two bedrooms held a wardrobe and chest of drawers each and small bedside cabinets. In the boys' room a thick bright rug stood between their beds, and Pearl had one at the side of her bed. She had also bought a small writing desk for her room. The top had a red-leather inset above three frieze drawers and three short drawers on each pedestal. This was where she intended to keep any documents and work on her business accounts in peace. Mr Casey had assured her the desk was French walnut. Certainly it was very attractive and the small chair which came with it was comfortable.

In the evening Pearl took the boys to the Old Market and did what she'd wanted to do ever since the day she had collected them from the workhouse. 'Choose some warm clothes,' she told them, indicating the stalls full of second-hand clothes. 'And drawers and socks too. Seth and Fred and Walter wouldn't want you to carry on walking about in those threadbare things the workhouse gave you.'

The boys, overcome by the events of the day and the wonder of their new home, just stared at her for a moment. Then, their faces beaming, they hugged her round the waist before darting off.

The next morning, the second stage of the enterprise began. Along with the pots, pans, crockery, cutlery and other utensils for the kitchen, Pearl had purchased a somewhat battered but strong kitchen table and four hardbacked chairs for mealtimes. Two smaller but equally stout tables – one for stacking dirty pans and dishes on and one for food preparation – now stood either side of the stone sink. A large dresser occupied one wall, and a pine and fruit-wood high-back settle with flock cushions another. Several pine wall-racks had been fixed in appropriate spaces to leave what remained of the floor area free.

Now the closed range was free of the dirt and grime of decades

Pearl considered it a thing of beauty. It was more than big enough for her purposes, with two ovens for roasting and baking. The flues for the two ovens were arranged so that the one around the baking oven passed underneath first, providing bottom heat which was more suitable for baking, whilst the flue of the roasting oven passed over the top first, providing top heat. The space above the hot plate was lined with cast-iron covings which would be useful for the warming of plates and keeping food hot, and the boiler providing hot water was a huge bonus. The range was going to be the means of their livelihood and Pearl felt quite emotional as she stared at it, newly blackleaded and gleaming, with an enormous black kettle and various other pots and pans stacked on it.

The shop itself now had several narrow old tavern tables behind the counter. A number of covered entrée dishes were standing on these, some on small metal stands with candles below which would keep the food warm, and some without. The other two thirds of the shop had numerous small tables and chairs scattered about. None of them matched, but Pearl didn't think her customers would care about that. She had decided they could either sit and eat at the tables or take the food away, although in the case of the latter – if they ordered soup – the customer would have to provide their own receptacle for carrying it home. The same would apply in the case of mushy peas or tripe and onions. She would provide cans for those who didn't bring their own dishes, but she would make a charge for these.

It took Pearl a further two days to sort out the kitchen, scullery and shop, and find a place for everything, but by the weekend she was straight at last and they moved into Zion Street. The day had been a bitterly cold one, with intermittent snow showers and a raw wind, but that night, as she tucked James and Patrick into their beds and then walked through to the sitting room where a good fire was blazing, she was thinking of Seth. It was he who had given them everything they had, this beautiful warm home and the chance to earn her own livelihood doing something she loved. She knew Fred and Walter had done their part, but they would have been led by Seth. It had always been that way. She wished, she so wished he could be sitting here tonight, slippered feet up in front of the fire; Fred and Walter too. But he wouldn't try to see them; his goodbye had been final.

She had been fighting all day – and not just this day – from allowing her thoughts to focus on Christopher, but tonight she was very tired and her resistance was low. It seemed a natural succession for her thoughts to flow on to him and when they did, the tears came. And she found she was crying for Byron too. He had saved her life and he had loved her, and he wasn't a bad man. At times like this, Halimena's words always came back to haunt her and tonight was no exception. *Born to trouble.* But she didn't want trouble, she was the last person in the world to court danger and tribulation, so why did they always find her? What was it about her which made things happen?

She indulged in an orgy of self-pity for a little while before drying her eyes and blowing her nose. Enough, she told herself forcefully. She had a lot to be grateful for. Bad things might happen but nice things came along too. Look at her now. Just over a month ago, the three of them had been stuck in one small room and she had been turning inside out wondering how she was going to feed and clothe them and make ends meet.

She stood up and walked over to the beautiful mirror which had so captivated Patrick. For a long time she stared into the pain-filled eyes of the girl who looked back at her.

She would never marry now, never have a family, bairns. She knew that. Folk might call her foolish but she knew it. Christopher had been . . . irreplaceable. But perhaps that wasn't a bad thing. Her life was going down a different path but it didn't have to be doom and gloom, just different. She would have the time to give herself wholeheartedly to the shop and take care of James and Patrick now, build them all a future. And she wouldn't fail.

The girl in the mirror's chin lifted, her eyes narrowing and her lips compressing.

No, she wouldn't fail. Whatever it took, however hard she had to work and whatever she had to sacrifice, she would climb the ladder of success – and take James and Patrick with her.

The next week saw sacks of flour, rice, green split peas and potatoes delivered to the shop in Zion Street, along with a myriad of other supplies which had the occupants of the houses thereabouts gossiping for hours. In the middle of the week when the signwriter came and the words *Croft & Bros. Pie Shop* were painted above the sparkling clean window on pristine white board, the neighbourhood fairly buzzed with the news. Was it true, the old wives murmured over their backyard walls, that a mere bit of a lass had taken over old Ma Potts's place? Not just that, but the lass had two bairns in tow, her brothers by all accounts. She didn't really think she could run a shop, did she? And her just out of nappies? She'd come a cropper, sure as eggs were eggs, but there were always them who had to learn the hard way. A bonny little piece like her would be better occupied getting herself a husband and having a bairn every year like other lasses her age.

Pearl didn't know exactly what was being said, but she had lived her childhood in the East End and she had a good idea. It didn't bother her, but it confirmed what she'd known already; the food she produced needed to be that bit better than any from other shops roundabout, but for the same price, or cheaper. And it would be, thanks to her time with the Romanies.

She planned to open the shop the following week, and for an incentive to encourage folk through the door she intended to give each customer a little bag of pickled onions with their order. A sprat to catch a mackerel, as James put it when she explained her plans to the lads. She laughed and nodded. In an area where more than a few of her customers wouldn't be able to read or write, word of mouth was vital, and nothing spread faster in the East End than news of something for nothing.

The weekend was a time of frantic activity and a hundred and one small panics, but at six o'clock on Monday morning Pearl opened the door of the shop wide despite the freezing morning. She had put a notice in the window the week before, declaring when business would start, but there was nothing like the smell of hot food to tempt a man on his way home in the morning from the night-shift. She intended to stay open all morning, but shut for a time in the afternoon so she could prepare food for the next day, opening once again for the evening trade at six o'clock. If she could have afforded to pay an assistant to take orders and serve in the front of the shop, so she was released to work in the kitchen, she could have stayed open all day, but for the time being that was out of the question. James and Patrick had promised to get to work peeling and chopping vegetables and other mundane tasks before and after school, but they could only be expected to do so much.

She stood in the shop doorway after propping the door open, the glittering pavement and white rooftops indicative of the heavy frost which had fallen overnight. Inside the shop the new paraffin heaters were warming up the interior nicely, and for a moment she considered shutting the door again to keep the heat in. But what use was a warm shop if she had no customers? Once word had spread and she had her regulars, she could shut the door then.

At ten past six a young lad about Patrick's age sidled into the shop, his huge eyes in a thin white face and hair streaked with nits immediately proclaiming his family's circumstances. Before Pearl could speak, he said, 'Me mam says what's the least you can buy an' still get the pickled onions?'

Pearl looked at the child. He wasn't wearing a coat and his boots were several sizes too big and more holes than leather. She wanted to reach behind her and fill a bag with meat pies and chitterlings and sausages, but she knew that kind of weakness would be seized upon, and within a few short weeks she would be as destitute as his family obviously were. Swallowing hard, she said, 'A bowl of soup is a penny, but you need a can for it. Have you got one?' As he shook his head, she swallowed again. 'A bag of battered pieces then.'

'What's them?' he asked suspiciously.

Corinda had used to grind up all the offal of any meat the menfolk brought back, mix it with a blend of herbs and wild garlic and coat it in a seasoned batter before frying it over an open fire. The end result had been delicious. Rather than go into a lengthy explanation, Pearl said, 'Meat bits.'

'Aye, that'll do.'

She gave him a generous bagful, along with the pickled onions, took his one and a half pence – all carefully counted out in farthings – and waved him out the door.

Her first customer. She stood staring after him, not knowing if she wanted to laugh or cry. Was she doing the right thing? Would she be able to stand it? She was still debating whether to run after the boy and make some excuse for giving him back his money when a couple of miners, still black from the night-shift, stopped by the open door.

'Somethin' smells good, lass.' One of the men, his teeth white in his coal-smeared face, smiled at her. 'Taste as good as it smells, does it?'

'You won't know if you don't try it.'

'Aye, true enough. What you got then?'

Pearl went through the list along with the cost of each dish.

'The soup sounds all right but I dare bet you don't want us sittin' down like this?' He indicated his sooty clothes.

Pearl smiled into the black faces. 'The way I look at it, you've done an honest night's work for an honest night's pay, so why not?'

'I don't know about the pay bit, lass. Them owners'd wring the last farthing out of you given half a chance with their measures an' all, but we'll come an' have somethin' to warm us.'

They drank the soup and then ordered a couple of pies and peas to go with their pickled onions, complimenting her on her cooking and declaring they'd spread the word among their pit mates. They left Pearl in a rosy glow of achievement which faded once James and Patrick had left for school and she had no other customers all morning. Several housewives stuck their heads in the door asking her this and that, but no one bought anything. By midday Pearl had changed her mind and decided to stay open all day in the hope of selling the food she'd cooked the night before and that morning. She had a huge cauldron-type pot of soup simmering on a very low heat on the hob in the kitchen, but was beginning to think it was all going to go to waste when mid-afternoon customers began to dribble in in their ones and twos. By the time James and Patrick got home from school she had a small queue and was glad of the lads' assistance. Customers again tailed off about eight in the evening, but a sudden rush just before ten meant Pearl didn't lock the shop door until after eleven o'clock.

James and Patrick had peeled another pile of vegetables before Pearl had sent them to bed just before the late rush, but even so she didn't fall into bed until gone three in the morning and by then she was dropping with fatigue.

The next few days were similar, and by the Saturday evening when she took stock she found she'd barely broken even and hadn't made a profit. She had decided beforehand to close most of the day on a Sunday and only open in the evening so she could spend some time with James and Patrick. In the event she slept most of the day away before staggering out of bed at four in the afternoon to begin work.

The next few weeks were hard. There were moments when Pearl even thought longingly of the pickle factory; at least she had been able to have eight hours' sleep a night when she had worked there. Christmas came and went in a blur. She had tried to make Christmas Day special for James and Patrick, and on Christmas Eve had pinned two stockings to the hearth in the sitting room. She filled them with nuts and all manner of sweets, along with an orange and apple each and a shiny half-crown. On Christmas Day they had a big fat turkey with all the trimmings and plum pudding to follow, but once the boys were in bed and asleep Pearl sat in front of the fire thinking of Christopher and wondering if he was thinking of her. She cried herself to sleep that night and woke up the next morning glad to return to the punishing pace which kept her from brooding.

On New Year's Eve it snowed heavily. It being a Thursday, Pearl opened as normal but she let James and Patrick stay up late. That night in the kitchen, as the clock chimed midnight and all the ships' hooters and whistles sounded and the streets round about were filled with shouts and laughter as neighbours first-footed each other and celebrated the start of a brand new year, the three of them toasted Seth, Walter and Fred with hot mulled wine.

James and Patrick went off to bed a little tiddly and once she was sure they were asleep, Pearl went downstairs and into the back yard. It was still snowing, a million starry flakes falling from a laden sky. It was quieter now, just the odd shout or dog barking breaking the silence of the hushed new white world.

'I thought you might come tonight, Seth.' She spoke softly, her breath a cloud of white as she stood on the doorstep. 'Stupid I know, you might not even know where we are, but somehow I think you do. I wish you'd come. I don't care what you've done in the past, you're my brother and I love you. Much more than you know.'

She hugged herself, wrapping her arms round her waist as she shivered. A couple of streets away there was a sudden burst of sound, someone calling and another voice answering, and loud laughter borne on the night air.

The beginning of a new year. A snowflake landed in her eye and she blinked before turning and shutting the door. Walking back into the kitchen, she looked at the row of bread tins proving in front of the range. The dough had risen nicely, and bending down she popped the first batch of bread into the oven and then checked the meat pies in the roasting oven.

She couldn't let this fail. Sinking down on one of the hard-backed chairs, she gazed into the light of the oil lamp in the middle of the table. She was dipping into what remained of the money Seth had given them each week to pay the rent and buy supplies, and although she wasn't losing money in the shop she still wasn't making any – and they couldn't carry on like that for much longer.

The flickering light was hypnotic; she felt her eyes begin to close and stood up sharply. She was tired, so tired – but she still had two or three hours' work in front of her before she could go to bed. And she didn't mind the hard work, she really didn't, but if only she could see some encouragement . . .

Fetching the meat pies out of the oven she put the next tray-fuls in and then straightened, stretching her aching back.

She had to *believe*. She nodded to the thought. Believe this had been the right thing to do, that it wasn't a mistake. Believe she could make a better life for James and Patrick, for all three of them. And her little band of regulars was growing, albeit slowly, and everyone said her food was the best they'd tasted. Mind, they probably would say that to her face, she reasoned in the next moment. They might be saying something quite different out of earshot.

Enough. Again she nodded and then said the word out loud: 'Enough.' If she didn't believe in herself, then for sure no one else would. Word *was* spreading. Only the other day a small group of workers from the candle factory had come in, saying how one of their number had recommended her. It wouldn't take too many incidents like that before she'd be making a go of things.

When Pearl did her accounts at the end of the week, she had to add them up twice before she believed what her eyes were telling her. Five shillings' profit! All right, admittedly it wouldn't even cover the rent for the week, but five shillings was five shillings nonetheless.

The next week it was just over one pound. The week after that, it doubled.

In March, Pearl felt the shop was doing well enough to justify the employment of an assistant. She hired a very capable widow-woman who was struggling to make ends meet. Nessie Ramshaw proved to be a blessing in all sorts of ways. Not only did she free Pearl up to concentrate on the cooking, but this motherly soul with a heart of gold also had a tongue that could cut the most awkward customer down to size; she was tailor made for working in the front of the shop.

James and Patrick soon adored the stalwart little woman, a feeling which Nessie fully reciprocated. Nessie's only child, a son, had died with the fever when he was eight, and it was soon clear to Pearl that her young brothers filled a heart-shaped hole in Nessie's life.

It was Nessie who prompted Pearl to go to the bank and see the manager with a view to taking out a mortgage. Shortly after this, towards the end of that year, Pearl put in an offer of eighty pounds for the premises through the good Mr Mallard. When the owner demanded ninety, Pearl didn't quibble. She knew if Ma Potts's cousin took it upon herself to pay them a visit and observed how she'd improved their living quarters and the shop itself, and how prosperous it was becoming, she'd ask more.

Pearl took out a mortgage for half of the amount; the other half she could afford to pay outright. When everything was done and dusted and she was officially a woman of property, she and Nessie and the lads went for a slap-up meal at the Grand Hotel to celebrate. They virtually tiptoed into the hotel feeling completely out of their depth in the impressive surroundings, but once they were seated at a table in the fine dining room – lit by the modern phenomenon of electricity – Pearl began to enjoy herself. They ordered their meal from the embossed menu and when the first course came, Pearl relaxed back in her seat.

This wouldn't be the last time they'd dine here, she vowed to herself, watching her brothers' faces as they stared at the smartly dressed waiters gliding about, a white cloth draped over one arm. She was going to rise in the world and take James and Patrick with her. Christopher's family had treated her as though she was something distasteful they'd brought in on the bottom of their shoes; she would never allow anyone to speak to her again in that fashion. And if she had to work her fingers to the bone to achieve what she wanted, so be it. It was a man's world – look how the poor Suffragettes were being treated – but already women in Finland had won a real taste of political power when they'd secured seats in the Finnish Parliament, and a few years ago no one would have thought that possible. So why not more women in all realms of society, including business? The bank manager had been faintly patronising when he'd agreed her mortgage facility; one day – and not in the far distant future either – she'd repay that and buy another shop, more than one . . .

'This soup's not a patch on yours, lass,' Nessie murmured in her ear. 'An' can you hear that man a couple of tables away? He might look like the gentry but he's got a mouth on him as big as the pithead.'

Pearl grinned. Nessie wasn't in awe of any establishment or person, and she was so glad the two of them were firm friends. She had never had a real friend of her own before; Freda had been kind to her, but Byron's sister's confidantes had been among her own kind, which was understandable. In the last months she had found she could talk to Nessie about almost anything. Her friend knew all about her life with the Romanies, and about Byron and Christopher, all her hopes and fears for the future and her poverty-stricken childhood. The only thing Pearl hadn't revealed was Seth's part in providing the wherewithal for the shop premises. As far as Nessie was concerned, Seth and the others were in prison and she'd last seen them as a child. She had explained away her means of setting up the shop by saying she'd had a windfall from a relative – which was true in a way – and, Nessie being Nessie, the little woman hadn't pressed her further.

Their meal was most enjoyable but Pearl sensed that the boys were somewhat uncomfortable in the opulent surroundings. On the way home they stopped at the Old Market; the carousel was there at the top and it being a Saturday night there was boxing and men playing accordions, as well as a stall where you had to get footballs through holes. Pearl gave James and Patrick sixpence each and she and Nessie watched them have fun in the more familiar surroundings. The carousel was a penny a ride for five minutes, and the lads had two rides each before trying their luck at a couple of games stalls. They finished up at the bottom end at the very large sweet stall, buying a bag of bullets and a liquorice shoelace each, along with some nuts and raisins for a ha'penny per bag from a man with a wooden barrel.

Tired but happy, they walked Nessie home to her lodgings in Northumberland Place before continuing on to Zion Street. It was a wet night and the rings of blue light around the gas lamps shone on the cobblestones, turning them blue too. When Pearl opened the door and ushered the boys upstairs to start getting ready for bed, she stood for a moment in the dark shop, counting her blessings and reflecting how, in a mere twelve months, their lives had been transformed. She had much to be thankful for. And if she cried for the moon occasionally, and the feel of a pair of strong arms holding her tight and a handsome face topped with corn-coloured hair close to hers, only she knew.

Chapter 20

'What the hell are you on about, boy? Who said we sent the chit off with a flea in her ear?'

'Don't bother to lie, Father. I know.' Christopher stood facing his parents and Nathaniel, his eyes blazing. 'You had her brought here and threatened her with all sorts of repercussions even before Mother and I left for Europe, and when she came back—'

'Came back?' Clarissa interrupted. Turning to her husband, she said, 'You didn't tell me she came back.'

'I didn't know.'

'She came back and was told I'd gone away.' Christopher came further into the drawing room. 'On your orders. All the staff were told to say the same.'

'So it's one of the staff who's been filling your ears with tittle-tattle?'

'No, it's not one of the staff.' Christopher could say this in all honesty. When Tilly the kitchenmaid had waylaid him in the stables that morning to tell him some very interesting facts, she'd also mentioned that she and one of the grooms were running off to get married. The butler had forbidden it, she'd added, since liaisons between members of staff were not allowed, but they loved each other, and the groom in question had already got a good job down

South through his brother. They were leaving within the hour but she'd had something on her conscience for over twelve months and she couldn't go without telling him. Christopher had listened to what the girl had to say and his blood had begun to boil.

'Then who was it?'

'That doesn't matter. Suffice to say I know this person was telling the truth, which means . . .' he looked straight at his brother now, 'you lied to me.'

'I lied to you?' Nathaniel reared up as though he had been stung. He and his father had recently arrived home and had been enjoying a pre-dinner sherry when Christopher had walked in. He felt sorry for his brother. Since Chris had decided not to return to Oxford he'd taken over the responsibility for the farm and had been spending a lot of time with Tollett, which must be wearing for anyone, but Chris's refusal to buck up and get over the gypsy wench had begun to annoy him. 'When did I lie to you?'

'When you pretended to help me find her. You never intended for us to get together, did you? It must have been a great relief when you found out she had drowned.'

'Don't be stupid.'

'Oh, I *have* been stupid – I see that – but not now. Now I'm *not* stupid, Nat. Now I understand what drove Pearl to kill herself.'

'You don't know she killed herself.'

'I know she went out walking in the dead of night and ended up drowned. That's enough.'

'It could have been an accident – that old crone herself seemed to think so. The river was in flood, she said so.'

'Accident or no, your actions,' he included his parents in the sweep of his head, 'killed her as surely as if you'd held her under the water yourself. We loved each other—'

'Oh, for crying out loud!' Oswald's patience, tenuous at the best of times, was being sorely tried. 'She was a gypsy, a common vagabond. All her kind are thieves and harlots—'

'One more word and I'll forget you're my father and strike you down where you stand.'

'That's enough.' Clarissa was white faced but regal as she stood up and joined her husband in his favourite place in front of the fire. 'Your father is right, Christopher. The match could never have taken place, you must see that? And look what a brush with those people has left you with. You still have difficulty with your left arm and tire easily.'

'I do not tire easily, I tire of life in this house! Of the shallowness and emptiness of it all. The only time I feel alive is when I'm with Wilbert.'

'Wilbert?' Clarissa's smooth brow wrinkled.

'He means Tollett, the farm manager.' Nathaniel had joined his parents and the three of them faced the angry young man in front of them as one united force.

'The farm manager?' Clarissa's expression suggested there was an unpleasant smell under her nose. 'I trust you aren't making the mistake of getting too familiar with a servant, Christopher.'

Christopher stared at them. He had known for some time that this moment would come. Either that or he would go insane, because there was no way he could continue living under his father's roof and retain his sanity. He could imagine what they had put Pearl through when she'd been brought to the house, how they had made her feel, but in spite of that she had loved him enough to come back a second time to try to see him. Such a flood of hate for the three people in front of him surged into his breast that if he had had a pistol in his hand he didn't like to think what he would have done. And Nat, for Nat to betray him like this . . .

'I'm leaving,' he said flatly, 'so you won't have to worry about Wilbert Tollett or anything else connected with me.'

'What do you mean, you're leaving?' Oswald's lip curled. 'If you think you're going to go off gallivanting, think again. You've had it too easy, m'lad. That's your trouble.'

Christopher looked into his father's hard little eyes. 'You're probably right.'

He turned away, only to be swung round by Nathaniel's hand on his arm. 'Wait, Chris. What are you going to do?'

'Why should you care?'

'I care, of course I care – you're my brother!'

Shaking off Nathaniel's hand, Christopher stared into the face which was so like his own. He had always seen his brother as an ally against their parents, someone who was more like him under the skin than their mother and father realised. He had also been conscious of being under Nathaniel's worldlywise wing, but his brother's protectiveness had never irked him because it was given with love. Or so he'd thought. Now he wasn't so sure. 'I have my allowance that Great-Aunt Estelle left me – I'll survive.'

'Your allowance?' Oswald said contemptuously. 'That wouldn't keep you in boot leather.'

'Then that will be my problem, not yours.'

'This has gone far enough.' Clarissa moderated her voice. Like Nathaniel, she had seen what was in Christopher's eyes. 'Let's have no more talk of leaving, Christopher. What we and your brother did, we did for the best. You must believe that.'

'The best for whom, Mother? Certainly not Pearl or myself; I fancy we came way down on the list of priorities. Anyway, it's of no matter now. I've never been a hellraiser and my account has accrued to a tidy sum in the bank, more than enough for me to purchase my own farm or smallholding somewhere.'

'What?' Now he really had his mother's attention. 'You aren't seriously considering demeaning yourself in such a fashion! You are just saying this to spite me, aren't you? To punish me.'

'I'm quite serious, Mother.' The dream of the little bookshop had died with Pearl. He found he didn't want to mix with people these days, but animals were different. They asked for nothing but to be treated well. In the last months, unbeknown to his parents, he had got his hands dirty working with Wilbert on the farm and it was only on those occasions he had found a measure of peace. It had been then this idea had begun to grow. He had no interest in being a gentleman farmer, someone who had umpteen employees and a manager to run things. He wanted – he *needed* – to work on the land and be able to breathe God's clean air, to be tired enough at night to sleep.

'I forbid it.' Clarissa's face had turned an ugly shade of red. 'Do you hear me, Christopher? I forbid it. I won't have you turn us into a laughing stock.'

'If you do this, you know you'll be cut off without a penny from me?' Oswald said grimly. 'Nathaniel will get the lot.'

'I don't want anything from you, Father. Or you, Mother.' Christopher's voice was calm. 'And Nat deserves his inheritance.'

Clarissa was stretching upwards, the poise that was a part of her gone. 'You ungrateful little cur. I won't let you do this, I won't!' She stamped her foot, an expression on her countenance that could only be termed hate. 'I'll never forgive you if you leave now, Christopher. I mean it. From this moment it will be as if I only have one son. Do you want that?'

Christopher's eyes moved to each face in turn. There arose in him a feeling of aloneness such as he'd never experienced in his life before, even though he had always felt alone within this family. But this was deep, devastating. It was the severing of blood ties. As he held his brother's eyes it was Nathaniel who glanced away first, the action a declaration of where his loyalty lay. But then he had always known his brother danced to their father's tune, hadn't he? None of this should have come as a surprise.

'Well?' Clarissa glared at him. 'Are you going to be sensible so we can discuss this in a civilised manner?'

'Goodbye, Mother.' Christopher turned and walked out of the drawing room and up the winding staircase to his suite of rooms. Packing a bag with his personal effects and a few clothes, he came downstairs again and paused for a moment in the hall. He could hear the low hum of voices from the drawing room. He stood looking around him. He would never set foot in this house again. He had been born here and had never known another home, and yet he didn't feel a thing for it beyond a wish to be gone.

Leaving the house, he made his way to the stables. He was taking Jet, since he wouldn't put it past his father to have the horse put down if he left him here. His mother talked of spite, but Christopher had never met anyone as spiteful as Oswald when he was provoked.

He had just mounted the animal and was about to canter out of the yard when Nathaniel appeared. 'Don't go like this, Chris,' he implored. 'Stay and talk things out. They'll be reasonable, I promise you.'

'They don't know the meaning of the word and you know it. Anyway, I've had enough – of them, this house, the life we're expected to lead. Hell, the banality of it.'

'All this for that gypsy wench? I don't understand you, man. You're my brother but I don't understand you.'

'I understand you and them only too well, Nat.'

The two men studied each other for a moment before Nathaniel said, 'I'm asking you not to go, Chris. I – I don't want to lose you.'

There was a long pause before the answer came: 'It's too late for that.'

Again there was a pause before Nathaniel spoke. His countenance had darkened, and for a moment Christopher could see their father in his brother's angry face. 'You only knew her for two minutes and you're prepared to sacrifice our brotherhood on the altar of this ridiculous whim? I agree with Mother and Father that—'

'I know.' Christopher cut into his brother's furious tirade and his voice was cool, even cold. 'Goodbye, Nat.'

He left with his brother's curses ringing in his ears, but kept his back straight and his head high until he had passed through the gates. Once away from the house he stopped Jet in a quiet lane, taking great gulps of the freezing air as he fought to keep back the tears which were stinging his eyes. He didn't know why he was crying – whether it was for Nat or himself or Pearl, or simply the end of an era. He just didn't know. His stomach churning, he made an effort to pull himself together. From a child he had shrunk from scenes, hating confrontation of any kind. Perhaps he had been too inclined to circumvent any unpleasantness?

He shook his head at himself. There was no perhaps about it. He had been content to take the easy road and let his parents ride roughshod over him, and now he was getting what he deserved. But Pearl . . . Pearl hadn't got what she deserved. The ache in his chest that came with thoughts of her made him want to groan out loud, but he was past that now. In the first few weeks after he'd visited the gypsy camp and learned of her fate he'd lain in bed at night biting his pillow in an effort to stifle the animal-like moans that made his guts writhe.

There was the odd snowflake drifting about in the wind and the night was as black as coal. He wanted nothing more than to put some distance between himself and the estate, but he couldn't leave without making his goodbyes to Wilbert and his wife. He turned Jet in the direction of the farm.

When he reached the farmhouse, the lights shining from its window looked welcoming in the darkness. He knocked on the door and it was one of the children who opened it, immediately calling over his shoulder, 'Da? It's Sir from the big house.'

The next little while was one of bustle and activity. Wilbert sent his oldest boy to lead Jet into the stables, and Mrs Tollett ushered the rest of her brood to bed, despite their protests, leaving the two men to talk in peace. Before she left the room she made it very plain that she wouldn't countenance Mr Christopher doing anything else but staying the night under their roof; she wouldn't sleep a wink at the thought of him riding out on such a night.

Once Christopher had acquainted the manager with the facts of the matter, Wilbert sat back in his armchair opposite Christopher's in front of the open range. He'd fetched a bottle of whisky on the young man's arrival. Now he poured them both a generous measure, drinking half of his before saying, 'You're serious about this small-holding-cum-farm idea?'

'Never been more serious in my life, Wilbert.'

'It won't be like here, sir. You do understand that? You'll be up to your eyes in it most days, come hail or shine, and farming is backbreaking work at the best of times. Are you sure you're up to it?' It said much for how their relationship had progressed that Wilbert could talk to the son of his employer so frankly.

'If I answer that truthfully I have to say I'm not sure, but I'm going to have a damn good try.'

'You'll need a couple of good men working with you, men with experience.' When Christopher would have protested, Wilbert held up his hand. 'Believe me, I know what I'm talking about. Even I, with fifty odd years behind me of working on the land, wouldn't want to take on a farm without help, and excuse me for saying it, sir, but you're still wet behind the ears in that regard.'

Christopher grinned. He finished his whisky and Wilbert poured them both another glass. It was then the manager said thoughtfully, 'I might know the very place . . . that's if it hasn't already been sold. I was talking to an old acquaintance of mine at the last cattle fair in October, and he was all set to move further south and live with his daughter once he'd sold up. His wife died a year or so ago, and he has the need to be with family; there are several grandchildren he's only seen once or twice. Mind, his holding is a fair distance, and as far as I know there's nowt in the way of modern conveniences, if you know what I mean. Back of beyond, Jed's place is.'

'Back of beyond would suit me admirably.'

'Aye, well forgive me again for talking straight, sir, but you've been used to a life of comfort and ease. The winters can be devilish, and spring and autumn can be mud baths on a farm. Going out riding and coming back to a stable boy who sees to the horse, and servants who take care of your every want makes the worst weather pleasurable. There'll be days – weeks at a time – when your body is aching and you feel wretched, and still you have to see to the animals' needs. And you're not a hundred per cent fit yet after the . . . incident, sir. You know you're not.'

Christopher stared at his friend in the mellow light from the fire. There was an understanding smile on his face when he said softly, 'I know you feel you have to point all this out, but it won't make any difference, Will. If I don't do this I might as well blow my brains out because I can't go on as I am. That's the truth of it. It's do or die – in the real sense of the words.'

'Oh, lad, lad.' Convention and propriety went out of the window and Wilbert spoke as he would have done to one of his own children. 'Bad as that?'

'Every bit as bad as that.'

'Still the girl, the gypsy lass?'

'Yes, and no. What I mean is, it's not just Pearl. Meeting her, falling in love, shone a light into my life and I didn't like what I saw. Or what I was, come to it. I think I'm a weak individual, or I have been. That has to change if I'm to live with myself. I've hidden in books too long. Now I feel I have to take life by the throat and find out what I'm made of. I might not like it at the end of it all, but at least I'll know. Does that make sense?'

Wilbert nodded. 'Aye. Reckon you think too much, lad, but if nothing else you'll have no time for that if you're running a farm, even a small one like old Jed's. I'll take you there in the morning but it's a fair ride, past Alnwick and then some. I understand since Jed's wife died, one of the wives of the couple of men who work for him goes in and does, so that'd take care of your meals an' such, which would be a blessing. Like I said, it's isolated though. Don't see folk from one month to the next, so Jed says. He didn't mind that, but it'd send some folk barmy.'

'Not me.'

'Aye, well hold your horses till we see what's what in the morning, eh? And in the meantime this whisky needs drinking. The wife'll make up a bed for you on the sofa in the sitting room later, once we've had a bite of supper.'

'Thanks, Wilbert.'

'My pleasure, sir. I've often said there's nowt but one good thing come out of the big house and I'm sitting talking to it right now. And if Jed's place don't suit, I'll make enquiries elsewhere, all right?'

Jed's place did suit Christopher, although Wilbert was full of misgivings when he saw how rundown the small farm was, certainly by his standards. They had followed the road to Alnwick, but when it divided they turned left, past the River Aln and towards Ditchburn. The day was bitterly cold but the snowclouds had cleared and a weak winter sun lit their journey. The sunlight brought a kind of charm to the lonely landscape, the bare trees and windswept hedgerows beautiful in their own way.

Christopher checked the thought. He couldn't afford to think like this if he was going to be a farmer. From now on he had to be practical and not given to flights of fancy.

They travelled up hill and down dale off the beaten track before they reached the huddle of buildings which made up Hill Farm. The farmhouse itself looked to be half the size of the one on the estate, and this proved to be so once they'd arrived and Jed had welcomed them in, his eagerness proclaiming the fact that the farm had not yet been sold. There were two rooms downstairs, a sitting room-cum-kitchen and a massive scullery complete with mangle and poss-tub and a brown stone sink. A wooden ladder led to the upstairs, which was one large room. The whole place was filthy, and an aura of neglect hung over everything.

After a cup of strong black tea Jed showed them the boiling-up room for pigswill which was reached by a narrow door leading off the scullery. From here an outer door led directly into a large stone-flagged farmyard. This was bordered on one side by the pigsties and on the other by a long hen run and hen crees. The dairy was situated at the end of the farmyard, and beyond this were the stables and several large barns. An outdoor privy was a stone's throw from the house in a corner of the yard next to the hen run. Jed admitted that a large part of the acreage he owned was devoid of crops or livestock; he had been 'running things down' since his wife had died. Wilbert's sniff at this point suggested he thought the farm had been running down long before this.

Christopher and Wilbert met the two labourers employed on the farm. They and their wives lived in two of a row of five terraced one-up, one-down cottages built some hundred yards away from the farmhouse on a slight incline. They seemed nice enough fellows, and the older of the two confided that in Jed's father's day all five cottages had been in use and the farm had been thriving. But, the man added hastily, he was sure that with a little money thrown at it the farm could be returned to its former glory.

The men's wives milked the herd of cows and worked in the dairy, joining their husbands in the fields when required to do so and looking after the hens and pigs.

One of the women, a red-cheeked matron of middle-age, was introduced to them as the lady who saw to things in the farm-house and Jed's meals. 'Not very well, by the look of it,' Wilbert had quietly murmured to Christopher once they were out of earshot.

The children of both couples had grown up and left, there not being a job for them on the farm. Christopher suspected there had been plenty of work for them to do, but Jed either couldn't or wouldn't pay to keep them.

None of this deterred him. The farm was sufficiently remote for the solitude he craved whilst providing a very real challenge. In due time he could visualise extending the farmhouse to make a comfortable home, and building a new boiling-up house and pigsties some distance away from his living quarters, along with utilising vacant fields for more grazing stock. There were plenty of gushing streams providing fresh water; he would see about bringing running water into the house and certainly digging a couple of wells on the property. But all that could wait for some time. Initially he could see he would have his work cut out just to get things shipshape.

By the time he left the farm with Wilbert a deal had been struck, and it had been agreed that he would take possession once the necessary paperwork and funds had changed hands, and certainly within the month. In the meantime he would find lodgings somewhere other than with Wilbert and his wife. He had no wish to place his friend in an awkward position with his father.

His head was whirling as he rode away, but for the first time since he had learned of Pearl's death, Christopher felt a glimmer of interest in life again. He didn't fool himself that the road he'd chosen was an easy one, but *he* had chosen it – and that made all the difference. Here, in this remote piece of Northumberland, he might find peace.

PART FIVE

Wartime

July 1914

Chapter 21

After many months when the European arms race had continually fuelled fears of war, events suddenly unfolded with bewildering speed during the July of 1914. By the end of the month it was clear that British ministers' efforts to avert the catastrophe of war in Europe had failed. As Britons returned from the annual Bank Holiday, Germany invaded Belgium. Britain's declaration of war against Germany sent cheering crowds surging through London to gather in huge numbers in Downing Street and outside Buckingham Palace, singing the National Anthem. Young men in their thousands crowded into the recruiting offices, volunteering to cross the Channel and put an end to what that maniac, the Kaiser, was doing to the poor Belgians.

The men of the British Expeditionary Force were hailed as the heroes who were going to finish the war by Christmas, and patriotism was at fever pitch. However, by the end of August, after a bitter struggle for the town of Mons which resulted in a bloodbath, what was left of the British forces had pulled back. In under a month the Germans had swept over most of Belgium, crossing the Sambre and Meuse rivers and forcing a French retreat to the Somme, the last barrier before Paris.

In September, Prime Minister Herbert Asquith called for another

500,000 men to sign up for the Army, and in October trench warfare began. By November a continuous line of trenches full of weary soldiers stretched from the North Sea to Switzerland, and December saw nearly 600,000 Allied prisoners in German hands. No one talked of the war being over quickly any more.

Pearl had been beside herself when war was declared, for the simple reason she was terrified that James and Patrick would enlist. Although recruits to the Army had to be at least eighteen, determined young men all over the UK were lying about their age and finding a way to fight for their country. James was sixteen now and Patrick fifteen, and boys of that age were particularly idealistic. When young Jimmy Hogarth two doors down, who was the same age as Patrick, joined the Royal Marines one day and was away the next, Pearl sat her brothers down and made them promise they wouldn't do anything rash. She needed them, she insisted. She and Nessie couldn't run the business on their own.

The last five years had been good ones, and the business had grown swiftly. The house next door had become vacant twelve months after they'd moved into Zion Street, and Pearl had remortgaged and bought the property. This had enabled her to extend both the shop and kitchen facilities, and their living quarters. She'd had the extra space upstairs converted to a kitchen-cum-dining room – thus making the flat independent of the shop – and added another bedroom. Once the alterations were complete, Nessie had left her lodgings and moved into the new bedroom, and the arrangement had worked very well. Not only did the two get on like a house on fire, but for the first time in her life Pearl had a friend to share any problems with, and in that regard Nessie was a tonic. Nothing seemed to get her down.

Once the lads were working in the shop Pearl's workload had lessened for a while, but the popularity of Croft & Bros. proved to be something of a double-edged sword. The success of the business meant Pearl was able to pay off the mortgage completely just before war was declared, but the shop was also a hard taskmaster. Not that she was complaining. The business meant the boys' home was secure, along with their future.

James in particular had a flair for cooking, and she had introduced him to all her secret recipes and tricks she'd learned whilst with the Romanies. She found she only had to show him something once and he remembered it perfectly. Patrick, on the other hand, burned everything he touched and couldn't get the hang of the simplest dish, but was great with the customers and had a gift with figures which meant she was beginning to teach him how to keep the accounts and so on.

For a short while life ticked on as usual, despite the news in the papers. There was great elation in January when British warships scotched a German plan to bombard East Coast towns and sunk the most powerful battlecruiser in the world, the *Blücher* – then outrage in February when German submarines began a blockade of the British Isles in a strategic gamble aimed at destroying the UK economy. Posters of Kitchener, his right arm stretched out and his forefinger pointing, were everywhere, stating *Britons (Kitchener) Wants You.* The bottom of the poster carried the message: *Join your country's Army! God save the King.*

But now the telegrams were starting to arrive, headed *On His Majesty's Service.* But it was after Yprès, and then Gallipoli, when British soldiers were caught on barbed wire on the beaches as they tried to land, and were mown down by enemy fire, that an ugly phenomenon really took hold. Women, angered that their loved ones were being slaughtered in their thousands, couldn't bear to see one able-bodied man walking the streets in a civilian suit. White feathers were thrust into male hands or tucked in jacket pockets or lapels, or sent through the post. It didn't seem to matter that the individual in question might be in a reserved occupation or genuinely exempt on medical grounds. Normally gentle and reasonable women targeted other women's husbands and sons and brothers with a cruelty that would have been unthinkable before the war began.

Whether it was the mood of the country's women or the fact that several of his peers had lied about their age and gone away to fight, Pearl wasn't sure, but at the beginning of February 1916 – a month before the Military Service Act that called for all single men between the ages of eighteen and forty-one to enlist came into force – James came home one day and said he'd enlisted. He was five months away from his eighteenth birthday. When Patrick, loath to be parted from his brother, followed suit the next day, Pearl felt her world had come to an end. Patrick was only sixteen, eleven months younger than James, and furthermore he didn't look any older than the age he was, but with the call for recruits ever more urgent due to the ongoing slaughter on the battlefields, the war machine didn't look too closely at things it preferred to ignore. Or that was how many mothers felt anyway. With the Navy already legally taking lads of fifteen, many a big burly Recruiting Sergeant had the idea that what was good enough for the Navy was good enough for the Army.

The next day, the boys left for training camp. Pearl didn't know what she would have done without Nessie. It wasn't so much the lads' work in the shop, although the two girls she hired weren't a patch on the boys, but the constant nagging worry once she knew they'd actually left for the front that had her beside herself. But with Nessie's help she finally accepted what she couldn't change. By May, when a brilliantly sunny day marked the start of the Government's new 'daylight saving time', and clocks throughout Britain were put forward by an hour to make the most of work output in long, lighter evenings, Pearl was able to sleep properly again most nights. The boys wrote to her when they could, cheerful letters which made light of their circumstances. This changed after the beginning of July. The carnage which began as the Somme campaign opened resulted in 19,000 men dying in one day, mown down by German fire, and over double that number maimed, blinded or crippled. Old Generals – elderly and unimaginative professionals from the peacetime Army – refused to contemplate the problems of trench warfare, and the result was a massacre. The slaughter was prolonged for weeks, then for months. It only came to a halt in November when it foundered in mud and both sides dug in for the winter, the zest and idealism with which nearly three million Englishmen had marched forth to war gone for ever.

Pearl received fewer letters now and their tone was heavy even though both her brothers tried to keep the horrors from her. But she read the papers. She knew the troops were choked with mud and dulled by death and tested to the limit of their endurance. But as long as the letters kept on coming, they were alive. It was a telegram she dreaded.

She and Nessie prepared for a quiet Christmas. Amazingly, with the price of a loaf at record levels of tenpence, and food costs soaring, Pearl found she was busier than ever. Or perhaps it wasn't so surprising. For the first time in England's history, over three million women were employed outside the home in war work and earning a wage of their own. Pearl's policy of keeping her prices down and providing tasty, filling food meant weary wives and mothers, exhausted after a day in the armament factories or delivering sacks of coal or any of the other hundreds of jobs women were doing with no menfolk available, could bring their families to eat cheap good food without having to cook it themselves.

Pearl's bank balance, already extremely healthy, rose sharply, and even when she decided to employ a third girl, her profits continued to increase.

As Christmas Eve fell on a Sunday Pearl had decided to close the shop for three days, re-opening on the Wednesday. It was the first time since she had started the business that she'd had three days off in a row and she knew she needed it. She was exhausted, in body, soul and spirit. And then, on the Friday before Christmas, she received a telegram. It was Nessie, all the colour drained from her face, who brought it through to the kitchen where Pearl was up to her eyes in dough. Pearl took it without a word, terror making her ears ring. 'I said I was you,' Nessie said shakily. 'I didn't want him to frighten you.'

Frighten her? Pearl stared at her friend. She felt sick, physically sick. Her fingers seemed to work independently of her mind because she watched them opening the telegram as though they belonged to someone else. For a moment everything was blurred and then her vision cleared. She read the printed words once and then twice before sitting down on one of the hardbacked chairs as her legs gave way. 'It's Seth,' she said numbly. 'My eldest brother. He's – he's hurt, dying. He's named me as next-of-kin. I – I have to go to him.'

Hilda and Martha, who had been helping Pearl in the kitchen, stared at their employer in surprise. They hadn't known she had any other family but James and Patrick. Nessie took control. Taking the telegram from Pearl's frozen fingers she read it swiftly. 'The hospital's in Gateshead,' she said briskly. 'One of them grand houses that's been converted since the war by the sound of it, Wynford Hall. Still, that's a lot better than him being somewhere down South. We can have you there in no time, lass. You go an' freshen yourself up and I'll get a cab, all right? We can manage here.'

'I – I have to go.'

'Course you have to go, he's your brother.' Seeing that Pearl was incapable for the moment, Nessie nodded at Hilda. 'Run and get a cab, an' you –' she looked at Martha '– make a strong cup of black coffee. Not tea, coffee. An' bring it up when it's ready.' Taking Pearl's arm she raised her to her feet and it was like that, Nessie leading her friend as though she was an old, old woman, that they left the two open-mouthed girls.

Pearl was ready when the cab came ten minutes later. Nessie had offered to go with her, but she had told her friend she needed her to stay and look after the shop. This was true, but the main reason was that she wanted to see Seth by herself. If he was dying – her heart stopped at the thought and then jerked into life so violently she put a hand to her chest – if he was dying she wanted to stay as long as he needed her, without worrying that she was putting anyone else out.

Seth, Seth . . . All the way to Gateshead his name reverberated in her head. He was a soldier. The telegram had said he'd been injured in battle. He had gone away to fight and he hadn't told her, hadn't come to see her . . .

Nessie was right, Wynford Hall was a grand old house set in extensive grounds on the outskirts of Gateshead. When the cab deposited Pearl at the foot of several semi-circular steps which led to magnificent oak doors, the building in front of her seemed vast. Once inside, a reception area with a number of comfortable-looking armchairs dotted around small tables confronted her. She made her way over to a desk, behind which sat a young woman who smiled at her as she approached. 'Can I help you?'

'I had a telegram this morning.' Pearl fetched it from her bag. 'My brother's here. I – I've come to see him.'

'It's not visiting hours.' The woman's words could have appeared officious but her tone was sympathetic. 'Do you have an appointment?'

Pearl shook her head. 'It says he wants to see me and he's very ill. I thought . . .'

The woman nodded. 'Sit down for a minute and I'll see what I can do.'

Ten minutes later, a young nurse came and escorted her to Matron Gordon's living quarters which Pearl suspected had once been a reception room. The Matron was sitting at a desk as Pearl entered, but rose and shook her hand before asking her to be seated. 'You are here to see your brother, is that right? Corporal Croft?'

Pearl nodded. She had read that Seth was a Corporal, but only now did it really register. 'I had a telegram.'

'I know. I arranged for it to be sent.' The Matron paused. 'You understand your brother is very ill, Miss Croft? He was hit by shrapnel which caused considerable internal damage and necessitated three operations. However –' again the woman paused – 'it's more the fact that he has no interest in getting better that worries me. In cases like his, the mind really can make the difference between life and death. He seems very troubled.' She flapped her hand. 'Of course all the men are troubled, why wouldn't they be after what they've been through? But somehow I feel it's different with your brother. Anyway, he told me he wanted to see you and I promised I'd contact you and here you are.'

'Yes, here I am.'

The Matron looked at her, a penetrating look. 'I don't know why your brother hasn't asked for you before in the two months he has been with us, but I don't have to know. All I would say to you is that he is something of a hero. I don't know if you're aware of this?'

'No. No, I wasn't.'

'He was mentioned in dispatches, I understand. Got several of his men who had been injured to safety whilst under enemy fire. Went back four times. The fifth was when he himself was injured.' The Matron paused. 'Whatever the family situation is, you can be proud of him.'

Pearl stared back into the discerning eyes. 'I've always been proud of him,' she said simply.

For the first time since Pearl had entered the room, Matron Gordon smiled. 'Good.' She rose to her feet. 'If you would like to follow me, I'll take you to see him.'

The patients' dormitories were all on the first floor, the Matron explained as she led Pearl into the hall and up the wide curving staircase. It wasn't an ideal situation, not with some of the men having been blinded or crippled, but in these times they had to make the best of things, didn't they?

Yes, Pearl replied, they did.

And of course these facilities doubled as a convalescent home once the patients were feeling better, and with the grounds as they were, this was a huge bonus. There were several acres for the men to walk or sit in, and a couple of the local carpenters had made over two dozen benches and tables free of charge for them. That was kind of them, wasn't it?

Yes, Pearl replied numbly. It was very kind.

A nurse – bright, brisk, young – had told Seth ten minutes ago that he was going to have a visitor. His sister. She was talking with the Matron at the moment, but she'd be along shortly so they were just going to make him nice and fresh for when she came.

He had submitted to the girl's ministrations without protest. He usually did. They had a job to do, after all, and they did it very well. It was thanks to Nurse Hardy and the rest of them that he was still here, he supposed, because if it had been left to him to eat, to physically put the food in his mouth, he wouldn't have bothered. But they'd fed him initially and then bullied and cajoled him to eat while they stood over him. But he was growing weaker. He knew this and he welcomed it. But with the knowledge had come the need to see Pearl one last time and explain. Just to explain.

He was looking at the door when Pearl and the Matron walked into the ward, and in the moment before her eyes found him he saw what a fine-looking young woman she had matured into. Of course, she had always been bonny, even as a little bairn, but now there was an air of . . . what? he asked himself. Something which had been missing the last time he'd seen her eight years ago. And then it came to him. Self-possession. The way she held herself, the tilt to her head – that was it, self-possession.

And then she was in front of him, her great blue eyes glittering with unshed tears and her arms outstretched. She took his hands, which had been resting on the starched counterpane as she bent over him, her lips brushing his cheek as she whispered, 'Seth, oh, Seth, I've prayed for this day, prayed that I'd see you again. Why didn't you let me know you were here before?'

He didn't answer this. 'Thank you for coming.' His words were low and husky.

'You don't have to thank me – of course I came! You're my brother.'

Matron Gordon cleared her throat. Speaking to Seth, she said, 'I've explained I don't want you tired, Mr Croft, so your sister will only stay a short while on this occasion. Fifteen minutes, all right?' Nodding at them both, she departed in a rustle of starched linen.

Pearl released his hands to sit down, but then she took the one nearer her and held it tightly between her own. 'How are you?' she said softly. 'Are you in much pain?'

Again he didn't answer this. 'I – I wanted to talk to you.' He carefully adjusted his position in the bed, but even then the knife-like pain speared one side of his abdomen. The other five occupants of the ward were asleep – or lying with their eyes closed, at least – it being the time for their afternoon nap. He knew he was lucky compared to them. Foster had lost both legs, and Davidson and

Bainsby an arm and leg each. Shaw was so badly burned his wife had fainted when she'd first seen him, and as for Alridge . . . He didn't like to think what Alridge's life would be like if he lived. How could a man exist as a torso and little else?

'Please don't tire yourself, you heard what the Matron said.'

'Pearl, I have to explain. I have to tell you about Fred and Walter.' He swallowed. 'They – they're gone, both of them. We joined up together in the first week of the war and Fred bought it as soon as we were shipped to the front. Walt went the first day of the Somme. It was quick for both of them – and believe me, that's something to be thankful for.'

She said nothing but clutched his hand tighter, her face white and strained.

'They paid their dues to their country, Pearl. We all have. If there's any justice in the hereafter, that'll count for something. Whatever anyone says, they were good lads at bottom.' He shut his eyes for a moment, trying to regulate his breathing so he could carry on. He had to say it all. There wasn't much time. He gazed into her face, his voice coming in gasps when he muttered, 'We knew what you'd done, the shop and all, and – and we were as pleased as Punch. Our baby sister running her own business – and not just running it, expanding and all sorts. An' the lads, James and Patrick. You've done 'em proud, lass.'

'Not me.' Tears were rolling down Pearl's face now, she couldn't help it. 'It's all thanks to you and Fred and Walter, all of it. I was at my wit's end that day you found us, and suddenly you turned everything round.'

Seth smiled. 'You turned it round with the shop. By, the number of times I had to bite my tongue when someone or other was saying what a grand little place it was. Croft and Brothers. We liked that.'

'Why did you bite your tongue? You should have told them I was your sister.'

'Nay, lass. I'd never have done that to you.'

'What do you mean, done that to me? Seth, I love you. Can't you understand? You're part of me and the lads, our flesh and blood.' She stared into the rough, coarse-grained face that bore little resemblance to the brother she'd known as a child. He looked tired and terribly ill, his big frame reduced to nothing but skin and bone.

She looked down at his hand in hers, the big knuckles and crooked little finger which had never healed properly after their father had deliberately broken it one day when Seth had tried to stop him hitting her. She had been only five years old at the time, but she remembered it distinctly. Their father had broken only the one finger on Seth's left hand because that meant he could still work for McArthur the next day as usual. Speaking softly, she said, 'From when I can remember you've been there for me, Seth – for us all. Trying to do your best and looking after us. I'm proud to be your sister.'

'You wouldn't say that if you knew the things I'd done.'

'I don't care what you've done. Anyway, that's all in the past now. You said yourself you've paid your dues.'

'I said Fred and Walter had.'

'It's the same thing. And I repeat, I don't care what you've done. I love you. I want you to get better. Please, Seth, I can't bear to lose you a third time. There's room at home, you could come and live with us until you're feeling better.'

'I won't get better, lass.'

'Not if you don't try – no, you won't.'

Seth moved his other hand over hers. 'Look, lass—'

'No. *You* look.' It probably wasn't the way to talk to a desperately ill man, but Pearl had heard the resignation in his voice and the words the Matron had said were fresh in her mind. *No interest in getting better. The mind can make the difference between life and death.* 'All your life you've been a fighter, so why are you taking the coward's way out now? I don't want to hear a nice little speech about you being proud of me, I want you to be part of my life. I need you. The lads need you. I don't know how they'll be when they come back from all this, but I do know they'll need you to help them make sense of it all. You'll need each other.'

'I couldn't take care of Fred and Walter. What makes you think I can do any better with James and Patrick?'

'Oh, Seth.' His face had undergone a change, and for a brief moment she had seen the pain he was trying to conceal.

'I miss them, Pearl. They followed me into war like they followed me in everything else. If I hadn't said I was going to enlist, they wouldn't have. I killed them.'

'No, you didn't! They were grown men with minds of their own, you know that at heart. And when you were lads you could have no more stopped Da putting them with McArthur than stopped him doing the same to you. Like you said, you all felt you were paying your dues for the past.'

'In – in my dreams they call out to me to save them, but I can't. I hear them. All the time in my head I hear them.'

'That will get better. I promise you, it will. And like you said, they both died quickly. Maybe if you'd waited until you were all conscripted they might have had painful lingering deaths.' Her fingers tightened on his. 'The thing is, Seth, it was their time to go. It's not yours. I know Matron Gordon thinks you can pull through if you try, and so do I.'

He shook his head on the pillow. 'Pearl, I know you mean well, but—'

'No buts.' She bent and kissed his brow. 'Please, Seth, no buts. I know you can get over this if you want to, and I need you. *We* need you. I know that sounds selfish, but that's how I feel. What – what if the lads don't come back . . .'

Seth interrupted her brusquely. 'Don't say that. Don't even think it.'

'I can't help it.' She made a small motion with her head. 'I think it all the time under the surface. I'll be all on my own then and I can't bear the thought of that.'

'Don't upset yourself. Now come on, wipe your eyes. James and Patrick will come home, I feel it in my bones.'

'Whether they do or don't, I want you too.' They stared deeply at each other again. 'Will you try, Seth? For me. Will you?'

He moved restlessly. 'Pearl . . .'

'Promise me.' The time was nearly gone and now her voice was urgent. 'Promise me, Seth. I know if you do you'll keep your word.'

Seth's lips moved in a wry twist of a smile. 'Your faith in me is humbling,' he said with a touch of mockery.

Pearl wouldn't be deflected. 'Promise me.'

He had wanted her to come today so he could clear his conscience, he had wanted her to be soft, sympathetic – accepting of his imminent demise. He was tired, so tired, and the thought of slipping away into a place where he didn't have to think any more, where he was responsible for no one, where there were no demands on him, was sweet. Some of the men here feared death, but it was life he feared – Pearl was right about that. He should have known she'd react as she had. She had called him a fighter and maybe she was right, but Pearl was the same. Fred and Walter hadn't had that in them – he didn't know about James and Patrick, they were virtual strangers – but he and Pearl were cut from the same cloth.

The thoughts whirled in his head. And she was right about something else, too: if he made her a promise he would strive to keep it. She knew him too well.

'Lass, you don't know what you're asking. The thoughts in my head, the things I've seen . . .' He shut his eyes. When he opened them again, the azure-blue gaze was still hard on him.

'Promise me,' she repeated.

Seth sighed deeply. How could he explain that he didn't want to live with himself any more, with the man he'd become? He had faced himself long before the war and he hadn't liked what he had seen. He liked it still less now.

For the fifth time, Pearl said, *'Promise me.'*

'All right. I promise.'

It was over two months before Pearl brought Seth home, but at the beginning of March she was finally able to get him installed in what had been her bedroom above the shop. Although the lads' room was empty she had wanted Seth to have his own room, besides which – and she couldn't explain this logically – she felt that if James and Patrick's room was waiting for them, they would come home to it one day. They'd moved her bed and wardrobe into the room she now shared with Nessie; her writing desk she'd fitted into a corner of the sitting room. Seth's room boasted a new bed and wardrobe, a big easy armchair and small table, and a bookcase.

Pearl tried to make the journey from the hospital as easy for Seth as she could, but by the time he'd climbed the stairs to the flat it was clear he needed to go straight to bed. When she opened the door to his room, Seth stood for a moment staring around him. A fire crackled in the grate, a large bowl of fruit stood on top of the bookcase, and the easy chair was close to the fire with a thick rug for his feet. Pearl had sewn new curtains and a matching bedspread in a cheerful red and cream material which was bright and warm but still distinctly masculine in appeal, and she'd covered two plump flock cushions for the chair in the same cloth. A pile of magazines reposed on top of the table, along with twelve ounces of the tobacco Pearl had noticed Seth smoke in the hospital, and a new pipe. On the long shelf underneath, two bottles of the finest brandy and malt whisky and several glasses nestled on a silver tray.

Seth was a big man, at least he would have been if there was any flesh on his bones. Propped against his pillows in the hospital or sitting in his chair he had appeared thin; now, with his clothes hanging on him, he was skeletal. But it was the look on the gaunt face as he turned to her that caused Pearl to swallow hard. 'You've done all this for me?'

In an endeavour not to burst into tears she kept her voice light. 'Well, I don't know anyone else who smokes that particular brand of tobacco.'

'It's grand, lass.'

'If the books aren't to your taste you'll have to blame Nessie. She was in charge of choosing them. She's tried to pick a mixture— Oh, don't. Don't, Seth. It's all right.'

As the tears began to rain down his face she guided him to the bed, not knowing what to do as he began to rock himself almost like a baby. It was Nessie who took charge. Coming to the door, she took in the situation at a glance.

'Go and make a pot of tea, lass,' she said to Pearl, sitting down on the other side of Seth and drawing him into her arms as a mother would a child. 'This is the best thing that could have happened – he needs to cry it out. There, there, lad.' She was patting Seth's back as he buried his head in her ample chest, her voice soft. 'Get it all out, that's right. It'll do you the world of good. I know, I've been there.'

Pearl was at a loss. She'd never known Seth to cry, not even as a child when their father had leathered him with his belt until the buckle had ripped his skin and the blood had run. He was strong, Seth. Rock-like. He had had the odd quiet day, of course. Days when she'd barely been able to get anything out of him when she'd sat in the ward, and once or twice when she had arrived at the hospital unexpectedly, he'd been staring into space with a frightening look on his face. But this. This was something else.

She took her time making the tea. When she carried the tray to the bedroom door it was to see Seth fast asleep on top of the bed just as he was with his coat still on, and Nessie carefully pulling the boots off his feet.

Nessie gestured for Pearl to leave and followed her out, closing the door quietly behind her. 'He's fair exhausted, poor lad.' Nessie shook her head as they sat down in the sitting room. Pearl poured them a cup of tea each as her friend continued, 'But now he's started to let it out, it's a good sign, lass. Take it from me. If you keep stuff in it takes over, like a poison.'

Pearl supposed Nessie was right. No, of course she was right, there was no question, she told herself, but it had shaken her more than she'd imagined, to see Seth's grief and pain. Putting down her cup and saucer, she said, 'Do you think I've bitten off more than I can chew having him here, Nessie? At the hospital there were doctors who knew about this sort of thing.'

'Lass, he's where he should be, in my opinion. And we'll see it through together, so don't fret. Them doctors don't know everything by a long chalk. But I'd better get meself downstairs and see what's what. Them girls are willing enough but there's times I think the Good Lord gave more up top to the milkman's horse than them three, bless 'em.' Nessie swallowed her tea, scalding hot though it was, and stood up, patting Pearl's shoulder. 'Put your feet up for a bit, lass, and don't fret. It'll all come out in the wash and old Meg's backside with it.'

As Nessie bustled off, Pearl stared after her. Dear Nessie. What would she do without her? And she had been so good with Seth. If only James and Patrick could survive the war unscathed, she would never ask God for another thing in her life. Unscathed. She tutted inwardly at herself. Of course they would have to bear mental scars after all they would have seen and done, but – she shut her eyes tightly, her stomach churning – if they could come home whole physically. Some of those poor men at the hospital . . .

Dear Lord, please help Seth get better. Immediately she'd said the prayer she berated herself. One moment she was promising God she'd never ask Him for another thing if He'd watch over James and Patrick, and the next she was already making more requests. But that shell of a man in there wasn't her Seth. Pearl bit down hard on her bottom lip. Her brother needed restoring, in body, soul and spirit – and she didn't have a clue how to do it.

Chapter 22

Most of the older folk were saying the world had officially gone mad. How else could you justify bit lasses in the armament factories earning two pounds and ten shillings a week – more than four times the wage of a trained parlourmaid? And now women no longer felt they needed male company if they wished to eat out; business girls dined alone or with each other, and housewives whose husbands were in the forces went in pairs to the pub or the pictures. Skirts were shorter, respectable women had taken to wearing make-up and smoking cigarettes in public – what sort of world was it going to be when the war was over?

For those women living with the daily fear of the black-edged telegrams, the problems of the future seemed trivial. Men were dying in unbelievable numbers, and America entering the war in the spring of 1917 hadn't seemed to make much difference. The carnage went on and the telegrams still came. In the summer, as the third battle of Yprès unfolded to the accompaniment of cease-less bombardments and remorseless rainstorms, it was hard to say which was feared most – the German machine-gunner or the Flanders mud.

James and Patrick wrote home that the fields around Passchendaele Ridge had been turned into quagmires. Men who had survived the relentless gunfire were being sucked to their deaths when they slipped from the duckboards. Stretcher-bearers, up to their thighs in mud, were having to be rescued themselves.

It seemed impossible to Pearl that her brothers could survive such conditions, and yet equally impossible that she would never see them again. It couldn't − it mustn't − happen, she told herself, and every time she looked at Seth and the progress he was making, she took hope.

The hearty, rosy-cheeked doctor who had spoken to her at some length before she had taken Seth home, had been at pains to explain that her brother would never be completely fit again. But, he'd added, with plenty of good home cooking and commonsense, there was no reason why Mr Croft shouldn't live to a ripe old age. If Pearl could see the doctor now, she'd add, 'And Nessie Ramshaw.'

From that first day ten months ago when she'd brought her brother home, Nessie had instinctively seemed to know how to deal with him. That Seth was a damaged and complex individual was in no doubt and, impaired though his body was, it was his mind that was the real battleground. But Nessie wouldn't let him brood. She'd breeze in on him when he was in one of his dark moods, talking to him at length, making him laugh, even teasing him on occasion. Other times they would talk for hours about the things he had seen and done in the war. At least, Pearl had thought it was only about that until recently, but then a casual remark Nessie had let drop had revealed that Seth had confided details about his murky life before the war too.

Pearl had been slightly hurt at first. Seth never talked with her like he did Nessie. But Nessie, sensing this, had been quick to re-assure her. 'You're almost too close to it all, lass,' she'd said softly, 'and he values your high opinion of him more than he could express. Now you and I know that'd never change whatever he told you, but he doesn't understand that, being a man.' She'd grimaced, making Pearl smile. 'But this is like a cleansing for him, I think. He needs to bring it all out into the light. Mind, I never imagined I'd ever be placed in the position of a Mother Superior.'

Now Pearl laughed out loud. Anyone less like the head of a

female religious order than Nessie Ramshaw was hard to imagine. But she was good for Seth.

By the summer Seth was feeling stronger and he began to help Nessie for an hour or two in the front of the shop. This proved so successful that when the girl who worked for Nessie left in the autumn, having been enticed away by the three pounds a week she could earn in the local munitions factory on the night-shift, Seth declared himself well enough to work full-time. Certainly a man's presence, especially one as big as Seth, was a curb on the more unruly element who sometimes came in late on a Friday or Saturday night after drinking in the pub. Being an ex-serviceman who had been invalided out of the Army, Seth was treated with respect by even the roughest of their customers.

So it was with a much more settled heart about her brother that Pearl prepared for the fourth Christmas of the war. James and Patrick had written to say that entertainers, from opera singers to jugglers, were now putting on shows regularly along the front to boost the spirits of the British 'tommies'. The one they'd been to the night before near Vérey had included light opera, a Scottish comedian, a Charlie Chaplin impressionist and a trick cyclist – along, of course, with a singalong. The letter was received with mixed feelings by Pearl. She was glad her brothers felt they hadn't been forgotten by the world in general, but the thought of popular songs such as 'Pack Up Your Troubles in Your Old Kit Bag' and 'If You Were the Only Girl in the World' being roared out by men who knew they could all be blown to bits the next day was very poignant.

On Christmas Eve, the night of hope, she prayed fervently for her baby brothers once she was in bed, and with her defences low she couldn't keep the usual guard on her mind regarding Christopher either. She didn't know if he was alive or dead, lost on some foreign field where so many had fallen, but when she closed her eyes she could picture him as he had been. Whole, handsome, hers. It was a long time before she slept.

On Christmas Day they lifted their spoons to James and Patrick when they ate their Christmas pudding. The War Office had supplied British troops in France with Christmas puddings, and Pearl hoped the day was another brief respite from the carnage for her brothers. Outside the house, a fresh fall of snow was adding to the inches packed hard on the ground, but inside was warmth and comfort – and the thought of loved ones so far away, fighting to preserve what they were enjoying now. It made for a sad, emotional day.

She and Nessie went to the evening service at the parish church, but Seth wouldn't accompany them. Pearl wasn't surprised at this. She knew Seth's views on a God who allowed the bloodbath and butchery of the war well enough now. He didn't force them on anyone, but if asked he didn't hold back either. She had listened to him and Nessie having long talks on a Sunday afternoon when they all took the chance to relax after dinner. She rarely joined in because Nessie's views were so similar to her own that she felt she didn't have to, besides which she enjoyed listening to the other two. They had some right set-tos.

'There'll be more and more folk thinking like I do when this lot's over,' Seth had said last Sunday afternoon.

'Then I pity them like I pity you,' Nessie had replied spiritedly. 'It wasn't God who made the guns and fired the bullets, Seth. It was men. Men started this war with their greed, and when it's over they'll still be greedy, that's the nature of the beast. If the world was run by women there'd be no wars, because what lass wants to send her da or husband or son into battle? Most women have more commonsense in their little fingers than men have in the whole of their bodies. There'll be some changes now women have won the right to vote, take it from me.'

'Oh aye, I thought we'd get back to this afore long.' Seth enjoyed teasing Nellie on this topic. 'But don't forget, it's only women over the age of thirty and it's not happened yet.'

'The Commons voted in June, so it'll be through next year – and we'll soon have it down to twenty-one, same as men,' Nessie declared passionately. 'Some countries have got women MPs already.'

'May this God you say is on your side help them, that's all I can say.'

'I don't say He's on the side of women any more than He is of men. I'm just saying you can't blame the wars and terrible things that go on, on God. He gave us free will to choose to do right or wrong, the Good Book tells us that.'

'And you believe it?'

'Aye. Aye, I do.'

Pearl remembered how Seth had suddenly leaned across to Nessie and patted her hand. 'Then go on believing, lass. I wouldn't want to take that away from you.'

'Don't worry, Seth Croft, you won't. It'd take a bigger and uglier bloke than you to do that.'

They had looked at each other for a moment and then burst out laughing.

Pearl glanced at Nessie now as they came out of the church. It had stopped snowing although the air was bitterly cold. 'I wish Seth had come with us,' she said quietly. 'It was a beautiful service and it might have given him some comfort.'

'He's got a long way to go before that day, lass, but we'll keep chipping away at him, eh?'

'It's you who does that, Nessie. He talks to you like he never talks to me, or anyone else for that matter.'

'Oh, I wouldn't say that.' Nessie was suddenly brisk, dismissive.

'He does,' Pearl insisted. 'I know he thinks the world of you. You're such a good friend to us both, Nessie.'

Nessie fiddled with her hat, a strange expression flitting over her round face. If Pearl hadn't known better she would have termed it sadness, but Nessie was never sad.

'Seth's a fine man,' Nessie said shortly. Then, her manner changing, she dug Pearl in the side with her elbow. 'Come on, get a move on. I know we had a bite before we came out, but me stomach's thinking my throat's been cut and that Christmas cake you made is calling.'

Pearl smiled back. 'Last one in the door makes the tea,' she said, tucking her arm in Nessie's, and slipping and sliding on the frozen ground, the two women made their way home.

* * *

Seth had been sitting in front of the fire while the women had been gone, his head bent and his big hands palm downwards on his knees. If someone hadn't looked too closely they would have supposed he was dozing, but they would have been wrong. Although his body was relaxed and still, his mind was very active – and it was dealing with the problem that had begun to assail it more and more in the last few weeks. *Nessie.*

A piece of coal slipped into the glowing cave beneath it, sending a momentary firework of sparks up the chimney before harmony was restored, the only sound now in the room the ticking of the clock on the mantelpiece.

What would she say if he told her how he felt? And then he immediately answered himself: she'd laugh her head off. Then, no – she wouldn't do that because she was kind; she was kindness itself, was Nessie. No, she wouldn't laugh at him but he would read the amusement in her face nonetheless. 'Eh, lad,' she'd likely say, 'I'm old enough to be your mother.' That was what one of the bairns had said the other day in the shop when Nessie had been pretending to rail at him for dropping a pie he'd been wrapping up for the child. 'Is she your mam then?'

But she wasn't old enough to be his mother, leastways not unless she'd had him when she was nowt but a bairn herself. There was eleven years' difference between them, that was all. *All!* He gave a 'Huh!' in his throat. And the stupid thing, the frustrating thing was if it had been the other way round, if he had been forty-two and she thirty-one, no one would have blinked an eye if they'd taken up together.

But all that was relative anyway, because he knew full well she would never look at him in that way. And who could blame her? He'd been in a bad way when he'd first come here – how bad he hadn't realised until that first night when he'd cried like a baby. He hadn't cried since he couldn't remember when, but once started he hadn't been able to stop, or so it had seemed.

A tide of red washed up his neck and flooded into his face as he squirmed in shame. Day after day he'd gone on, he couldn't remember half of it. And then had followed the need to talk. He'd told her things about the years before he joined up that could send him down the line if she opened her mouth – not that she would, he knew that. And then he'd started on about the war, about Fred and Walt, the slaughter that had gone on, the constant deafening blast of artillery and the screams and groans of the dying and injured. The way men had turned into dumb killing machines, with vacant eyes and loose mouths. And the mud. Oh yes, most of all the mud . . .

She must think him a weak-kneed nowt. His head jerked as though he was attempting to toss the thought aside. And she was right, he was. For years he'd played the big fellow – it had been the way he'd survived – but he was the big fellow no more, certainly not in Nessie's eyes.

Rising abruptly to his feet he left the sitting room and walked through to his bedroom where he had left his pipe. After lighting it he poured himself a large glass of brandy and then walked back into the sitting room.

Deep down, Nessie must think him an excuse for a man but because she was kind she didn't condemn him as many would have. But she pitied him, which was worse. He'd seen a look on her face sometimes when she glanced at him. *Damn it.* He stared into the fire again. But he owed it to Pearl to stay and help with the shop, labour being scarce, at least until James and Patrick came home. And then he bit his lip. Who was he kidding? If Pearl had girls queueing at the door for a job, he'd still stay – because Nessie had become as necessary to him as breathing. It was as simple as that.

Chapter 23

As the carriage wheels bumped over yet another deep rut in the lane they were travelling along, Clarissa Armstrong glared at her husband. 'I'm going to be black and blue at the end of this. You should have summoned Christopher to the house as I told you to.'

'You know as well as I do that he wouldn't come. I tried, damn it.'

'You should have *made* him come.'

'For crying out loud, woman, talk sense! If three visits by Parker wouldn't persuade him, what would? You tell me that. Do you think I want to travel to the back of beyond?' He almost added, 'With you,' but he was too weary of her perpetual harping to provoke a scene. He'd cursed Christopher every inch of this hellish journey himself, but silently. He hadn't felt at all well for the last few months and the pains in his body were getting worse, not better, in spite of the pills and potions the doctor had prescribed. Damn quack, he was. Tension and worry, he'd said, and put in a bill for two pounds ten shillings.

Oswald snorted to himself. Was it any wonder he was worried? He didn't know if he was on foot or horseback half the time these days. The war had played havoc with his business dealings but his home life had been worse hit. The damn Government, insisting that servants needed to be given their marching orders so as to release them for what was called 'more useful purposes'! This had decimated his staff. He hadn't long bought a motor car and employed a chauffeur, but the latter had skedaddled and joined up. With Clarissa bleating in his ear that all their friends travelled by car he'd tried driving the thing himself and crashed it into a tree. After that, they'd reverted to the carriage and horses, and his wife hadn't stopped complaining ever since.

They had only halved their staff, which was nothing compared to others he could name. The Steffords were left with only their housekeeper, cook and one maid, and had shut up part of their home for the war effort, but when he'd suggested doing the same, Clarissa had bitten his head off. Kate Stefford had thrown herself into this and that, organising food and clothing parcels for the troops and heading umpteen committees, but to his knowledge Clarissa hadn't lifted a finger.

But it was the death of Nathaniel that had hit him the hardest. He hadn't expected to miss him so much, hadn't realised how much he'd relied on him. He'd been proud of him in his officer's uniform, of course, proud that his son had been willing to fight for his country and hadn't waited until he'd been conscripted like many he could mention, but when they'd received the telegram . . . Now they were going to see this one who wasn't worthy to lick his brother's boots. It was true what they said: the devil looked after his own.

Clarissa was holding a handkerchief scented with cologne to her nostrils as though they were travelling through a Newcastle slum area rather than the fresh countryside. It was one of many of her 'genteel' habits which drove him to drink. 'You didn't have to come,' he said irritably. 'I told you I could handle this on my own.'

'I don't think so.' Clarissa's voice was cutting. 'You have an unfortunate penchant of alienating even the most reasonable of men, and Christopher is not reasonable. You will lose your temper if I'm not there to check you, and then we'll be worse off than we are already.'

'I don't know why the hell we're going to him cap in hand anyway. It should be him grovelling to us.'

'No one is "grovelling", Oswald, but this attitude is just the sort of thing I was talking about. You're bent on confrontation and you should have learned by now that Christopher does not respond to your bully-boy methods. You could employ them with Nathaniel – he was a different kettle of fish.'

How she could talk so calmly and coldly about her own child he didn't know. Oswald rubbed his perspiring face with his hand. The April day was unseasonably warm. She was an unnatural woman. He had found her lack of emotion chilling even before they married, but since they had heard about Nathaniel this flaw in Clarissa's nature had got worse. Or perhaps he was just noticing it more? Whatever, he would have given the world once or twice for her to feel as he was feeling about their son. It would have been bad enough if Nathaniel had died quickly, blown to smithereens in a moment like so many were, but to know he had died slowly of blood poisoning from the wounds he'd received made his stomach heave if he thought about it. His voice harsh, he said, 'Leave Nathaniel out of this.'

'Don't be so stupid. The only reason we're making this journey is because Nathaniel has gone. You know it, I know it – and Christopher knows it.'

'I didn't want to make it, if you remember.'

'Oh, I remember, Oswald. I remember very clearly what you said to me. But, unlike you, I want the estate to pass to our own flesh and blood, perverse though Christopher is.'

Oswald ground his teeth together. 'Don't make me lose my temper, Clarissa. You know I want that too but like I said, Christopher won't look a gift horse in the mouth. He might be a fool where the women are concerned, but he'll fall in line. No one turns their back on an inheritance like he'll come into when we're gone.'

'Really? If that is so, why, pray, didn't he come when you sent Parker, not once but three times? You underestimate him, Oswald. You have always underestimated him.'

'Is that so? Whereas you've always handled him perfectly?'

'Don't raise your voice to me. I'm not one of your employees or a common wench you've set up in a house for your pleasure.'

Oswald shot a glance at her. Did she know about Peggy? No, it wasn't possible – *was it?* Surely she would have said something before this. No, she'd been talking generally, of course she had. Nevertheless he moderated his voice when he said, 'You were with me on the gypsy chit, you know you were.'

'Of course I was, we're not disputing that. But one of your weaknesses is that you always suppose people come down to your level, Oswald. I'm sure it would come as a surprise to learn that not everyone is motivated by greed or power or . . . lust. I consider Christopher unworthy in every respect, but I understand him enough to know that he has a peculiar code all of his own. He associates with the riff-raff of society as naturally as his own class, he has no sense of decorum in that respect. He may be an embarrassment and a disgrace but he is the only son we have now, and I won't have you jeopardising his return to his rightful place in society.'

The way she had said lust, she *did* know about Peggy. Oswald stared at his wife but Clarissa was looking out of the window, the handkerchief in place once more. Not that she could take him to task on the matter. Once Christopher had been born, Clarissa had informed him that her duty had been fulfilled. He was free to have 'diversions' as long as he was discreet. Her bedroom door had been firmly closed after that, and the once he had dared to try to resume intimate relations, she had frozen him out of the bedroom. And he had been discreet. He still was discreet, but Peggy was the first woman he had actually set up in her own place. It had either been that or lose her, as Peggy herself had made very plain, and he'd discovered he needed her. He might be getting old but Peggy suited him and he'd found he didn't want the bother of seeing to his needs elsewhere. Peggy was earthy and bawdy and she enjoyed a bit of rough stuff on occasion, but she could be kind too. She'd held him when he'd cried about Nathaniel and she hadn't thought any the less of him afterwards. Or if she had, she hadn't shown it, which was all he asked.

'Is this the place?' Clarissa's voice was one of horror as she peered more closely out of the window. Oswald leaned across to see. Parker had told them they had to follow the rough stone road which Mr Christopher had had laid a couple of years back for the last part of the journey, and it would bring them to the farm. 'It can't be, can it? It's . . .' Words failed her.

Oswald wasn't so surprised. He had asked his butler what Mr Christopher's farm was like, and Parker had been frank. The nearer they got to the farm the more he agreed with his butler. 'Not a patch on the estate farm, sir.' Mind, at least you could get to the place without travelling across fields and rough ground. Apparently, according to Parker, that hadn't been the case when Christopher had taken the place on. And the fields filled with grazing cattle and sheep and lambs he could see now through the carriage window had been practically bare of livestock.

The carriage trundled down the bumpy road and into the farm-yard itself eventually. The coachman jumped down and helped them alight, his face impassive when Oswald ordered him to resume his seat and wait. The servant grapevine had been active, and what Parker had related in confidence to the housekeeper had winged its way down to what was left of the rest of the servants. Personally he thought the place was a whole lot better than Mr Parker had described.

Clarissa stared at the hen run and hen crees. When her gaze moved to the pigsties she visibly shuddered. 'Do – do you think Christopher is at home to visitors?' she asked Oswald faintly, for all the world as though they were making an afternoon call on one of their circle of acquaintances.

Oswald was taking a perverse pleasure in his wife's distress. Taking Clarissa's arm none too gently, he virtually hauled her across the muck-strewn farmyard. He'd noticed a front door to the house as the carriage had approached the building, but the yard led to what was clearly a back door. It was on this he hammered, thinking grimly that Clarissa needed her handkerchief for once. The stink from the pigsties was ripe in the warm air.

When it became clear that no one was going to answer, he tried the door which opened into a stone-flagged scullery. A pile of dirty dishes were in the sink and stacked on a table, and stuff was strewn everywhere. When they walked through to the kitchen–cum–sitting room it was equally messy and devoid of comfort. The remains of a meal were still on the kitchen table, and the fire in the range had all but gone out.

They were standing looking at each other when they heard footsteps and then a man appeared in the doorway to the scullery. It took them a moment to realise it was Christopher, he was so changed. He was clad in a workingman's clothes for one thing, and he had a full beard which was threaded with grey, as was his shock of thick hair.

'Mother. Father.' He nodded at them but made no effort to come towards them. 'I was in the upper field and saw the carriage, but it takes a few minutes to reach the house.'

Clarissa had her hand to her throat and uttered not a word. She didn't have to. Her horror was written on her face.

After dragging his eyes from his son and glancing at his wife, Oswald cleared his throat. 'Hello, Christopher. We've come to have a word with you, as you can see. Parker said you couldn't spare the time to leave here.'

'Lambing,' said Christopher briefly.

'Quite.' For once in his life Oswald had had the wind taken out of his sails. Clarissa had insisted she was going to do all the talking but she was simply staring at her son and he could understand why. He felt at a loss himself to deal with the weatherbeaten individual in front of him.

Clearing his throat again, he said, 'I understand Parker told you about Nathaniel.'

'Yes, he did. I'm very sorry.' Christopher came into the room now, waving his hand towards the old sofa. 'Won't you sit down?'

Clarissa glanced at the sofa which had seen better days and which at the moment had a large ginger cat curled up on it. Pulling one of the hardbacked chairs away from the kitchen table she placed it in the middle of the floor and wiped the seat with her handkerchief before sitting down. Oswald remained standing. 'Do you understand what Nathaniel's going means to you?' she asked coolly, her composure restored.

'It means I have lost a brother of whom I was fond.'

'Fond?' Oswald turned his head sharply. 'You had a funny way of showing your affection, that's all I can say.'

'*Oswald.*' Clarissa's beautiful face was calm but her voice carried a warning.

'We were fond of each other, as it happens. The last time Nat came here—'

'Your brother came *here*?' Christopher's words had startled Clarissa, and Oswald was looking thunderstruck.

'Several times. The last occasion was shortly before he left for France again after his last leave.'

'He didn't mention this to us.'

'He didn't think you would approve,' Christopher said simply.

'He was damn right.' Oswald looked as though he was going to explode.

This time Clarissa's voice was sharper when she said, '*Please*, Oswald.'

'He stands there with a smirk on his face and tells us Nathaniel came to see him before he got himself shredded with shrapnel, and you expect me to say nothing?'

Christopher's face was white but his voice was low when he said, 'The smirk is in your imagination, Father.'

'And you hiding here while your brother fights for King and country is in my imagination too, I suppose?'

'As it happens I tried twice to enlist but the injury to my arm and chest means I'm classed as unfit. Satisfied?'

'Unfit? And you work on a farm?'

'Take your argument to the doctors, Father. Not me.'

'I don't believe a word of it. You never attempted to enlist.'

'*Oswald!*' For the first time any of them could remember, Clarissa had shouted. She hadn't merely raised her voice, she had shouted. It shocked Oswald into silence and it was into that silence Clarissa said, 'I am sure you would have gone to war if you could, Christopher, but I am glad you did not. Losing one son is quite enough.'

Christopher could have reminded his mother at this point that according to her she'd only had one son *to* lose, but he did not. He knew why they had come to see him. Funnily enough, Nathaniel himself had predicted it as they were saying goodbye that last time. They'd shaken hands but then Nathaniel had hugged him hard, slapping him on the back as he'd let him go. 'Look after yourself, little brother. I'm glad we're back as we were in the old days.'

Christopher had been able to say in all honesty, 'So am I.' Something he was glad about now.

'If anything happens to me, you know the pair of them will be hotfoot here to lay the royal robe of inheritance over your manly shoulders, all forgiven?'

'Nothing is going to happen to you.'

'Perhaps not, but be warned just in case.'

'Nat, I don't want a penny of their money, never have. I've got all I want here. I'm gradually getting it round and in a year or two I'll start on the house. Get running water piped in from the stream and do the building work I told you about.'

'I never thought you'd stick it, you know.' Nathaniel swung himself up on to his horse. 'I thought the winters would do for you, and the loneliness.' He'd clicked at his horse and as it had trotted off, called over his shoulder, 'See you when the swallows come home, little brother.'

Only he hadn't.

Christopher brought his mind back to what his mother was saying. '. . . And so your father and I think it's high time we all let bygones be bygones. None of us wants a family feud, do we? So many people have lost loved ones and it's made us all realise what is important, I'm sure. Isn't that right, Christopher?'

The hypocrisy was too much. He had told himself that if they came, he would be polite but firm. He wouldn't be drawn into an argument and he would be civil. Nothing was gained by further animosity and when all was said and done, they had just lost Nathaniel on whom all their hopes of a good marriage and grand-children to carry on the family name had been pinned. But for his mother to sit there so cool and calm and lie through her back teeth made his blood boil. He preferred his father's hostility.

'And what, exactly, do you think *is* important, Mother?' he asked grimly.

'Well, it's obvious, isn't it?'

'Your mother and I are prepared to put the past behind us.' Oswald felt he'd been silent long enough. 'If you knuckle down, I see no reason why you can't do as well as Nathaniel, given time. It might take a while for you to pick up the strings but you're not unintelligent.' When Christopher continued to stare at him without speaking, Oswald said, 'Do you understand what I'm saying, boy?'

'Perfectly. You want me to step into Nathaniel's shoes.'

'Well aye, in a manner of speaking.'

'We want you to come home, Christopher,' Clarissa said with what she fondly imagined was a winning smile.

'I am home, Mother.'

Clarissa blinked. 'This – this building can hardly be called that.'

'On the contrary. This is my home, bought and paid for. The cattle and sheep are mine, and the crops in the fields. I have men and women working for me who give a good day's work for a good day's pay. I am satisfied with what I have.'

'As our only child the estate and all we have will come to you. We are talking of great wealth and influence, Christopher.'

'I don't want it. I told you I didn't want anything from you and Father once before – I meant it then and even more now. I have no intention of stepping into a dead man's shoes, Mother. I couldn't fill them as Nathaniel did.'

'Too damn right you couldn't.' Oswald's patience had run out. 'Your brother was ten times, twenty times the man you are. He knew where his duty lay and there was no snivelling about it. But you'll come cap in hand one day, boy. You see if I'm not right. You were spoonfed all your life and leopards don't change their spots.'

'This one did.' Strangely, he wanted to laugh. He couldn't blame them for thinking the dreamy, easygoing, impractical youth they'd known would fail. In that first bone-weary year he had often thought it himself. But he hadn't failed. And he had improved the farm and was still improving it. He had found another part of himself, that was the only way he could describe his love of the land and this life. It didn't negate his enjoyment of poetry and books, and there were times when he longed for the luxury of a whole morning or afternoon to himself just to read or think, but one couldn't have everything. And he was lonely oft-times, but not for people. Just one person. He had expected the ache of losing her to get better over the years, but it had not.

His mother had risen to her feet, her face icy. 'We came here holding out the olive branch, Christopher.'

'And will that still apply if I don't fall in with what you wish?'

Her answer was to sweep past him. 'Come, Oswald. There is nothing more to be said.'

His father paused. 'You'll want us before we want you, boy. Remember that.'

As always, his father had to have the last word, Christopher thought with grim amusement. He made no effort to follow them or move to the window, not even when he heard the sound of the carriage moving off. Instead he threw some logs on the fire and a small amount of coal, and once the fire was blazing he put the kettle on the hob to make himself a pot of tea.

Going to the cupboard, he brought out a breadboard on which half a loaf remained and put it on the table after he'd pushed a couple of dirty dishes out of the way. Mabel, who 'did' for him and looked after his meals, had sprained her ankle badly a couple of days ago and was laid up, so he'd been fending for himself with the help of the odd bit of baking from Ivy, the other labourer's wife. Fetching a pat of creamy butter and a large chunk of cheese from the cold slab in the pantry he placed them beside the bread, and then mashed the tea, letting it draw while he again went to the cold slab, this time for the big joint of ham Mabel had brought over before she'd had her accident. He cut himself two thick slices. He was hungry. He'd been up most of the night with a ewe who'd had trouble delivering, but the end result had been two healthy lambs and a delighted new mother, so he wasn't complaining.

He sat eating his meal at the cluttered table, and as he glanced round the shabby surroundings he could have been surveying a palace. After the first arduous year was under his belt and he had survived what had been an uphill and painful struggle to pull through, he had begun to draw strength from the wood and bricks and mortar which made up his home. He had found a date carved into one of the ceiling beams in the kitchen. 1775. That meant this house had been standing for coming up to a hundred and fifty years, impervious to the cruel winds and rain and snow which lashed it daily in the worst of the weather. It had nurtured generations of children born under its protection, and it had served them well. It deserved the best he could give it.

This oneness with his surroundings had never diminished, not even when he had been forced to acknowledge that old Jed had sold him something of a pig in a poke. Everything in and about the farm was tired and old, and his three hundred pounds a year only stretched so far. But he *was* improving things, bit by bit. And his men, Ray Fletcher and George Irvin, were with him, their wives too. When he'd bought more cattle and sheep, knowing he had to make the farm work for him if he was going to make a profit, they had stepped up to the extra toil involved, understanding he couldn't afford to take on more men for the present. And the additional fields of wheat and barley and all they involved, they'd been with him there too. Sometimes the three of them, he and Ray and George, had worked eighteen hours a day, and their wives had done their bit and more. He wouldn't forget it. Finishing his tea, Christopher wiped the back of his hand across his mouth. No, he wouldn't forget it. They'd get their reward, God willing. How long they'd have to wait for it was something else.

His mouth curving wryly, he shook his head. Most folk would think he was mad, barmy, not to take what his parents had offered. He knew that. And there was no doubt that even a smidgen of the Armstrong thousands would be useful here. But that was the thing. They weren't offering his farm a lifeline, just the opposite.

His stomach full, he stretched his arms over his head and yawned. He had to sleep for a while. Ray and George would fetch him if they needed him. Walking across to the sofa, he nudged the cat off with his hand and threw himself down. He was too tired to think about his parents or Nathaniel or any of it. The cat jumped back up — it had figured out long ago that its master was a soft touch — and nestled itself across Christopher's chest, gently kneading the rough material of his jacket and purring before settling down to sleep.

Chapter 24

There was talk that the war would soon be over, as the Allies were sweeping all before them along the whole Western Front, from the Schedlt River in the north to the Sedan in the Ardennes. All along the line, the Germans were avoiding battle wherever possible, if the newspapers were to be believed, making a stand only in order to cover their retreat. Elsewhere, Germany's allies were collapsing. But for the people of Britain, weakened by wartime hardships, one last tribulation was gathering strength as September unfolded. The virulent strain of influenza known as the 'Spanish flu', which had already caused millions of death around the globe, had reached Europe, and already doctors were predicting that more people would die of influenza than were killed by the war.

Pearl and Nessie were terrified that Seth would be stricken by the flu after all he'd been through. Although some patients recovered, others died swiftly in agony.

Pearl tried – unsuccessfully – to persuade her brother to stay upstairs in the flat rather than serve in the shop where he came into contact with hundreds of people in a week, but he was adamant that he wasn't going to leave Nessie to do all the work when he was perfectly healthy. In the event, it wasn't Seth who succumbed to the disease. In the middle of October, when 2,000 deaths a week were being reported in the capital, which completely over-shadowed the fact that the House of Commons voted by 274 to 25 to allow women to become MPs, Nessie became ill.

At first she dismissed her fever and blinding headache by saying she'd caught a chill, but within a few hours it was clear she had the flu. The rigors and severe muscle pain, wracking cough and inability to stand and walk all proclaimed that Nessie had contracted the severe form of the disease. The newspapers had reported that some victims could die within twenty-four hours of showing symptoms, a blue tint to their faces and coughing up blood.

The doctor was no help when he came to the house. Nessie's normal rosy complexion was a dull, pasty white apart from two spots of burning colour on her cheekbones and her eyes appeared sunken in her head. 'It's the flu, sure enough.' The doctor was exhausted; he had been on his feet for hours visiting patient after patient. 'Try to get liquids down her and I'll leave you an elixir to be taken every four hours. It might help.'

'Is that all I can do, give her liquids?' Pearl had taken the doctor through to the sitting room after he'd examined Nessie, and now she and Seth stared at the tired man. They'd shut the shop earlier, putting a notice in the window to say that due to illness, the business would be closed for the next few days.

'I'm afraid so.' The doctor rubbed at his gritty eyes. 'I can try to get her into hospital, but to be honest they're full and half the staff are off ill. She'll probably get more care here with you if you're prepared to nurse her, although . . .' He paused.

'Although?' Pearl prompted.

'Patients stricken this quickly and severely often die within hours. It's a form of hemorrhagic pneumonia, although we don't understand what the actual strain is. I'm sorry to be so blunt.'

'But she's strong and healthy,' Seth said roughly.

'This flu is unusual in that it seems to target those people usually least vulnerable.' Taking in their shocked faces, the man added, 'I'm sorry, that's no comfort, I know, but it's one of the few things we do know about this disease. Have either of you been feeling unwell?' When they shook their heads, he said, 'Let's hope that continues.

I have visited patients in homes where other members of the family are unaffected. Of course, in some places the whole family are ill. If either of you starts to feel unwell, go straight to bed and wait for the worst to pass. I'll call to see Mrs Ramshaw tomorrow.'

Seth saw the doctor out. When he returned, Pearl was in the kitchen making Nessie a warm drink. 'I'll take it in to her.' Seth held out his hand for the mug of sweet milk.

'No, I'll do it.' She and Nessie had agreed that Seth mustn't enter the sick room, and up to now she had managed to keep him out. 'It's silly for both of us to risk catching it, Seth, and I've been seeing to her thus far.'

'I'll take it in to her,' he repeated. 'I want to.'

'Well, I don't want you to – and neither does Nessie. You've made wonderful progress since you came home, and you don't want to undo all the good you've done.'

'Pearl, I'm a grown man, not a bairn, and you're not my mother. I'm not ungrateful for the thought and your care, you know that, but allow me to decide what I can and can't do.'

'This is ridiculous.' Pearl glared at him. As though she hadn't enough to concern her with Nessie, here was Seth acting up. 'If you think you're helping me by doing this, you're wrong. I don't want to have to worry about you as well.'

Seth looked at his sister. A straight look. 'I wasn't thinking about you,' he said bluntly. 'I was thinking about Nessie. I need to be with her, Pearl.'

Pearl stared at him, her mouth opening slightly before she shut it with a little snap. 'You . . .' She was lost for words. 'I didn't . . .'

'Know how I feel?' Seth finished for her. 'Why should you have known? No one does, not even Nessie. I'm not stupid, Pearl. I know I've got no chance with her.' He smiled grimly. 'I've told her too much, that's the thing.'

'You care for Nessie.' It was a statement, not a question.

Seth answered anyway. 'More than life itself. If she dies . . .' He shuddered and sighed. 'But she won't die. I won't let her. Matron Gordon used to come and talk to me sometimes when the others were asleep. She was a canny old bird, the Matron. She knew full well I wanted to die. "Fight, man, fight," she used to say. Even when I swore at her, she still used to come back the next night, like a little wise owl. And she *was* wise in her way, even if I wanted to strangle her at the time.' He looked his sister in the face. 'Give me the drink, Pearl.'

Pearl gave him the mug.

Nessie was coughing and struggling for breath when Seth entered the room, her forehead wet with perspiration. She could barely speak when the paroxysm passed, but as he sat down on the edge of the bed and wiped her face with a flannel, she whispered, 'Get out of here.'

'That's nice.' Seth forced a grin. 'Very friendly.'

'I – mean it.' She coughed again, holding a handkerchief to her lips, and when she removed it Seth was terrified to look in case there was blood. There wasn't.

'Drink this, it'll help the cough.' He lifted her slightly and held the mug to her lips.

'Seth, please. You'll be ill.'

'Stop talking and making yourself cough and drink, woman.'

'Not till you go.'

'I'm not going, Nessie, so make up your mind about that. Pearl's putting her feet up for a bit and I'm staying here. For the record, she tried to stop me and I told her what I'm telling you. I'm not a bairn and I won't be treated like one. *I* decide what I do and don't do.'

'You – haven't got – the sense you – were born with.'

'Very probably.' The doctor had talked about a form of pneumonia and he could believe it, listening to her trying to breathe. How could this thing rage through a healthy body so quickly and devastatingly? 'Now drink the milk.'

She had a few sips, her eyes shut against the pounding headache she'd complained of earlier and her face screwed up in pain. Pearl came in and handed Seth the medicine. When they'd given her a dose, Pearl took the bottle away and Seth laid Nessie gently down, stroking the hair back from her damp forehead. 'Go to sleep, I'm here.'

'You shouldn't be,' she gasped.

'Yes, I should, Nessie. Now shut up and go to sleep.'

The doctor came for the next five days. When on the sixth day Nessie still hadn't coughed up blood, he seemed more hopeful, and on the seventh day he said he wouldn't call again unless he was needed. Once in the sitting room with Pearl and Seth, he said quietly, 'I think she's past the worst, but convalescence is protracted. Expect her to be weak and easily fatigued and low in herself for some weeks.'

'She sleeps all the time now.'

'Good. Let her. Better than any medicine I can give her. I think she escaped the hemorrhagic pneumonia but she's certainly had a touch of the bacterial kind, and recovery will be slow.'

Once the doctor had left, Seth sat down very suddenly on the sofa. Pearl looked at her brother. 'You're exhausted,' she said softly. 'You haven't slept properly for days.' Seth had insisted on sitting up nights on her bed while she slept in his and she knew he'd only dozed and catnapped because Nessie had told her that every time she'd opened her eyes, he had been awake and looking at her. 'Nessie's sleeping so go and get in your bed and have a few hours. I'll keep looking in on her.'

He scrubbed at his face, his eyes bleary. 'We're going to have to think about opening up downstairs now Nessie's out of danger.'

'Maybe, but not today. Today you're going to sleep and I'm going to be in charge for once. I'd forgotten what a bossy individual you are, Seth Croft, till this little lot.'

'Pot calling the kettle black.'

Pearl smiled. 'Go on.' She gave him a little push. 'Go and sleep for as long as you can. I'll see to her.'

She followed him out of the room and stood with him when he stopped and looked in at Nessie through the open bedroom door. Nessie's eyes had been shut but she opened them and smiled. 'Give it a day or two,' she whispered, 'and I'll be back downstairs.'

'Not if I have anything to do with it.' Seth surveyed her pallid face. She had been on the plump side a week ago, now she seemed all skin and bones. 'You'll do as the doctor said and take it easy for the next few weeks. We'll manage just fine in the shop. You're not indispensable, you know.'

Nessie's smile disappeared. 'I know that,' she said quietly.

Pearl pushed Seth again. 'Go and lie down.' Looking at Nessie, she said, 'I've told him to rest, he's done in.'

Nessie nodded but said nothing. When Seth had shut the door to his room, Pearl smiled at her friend. 'Fancy a cup of tea?'

Once Nessie had drunk her tea she lay dozing, and Pearl caught up on a few chores she'd been putting off for days. The October day was cold but sunny, and Pearl opened all the windows in the flat apart from those in the rooms where Nessie and Seth were sleeping. It was wonderful to let the fresh north-east air blow through for an hour or so; she felt as though it had taken the last of the sickness with it. At least, she hoped it had. She'd been watching Seth like a hawk all week, but to date God had answered her prayers and neither she nor her brother showed any signs of falling ill.

It took a while for the flat to warm up again when she closed the windows, but after making herself a warm drink she sat down in the sitting room to darn some of Seth's socks. She must have fallen asleep immediately, because when she came to she was still holding the first sock and the room was lit only by the glow from the fire, it being dark outside.

Jumping up, she went quickly into Nessie's room, worried that her friend might need something. Nessie was wide awake, staring at the door as Pearl lit the gas mantle. 'Is Seth all right?'

'Seth? I think so. He's still asleep. Hang on a sec, I'll check on him.' Opening Seth's door, Pearl saw he was lying facing the wall, his regular, steady breathing telling her he was still out for the count. She reported back to Nellie, made her friend a fresh hot drink and plumped up her pillows, then went into the kitchen to see about dinner.

It was another hour before she popped her head round the door to Nessie's room. 'All right?' she asked brightly, then, 'What's the matter? Are you feeling ill again?'

'Seth's sleeping a long time. You – you don't think he's going down with the flu, do you?'

'He's just tired, Nessie. We all are.'

Nessie nodded, then stared at Pearl. Stifling a sigh, Pearl said, 'You want me to check on him again?'

'Oh, please, Pearl. I've got a feeling on me . . .'

A few moments later, Pearl was back, saying, 'He's sleeping, Nessie, that's all. Look, read one of those magazines by your bed and don't worry. Dinner will be ready soon and his stomach will wake him. You know Seth and food.'

Pearl had cooked stuffed cod for dinner. Nessie had no appetite at all but the dish was light and tasty and she thought it might tempt her. When it was ready, Seth was still deeply asleep and she was loath to wake him. He hadn't slept properly in days and was completely exhausted; she'd keep his food hot and he could eat when he awoke. She took Nessie's meal into her on a tray and the first thing Nessie said was, 'Is Seth up yet?'

'No, but I'll keep his food hot.'

'He's ill, isn't he? You're not saying, so as not to worry me. He should never have looked after me, it's all my fault.'

Reminding herself that the doctor had said depression was a factor in recovery, Pearl said patiently, 'Look, lass, he's exhausted, which is only to be expected. And if he did go down with anything, it wouldn't be your fault anyway.'

It was the wrong thing to say. Nessie's chin wobbled and the next moment she'd burst into tears. Putting the tray on her own bed, Pearl knelt down by Nessie and patted her hand. 'You're just feeling low and no wonder, you've been so ill.'

'P-promise me he's all right.'

'Seth? I promise.'

'I – I couldn't live with myself if anything happened to him because of me. He's come through so much and he's so brave and good . . .'

A light had clicked on in Pearl's mind. Still patting Nessie's hand, her voice soft, she murmured, 'You like him, don't you?' Why hadn't she seen it before? Thinking back, a hundred little things should have alerted her. Oh, what a muddle.

Nessie retrieved her hand and wiped her eyes. Her face burning, she whispered, 'Promise me you won't ever tell him, Pearl. He'd be so embarrassed. Here's me old enough to be his mother—'

'Hardly,' Pearl interrupted.

'Well, nearly. There was a bairn in the shop a few weeks ago who asked Seth if I was his mam.'

'I don't know why,' Pearl said stoutly. 'You look younger than your age and Seth looks older than his.'

Nessie smiled shakily. 'You don't lie very well, lass. I look what I am, a middle-aged woman with not much to commend her. Seth – Seth's in his prime. He'll want to marry one day, have a family, bairns.'

It was on the tip of Pearl's tongue to tell her, but then she bit back the words. She had promised Seth, but she hadn't promised Nessie and she didn't intend to. Her voice brisk, she said, 'No more crying, that won't help you get better.' Standing up, she placed the tray on Nessie's lap. 'You get on the other side of that and I'll be back in a minute when I've ate mine, all right? And don't worry about Seth. He's as tough as old boots, all us Crofts are.' She nipped out of the room before Nessie could say anything more, shutting the door behind her.

Seth was just beginning to stir. As she reached his side he opened his eyes. 'What time is it? It's dark outside – how long have I been asleep? You should have woken me.'

Ignoring all that, Pearl said urgently, 'Nessie's been crying.'

Seth shot up, swinging his legs over the side of the bed. 'What's the matter?'

'You.'

'Me?' He ran a hand through his hair. 'What are you on about?'

'She'd got it into her head you were going down with the flu.'

Seth stated the obvious. 'I'm not.'

'I know that, but she thought you were and she got terribly upset.'

'But you told her I was all right?' Seth said as though that settled the matter.

Wondering why men in general and her brother in particular were so thick, Pearl said tersely, 'She was crying over you, Seth.'

'I know, you said.'

'She said she couldn't live with herself if anything happened to you.'

'Nothing *is* going to happen to—' Seth stopped abruptly.

'She thinks you're brave and good and you've come through so much, but she's older and one day you'll want to marry and have bairns with someone. She thinks you'd be embarrassed to know how she feels.'

Seth stared at her, the look on his face making Pearl relax and take a breath. She'd done her bit, now it was up to him.

She wasn't privy to what went on between them once Seth had closed Nessie's bedroom door behind him, but some time later when Seth called her, his face was beaming. She came into the room to see Seth sitting holding Nessie's hand and in that moment Pearl really did think Nessie looked like a young lass. 'We're going to be married as soon as Nessie's well.' Even Seth's voice was different, lighter.

Pearl squealed and then the three of them hugged each other, Nessie keeping her arms round Pearl for a long time. 'Bless you,' she whispered. 'Bless you, lass.'

PART SIX

A Kind of Peace

November 1918

Chapter 25

'It's over. Germany signed the Armistice days ago, and they've taken down the blackout curtains and unmasked the streetlights. Everyone went mad in the town, with dancing and fireworks and street-parties for the bairns.'

Christopher stared at Ray Fletcher. He had known the end was near, of course. Even somewhere as remote as Hill Farm had the odd tinker or two pass by, and the last time he'd gone to the cattle market, the townfolk had been talking about the Germans being pushed back to the old Hindenburg Line. He took the newspaper Ray had bought for him when Ray and his wife had visited their eldest girl in Sunderland, who had just presented them with their first grandchild.

Reading swiftly, he scanned the front page, passing over the reports of the jubilation in the capital which had marked the end of the war. The terms of surrender were hard: Germany had to hand over 5,000 heavy guns, 30,000 machine guns, 2,000 war planes and all her U-boats; the surface fleet would be interned in British waters, with only caretaker crews. Thousands of locomotives, wagons and lorries were to be delivered to the victors, and Allied troops would occupy the Rhineland, their upkeep to be paid for by Germany. Finally, the Allied blockade of Germany was to remain in force.

Christopher read on. Apparently the Kaiser had fled Germany and revolt had swept the country. Socialist demonstrators were filling the streets, sailors had mutinied and army troops had seized their command posts. If it wasn't all-out revolution, it wasn't far off. And not before time. Because of this madman, ten million men and boys worldwide had died, Nathaniel among them. The newspapers were already calling them 'a lost generation'.

Stuffing the newspaper into his jacket pocket to read later, he pulled his muffler further up his face. It had been trying to snow all day and the wind was enough to cut you in two; all he wanted was to get indoors in front of the fire and toast his toes with a glass of whisky in his hand, but he still had one or two things to do outside first. He smiled at Ray. 'What's the baby like?'

'Best ask the wife. Far as I can see, he's got two arms and two legs same as any bairn, but according to her there's never been a bab to match him.'

'Proud grandma.'

'Oh aye, she's that all right.'

As the two men parted, the first fat snowflakes began to fall out of a laden sky. Christopher knew the signs. They were in for a packet. Last winter had been a bad one; the wind had been like a carving-knife, cutting hands and cheeks until they bled, and the cold had frozen his gloves like boards day after day. The oldtimers were saying this winter wouldn't be any different. Before he had come to live here he had never regarded the weather as friend or foe, but he did now. Wall-mending, milking, cattle-feeding and watering still had to go on whatever the conditions. The cowhouses and stables had to be cleaned and the hens, calves, pigs and sheep had to be fed. A good winter made all the difference, if such a thing existed in this part of the country. He understood now why the weather was the favourite topic of conversation with countrymen: it was the foundation on which all their livelihoods was based.

During the winter months all the cattle were kept indoors at night and food was fed to them in their cribs in the form of pulped turnip, hay or crushed corn. Christopher found he felt an abiding satisfaction when he surveyed the animals settled down for the night. It made for more work in the winter, and before bedtime a visit had to be paid to all the animals in their various buildings to ensure they were safe and in no danger from their tethers, but nevertheless this gathering-in touched something fundamental deep inside.

It was quiet in the cattle-shed apart from the chinking of tie-chains, and puffs and snorts. Outside, the wind was howling and the storm was gathering force; inside, was lamp-lit serenity. Christopher experienced a shaft of pure joy that came from knowing that at this precise moment there was no place he would rather be on God's good earth. He grinned at the fanciful thought. The men and women who worked for him were not given to such whimsical notions, or if they were, they didn't admit to it. He was an oddity, caught between two worlds, and there had only ever been one person who had allowed him to be himself and loved him for it.

If she had lived, Pearl would be a mature woman of twenty-eight or so now. They would likely have had children. A son maybe, and two daughters. He would have liked daughters, little minia-tures of Pearl, and his son would have been tall and gentle. Charles Armstrong. That had a ring to it.

He gazed over the cattle, their warm breath like steam as they contentedly chomped.

Pearl would have been a good mother and he would have been a good father; they both, in different ways, had had bitter child-hoods. They would have made sure Charles and his sisters knew they were loved and cherished.

The shed door opening brought him swinging round to see George stomping in, his cap and shoulders covered in a mantle of white. 'Comin' down thick and fast now, Mr Armstrong. We'll be diggin' ourselves out in the mornin', you mark my words.'

George always looked on the bright side.

'Well, it won't be the first time, George, and I don't suppose it will be the last.'

'Aye, you're right there.' George picked up a bale of hay. 'I'll be after seein' to Bess and Gracie,' he said, naming the two shire-horses, 'and I can manage the rest the night. Why don't you get yerself in front of the fire, Mr Armstrong? You've been hard at it the last couple of days, with no let-up.'

'There was extra to do with Ray not around.'

'Aye, well he's back now an' he's seein' to the cattle in the other shed.'

Christopher nodded. He liked George and he knew George liked him. George was getting on a bit, and the old Northerner treated him much as Wilbert had done, giving him the respect due to his position but with a fatherly edge to his manner. He had struggled in the early days, but George and Ray hadn't condemned him for his lack of experience, rather attempted to ease his way as much as they could – and he was grateful to them for it.

Once in the house, he fetched the beef stew and dumplings Mabel had left on a low heat in the oven. She was a good cook but a plain one, and that suited him fine. He had never particularly enjoyed the elaborate dinners in his parents' home. The cat wound round his ankles as he ate his meal and he left a good saucerful of food for it, although it was supposed to earn its living mousing.

Once he had finished, Christopher lit his pipe and poured himself a glass of whisky before settling in front of the fire. It was then he remembered the newspaper. Fetching it from the pocket of his jacket, he resumed his seat. After quickly going over the front page again, he opened it up and began to read the local news.

Many schools were closed because of the current influenza epidemic, and absences from work had risen sharply, but those who were able had celebrated Victory Day, some a little too heartily. The article showed a picture of an inebriated man clinging hold of a lamp-post with a silly grin on his face. Christopher smiled to himself.

Local women up and down the town had got together to throw street-parties for the children which were thoroughly enjoyed by all. In spite of the restrictions on meat, butter and tea, there were veritable feasts to be had and the children had a wonderful time.

The lucky children in Zion Street in the East End had a real treat when a local shopowner baked two hundred fishcakes for their supper. Christopher barely glanced at the photograph of a long trestle table covered with food, and benches upon which so many children were squeezed it didn't look as though they'd be able to move, let alone eat anything. A woman was holding a large tray on which the said fishcakes were piled.

He had actually turned the page when he felt every nerve in his body jangle. His heart beating fit to burst, he whipped the page back and stared at the photograph of the woman and children again. *It was impossible.* Of course it was impossible, he knew that, but it was Pearl's face smiling up at him. He stood up, holding the newspaper close to the oil lamp that was on the mantelpiece above his easy chair. The likeness to Pearl had his stomach churning. It wasn't her, since this woman was a shopkeeper and obviously fairly prosperous if she could afford to provide a host of children with free food, but the similarity was uncanny.

He stared at the photograph for a long time before refilling his whisky glass and sitting down again. He tried to read the rest of the paper – it was rare they had the luxury of obtaining such reports from beyond their little world – but he couldn't concentrate. He felt disturbed, restless.

After throwing some more logs on the range fire, Christopher walked to the window, staring out at what was fast becoming a blizzard. Last winter they'd been snowed in for a couple of months, but that hadn't been till January. It was going to be a long hard time of it, if this little lot persisted. Still, with the war over he could maybe see about taking another man on in the spring. It might be a bit tight financially but they needed more help if the farm was going to thrive and grow. What was it his father had always said? 'You need to speculate to accumulate.' That was it. But then with thousands behind him, Oswald Armstrong hadn't exactly been gambling his last penny.

Stretching, he turned away from the window. With Ray visiting his daughter he and George had been hard pushed the last couple of days, and he was dog tired. Last night he'd shut his eyes for two minutes in the chair and woken up to daylight pouring in the window and a stiff neck. He'd have a sluice down in a minute and get to bed – he needed his rest. But still he stood surveying the room, without really seeing it. She did look like Pearl, that girl in the paper. Could it be a relation? He remembered Pearl saying she had brothers but she hadn't mentioned a sister. Perhaps a cousin? It could happen like that sometimes. How old would this girl be?

He picked up the newspaper again and studied the picture. It was hard to tell. Twenty-three, twenty-four maybe, but the camera could lie, and unless the girl had inherited the business it was unlikely she'd be that young. Anyway, it was no good going digging up the past. Pearl was gone and he'd learned to live with the fact. He was married to this farm now and she was a possessive wife. Flinging the paper down, he put the kettle on to boil. He'd spoil himself and wash with warm water tonight instead of making do with cold as he normally did, being too tired to bother.

By the time he climbed the rickety ladder to the long room under the eaves, he felt more settled. The girl in the newspaper might be a relation of Pearl's or she might not; either way it was irrelevant. There would be nothing gained in trying to find her. The manner of Pearl's death and the loss of the future they'd planned together had nearly sent him mad for a while; he couldn't resurrect all those feelings and he didn't want to.

Settling himself down on the straw mattress that made up his bed, he pulled the heap of covers over him just as he was, fully dressed. The roof had so many draughts he'd learned early on that he needed to sleep with his clothes on.

Not that it would always be like this, he told himself, smiling in the dark as the cat padded into the room and, purring loudly, curled up beside him. For a supposed farm cat, she liked her comfort, did Daisy. He'd restocked the farm over the last years and got the barns and cattle-sheds into good order. He'd done quite a bit, when he thought about it. Next year he could think about moving the pigsties and boiling-up room, and then perhaps start on the house. Everything in good time.

On this comfortable thought and in spite of the wind howling like a banshee, Christopher went straight to sleep.

He slept soundly all night, curled up like a dormouse, barely moving, waking at five o'clock as he always did when some inner alarm clock told him it was time to start the day. Once downstairs, he stoked up the fire which he'd banked down with wet tea-leaves the night before, and made himself a cup of tea. That would suffice until eight o'clock, when he came in from seeing to the animals and Mabel would have a pan of porridge laced with fresh cream ready for him. Nothing in his life had ever tasted as good as that porridge did first thing.

The storm of the night before had burned itself out, leaving a few inches of snow behind it. A few inches was nothing – it was when it was a few feet and reached the top of the hedgerows that it became a problem. George and Ray and their wives were already in the cattle sheds when he left the house, the women seeing to the milking and the men mucking out. It was to the men he spoke. 'I'm taking Jet and riding into Sunderland – there's some business I need to see to.'

He was speaking the words before he realised that some time during his sleep he'd reached the decision. Perhaps it had always been there in the back of his mind.

George and Ray stared at him with some consternation. It wasn't the best of times for the young master to be taking himself off on a trip. Still, he was the boss.

Christopher read their minds. 'I'll be back tonight, at the latest tomorrow, but it can't wait, all right? I want to go before the weather closes in.' Calling to Mabel, he said, 'I'd like an early breakfast today, I'm leaving shortly for Sunderland.'

By seven o'clock, when a murky half-light was struggling to bring in a new day, Christopher was already on his way, Jet thrilled to be out on an early-morning jaunt. The narrow road of smashed stone and pebbles which had taken months to complete was buried under its white blanket, but still made for far easier riding than had been the case before it was laid.

In spite of the excitement and fear and a whole host of other emotions which were making his insides churn, the white landscape gave Christopher pleasure. The vivid scarlet of wayside rosehips gave him just as much satisfaction as ever the best of his father's paintings had done, and so it was with the glinting sparkle of spider-webs as a reluctant sun rose like a feeble lantern over the scene.

When he was a child, Nathaniel had frightened him with stories about the month of November marking the Celtic 'Samhain', associated with the cult of the dead. In pagan times, Nathaniel had murmured so their nanny hadn't heard him, massive bonfires were lit to ensure the sun's safe return. The natives believed that as the flames licked into the winter sky, the Sun God grew stronger. November was the 'silent' month, full of days so stark and bare that it suspended natural laws and left spirits, ghosts and demons free to roam the earth. The little boy he'd been then had had nightmares for weeks.

Oh, Nat, Nat. Christopher lifted his head and stared into the fleeting wisps of silver tingeing the sky where the sun touched it. *What would you think of me now, chasing a ghost all of my own in the vain hope that maybe – just maybe – there's been some mistake? Has death mellowed you to the point where you would say, 'Try, little brother,' or would you be filled with pity or condemnation for my foolishness?*

He would like to think the former, but he rather suspected it would be the latter. His mouth curved in a wry smile. Whatever, it didn't matter. Foolishness or not, he had to make sure. The old crone at the gypsy camp might have dealt with him falsely for reasons of her own, even though he had held his hand with the man who had done him so much damage. Pearl had always said the Romanies were a law unto themselves.

Her name brought the familiar ache to his chest and for a moment he wondered on the wisdom of what he was doing, re-cognising how he would feel when he had to return home – as he surely would – disappointed and alone. Well, he'd put a face on things. That's what people did. All the women, young and old, who had lost loved ones, the men who'd lost sons and fathers and brothers, they faced the choice of wallowing in their own misery or going on. Only children thought life was fair.

He'd just passed through the hamlet of Ditchburn when Christopher's eyes narrowed as he peered ahead. Could that be Parker in the approaching trap? Yes, it was the Armstrongs' butler. What now?

By the time he was abreast with the trap he knew something serious was afoot.

'Oh, Mr Christopher.' Parker was red faced and agitated. Twice the trap had got stuck in thick snow since he'd left the house in pitch black in the early hours. Only fools and those with a death wish would attempt to travel in such conditions, but the mistress had been adamant. When he had suggested he wait until first light before leaving the estate she had been quite unlike herself. Of course it was her worry about the master, he understood that, but for the mistress to speak to him in such a fashion . . .

'What's wrong, man?'

'It's the master, sir. He collapsed two days ago and we understand he's poorly. Very poorly, sir. The mistress said he's been asking for you.'

'Collapsed?' If it wasn't impossible, he would think his parents had done this on purpose. 'What do you mean, collapsed? What have the doctors said? Is it his heart?'

'Not his heart, sir, no. It appears the master has had some trouble with his stomach for months – an ulcer possibly. The mistress has called for a physician from London to come and look at him, but the master seems to be getting worse by the hour. He –' Parker swallowed hard – 'he's sinking, sir.'

Christopher stared at the servant. Not his father. Oswald Armstrong was the very quiddity of life at its rawest: loud, crude, objectionable but always vital.

'Will you come, sir?'

'Of course.' What else could he do? Perhaps his father wasn't as ill as Parker imagined. He had told his men he would possibly be home tomorrow rather than today, so he could still fit in a visit to Sunderland to seek out this woman who bore such a remarkable resemblance to his Pearl.

Everything in Christopher longed to let Jet have free rein and make short work of the journey to the estate, but apart from the obvious danger of the horse breaking a leg if he acted in such a foolhardy manner, he couldn't leave Parker, who was clearly terrified of becoming stranded. Curbing his extreme frustration, he said to the butler, 'Let us proceed as swiftly as we can. I have business in Sunderland to attend to once I have seen my father.'

Oswald Armstrong was dying and he wasn't dying easy. Apart from the pain, which seemed to be tearing him apart, he wasn't ready to leave the trappings of the life he'd spent his whole life acquiring. He turned his head on the pillow and glanced towards the window where Clarissa was standing looking out. The last few days were the first time in thirty years she had set foot in his suite of rooms, and he hadn't been allowed in hers in all that time. She was a cold, calculating shrew of a woman, without natural warmth and affection, and yet he knew there was still a small part of him that was in awe of his wife. He had been amazed when she had agreed to marry him. Oh, he'd known it was for the Armstrong wealth, no one had made any bones about that, but he'd still been surprised that a woman of her breeding and class had consented to take him. And she knew, she'd always known that at bottom she had the upper hand. And now she was waiting for Christopher to come so she could play on what she saw as his weakness and soft heart, and draw him into her web again.

Oswald shut his eyes tightly for a moment as the pain became unbearable. When the spasm passed and settled down into mere agony he opened them to see her surveying him dispassionately. 'I'll leave you to rest,' she said, then nodded at the nurse sitting in a corner of the room and swept out. She could always sweep in and out, could Clarissa. Damn her.

Would Christopher hold out against her? Oswald asked himself silently. He knew at heart that he himself had never been able to. Oh, she let him have his little victories now and again if they didn't impinge on her too much, but that was all. Nathaniel had been the same, she'd been able to play their elder son like a violin. But Christopher had surprised her that time they had gone to see him; she'd been beside herself for weeks after that. Christopher had surprised him too. The namby-pamby child and ineffectual youth had grown into someone he didn't recognise, not that he had ever understood him.

The last lot of medicine the nurse had given him a few minutes ago was beginning to take effect at last, he could feel it taking the edge off the pain. He wouldn't have believed pain like this could exist, he'd have thought the heart would give out before it. He prayed the London physician would be able to do something, but he knew it was a lost cause. Once he'd started bleeding heavily from the rectum he'd been sure of it.

He must have dozed a little because when he next opened his eyes it was to see Christopher sitting by the bed with Clarissa at the side of him.

'Hello, Father.'

Oswald focused his eyes on his son's face. Weakly, he said, 'You came then.'

'Of course I came when Parker said you wanted to see me.'

Oswald began to cough and the nurse came swiftly to the bed, holding a linen square to his lips. The square was stained red with blood when she dropped it into the bowl she was holding and then resumed her seat in the corner of the room. With difficulty, Oswald muttered, 'It – was your mother's idea.'

'Because I know how your father feels,' Clarissa put in smoothly, 'and because I felt it only right for you to have the chance to say goodbye.'

Seeing the look that passed over his son's face, Oswald said thickly, 'It's all right. I – I know I'm on my way out.'

'But this London doctor? He might be able to do something.'

'Maybe, if I'd had the sense to – to go to him – months ago.'

'How long have you been feeling ill?'

'Months, probably twelve months or more.' The pillows had slipped but when he tried to move, the pain was so intense it brought an involuntary groan.

'Wait. Let me.' Christopher bent over his father, adjusting the pillows and gently easing Oswald against them. He could feel his father's bones through his pyjamas and realised the weight had fallen off him.

'Th-thanks.' It was the first time in his life Oswald had thanked his younger son for anything, but neither of them noticed. 'You – you were able to leave the farm for a bit?'

Christopher waved his hand, signalling that the farm was of no consequence in this situation.

A knock at the door was followed by Parker entering. Looking at Clarissa, he said, 'The London physician, Mr Grimmett, has arrived, ma'am.'

Clarissa rose to her feet. 'Thank you, Parker.' Looking at Oswald, she said, 'I'll bring him up shortly. Come along, Christopher.' With that she left the room.

'W-wait.' Oswald made a feeble movement with his hand as his son stood up. 'I want to t-talk to you. Privately. You're not leaving yet?'

Christopher's voice was quiet when he said, 'Not yet, no.'

'Good, good. Once this quack's gone then. All – all right?'

'Of course.'

Christopher had a tea tray in the drawing room while the doctor and his mother were upstairs. They were gone for some time. When Mr Grimmett came downstairs he left immediately in the very shiny and large car he'd arrived in, and the housemaid came to fetch Christopher. When he entered his father's bedroom his mother said immediately, 'Your father is very ill, Christopher, very ill. Do you understand?'

He wanted to say of course he understood, he wasn't dimwitted. 'Yes, I understand, Mother.'

'I'll leave you two to talk for a while.' Clarissa looked directly at her husband. 'I'll return once I've instructed Mrs Peterson about lunch. You'll stay for lunch, Christopher?'

'Thank you, yes.'

The nurse was still seated in her spot in the corner when Christopher sat down close to the bed. His father looked worse, if anything, after the doctor's visit. 'What did Mr Grimmett say?'

His father had shut his eyes as his wife had left, now he seemed to open them with some difficulty and his voice was weak when

306

he said, 'Grim by name and grim by nature. Poked and prodded and told me what I already knew. A growth, likely as not. Several of them. Nothing – nothing he can do. Look, lad, your mother . . .'

As a spasm of pain cut Oswald's voice off and his face contorted, Christopher said quickly, 'Don't try to talk, Father. Rest now.'

'I'll – be doing all the resting I – I want shortly. Listen to me.' He gasped in air and after a few moments, went on, 'Your mother wants me to make you promise you'll pick up the reins when I'm gone. A – a deathbed promise. But I'm not going to.' He reached out a hand and as Christopher took it, he continued, 'We've never got on, you an' me. Chalk an' cheese. Nathaniel – Nat was more like me. Thought a bit of him, both of us, didn't we?' He didn't wait for a reply. 'But in all the – the time I was with him, I never once – told him I loved him.'

'Don't distress yourself, Father.'

'Woke me up to a lot of things, him going like that. You – you need to go your own road, lad. You hear me? Your mother – don't – don't let her – squeeze the life out of you. Be – be strong.'

As Oswald began to retch, the nurse hurried over with the bowl. There was a lot of blood. When she had wiped his mouth and he was lying back on his pillows, his face ashen, she murmured to Christopher, 'He's fading fast. Perhaps you should fetch Mrs Armstrong, sir?'

'What? Oh yes, yes.' But he didn't move. He couldn't take in that his father was dying.

Oswald forced his lids open. 'Chris-to-pher.'

'I'm here, Father.'

'Stay with me – till – till it's over.'

'I promise.' Turning to the nurse, he said, 'I'm not leaving him. Please will you get my mother,' even as he wondered whether Clarissa would get there in time.

In the event it was another twenty-four hours before Oswald breathed his last, although he didn't open his eyes again or speak. Nevertheless, his grip on his son's hand did not falter and Christopher remained at the bedside all of that time.

★   ★   ★

'So? What did your father say to you when you were alone?'

Christopher had had a bath and something to eat, and was sitting with his mother in the drawing room. It hadn't snowed while he had been sitting with his father but now the sky looked heavy with it. He finished the cup of tea he was drinking before he looked at his mother. 'We talked about Nathaniel.'

'And?'

'Other things.'

'Don't be obtuse, Christopher.'

'Like I said, we talked about Nathaniel. Father missed him.'

Clarissa's eyes had become icy. 'Did your father ask you to take over the estate?'

He had wondered if she would come right out and say it. 'No.'

'No? I don't believe you.'

'Be that as it may, it's the truth. In fact, Father advised me to steer my own course with regard to the future and not to be persuaded to do anything I don't wish to do.'

Clarissa had stiffened. 'He wouldn't say that.'

'I'm sorry, Mother, but that's exactly what he said.'

Outside the window, the first desultory snowflakes were beginning to drift in the wind. He'd been away from the farm for over twenty-four hours and the weather was set to turn nasty, he knew the signs. If he didn't make it back quickly he could find himself in trouble, as well as being unable to reach the farm for weeks. There was no chance of travelling on to Sunderland now. Standing to his feet, he said, 'There's nothing more to be done here and I need to get home. I'll try to make the funeral, weather permitting.'

'What do you mean, you'll *try* to attend the funeral?' Clarissa's voice was whip-sharp. 'And stay where you are, boy. I haven't finished with you yet.'

Christopher walked across the room pausing once his hand was on the doorknob. Staring at his mother's imperious face he was suddenly overcome with a wave of pity for the man lying upstairs. He'd been eight years old when Nathaniel had explained why their parents had separate suites. How Nat had come by the knowledge, he didn't know, but his brother had had a penchant for listening at keyholes. At the time he had felt more in sympathy with his mother than his father. His father had been a terrifying figure in those days, and nothing he'd done had pleased him. Keeping his voice level and low, he said, 'I am not a boy. I am a man with a farm to see to and responsibilities. Like I said, I'll try to come back for the funeral.'

'If you walk out of that door now you needn't bother to attend the funeral.' Then her manner undergoing a lightning change, Clarissa held out her hand. 'Christopher, please, come and sit down for a few moments. You know it was your father's dearest wish and mine too, for you to take your place here. When I die all this can be yours – yours and your children's.'

'I have no children, Mother.'

'But you will one day.'

'I think not. Any hopes I had in that direction were dashed years ago, as you're well aware.'

'You mean the gypsy wench?' Her hand fell to her side.

'I mean Pearl, yes.'

'I thought you were over that unfortunate episode.'

There was no softening in her, not an ounce of compassion. Her husband had just died in dreadful pain and yet it hadn't touched her. Wishing only to be gone, he opened the door. 'Goodbye, Mother.'

'I forbid you to leave.'

He closed the door quietly behind him and made his way across the hall. Parker appeared like the well-trained servant he was and Christopher was touched to see the man's eyes were red. He'd rarely heard his father say a kind word to him, but the man's grief was genuine. 'You're not leaving so soon, sir?' the butler said quietly.

'Afraid so.' Christopher knew Parker would form his own opinion as to why. He was a wily old bird. 'Is my horse stabled?'

'I'll send someone to fetch him round, sir.'

'No matter, I'll go there myself. Goodbye, Parker.'

'Goodbye, sir.'

He saddled Jet himself, much to the consternation of the stable boy, and once he was cantering down the drive he didn't look back. After the lodgekeeper had opened the gates and he was in the lane, Christopher paused for a moment. What had he been thinking of, travelling all the way to Sunderland following pipe dreams? People didn't come back from the dead. In the flesh, that girl in the newspaper probably wouldn't resemble Pearl at all. Photographs did that sometimes. Distorted things. It was time to let go. He'd never really done that, let go of Pearl.

The snow was falling more thickly and although it was only two in the afternoon, the heavy grey sky promised an early twilight.

He was a fool. Sighing heavily, he turned Jet back in the direction of Hill Farm. But no more fanciful notions. He had just said goodbye to his father and cut all ties with his mother. *That* was real life.

Chapter 26

December was a month of deep snow, unrelenting winds and bitter cold. The appalling weather wasn't made any more tolerable by the flu pandemic, nor the announcement that the demobilisation of Britain's vast army was going to be a slow process. For Pearl, secure in the knowledge that her beloved James and Patrick had survived the war and were coming home, and witness daily to Seth and Nessie's happiness, it was a good month.

Nessie wasn't strong enough yet to resume work behind the counter of the shop, but Pearl and Seth put in long hours and their staff rose to the occasion and went the extra mile. By Christmas week, everyone was tired and ready for a break. Christmas Day falling on a Wednesday, Pearl closed the shop until the following Monday and they had a restful Christmas, eating and sleeping most of the holiday away.

It was the day before New Year's Eve at ten o'clock in the morning that Pearl received the telegram bearing the dreaded words *On His Majesty's Service*. She had been laughing and joking with a customer when the telegram boy had arrived. The customer was an ex-Army man who'd lost a leg at the Somme, and who engaged in a little harmless flirting along with his pie and peas.

Seth came immediately to her side and they read the telegram together. The words *It is with deep regret* and then *James Henry Croft* and *Patrick Edmund Croft* swam before her eyes before she collapsed in Seth's arms, moaning piteously before fainting clean away.

When she regained consciousness, she was lying on the sofa in the sitting room of the flat and Nessie was kneeling by her side, her face awash with tears. 'Oh, lass, lass.' Nessie took her hands, holding them tight. 'I'm so sorry, lass.'

'Where's Seth?' Pearl asked vaguely, her head muzzy.

'He's seeing to things downstairs.'

'It can't be true.' Pearl struggled into a sitting position. She felt physically sick and fought the weakness. 'James wrote to me – he said they're all right.'

Nessie's eyes looked back at her, shining with tears and a deep sorrow. 'It was the flu, lass. It's taking so many, especially men drained by the fighting and all they've gone through.'

'No.' It couldn't be. She wouldn't let it be. They were going to come home and work in the shop, their future secure. She drew in a long shuddering breath. 'No,' she said again. They had survived all the fighting, all the terrible slaughter, and they were coming home. Anything else was unimaginable.

'Lass—'

'*No!*' She wrenched her hands from Nessie's, the screaming in her head erupting from her mouth.

When Seth burst into the room a few moments later he took in the situation in one glance. He slapped her once, hard, across the face and then gathered her into his arms, holding her tightly as a grief so intense as to be unbearable shook her body, causing her to fight him for a few moments before she went limp.

They were gone. Her boys, her babies, her precious babies. She clung hold of Seth as he rocked her back and forth, his own face wet. She couldn't stand any more. What had it all been for, if not for her boys? Without them there was nothing. And death was so final, so cold. She wanted to be able to hug them, to tell them she was proud of them, to see their faces and hear their voices. They couldn't be dead. She wouldn't let them be dead. Oh, James, Patrick. Patrick, James.

★   ★   ★

It was midnight. Pearl was asleep, partly through exhaustion and partly because of the medication the doctor had prescribed when Seth, frightened by her sobbing, had sent for him. Seth and Nessie were sitting together on the sofa, their hands entwined and Nessie's head on Seth's shoulder. 'She won't get over this,' Seth said softly. 'That's my fear.'

'She will, she will. She's strong, Seth. You know she is.'

'Aye, but the lads were her world. They were when she was nowt but a bairn, and after that time with the gypsies it was like she'd never been away from them. Me mam . . . well, she wasn't a mother if you know what I mean.'

'Aye, I know what you mean.'

'It'll take the joy out of her life – I've seen it before with folk. Oh, they go on, they walk and talk and breathe, but something's gone. I – I was in danger of that before I met you, lass.'

'Oh, Seth.'

'Straight up, I was. And through Pearl we met and here we are.'

Nessie raised her head and they looked at each other. She touched his cheek with her hand. 'You can't do this for her, Seth, whatever she's done for us.'

'I know. That's what's twisting me guts.'

'But she has us and the shop – she's not alone.' And then she said, 'That was a silly thing to say, wasn't it?'

'You could never be silly.' He sighed deeply. 'I want her to be happy, Nessie. That's all. From when she was born she's had it rough and I really thought, with the lads coming home and all, things were looking up for her. You know, me and Pearl had been talking about perhaps inviting the neighbours in on New Year's Eve for a bit of a shindig just minutes before the telegram came. "Plenty to celebrate", that's what she said. Dear gussy . . .'

They sat in silence for a little while, each lost in their own thoughts, and then Seth said, 'Come on, lass. You need your rest and tomorrow's going to be a difficult day.'

'I'm coming back to work, Seth. Pearl's in and out of the kitchen, cooking, seeing to customers, then back cooking. It's too much. I know the girls try hard, but you and I serving are a good team and it leaves Pearl free to be in the back. That way she won't have to talk to folk if she doesn't feel like it.'

They had stood up and now Seth pulled her hard against him, kissing her long and deeply. 'We're a good team all right, lass, and not just in the shop. I don't know why the Good Lord saw fit to give you to me, me being the man I am, but I'm thankful for it. We'll get the Banns read in the New Year and I'll come along with you to church – you'd like that, wouldn't you?'

'You know I would.'

Seth rubbed his chin, his manner sheepish. 'I prayed today, down there in the shop while I worked. First time in years. I said if He'd just get Pearl past this and on an even road again, I'd go to church every Sunday for the rest of me life.'

Nessie smiled, a little sadly. 'You can't bargain with God, Seth. Anyway, only the other day you said you weren't sure if He exists, the mess the world's in.'

'Aye, I know that, but if He does, it won't do any harm to hedge me bets, will it?'

'Oh, Seth . . .'

The thaw which had set in after Christmas had turned the back lanes to quagmires and filled the streets with brown slush. An icy rain battering at the bedroom window woke Pearl in the early hours and instantly she remembered. She lay in the darkness listening to Nessie's gentle snores and feeling she was in a nightmare, but one from which there was no awakening. Every month her younger brothers had been gone she'd had a dread of the telegram boy. Each time the shop bell had tinkled, her heart had jumped: she'd never got used to the sound. She'd heard of other brothers, sons, husbands and fathers dying, and every single time she'd sent up a prayer for James and Patrick. And then in the last weeks, the heavy weight had been lifted from her heart and she had relaxed, knowing the war was over and they were coming home. Somehow, that made it all the worse now. Her brothers had been cheated – they all had. It was cruel, pointless.

Wearily she glanced towards the window where a glimmer of

light from the streetlamp outside showed through a chink in the curtains. The words Halimena had spoken so long ago were dancing in her head. She didn't think of them so often these days, but now they had come back to haunt her once more. Was it possible to be born to trouble, to take it wherever she went? Did she have a curse on her that affected those she loved? She felt herself slipping into the old abyss of self-recrimination and guilt and sat up sharply, hugging her knees in the cold room.

No, she wouldn't let that wicked old woman bedevil her. It was the flu that had taken the boys, just as it was taking thousands, millions worldwide, but how could she go on without them? She'd had such plans . . .

Her eyes dry but her heart aching so much it was a physical pain, she listened to the rain beating down as she went over her hopes and dreams for her lads. The shop had prospered so well and her bank balance was so healthy she had the notion she'd start two other shops in different parts of the town, each with living accommodation above. Smaller shops than this one, but places where, in due course when James and Patrick found wives, they could start a family while they managed their own premises. That way they would have been independent. A man needed to be independent.

She bowed her head, a small moan escaping her lips. Oh, her babies, her boys. Pray God it had been quick, she couldn't bear to think of them suffering and dying slowly on foreign soil.

She sat for a long time lost in a morass of utter despair before sliding out of bed and reaching for her dressing-gown. It was still early and quite dark, but she felt her way downstairs to the shop kitchen. She didn't want to use the one upstairs; Nessie or Seth might hear her and they needed their sleep.

Once in the kitchen she lit the gas mantles and gazed around her. She was the owner of all this and had several hundred pounds in the bank, something she would have considered impossible when she'd first had the idea of the shop. Everything she'd touched in the business had turned to gold. But she would gladly swap it all and live in a hovel if she could have James and Patrick back.

She felt as though the mainspring in her life had snapped. When she'd peered down the years she'd seen herself as a kind of grandma to the lads' bairns, imagined little arms round her neck and James or Patrick smiling at her as she held their offspring. Christmases filled with noise and life and little ones, people she could love and be loved by. When she had lost Christopher she had known she would never feel like that about anyone else, and time had borne this out. Partly, she supposed, because she didn't *want* anyone else to take his place.

When Christopher had been wrenched from her, a curious feeling of emptiness deep within had been established, and she knew it would prevail until the day she died. She was glad Nessie had been able to find love again – and thousands of other women did – but she wasn't made like that. Perhaps she had been wrong to pin all her future happiness on James and Patrick, to expect to live the life she'd been denied as a mother and grandma through them. If so, she was paying for it now.

She made a pot of tea and once it was mashed drank three cups with plenty of sugar. It still felt like a luxury even after all these years, having sugar in her tea. They had been lucky to get a warm drink of any description when she'd been growing up, but at least she hadn't been incarcerated in the workhouse like James and Patrick. She'd thought she was all cried out, but now she laid her head down on her arms and wept afresh for her beautiful, brave boys.

After an hour or so she washed her face and crept upstairs to get dressed before returning to the shop kitchen. Work was a panacea. By the time Nessie and Seth came down at half-past five everything was in order. Soup was simmering on the stove and the ovens were full, fresh bread permeating the air with its fragrance.

'Lass, we didn't expect you to work today. You should be in bed,' Nessie scolded.

'You shouldn't be working either.'

'There's nowt wrong with me now and it was driving me barmy up there by myself.'

Pearl nodded. 'That's exactly how I'd feel,' she said quietly.

After that, nothing more was said about her resting.

It was a busy day, in fact they were rushed off their feet as folk bought extra to take home for the jollifications that evening. Pearl was grateful that Nessie had resumed her place in the front of the shop, even though she was worried that her friend might not be fully recovered. She just couldn't have coped with having to be cheerful with customers today. Hilda and Martha had offered her their condolences but then had worked in silence – unusual for them – and with demand so high she had to concentrate on what she was doing, even though the feeling of desolation was there all the time.

Nessie came bustling into the kitchen midday, insisting Pearl take a break and eat something. Pearl knew her friend meant well and so to please her she forced down a bowl of soup she had no appetite for, and then went straight back to work.

At two o'clock, traditionally a quieter spot in the day after the lunchtime rush and before the evening trade, Seth was busy in the storage room-cum-scullery off the kitchen sorting out a recent delivery, and Hilda was helping Nessie in the front of the shop, when Nessie again appeared in the kitchen.

Pearl took one look at her flushed face and said, 'What's the matter? Do you feel unwell?'

'There's a man.' Nessie stared at her, seeming to struggle for words. 'He – he's asking for you.'

'A man? What's his name?'

'He wouldn't say, but from your description . . . Oh, I don't know, lass. It might not be.'

Her mind still steeped in grief, Pearl wondered what on earth was wrong with Nessie. What did anything matter, in view of the news they'd had the day before?

'Do you want me to come and see him?' she asked dully.

'Aye, yes, but I'll just get Seth.'

Bemused, Pearl watched as Nessie hurried past her to the storage room. Turning to Martha, Pearl said, 'Keep an eye on those pies, they're nearly done,' and walked out of the kitchen into the front of the shop. There were a few customers sitting eating and one or two waiting to be served by Hilda. Pearl sensed rather than saw this because her whole being was taken up with the tall figure standing to one side of the counter near the window. He was wearing the clothes of a workingman, except for his high-topped boots, but unlike most workingmen there was no cap on his head.

She caught hold of the doorpost as her head swam. It was Christopher, yet not Christopher. It had been ten years since they'd met and then he'd been a handsome, blond-haired young man. This man was still handsome, but his hair was deeply threaded with grey and he had a neatly trimmed beard, but it was the fact he looked so much older that had her doubting her own eyes. Christopher would be thirty, thirty-one now, but this man appeared all of forty-five and he was big, broad in the shoulders.

And then he spoke. 'Pearl?'

She couldn't move, couldn't speak, her mind telling her she couldn't faint twice in twenty-four hours, she wasn't the fainting kind. He walked towards her and she watched as he lifted the trap in the counter and came to stand in front of her.

'Christopher?' Her voice was a whisper. 'It's not possible.'

'That's what I told myself when I saw your photograph in the newspaper. They'd told me you were dead.' She watched him swallow hard but still he didn't touch her.

Becoming aware they were the focus of attention, Pearl straightened, her voice shaky as she said, 'Come through to the flat.' As she led the way to the stairs, Seth and Nessie came out of the kitchen, Seth wiping his hands on his trousers and his face worried. 'This – this is Christopher Armstrong,' she managed fairly steadily. 'My brother, Seth, and his fiancée, Nessie,' she added, turning to meet the grey eyes of her dreams.

The two men shook hands but no one smiled.

'I shall be upstairs for a while,' Pearl said to Nessie, who immediately replied, in a tone that brooked no argument, 'I'll bring you a tea tray in five minutes, lass.'

Pearl was aware of Seth and Nessie watching them as she led Christopher upstairs to the flat. He followed her into the sitting room. The room was cold, the fire all but out in the grate. 'Please sit down,' Pearl said, as politely as if he was an ordinary caller. 'I'll just see to the fire.'

He was still standing when she'd put wood and coal on the fire with the brass tongs. She had tried to pull herself together while she'd busied herself with the fire but now, looking at him, she felt weak at the knees. 'How – how are you?'

He didn't answer this. His voice low, he said, 'I didn't know you were alive for sure until I spoke to the lady downstairs. I looked for you after I came back ten years ago, but they – the gypsies – they said you'd been drowned. Pearl,' he hesitated as though nerving himself, 'are you married or betrothed?'

Dumbly, Pearl shook her head. She couldn't believe he was here, but it was too much coming on top of the news the day before. She felt numb, disorientated.

'I've never stopped loving you.' His voice came softly, uncertainly. 'I've mourned you for ten years but I've never stopped loving you. There's never been anyone else.'

The numbness was fading, a feeling welling up that was so fierce she had to put her hand to her breast. 'Nor for me,' she whispered weakly.

'Really?' A smile lit his face. 'But you're so beautiful, so exquisite. I didn't dare hope . . .' His arms went around her and she fell against him as the last of the numbness melted.

'Beautiful, exquisite'. Only her Christopher had ever spoken like this. It was real, he was here.

His mouth on hers, he kissed her as he'd done all those years ago, but now it was the man, not the boy, who was making love to her, and it was the woman in her who answered with her own lips and body. He was kissing her face, her throat, her hair, murmuring that she was his sweetheart, his beloved, his dear one.

The madness was only brought to a halt by Nessie – tactful for once – knocking on the sitting-room door. It was a few moments before Pearl said, 'Come in.'

Nessie was holding a tea tray but her eyes went straight to Pearl's face, and what she saw there must have reassured her because she visibly relaxed, her voice soft when she said, 'All right, lass?'

Still within the circle of Christopher's arms, Pearl nodded.

'I'll tell Seth. He's beside himself down there.' Looking straight at Christopher, Nessie said, 'He thinks a bit of his sister, we all do.'

'So do I, Nessie.'

'Aye, well, that'll be what he wants to hear.' She nodded at them both, put the tray on the table and marched out.

When Pearl glanced up at Christopher he was smiling. 'A good friend?'

'The best.'

'I can understand their distrust of me, but I swear to you I came looking for you . . .'

He stopped as Pearl laid a finger on his lips. 'Come and sit down,' she said. 'We've got ten years to catch up on.'

He nodded. 'But first . . .' He cupped her face in his hands, his mouth coming down to hers once more.

They spent all afternoon and evening in the flat, talking, loving, crying more than once. Christopher held her tight when she told him about James and Patrick, sobs shaking her yet again. Pearl held his hand in hers, stroking his fingers as he told her about Nathaniel and then his father. Slowly the events of the last decade in their lives were unravelled and both were amazed at what the other had accomplished, and the twists and turns their lives had taken. Afterwards, Pearl was shocked that she didn't once think or worry about the shop, but the truth of it was, it had ceased to exist. It didn't matter – nothing mattered beyond the miracle of Christopher seeking her out and finding her.

It being New Year's Eve they'd planned to shut the shop earlier than usual, and at eight o'clock Seth and Nessie came upstairs. Pearl could sense that Seth was very wary at first, but within half an hour he'd satisfied himself that Christopher was genuine and the four of them ate a meal together, Pearl and Christopher holding hands under the table.

It had been decided that Christopher would stay the night and sleep in the boys' room, but in the event Pearl and Christopher sat up all night once the four of them had welcomed the New Year in with a toast to lost loved ones and tears from Pearl and

Nessie. Christopher had explained that he had to get back to Hill Farm the next day and both were loath to waste a minute of the precious time they had together.

Pearl was lying in Christopher's arms on the sofa as a rosy dawn stole tentatively into the room. She was exhausted but had been fighting falling asleep all night. They had been separated for a decade, had grown and matured into different people from the ones they'd been that hot summer ten years ago, and yet the feeling between them was stronger than ever. She shut her eyes, breathing in the smell and feel of him, and still slightly dazed by the enormity of what had happened.

His voice came soft and tender above her head. 'How soon will you marry me? I'm terrified to leave you, terrified something will separate us again.'

She turned in his arms, their faces so close their breath mingled. 'As soon as you want.'

'Today? Tomorrow?' He laughed. Then, his face sobering, he said, 'The farm isn't a grand one, Pearl, far from it. In fact, it's nothing like you've been used to − the house I mean. I was going to start on it this year, but for now it's—'

'Home, because you're there,' she interrupted gently. 'And don't forget where I was born, Christopher, or where we lived when I first came here. One room for the three of us. But I've got savings − we can start on the house straightway.' Now her face was sober when she said, 'I'd like to make the business over to Seth and Nessie − all of it, the flat too. As a wedding present for them. Would you mind if I did that, rather than selling it?'

He traced her mouth with one finger. 'It's a wonderful idea and of course I don't mind. I wasn't sure how you would feel about leaving all this, to be honest, having built it up from scratch.'

She considered this for a moment. 'Perhaps if James and Patrick had lived I'd have felt a pull, I don't know, but now I feel I don't belong here any more. It's strange because even a week ago I wouldn't have dreamed I could ever say that. Do you think I'm a fickle creature?'

'I think you're a wonderful creature.' He kissed her soundly. 'The

321

rest of our lives won't be long enough for me to show you how wonderful.'

'I'll be a good farmer's wife.' She smiled at him.

'I know it. And you won't mind the remoteness after the town?'

She shook her head. 'I prefer it. Corinda always used to say that if you scratched me you'd find a Romany under the skin.' She touched his face. 'You don't mind me talking about them, the gypsies? They were good to me, Christopher. They saved my life and treated me like one of their own – all except Halimena, of course. It was only the last days that were bad.'

'Because of me.'

'No, because of Byron.' She gazed at him, her blue eyes intent. 'I never pretended I loved him, not in that way. All along he knew I regarded him as a brother, but even if that hadn't been the case, it still wouldn't excuse what he did. For a long time I blamed myself, but how can you choose where to love? It just happens. But the things Halimena said to you, that was so cruel.'

'She was a cruel woman.'

'Yes, she was.' It was the only thing she hadn't told him, the words Halimena had thrown at her that last time. Ridiculous, but she felt if she voiced them, they gained power. Shaking off the shadow, she pulled Christopher's head closer.

'Kiss me,' she whispered. 'Please kiss me.'

Chapter 27

For several days after Christopher had returned to the farm Pearl had to keep reassuring herself that it hadn't all been a dream. Before he had left they had decided on a May wedding. That would give Pearl time to sort out her affairs and Christopher was anxious to at least pipe running water from the stream into the house for his new bride. They were going to use Pearl's savings on building an extension to the house and moving the pigsties and boiling-up house, as well as refurbishing the present building and buying new furniture. This would all happen once they were wed though, through the summer months.

More deep snow in January meant Christopher couldn't come to Sunderland again until the second week of February, when they had the weekend together before he left again. Although this was onerous for them both, Pearl had plenty to do to keep her busy in the day. It was the nights when a strange feeling of foreboding would come upon her, colouring her dreams so that she woke feeling far from refreshed. Sometimes she was back at the gypsy camp with Halimena shouting at her, other times she was being sucked down in deep mud like James and Patrick had described, vainly trying to reach Christopher who was standing some distance away. Another dream had her running towards a distant figure but without ever getting nearer, something pursuing her in the darkness. But the dreams all had one message. She was born to trouble, doomed to lose Christopher again.

In the bright light of day she told herself she was being silly. The dreams were a result of the huge changes which had taken place in her life: the loss of her brothers, Christopher seeking her out, their proposed marriage and all that it entailed. And she could believe it – in the daytime.

Night-time, those hours of darkness when the subconscious has sway, was different. Then she could almost smell the gypsy campfires, see Halimena's piercing eyes and taloned hands, hear the low chanting of her ancient incantations. At those times, Pearl felt sure that her marriage would never take place.

Seth and Nessie married very quietly in the first week of March, and Christopher was able to attend, which was good considering Seth had asked him to be the best man. Only Pearl and Christopher were present at the wedding and afterwards they went to the Queen's Hotel in Fawcett Street for lunch, Christopher's wedding present to the couple. He had first suggested the Grand, but Pearl had quickly asked if they could go to the Queen's Hotel instead. Nessie had said nothing at the time, just squeezing her friend's hand as they both remembered that other celebratory meal years ago and the two happy little boys who had finished the day with a bag of nuts and raisins from the man with a wooden barrel in the Old Market.

'This is nice.' Seth glanced round the fine dining room which could hold over a hundred guests, adding as the waiter brought a bottle of champagne to the table and presented it for Christopher to read the label, 'Ee, man, we didn't expect this.'

'My pleasure.' Christopher smiled at Pearl's brother and his new wife as the waiter opened the champagne and proceeded to fill four flutes with the effervescent wine. 'A toast, to Mr and Mrs Croft.'

'Mr and Mrs Croft,' Pearl repeated as Nessie blushed and Seth kissed her full on the mouth, causing her to blush still more.

'And to those who are with us in our hearts on this special day,'

Christopher added, reaching across and taking Pearl's hand as they raised their glasses once more. With tears in her eyes Pearl smiled at him. Her darling Christopher, she loved him so much. The shadow was there again, flitting across the poignancy of the moment and causing her fingers to tighten on his.

An hour and a half later they had finished the baked lemon chiffon and were waiting for coffee to be brought to the table, when Pearl reached into her handbag. 'I didn't buy you a wedding present because I wanted to give you this,' she said quietly, handing Seth a brown envelope. 'It comes with all my love to you both.'

'No, Pearl, no.' When he'd opened the envelope and seen what it contained, the colour had surged into Seth's face and Nessie looked equally shocked. 'We wouldn't let you do this. You and Christopher will need every penny, and—'

'It's done.' Pearl put out her hand and clasped Seth's, stroking the crooked finger. 'No going back. It's yours anyway, Seth. The money to start the shop came from you and I want to do it. I owe you so much.'

'Owe *me*? You owe me nothing, lass, it's the other way round.'

'Seth, do you remember why our da did this?' She lifted up the damaged finger and when he shook his head, his eyes narrowing in bewilderment, she said, 'I do. You've loved and protected me all my life and I couldn't have a better brother. Or a better friend,' she said to Nessie, who was crying openly. 'There were six of us once, Seth. Now there's only two. Let me do this. I need to.'

Seth stood up, drawing her into his arms, and careless of everyone in the restaurant, he hugged her tightly. 'Lass, when I look back over my life I'm deeply ashamed,' he muttered, tears running down his face. 'It'd eat me up if I let it. And yet you persist in seeing the best in me.'

'You've only ever shown me the best and the rest doesn't matter, it's history. I'm proud to be your sister, I always have been.'

They sat down just as the waiter arrived with the coffee. In the bustle of the man pouring each of them a cup, and the women oohing and ahhing over the beautiful handmade chocolates which accompanied the coffee, Seth had time to surreptitiously wipe his eyes and compose himself as they intended he should. As they left the restaurant, Seth pulled Christopher to one side. 'You knew what Pearl intended to do with the shop?'

'Of course.'

'And you didn't mind?'

'Mind?' Christopher looked into the tough face in front of him. He was beginning to understand that the toughness was only skin-deep. 'I agree wholeheartedly with her. The way Pearl sees it, she's just been minding your investment in her the last few years.'

'Thanks.' Seth rubbed his hand over his mouth. 'I mean it, thanks.'

It was from that moment on the two men became firm friends.

March saw another period of deep snow in the middle of the month, the wicked easterly winds and icy cold making it clear it had no intention of leaving 'like a lamb'. Despite her joy at Seth and Nessie's transparent happiness, Pearl found herself fretting for Christopher. She hadn't seen him since Seth's wedding day and was feeling the separation keenly. They had arranged that Seth would take her to Hill Farm for a visit, but it was the first few days of April before this became possible, weatherwise.

Seth hired a horse and trap for the day and they left Sunderland very early in the morning just as it was getting light, leaving Nessie in charge of the shop. An infant spring was evident once they left the town for the countryside, blackthorn and hawthorn beginning to sprout along the hedgerows, and wild flowers such as violets and primroses peeping shyly at them as they passed. The white, star-like flowers of the stitchwort dotted the hedgebank, reminding Pearl of the times she'd seen Halimena grinding up the flowers with powdered acorn to make a mixture to add to wine which was said to relieve the stitch, a pain in the side. Her corner of the caravan had been full of creams and potions the old woman had made, along with dead newts and bugs and even a snake or two suspended in bottles filled with liquid. Pearl shivered. A witch's den.

'Cold?' Seth wrapped the rug he'd tucked round her earlier more securely about her legs. She thanked him but didn't say the chill was from within rather than without.

It was an uneventful but blustery journey. In one or two places, the roads and lanes were caked with thick mud, which made the going slow; in others, the wild winds had dried the ground and it was hard. By the time they reached the road Christopher and his men had made, which led directly to Hill Farm, Pearl could appreciate how easily the farm could be cut off from the rest of the world. This worried her not an iota. In fact, she couldn't think of anything she'd like more than being in a place where the rest of the world couldn't impinge on them.

Once the farm came in sight Seth stopped the trap for a moment or two and they both stared at the huddle of buildings in the distance surrounded by fields of grazing cattle and sheep and lambs. Lambing was always a difficult and arduous time for farmers, Christopher had told her, which was another reason they had decided to wait until May to get married. 'Your future home,' Seth said gruffly. 'Nessie and I will miss you, lass.'

'We'll visit each other.' She turned to him reassuringly. 'It's not too far away.'

Christopher must have seen them approaching because long before they reached the farm he was waving and running along the road to greet them. 'He's actin' like a lad still wet behind the ears,' Seth said, shaking his head, although Pearl had the feeling her brother was pleased, nonetheless.

'I've been looking for you every day.' As they reached him, Christopher held out his arms and Pearl jumped down into them. 'Even in the thick snow when I knew it was impossible I still hoped.' He swung her round and round until she was dizzy and then kissed her thoroughly. 'Why didn't we say April instead of the beginning of May? I won't last another four weeks.'

'You'll have to.' Laughing, they followed the trap to the farm, arm-in-arm.

Pearl fell in love with the farm and wasn't even slightly daunted by the farmhouse, immediately seeing in her mind's eye how their home would look once the alterations were done. Christopher proudly showed them how he and his men had routed water into the farmhouse from the stream by means of pipes and a pump, insisting Pearl and Seth both took a turn pressing the handle of the pump so water spurted into the deep stone sink. 'I intend to have a well dug at some point too, but that'll be in the future, once the house is done.'

'It's lovely,' Pearl said, and she meant it. She knew the lot of a farmer's wife wasn't an easy one but it was satisfying and she had never been afraid of hard work or long hours. They would work together to build a good life for them and their bairns. Bairns . . . Her heart leaped and raced. Christopher's babies.

By the time she and Seth had to leave, Pearl had met the farm hands and their wives, seen every inch of the farm and even taken a turn feeding an orphan lamb Mabel had ensconced by her fireside. She was tired but contented as she left Christopher, the two of them clinging together until Seth lost patience and bodily lifted her up into the trap. The next time she would see him would be on their wedding day, just under four weeks away. She hugged the thought to her as the farm and his distant figure were lost to sight and she turned to face the front.

'We should have left a couple of hours ago. It'll be long since dark by the time we get home,' Seth worried as they bowled along.

'It's all right, it's a fine night.'

'Aye, but it'll be bitter once the sun's down.'

'Nessie'll warm you up once you get home.'

'Pearl!' Seth's voice expressed shock and Pearl giggled.

She was feeling more at peace than she had since the New Year. Seeing the farm and what her new life was going to be like, and the hours with Christopher, had been satisfying. She would never forget James and Patrick. They would always be close to her, carried in her heart along with Fred and Walter. But starting afresh like this, away from Sunderland and all its memories, she could remember the good times more easily and not dwell on the bitter 'what–ifs'.

Dusk was falling and birdsong was filling the air as they approached Morpeth. The road split here. One way led to the outskirts of Newcastle and then the town itself, while the other veered right towards the coast, leading to Tynemouth and South Shields and then Sunderland. It was as they reached the fork in the road that Pearl glimpsed the blue smoke curling up amongst the trees in the distance. Her heart seemed to stop beating and then resumed at a furious pace. She recognised those thin wisps spiralling into the evening sky.

'Seth, stop.' As her brother went to steer the horse towards the right, Pearl clutched his arm.

'What's the matter?'

'There's something I need to do. The smoke . . .' She took a deep breath. 'Seth, I think that smoke is from campfires, gypsy campfires.'

His eyes followed her pointing finger. 'Oh no, lass.' He turned to her, his face grim. 'If you're thinkin' what I think you're thinkin' . . .'

'Please, Seth.'

'Why, Pearl? You said yourself the past is just history. It's turned out all right, you've got Christopher.'

'I can't tell you why, I just need to see if it's them. It might not be.'

'This is foolishness. There was bad feeling when you left and there's only the two of us.'

'They wouldn't hurt us,' she said softly.

'Oh aye? Tell that to Christopher. He still bears the marks of what that man did to him, and will do till the day he dies.'

'But it saved him. He didn't have to go away to fight.'

'That's warped thinking and you know it. Your gypsy friend meant to do for him.' Seth turned her to him, his hands tight on her forearms. 'They live by their own rules, you told me so yourself. And the old grandmother, the one who told Christopher you'd drowned, what do you think she'd do if you turn up all bright eyed and bushy tailed?'

Halimena. It always came back to Halimena. Seth would never understand in a hundred years and she wasn't sure if she understood herself, but Halimena was the reason she had to see if it was 'her' gypsies making camp a mile or so away. And it could be. This was their territory, come the spring. 'I have to go.' She pulled herself free. 'With you or without you, Seth, I have to go and see.'

He swore succinctly. After sitting undecided for a moment or two he turned the horse and trap to follow the left fork.

'Thank you.'

'Don't thank me. This has all the makings of a disaster and I must be doolally.'

They heard the camp before they saw it. The gypsies were en route, Pearl thought to herself. It was always pandemonium when they stopped en route, especially for the women who had the children to see to as well as the evening meal. As they drew closer they caught sight of the camp in a pasture of several acres. It was a sea of caravans of all shapes and sizes, along with Romany, beehive and old Army belltents. The lithe figures of women and children and men with brown faces and black hats and shirts were everywhere, along with lurcher dogs and horses of all kinds. The noise, and the smell from the great black pots hung over the fires were all so familiar that for a moment Pearl felt she had come home.

'Well?' Seth growled at her side.

'I don't know, I can't tell if it's them. We need to go nearer.'

Muttering under his breath, Seth drove the horse and trap close to the hedges bordering the pastureland and then stopped. Pearl's heart was in her mouth. Likely the gypsies had been coming back to their site near Newcastle every year since she had been in Sunderland; these things were handed down from generation to generation and didn't change. They might approach from a different direction or be late or early by a few weeks, but that was all.

She climbed down from the trap and walked to the open gate which led into the pasture, and almost immediately saw a face she recognised. It was Naomi, one of Freda's friends, and she had a couple of black-eyed children about her skirts. As Naomi saw her she stopped dead, the bundle of twigs and wood she had been carrying dropping from her fingers. Reaching for the children's hands, she turned and disappeared into the mêlée.

Pearl had been about to speak but now she didn't know what to do. Turning to Seth, she said, 'It is them, Seth. I know that woman.'

'Aye, and she knew you an' all by the way she skedaddled,' he said drily. 'So, what do you want to do? Are we going to find the family who took you in?'

By now several more of the gypsies had become aware of their presence and had stopped what they were doing to stare. Pearl felt uneasy. Perhaps it *had* been foolish for the pair of them to come unannounced to the camp, especially in view of the way she had parted company with the tribe. Nevertheless, she felt this had happened for a purpose somehow, like the last link in a chain. Or perhaps it was just that Halimena had been playing on her mind since she and Christopher had found each other again. Or – and the unease deepened – was it possible that Byron's grandmother had summoned her to the camp this evening?

She was about to turn to Seth and suggest they leave when a tall aristocratic figure emerged from the crowd. Pearl stared at Corinda. It had been ten years, but Byron's mother didn't look any different. Pearl felt her face burn. The whole camp had become silent and Seth was as tense as a coiled spring beside her. Corinda came right up to them, her eyes fixed on Pearl. When she spoke, her voice was low.

'I knew you would come one day.'

Pearl licked her dry lips. 'I saw the smoke and wondered if it might be you.'

Corinda nodded. 'You look well.'

'I am well. And you?'

Instead of answering this, Corinda looked at Seth. Her gaze returning to Pearl, she said, 'He knows you lived with us?'

'Yes, he knows it all.' She had to ask. 'How is Byron?'

It was a moment before Corinda replied. 'He is happy. He married my cousin's daughter and they have three fine boys. He never went back to the horse trading after leaving here but he has become very skilled at cabinet-making and such things. I understand from my cousin that his goods are much in demand wherever they go. Yes, he is content.'

'I'm glad.' She hadn't realised until this moment how much Byron had weighed on her conscience, whatever she had said to the contrary to Christopher.

'And you have found happiness?' Again Corinda glanced at Seth. Pearl realised Byron's mother thought they were a couple.

She was about to explain when Seth said, 'I think she is very happy, isn't that right, Pearl?' as he pressed her hand warningly. Pearl was startled for a moment but then saw the wisdom of leaving things as they were. If she said Seth was her brother and that she was about to marry someone else, awkward questions might follow. It would hardly be tactful to inform Byron's mother that she was marrying the man who'd been instrumental in Byron fleeing his family.

She nodded. 'Yes, I'm happy.'

'If we're not going to make the whole journey in pitch blackness we need to leave, Pearl.' Again Seth pressed her hand. *So far, so good,* his touch said. *Don't push your luck.*

She nodded again, but instead of making her goodbyes, said, 'I'm sorry for everything that happened, Corinda. Byron saved my life when he found me that day and I'm grateful for the way you took me in. I never wanted to hurt anyone. That was the last thing I wanted.'

Corinda hesitated only a moment. Then she sighed. 'What is done, is done, and I see now you weren't altogether to blame. When all the facts emerged, I came to realise that Mackensie's mother played her part too. She was a . . . difficult woman at times.'

'Was?' Pearl found she was holding her breath.

'Halimena died just after Christmas.'

Pearl knew she ought to offer her condolences but she couldn't. She and Corinda looked at each other, their shared glance holding for a long moment. Then Corinda turned to Seth. 'You need to get home,' she said quietly.

Pearl wanted to thank this woman who had treated her as one of her own while she lived with them. Watching Corinda, she had understood what real motherhood was all about. The words hovered on her tongue but in the end all she said was, 'Goodbye. I'm glad we've seen each other again.'

Corinda looked deep into her eyes again and then smiled one of her rare smiles. 'I, too, am glad,' she said simply, before turning and melting away into the camp.

'Now can we get the hell out of here?' Seth still had hold of her hand and pulled her none too gently back up on the horse and trap. It had turned out better than he'd feared, but he wouldn't trust them gypsies as far as he could throw them, whatever Pearl said. Gave him the willies, they did, the lot of 'em.

Seth only breathed a sigh of relief once the sounds of the camp were lost behind them. Pearl had gone very quiet by his side. He glanced at her. 'All right, lass? Has it upset you?'

'No, it hasn't upset me.' She just couldn't take in that the evil old woman was dead. Somehow, she had imagined Halimena being immortal, there had been such a strong lifeforce in her. She had lived under that woman's shadow for years even though she hadn't wanted to acknowledge it. Now there was a lightness in her, as though something had lifted.

Had Halimena dying just days before Christopher came to find her released him in some way? And then she chided herself for the fanciful thought. She mustn't credit Halimena with powers she'd never had. It was a coincidence, that was all. They happened all the time, life was full of them. And in one way it didn't matter. Halimena was dead and she and Christopher were alive. Against all the odds they'd found each other, and nothing would separate them now. For the first time since she had seen him again she really believed it.

She lifted her face to the darkening sky that was ablaze with colour as though all nature had conspired to herald the moment. She felt giddy, drunk with relief as her spirit soared and rose on the wings of the night, and as she gazed upwards, the magnificent shape of a large barn owl flew straight across her vision, its pure white breast and richly covered brown and grey feathers clearly visible.

Pearl caught hold of Seth's arm and together they watched as the powerful bird circled once above them. Shrieking its supremacy, it swooped down so low she could see the beautiful tawny eyes gazing straight at her as though it knew her, before it disappeared into the shadows of evening and was gone.

Epilogue

Pearl and Christopher married on a day when the warm breeze carried the sweet scent of May blossom and all was sunshine and light. They'd chosen the little parish church of Ditchburn for the nuptials. It was the nearest church to the farm and meant that Ray and George and their wives could attend the service. Wilbert and his wife and children were there, and Seth had shut the shop for the day so the three shopgirls could attend with him and Nessie. It was a merry party who returned to the farm once the parson had pronounced the couple man and wife.

Ivy and Mabel had laid on a veritable feast in the hay barn. It had been swept out, the cobwebs brushed down from the rafters, and bunches of wild flowers fastened on the walls. A long trestle table was set up in the middle of the floor with two long forms either side. After the excellent wedding breakfast the table was pushed to one side and everyone danced to the accompaniment of music provided by Ray's fiddle, the hilarity aided by the bottles of homemade wine and ale which were consumed liberally. Everyone said they'd never been to such a wonderful wedding.

That night, Pearl slept wrapped in her husband's arms, and that the wedding night had been successful was borne out by the fact that exactly nine months to the day, Pearl gave birth to healthy twin girls. Nessie came to stay for a few weeks to help the new mother cope and had the time of her life.

Little Charlotte and Lucy were joined by their baby brother, Charles Christopher, two years later, and by the time the farm had almost doubled in size and the house had been extended yet again, another boy and then a girl completed the family. Pearl had her Christmases full of love and laughter and fun, and Seth and Nessie were regarded by the little ones as Granda and Grandma rather than Uncle and Aunt, and were greatly loved. Of Christopher's mother they'd heard no word since he had written to invite her to the wedding; Clarissa hadn't replied.

As they'd determined to be, Pearl and Christopher were good parents. With five children there were plenty of ups and downs, but it was a deeply satisfying life. Rewarding. With Christopher at her side, Pearl didn't want anything more. As she watched her children grow sturdy and strong, she knew the legacy of Halimena's curse was broken. They had been born to wholeness, unity and good fortune. They had been born to love.